G.I. BONES

By the author

Jade Lady Burning
Slicky Boys
Buddha's Money
The Door to Bitterness
The Wandering Ghost

G.I. BONES

MARTIN LIMÓN

Published by
Soho Press, Inc.
853 Broadway
New York, NY 10003

Library of Congress Cataloging-in-Publication Data

Limón, Martin, 1948-
G.I. bones / Martin Limón.
p. cm.
ISBN 978-1-56947-603-1 (hardcover)
1. Sueno, George (Fictitious character)—Fiction. 2. Bascom, Ernie
(Fictitious character)—Fiction. 3. United States. Army Criminal
Investigation Command—Fiction. 4. Americans—Korea—Fiction.
5. Korea (South)—Fiction. I. Title.
PS3562.I465G3 2009
813'.54—dc22
2009014766

10 9 8 7 6 5 4 3 2 1

"Success is always and everywhere a racket."

—RAYMOND CHANDLER (1888–1959)

1

Cloth streamers hung from the front door of the fortune teller's hooch; bright red, yellow, and green. Tiny bells tied to the streamers tinkled in the late afternoon breeze. Doctor Yong In-ja, chief of the Itaewon branch of the Yongsan District Public Health Service, pulled three sticks of incense out of her pocket, struck a single wooden match against a dirty brick wall, and lit all three. She handed one to me, one to the young business girl I knew only as Miss Kwon, and kept the last for herself. Pungent smoke assaulted my nostrils. Turning, Doc Yong pushed open the small wooden door in the front wall and crouched through into the fortune teller's courtyard.

My name is George Sueño. I'm an agent for the Criminal Investigation Division of the 8th United States Army in Seoul, Republic of Korea. Normally, I don't seek consultations with fortune tellers. But when Doc Yong asked me to accompany her and the traumatized Miss Kwon to see the woman whom she referred to as "the most famous *chom-cheingi* in Seoul," I didn't refuse.

Miss Kwon was a cute kid, about nineteen years old, with cheeks that quivered like a chipmunk's. I had first seen her in Doc Yong's office some twenty minutes ago. She had been so nervous at meeting me that her hands shook. I spoke to her in Korean, using polite verb endings, and she calmed down, but only a bit. Miss Kwon's fear of men—especially Americans—was vast. Doc Yong had asked me to meet with her, talk to her, and eventually to accompany the two of them on this outing to the fortune teller, thinking I could show Miss Kwon the positive side of Western manhood: not drunk, not aggressive, not treating women as objects to be bought and sold. I'd been flattered by Doc's confidence and, more to the point, grateful that she had never seen me running the ville on a Saturday night.

Although she was escorting a superstitious young country girl to a fortune teller, Doc Yong had confided in me before we left that as a modern woman and a medical doctor, she did not believe in such nonsense herself. But Doc Yong felt that a visit to Auntie Mee, the fortune teller, would reassure Miss Kwon, give her hope that she had a future worth working toward, a future that would be better than the present she was suffering through now.

And, Doc Yong finally admitted, when we were already halfway there, that the *chom-cheingi* also wanted to speak to me. *Me specifically*, I'd asked, or just anyone representing 8th Army law enforcement? *You specifically*, Doc Yong had replied. The fortune teller had asked for me by name: Sueño. I asked how she had known my name. Doc Yong shook her head. But I could figure it out. Itaewon was a small village and word gets around. Quick. The fact that my partner, Ernie Bascom, and I were Criminal Investigation Division agents was no secret. What did this *chom-cheingi* want to talk to me about? Doc Yong shook her head again. I'd find out soon enough.

I wasn't sure I liked being maneuvered into meeting someone I wouldn't normally encounter. I consider fortune tellers to be charlatans, people who use trickery to prey on the insecurities of people—mostly women—who shell out hard-earned money and receive little or nothing in return. But if Doc Yong considered it worthwhile for me to talk to this woman I'd set my misgivings aside. That was good enough for me.

Frankly, I would've followed Doc Yong anywhere. We did a lot of work with her—what with Korean "business girls" being constantly beat up or raped or even occasionally tortured by our brave American fighting men—and I wanted to retain her goodwill. But the main reason I decided to join her on this gray afternoon was that I had a crush on her. She was probably in her early thirties, about seven or eight years older than me, and she had legs that were maybe a little too short and a chest that wouldn't make any Hollywood starlet jealous. Her face was round and never made up and, on top of that, she wore thick-rimmed glasses and cut her hair in a straight bob that hung just past her ears.

But I found her attractive because of her smile. It was brighter than the sun coming up over the Eastern Sea and filled whoever was lucky enough to see it with a sense of vibrant optimism. And her skin was pure, unblemished, the color of light gold with just a hint of brown. It sounds like a lousy pick-up line but I was also attracted to her mind. When I gazed into her eyes I could see her evaluating me, turning everything I said this way and that, not coming to a conclusion but storing data, ready to reach a conclusion when, and only when, it became necessary. She was the only person I knew who, when I gazed into her eyes, I was certain was more intelligent than me.

Admittedly, I didn't live in a world of massive brain power. Most of the people I worked with were Army MPs, Korean cops, or miscreant criminals of either Korean or American vintage. Every time I talked to Doc Yong I felt as if I'd been hit by a breath of fresh air blowing in off the cold Yellow Sea.

Now we sat in the courtyard holding our sticks of burning incense for what seemed a long time, squatting on our haunches. Or maybe it just seemed like a long time because my thigh muscles had started to cramp. After a few minutes I had to stand up and stretch. Doc Yong motioned me back down.

The courtyard was like most courtyards of the working class poor: a *byonso*—an outhouse—made of cement blocks sat in one corner, earthenware kimchee pots lined the side walls, and in the center of the courtyard were a few scraggly rose bushes, barren now in the middle of winter, reaching toward gray clouds like the gnarled fingers of the dead. Miss Kwon held her stick of incense straight up in front of her face with both hands and remained totally immobile, except for her lips which mumbled an incomprehensible prayer. Doc

Yong did pretty much the same except her eyes darted about occasionally. My legs were so stiff and the joints of my knees ached so badly that I was about to stand and call the whole thing off when footsteps pattered on the raised wooden floor of the hooch. Silently, the latticework door slid open. A woman stepped onto the porch and bowed.

She wasn't what I expected; not a withered crone with a hooked nose and warts. Auntie Mee was a slender Korean woman, maybe in her thirties, clad in robes of embroidered blue silk. She bowed at the waist, and thanked us in a melodious voice for being good enough to join her in her humble household. We all stood. Doc Yong bowed first and then Miss Kwon and then me. Following Doc Yong's lead, we placed our burning incense sticks into a bronze holder encircled by rose bushes. Auntie Mee motioned for us to enter. We slipped off our shoes, stepped up onto the varnished wooden porch and ducked through the doorway onto the vinyl-covered floor of the home of the fortune teller.

We followed her down a dark hallway and emerged into a rear courtyard. This one was far better kept, with bonsai trees, ponds with tiny waterfalls and golden carp frolicking in the green water. Fortune-telling paid well. We followed a long porch around the edge of the courtyard to the rear. Auntie Mee bowed once more and led us into a room, twice as big as the hooch up front. It held a shrine. Above flickering candles, many pairs of huge round eyes glared at me: the Conquering General of Heaven, the Goddess of the Land Below, sleek copper Buddhas, fat bronze kitchen gods. Just about every sort of religion was represented here. A bearded figure in one of the murals seemed to be Jesus Christ.

Miss Kwon appeared completely awed. She knelt in the center of the room and bowed her head to the floor. Turning from us, Auntie Mee covered herself in a thick red robe, strode into the middle of the room, and squatted in front of Miss Kwon. Gently, she took the girl's quivering hands in hers. Auntie Mee closed her eyes and began to chant. The two of them seemed to be engaged in a spiritual communion. Neither moved but they held on to one another firmly. Finally, softly, Auntie Mee began to speak.

She asked Miss Kwon for her date of birth and then her hour of birth. After that she pulled a small table away from the wall and began to thumb through a sheaf of loose-leafed pages, tattered at the edges and held together by copper studs. In the center of the title page sat three characters; the one in the middle was too complicated for me to read but those on either end were composed of only a few strokes. By the flickering candlelight, Auntie Mee's finger traced row after row of Chinese characters, elegantly slashed thick lines made by an ink-dipped horsehair brush. Many of the manuscript pages were partially blank, as if chunks were missing.

Auntie Mee stopped—still mumbling to herself—and seized three large bronze coins with small squares punched in the middle. She threw them up in the air and allowed them to clatter to the surface of the wooden table. When they had stopped moving, she took note of how they landed and resumed her search through the grimy stack of curled paper. Finally, she grabbed Miss Kwon's hand, and started chanting again.

I could follow little of what she said. Much of the incantation was whispered in Miss Kwon's ear, so only she could hear it. Also, my Korean is conversational, not completely fluent. If I steer the topic of conversation to areas where my vocabulary is extensive, and if the person I'm talking to keeps the words and syntax simple, I can communicate effectively. But when someone takes off into the exotic realms where Auntie Mee was heading, into ancient incantations pulled from the hoary recesses of time, I become lost. Only a few words or phrases seeped in: "trouble with your family;" "men who don't respect you;" "foreigners who treat Koreans badly."

I wondered how much of this was fortune-telling and how much common sense. The Korean economy was desperately trying to rebuild itself in the early seventies, some twenty years after the devastation of the Korean War. Things were tough for the working poor in Seoul and, when crops failed, even tougher for the farmers in the countryside. Despite massive population growth in the cities—Seoul was up to eight million people—most of the Korean population still lived in agricultural areas. When girls reached marriageable age, they found it difficult to find a husband. Landless boys were not only drafted into the army for three years but afterward they ran off to the cities to find work. The girls were left to labor in factories hoping to build a dowry or, if their grades weren't so good in school, as bus attendants or janitors or scullery maids if they were lucky. The unlucky ones signed contracts with labor recruiters. Money would be sent home to their parents. They would work as "hostesses" in bars or nightclubs. Hostesses are expected to perform additional duties, duties that encompass prostitution. Often, after poverty and the system has broken them down, the girls give up all hope of living a decent life and plunge into drunkenness and drugs and sex-for-sale. These are the ones who end up being hauled into jail by Korean cops or, occasionally, G.I. cops like me.

I'm not a fortune teller but I saw all this in Miss Kwon's future. So did Doc Yong. The difference was that Doc Yong was trying to save her. I didn't know how.

Now Auntie Mee spoke in a strong clear voice. Miss Kwon was crying and bowing. Auntie Mee asked her an occasional question. Miss Kwon answered. Auntie Mee made what seemed to be pronouncements and Miss Kwon nodded vigorously.

During all this, Doc Yong had been sitting quietly, her head bowed. But now her fists clenched and she stared directly at Auntie Mee.

"Weikurei?" Doc Yong demanded. Why this way?

Auntie Mee shrugged and gestured toward the tattered manuscript, as if to say, That's what the book told me.

Finally, the reading was done and Auntie Mee and Miss Kwon hugged one another. Then Auntie Mee slid backward on her bent knees, and Miss Kwon, crying more than ever, bowed twice. Doc Yong, still scowling, comforted her and dragged her off to the side of the room, away from the glow of the flickering candlelight. They whispered to one another, conferring over the full meaning of the fortune that had just been told.

Auntie Mee motioned for me to sit before her. I slid across the floor and knelt, although my butt wouldn't descend as low as Auntie Mee's. My head towered a foot above hers. She backed up a little, uncomfortable looking up at me.

Many Koreans find Westerners unattractive. Upsetting, even. Our features are too gross, our bone structure too oddly shaped, our bodies too massive and reeking of the odor of meat. Apparently, that was Auntie Mee's attitude.

When she had put some distance between us she relaxed, arranged her blue robe around herself and began to talk, speaking Korean slowly and simply so I could understand.

First, she asked me for my date of birth. I wouldn't give it to her.

"Why? Don't you want your fortune read?"

I shook my head. "I don't believe in these things," I said.

She seemed greatly amused. "But many people do."

"Many people do a lot of things," I replied.

"As you wish." Auntie Mee sighed and slammed shut her pile of dog-eared pages. Then, still in Korean, she said something to me. It was a jarring change of subject and it took me a few moments to translate the sentence, mentally, into English.

"I want you to arrest someone," she told me.

I waited.

"A compatriate of yours," she said. "An American soldier."

"What has he done?" I asked.

"He bothers me every night. Wakes me. Makes me rise from my bed and forces me to light sticks of incense and speaks to me through the Conquering General of Heaven. He even interrupts me when I'm working with my clients, causing delays and confusing my readings. He's quite a pest. Rude, like so many of you Americans. And impatient too."

"Impatient?"

"Yes. Why doesn't he wait to take his revenge in the land of the dead like everyone else? Why must he bother me to take action on his behalf, here in the land of the living? What has he ever done for me?"

I was more confused than ever. "This American soldier," I said. "He is your boyfriend? He lives with you?"

The smooth contours of Auntie Mee's face twisted into a sneer. Doc Yong and Miss Kwon had both stopped talking.

"*No!*" Auntie Mee shouted so emphatically that I could scarcely believe the sound emanated from so slender a woman. "He visits me at night," she said. "He awakens me. He interrupts me when I am in trance. He bothers me always and he won't go away until someone finds his bones."

"His bones?"

"Yes. His bones. They are buried in Itaewon. I don't know

exactly where, but as to when he said something about 'at the beginning of peace.' Shortly after the end of the war."

The cease fire ending the Korean War was signed in July of 1953. That was over twenty years ago. Still, the implications of Auntie Mee's words hadn't fully sunk in.

"Whose bones is he talking about?" I asked.

"*His* bones."

"Then he's dead?"

Auntie Mee sighed, sat back, and crossed her arms. "Of course."

I glanced at Doc Yong. She nodded her head slightly in agreement.

I turned back to Auntie Mee. "What do you want me to do about it?"

"Find his bones. Send them back to America, back to his family, so they can be consecrated or whatever you people do with them. Then he will be happy and he will stop bothering me."

"How will I find his bones?"

"You are a detective," she said, as if that solved everything.

"I can't dig up all of Itaewon looking for old bones. I need somewhere to start."

"He said he was killed 'at the beginning of peace.'"

"Wait a minute," I interrupted. "You said 'killed.' Are you saying this American G.I. was murdered?"

"Yes. That's why he's so upset. He wants someone to find his bones. He was murdered here in Itaewon, when the fighting had stopped and people were able to return to Seoul and start rebuilding."

"Who killed him?"

She shrugged.

"Koreans or Americans?"

She shrugged again. "Find the bones," she said.

"Why did you choose me?" I asked.

"I heard about you through my clients. You speak Korean, you understand Korean people and, they all tell me, you do good things. Like him."

"What was his name?"

She shook her head. "At first, he wouldn't tell me."

"You asked him?"

"Of course. The first time he arrived. But he wouldn't tell me. It was as if he didn't trust me right away. He couldn't be sure that I would actually do something to help him. Then, finally, he made his decision."

"He told you his name?"

"Yes."

Auntie Mee reached into the folds of her thick red robe and pulled out a yellowed piece of paper. She handed it to me. I unfolded it. There, written in *hangul* script, were two words.

"I wrote it down," Auntie Mee said, "in the middle of the night, while he was bothering me."

"What was he doing?"

"Touching me," she said, squirming beneath her robe. "Everywhere."

I stared at her, keeping straight-faced, wondering if she was serious. She was. So were Doc Yong and Miss Kwon. They accepted her statement as if it were the most natural thing in the world. An American G.I. in bed with a Korean woman, what else would he do?

By guttering candlelight, I read the two words. The first was *mori*. This can mean either "head" or "hair" in the Korean language. The next word was *di*. This meant nothing in Korean. Perhaps the spirit was referring to the letter *d* as in the English alphabet.

"Does this name have any meaning?" I asked.

"That's what I'm asking you," Auntie Mee replied. "He's an American; that's his name. I thought you would understand."

"There's no such name as Mori Di. And no such word in English."

I gazed at the script again and then held the paper up to the flickering candlelight, turning it over to make sure I hadn't missed something. Maybe it was the absurdity of the situation or maybe I was just peeved at Auntie Mee's sense of assurance, but I felt impish.

"Is the American G.I. here now?"

"No. Not now."

"Could you call him?"

"Why?"

"I have questions for him."

"Never question the dead," she said. "What they want you to know, they will tell you."

"You asked him his name."

"Yes. And he didn't answer me until he was good and ready."

I turned to Doc Yong. My incredulity must've shown on my face. She nodded, encouraging me to accept the assignment, no matter how odd I thought it might be.

Auntie Mee sensed my hesitancy. "The reason Miss Kwon was upset a few minutes ago, and why Doctor Yong was angry on her behalf, is that they don't like bad news about the future. But the fault doesn't lie with me! It lies with the codex and with Mori Di."

"The codex?"

"Yes. This." She pointed to the pile of tattered pages. Now I could make out the title on the front page. *Chom*, which means "fortune-telling" or "divination", was the first word. The second character was sketched in eleven precisely printed strokes. I didn't recognize the character but I committed the lines to memory and made a mental note to look it up later. *Ki* was the last word, an ideograph meaning "narrative" or "account."

"What does Miss Kwon have to do with any of this?" I asked.

Auntie Mee shrugged again. "Who's to say? The fates of the living, and sometimes the dead, are intertwined in mysterious ways. If the bones of Mori Di are not found soon, and consecrated in a holy shrine then, unfortunately, Miss Kwon will meet an unpleasant fate."

"What sort of fate?"

"Not good. Most likely she'll die."

This enraged Doc Yong. She leapt out of her crouch, stomped across the wood-slat floor and kicked the table in front of Auntie Mee. Candle and codex and votive urn flew straight up in the air. Before they landed, Doc Yong grabbed a chunk of the fortune teller's thick black hair and yanked as if she wanted to rip it out of her skull. The two women grappled, screeching, and throwing ineffectual punches, but Doc Yong wouldn't let go of her grip on Auntie Mee's hair.

I bulled my way between the two women, trying to break it up. Doc Yong cursed like a Korean sailor. As the three of us struggled, Miss Kwon curled into a ball in her dark corner, her shoulders heaving. From what I could understand between screams, Doc Yong was telling Auntie Mee that she shouldn't have brought Miss Kwon into this; she shouldn't have frightened her by letting her know that if I failed in my mission to find Mori Di—or if I refused to accept the mission—Miss Kwon would die.

Auntie Mee, for her part, said that it wasn't up to her. It was foreordained by the codex.

Finally, I broke them apart. Doc Yong was still fuming. Auntie Mee straightened her robe, acting like a queen who'd been rudely offended.

Once they calmed down, Doc Yong returned to the whimpering Miss Kwon, comforting her, cooing, apologizing. Auntie Mee relit a couple of candles that had sputtered out, repinned stray hairs in her coiffure, tidied up her table and codex, and resumed her place of power in the center of the room.

"Mori Di," she told me, pointing at my nose, exasperated. "You find?" she asked. "No find?"

I glanced at Doc Yong. She was still angry but, reluctantly, she nodded.

Maybe it was Doc Yong's encouragement. Maybe it was the curiosity that had been aroused in me, both by the passion of these two women and by the oddness of the assignment. Maybe it was the pitiful whimpers of Miss Kwon who still huddled in her dark corner. Maybe it was the nagging worry that maybe—just maybe—the fortune teller was correct and Miss Kwon would die if I didn't find Mori Di's sbones. But more likely my decision was based upon a feeling of kinship with a man Auntie Mee called Mori Di, a young American who'd traveled halfway around the world to a country he'd probably never heard of before and somehow, for some reason lost now to time, had met a cruel fate.

I found myself turning back to Auntie Mee and telling her, "I'll do what I can."

Doc Yong, still breathing heavily, hugged Miss Kwon, stared directly into my eyes, and smiled her fabulous smile.

2

"**Y**our black-market stats are for shit," Staff Sergeant Riley growled.

He tossed a printout to Ernie Bascom, my partner, who caught it on the fly.

"So what else is new?" Ernie replied and tossed the printout into the trash.

"You'd better retrieve that," Riley said. "The First Shirt has a case of the ass and later this morning he's going to be reviewing your lack of performance."

"Screw the First Shirt." Ernie grabbed Riley's issue of today's *Pacific Stars and Stripes* and snapped the pages open.

The three of us sat in the headquarters of the 8th United States Army Criminal Investigation Detachment on the first floor of Building 306-A on Yongsan Compound Main Post. Riley, his skeletal body lost in the starched folds of his khaki uniform, glared at Ernie. As the Admin NCO, it was Riley's job to make sure that our statistics looked good in the reports that wound their way up the labyrinthine corridors of 8th Imperial Army. But in the day-to-day grind of criminal investigation, not everything can be quantified. I had little patience for Riley's reports. Ernie had none.

Miss Kim, the statuesque Admin secretary, did her best to ignore the three of us. She pecked away at her *hangul* typewriter, theoretically translating documents from English to Korean. Actually, I believed most of her attention was on Ernie. They'd been close once but after reading some of my reports, which often included Ernie's dealings with the fair sex, she'd begun to pull away from him.

He didn't seem to mind. Ernie Bascom was just over six feet tall, slender, with short sandy blond hair and green eyes behind round-lensed glasses and for some reason he drove women mad. I'm not sure why. I could only guess that it was because he was unpredictable; no woman ever knew if he was going to take a flying leap off a fast moving train or kneel and present her with a bouquet of spring roses. Ernie kept women guessing and once he had them confused he took his gratification where he found it.

Miss Kim had realized this and the realization made her furious at both of us. I tried to mollify her by being kind, occasionally placing a small gift on her desk, like a box of chocolates or a bottle of hand lotion from the Yongsan Main PX. It didn't help. She blamed me, Ernie's investigative partner, for leading him astray. Unfair. That was like blaming a canvas salesman for forcing Picasso to paint.

The time was now 0815. I clapped my hands. "Time to get cracking," I said to Ernie.

He stared at me dully. He didn't ask, *Cracking on what?*—not in front of Riley.

I half expected Riley to say that we had to wait for the first sergeant to return from his morning meeting with the provost marshal. He didn't. That gave us deniability if the First Shirt later asked us where we'd been. Mentally, I rehearsed my line: "Nobody told us that we were supposed to wait around the office, Top."

I rose from the gray, army-issue chair. Ernie stood too.

"Where the hell you two guys going?" Riley asked. "The commissary doesn't open until ten."

The 8th Army Commissary was where we monitored black-market activities. G.I.s, or more often their wives, bought goods from the commissary—bananas, maraschino cherries, instant coffee, soluble coffee creamer, sliced oxtail—all items difficult and expensive to obtain in Korea. Then they carted them out to Itaewon and sold them to one of the local black-market operators. The profit margin on most items was 100 percent, sometimes more. Despite the fact that there was a limit on how much a family could purchase each month, an industrious *yobo*—the Korean wife of an American G.I.—could pull down thousands of dollars per year; all of it strictly against Army regulations and strictly against the ROK–U.S. Status of Forces Agreement.

Black-marketing drove the honchos of 8th Army nuts. They didn't like seeing all those Korean women scurrying around their PX and their commissary and they didn't like the insolent attitude a G.I. developed when, for the first time in his life, he amassed ten thousand dollars in his bank account. That's where the law enforcement officers of 8th Army CID came in. It was our job to bust blackmarketeers. And at 8th Army staff meetings, the honchos considered this job just as important, if not more so, than solving assaults, rapes, murders, and other sorts of mayhem.

"We'll be at the commissary by ten," I replied.

"Yeah," Riley said. "But where will you be till then?"

"At the SIR warehouse."

SIR. Serious Incident Report. Riley didn't ask us what we'd be doing there but, whatever it might be, it sounded like official business so he was satisfied. If he was questioned later by the First Shirt, his butt would be covered.

CYA. That's what army bureaucracy is all about. Or as the Koreans say, cover your *kundingi*.

The warehouse was musty and the wooden door leading into the main storage area creaked when it opened. Fred Linderhaus, the NCO-in-charge, pointed us in the right direction.

"First thing in the morning," he said, "two CID agents want to look at some old files. Must be something big."

"Nothing big," I said.

"Then what?"

Ernie stopped and turned to block Linderhaus's way. "Do you have a freaking need to know?" he asked.

Since I'd first started working with Ernie Bascom, he'd been confrontational. This is a good thing in a criminal investigation agent and more than once his belligerent attitude had helped us gather information we needed or, more importantly, escape unscathed from a tough situation. Ernie's temper also had its downside, like unnecessarily earning us enemies when what we needed was friends. His hometown was Detroit, the white suburbs not the black inner city, and I often thought that maybe it was something in the way he was brought up that caused him to be such a hothead. Or maybe it was the two tours he'd spent in Vietnam, under fire, buying pure China White from the snot-nosed boys on the other side of the concertina wire. Whatever the cause, lately Ernie had been more temperamental than usual. Almost anything would set him off. For the last few days, the chip on his shoulder teetered there like a claymore mine ready to explode. I hadn't asked him about it. I hadn't had the nerve.

Linderhaus's eyes widened. "Hey," he said, shrugging his big shoulders. "Just asking."

"We're doing research here," Ernie continued, "because we're writing a book. That's *all* you need to know. You got it?"

"Got it," Linderhaus replied. He stuck his hands in his pockets, turned, and shambled back down the dusty corridor.

After he'd left, I said, "You really know how to encourage voluntary cooperation, don't you?"

Ernie snorted and grabbed his crotch. "He can voluntarily cooperate this."

The warehouse was a large Quonset hut on a cement foundation divided by a series of plywood walls painted a shade of green the army calls "olive drab." G.I.s call it "puke green." Fluorescent lights, hanging from wooden rafters, buzzed overhead. Wooden shelving reaching ten feet high bearing cardboard boxes teetered above us. Each box was labeled. We were in a section marked SIRs, JUNE 1962. Each box contained anywhere from thirty to a hundred SIRs for that month, statements concerning incidents that military police units throughout the Korean Peninsula considered important enough to report up the chain of command. If the 8th Army provost marshal agreed that the incident was serious, he included it in the blotter report that was presented daily to the commander, 8th United States Army. Once an incident was classified as a SIR, a file would be created, assigned a number, and an investigation launched, its progress tracked. The SIR remains open until the case is solved or otherwise declared closed.

Black-market cases usually don't get SIR treatment, not unless the case is particularly egregious like the wholesale pilfering of a few tons of army-issue copper wire. Normally, SIRs are made about assaults, thefts, rapes, and murders involving US Forces personnel. Often, a Korean citizen is also involved—sometimes as the perpetrator, more often as the victim.

With 50,000 American G.I.s stationed in Korea since the war ended more than twenty years earlier, there had been plenty of serious incidents to report. Eighth Army's purpose, according to military press releases, was to protect "Freedom's Frontier." That is, to deter the 700,000 North Korean Communist soldiers positioned just north of the Demilitarized Zone from invading their brethren in South Korea. Our real purpose, I believed, was to hold on to our empire. And many G.I.s who came to Korea and suddenly found themselves living in the lap of luxury—with houseboys to do their laundry and business girls to satisfy their needs after duty hours—took on the airs of potentates. And sometimes these petty potentates abused people they saw as their servants, which is why this SIR warehouse was stuffed full of box after box of paperwork reporting criminal activity.

The military, always mindful of its choirboy image, likes to keep this information under wraps. That's why Fred Linderhaus doesn't allow anyone in here unless they have a "need to know." And the outside world—the world the military considers to be its enemy—*never* has a "need to know."

We kept walking down the dusty hallways. Fleas flew in tight formations. I knew it was just my imagination but from within the boxes it seemed as if I heard the sobs of victims and the muffled screams of those who would never again draw the sweet breath of life.

"Doesn't Linderhaus ever sweep up around here?" Ernie asked. He wasn't listening to the same voices.

"They don't allow Korean cleaning crews in the warehouse," I replied. "The material's too sensitive."

"OK. So Eighth Army doesn't want anybody nosing around in their dirty laundry. But they ought to allow a fumigation team in once in a while." Ernie swatted at the swirling insects. "What the hell we looking for, anyway?"

"I told you. A G.I. who was murdered in 1953."

"And for what again?"

I told him about Auntie Mee.

"You say she's good looking?"

"Not bad."

"But you couldn't tell much beneath those thick robes."

"I wasn't looking that close," I said.

"Because you're stuck on Doc Yong. That's the problem with you, Sueño. You like those smart chicks, the kind who wear glasses."

I was about to tell him that not all women who wear glasses are smart but decided against it.

"So this fortune teller," Ernie continued, "this Auntie Mee, is ranting about something that happened twenty years ago?"

"Right."

"You didn't pay her, did you?"

"No. She just asked me to check this out as a favor. Really, I'm doing it for Doc Yong."

"Of course you are. You getting any of that?"

I ignored him.

I'm six foot four, Hispanic, with dark hair and dark eyes and some people have told me that I present a good appearance. But I have never had the success with women that Ernie has. I suppose I'm too serious. Growing up as an orphan in East L.A., as a foster child farmed out from family to family, I was forced to be serious. And observant. And cautious. Qualities that most of the silly girls we met in nightclubs didn't prize but qualities that I hoped Doctor Yong In-ja would respond to. I wasn't about to brief Ernie on my romantic progress—or lack thereof—with Doc Yong.

The boxes above us had reached the late fifties now and the

color and sturdiness of the cardboard was rapidly deteriorating. We reached 1953, DECEMBER, and then SEPTEMBER and finally, after shifting a few boxes, JULY.

It was on the top shelf, the cardboard crumpled and the rectangular shape distorted. Probably because the box had been dripped on through a porous roof at one time and then dried out. According to Linderhaus, this tin-roofed Quonset hut had been built only a few years ago. Who knows where they'd stored stuff before that? We used a small stepladder. Ernie steadied me as I grabbed hold of the big box, slid it to the edge of the wooden shelf, and let it drop onto the cement floor with a *thump*.

A squadron of fleas swirled into action. Ernie cursed and swatted.

"Christ, Sueño. You and your freaking fortune teller."

After the insects calmed down, I opened the box. It held a jumble of papers, some of them in brown folders, some not. I thumbed through the names typed on white labels at the top of each folder. Occasionally, I pulled a folder out and glanced at it.

Doravich, Peter T., Corporal, had been the perpetrator of an assault in the barracks up at the old 1st Cavalry Division, when the 1st Cav had been stationed near the DMZ. Doravich had beaten up another G.I. using an entrenching tool and the victim had lost an eye. Hardenson, Arthur Q., Staff Sergeant, had been tried and convicted for pistol whipping and then robbing a Korean bus driver. The bus driver's family had also filed a claim against the United States government for the then princely sum of $5,000. Marcellus, Oscar S., Private First Class, had been accused of raping a Korean business girl. The military court found that he'd merely been guilty of not paying her as agreed in their preexisting verbal contract. The court martial ordered him busted down two stripes to Private E-nothing and had him shipped back to the States.

None of the men had been murdered. So, presumably, their bones wouldn't be found in Itaewon.

The Korean War ended when a cease-fire was signed between North and South Korea—and their respective allies, Communist China and the U.S.A.—in July of 1953. Auntie Mee claimed that Mori Di had been murdered "at the beginning" of the reconstruction period. That is, shortly after the end of the war. I left the box marked

JULY, 1953 and moved on to AUGUST, 1953. Ernie switched on a flashlight because the glow from the overhead fluorescent bulbs didn't reach down here very well.

"You don't believe any of this fortune teller shit, do you?" he asked.

I shrugged. "Let me search these files," I said, "then we'll talk."

August didn't seem to have anything that matched Auntie Mee's words. Neither did the box containing the SIRs for September, October, nor even November. Ernie was becoming antsy and the time was close on to ten o'clock, when we would have to make our appearance at the commissary. I decided to at least finish the box marked DECEMBER, 1953 and then, like a sharp slap across the face, I spotted a thick manila folder.

"What is it?" Ernie asked.

I pointed.

There, typed neatly across a yellowed label affixed to the folder, was a name and a rank: MORETTI, FLORENCIO R., TECHNICAL SERGEANT, (MISSING, PRESUMED DEAD).

I pulled the folder out, rubbed the flat of my palm across its smooth surface, and felt a thin coat of dust trickle through my fingers. I thumbed quickly through the folder, every new fact confirming what I'd known from the moment I'd seen the name *Moretti*.

Ernie waited, hardly breathing.

Finally, I looked up at him and said, "We've found Mori Di."

We spent the rest of the morning sitting in Ernie's jeep in the parking lot out front of the Yongsan Commissary. People went in and people came out: G.I.s, officers, American female dependents, Department of Defense civilians, but mostly Korean wives. I paged through the Serious Incident Report and made notes. Ernie chomped impatiently on ginseng gum.

The Koreans would have called him Mori Di because that's how they would've heard his last name. There are too many syllables in American names for them so they try to pare them down somewhat. The Koreans wouldn't have called him by his first name, Florencio or Flo, for two reasons. First, G.I.s refer to one another by last names;

the Koreans would've mimicked that. Second, Koreans have trouble pronouncing the English letter f. The sound doesn't exist in their alphabet. The closest they can come is to couple a hard p with a u and then continue on with the word. For example, when you hear a Korean refer to France, if you listen closely, you will hear them say "Pu-ran-suh." Said quickly enough it sounds almost like "France."

So "Mori Di" would've been what they called him.

The next question was how had Auntie Mee known about him? I didn't believe for a minute that the ghost of Technical Sergeant Florencio R. Moretti had visited her from the spirit realm. Also, why did she care about his bones or where they were buried? At this point, the answers to these questions didn't really matter. I'd promised Doc Yong I'd try to find the remains of Mori Di and, for her sake, I would.

By noon the commissary was bustling and one Korean woman in a tight-fitting dress caught Ernie's attention. She was filling up the trunk of her PX taxi with every imaginable black-market item, from Tang to Spam. When she was finished, she hopped in the back seat of the taxi and gave the driver instructions. They pulled away from the long line of vehicles waiting in front of the Yongsan Commissary.

"That's our lady," Ernie said.

I looked up from the SIR. "You're just choosing her because she's the best looking you've seen so far."

"You've discovered my criterion. Are you a detective or something?"

Ernie started the engine and was just shifting into first gear when, in the distance, we heard a siren. The sound grew louder. Within seconds a canvas-sided MP jeep with a flashing red light atop its roof swerved into the commissary parking lot, hesitated for a moment, and then headed straight toward us.

"What the—" Ernie said.

Tires screeched and the jeep pulled up in front of us, blocking our way. Two armed MPs jumped out. Each kept his right hand atop the grip of his .45.

Ernie shouted at them. "You're blocking my way, morons!"

"Tough shit, Bascom," one of the MPs said. He was a buck sergeant and his name tag said POLLARD. I knew him. He was a good MP.

Sergeant Pollard stood in front of Ernie and told him, "You're off the black-market detail."

"So what took you so long?" Ernie replied.

"Break-in," Pollard said. "Field grade officer's quarters. You and your partner have caught the call." He pulled a small notebook out of his breast pocket, thumbed through it, and said, "Yongsan South Post, Unit 43-B, Artillery Drive. Assigned to the J-2, Colonel Oswald Q. Tidwell."

This is where two guys with less savoir faire would've whistled in awe. J-2 meant military intelligence. The *J* stood for "joint command": the United Nations, U.S. Forces Korea, and the 8th United States Army. So Colonel Oswald Q. Tidwell was in charge of military intelligence on the Korean Peninsula and answered only to the commander, 8th United States Army. In army parlance this is the equivalent of sitting at the right hand of god.

"Anybody hurt?" I asked.

Pollard studied his notes. "Not that's been reported so far. But Mrs. Tidwell is hysterical."

"Why?"

"Her daughter is missing. Hasn't reported in since fifteen hundred hours Tuesday."

"You mean Jessica?" Ernie asked.

Pollard checked his notes again. "Right. That's her name."

"Shit," Ernie said.

He jammed the jeep in gear and swerved past Pollard and around the other jeep. The two MPs looked after us, shaking their heads, glad that they weren't going to have to delve into the messy family life of Colonel Oswald Q. Tidwell.

Jessica Tidwell was notorious in the 8th Army. Only seventeen, she'd already become a legend. Last year, when she was a junior at Seoul American High School, the Department of Defense school on post for military dependents, she'd become involved with some fast-talking G.I. who worked at the 9th Support Group, the personnel unit on post. She attended a party at the barracks and, apparently, she'd first turned her amorous attentions on the guy who invited her and then on at least a half-dozen other young soldiers. Word leaked out. Ernie and I hadn't investigated the incident and I was grateful for that. Nobody thanks you when you air the dirty laundry of the family of a field-grade officer. But after the official report wound its way up the chain of command, the half-dozen or so G.I.s involved were brought up on charges—statutory rape and disrespect to the dependent of a field grade officer. Within days, they were not only convicted but two of them did some time in the stockade and all of them were summarily dismissed from the army.

But punishing the guilty wasn't enough for the honchos of 8th Army, not when one of their own was involved. They went one step further. The entire 9th Support Group—personnel, offices, barracks, equipment, vehicles, everything—was transferred to a small logistics compound about twenty miles outside of Seoul. In other words, banished for their sins.

Since then, Mrs. Tidwell had been keeping a very tight reign on her willful teenage daughter. Ernie knew of her from reports and gossip but even he was smart enough to stay strictly away from Jessica Tidwell. Or at least I hoped he was.

The Tidwells lived in a sprawling split-level home on Yongsan Compound South Post. A squad of MPs had already secured the perimeter and I recognized a sedan parked in the driveway as belonging to Colonel Cosgrove, the Chief Chaplain of the 8th Army. Inside, the chaplain sat on a leather upholstered couch, comforting Mrs. Tidwell. She held an embroidered handkerchief to her mouth and rose to her feet when we walked in.

"Are you the investigators?" she asked.

I nodded. "Yes, ma'am."

"What took you so long?"

I didn't know how to answer that one so I didn't.

She held her body stiffly and wore a cotton dress that was shaped by petticoats and elastic undergarments.

"I don't care about the money," she said, waving her arm. "They can have all that. I just want you to find Jessica." Her face wrinkled into a mask of rage. "And I want you to find her now!"

Neither Ernie nor I moved. The chaplain, a tall man with thick gray hair, moved toward her and grabbed her elbow. "Now Margaret," he said, "these young men are professionals. Let them do their jobs. And don't worry, they'll find Jessica."

We proceeded into the den, the room that Mrs. Tidwell told us was used by her husband as his home office. She explained what was missing. As we examined the evidence, she said, "I know you're afraid to ask but you must want to know why Oswald isn't here."

Both Ernie and I gazed steadily as Mrs. Tidwell, not speaking. The chaplain grimaced.

"My husband is a very busy man," Mrs. Tidwell said. "His responsibilities are massive. If he could, he'd be here right now, looking for his daughter.

"Don't smirk like that," she said to us. "I won't have it! Not in my own home. There is such a thing as silent contempt, you know," she screamed.

The chaplain stepped toward her. She lashed out at him with a fist. He dodged it easily, waited a moment, and then touched her shoulder. She turned and crumpled into his arms, where she stayed for a few minutes, sobbing.

None of the windows leading into Colonel Tidwell's home office had been broken or jimmied in any way. He normally kept the door leading into the den padlocked from the outside. Mrs. Tidwell told us that when she checked the room shortly after her husband left for work that morning, she'd found it open. At the time she hadn't thought much of it. But later, while airing out the house, she noticed that the door to the safe was open also. She called her husband and he told her to make sure that the thousand dollars in U.S. greenbacks he kept there for emergency use was still intact. It wasn't. The envelope was gone. Colonel Tidwell called the MPs from his office.

Technically, no American personnel in Korea are supposed to be in possession of U.S. currency. When a G.I. or his dependents arrives in country, all cash is converted into blue or red Military Payment

Certificates. The idea is that it will make it more difficult for the North Korean Communists to get their hands on U.S. currency which they could then use as international exchange. Despite this restriction, greenbacks are still available, illegally, on the black-market and fetch a higher price in *won*, the Korean currency, than MPC.

A full colonel who is the 8th Army J-2 was not going to be criticized for keeping a small pile of American cash on hand; an enlisted G.I. would be locked up for it.

Clearly, the theft of the money had been an inside job. There was no sign of a break-in and whoever had entered the den had used a key. The safe had been opened by someone using the combination.

The household help consisted of a Korean maid and a Korean "serviceman," what G.I.s would call a houseboy. I spoke to both of them. They were nervous they might lose their jobs. Neither admitted seeing anyone entering the den but they'd left the previous evening and hadn't returned until dawn. There were also two contract Korean security guards outside, supposedly to protect the J-2 and his family from possible attack by North Korean commandos. I didn't bother to speak to them because neither had entered the house. But I took note of which guards had been on shift the previous night in case I needed to speak to them later.

Mrs. Tidwell was less concerned about the theft of the greenbacks than she was about the whereabouts of her daughter, Jessica.

"She didn't come home last night," Mrs. Tidwell told us.

Mustering a neutral tone, Ernie asked, "Is that unusual?"

Slowly, Mrs. Tidwell shook her head. "Not anymore."

"'Not anymore?'" I asked.

"Not since she met that *Mexican.*" She spat the word out. Then she looked up at me. "Oh, I'm sorry. You're Hispanic, aren't you."

"Doesn't matter," I said. "Who is the Mexican you're referring to?"

"The driver," she said. "Nothing but a damn driver, when she could be dating any of the young officers at the O Club." Mrs. Tidwell's words fairly sizzled. "I don't know his name," she continued. "Jessica and I never speak of him. About a month ago he was assigned to drive for the Officers' Wives' Club and I dragged her along to a meeting on Daughters' Night, hoping that she'd hit it off with some of the other girls her age. Instead, she went outside to smoke and struck up a conversation with the driver."

"How do you know she's been seeing him?" Ernie asked.

"She tells me," Mrs. Tidwell replied, "every chance she gets."

Our first stop was the Orderly Room of the 21st Transportation Company, also known as Twenty-one T Car, the 8th Army motor pool. It wasn't difficult for Ernie and me to narrow down our search given the clues we had: Hispanic, assigned to drive for the Officers' Wives' Club. The first sergeant had the answer for us in less than two minutes: "Bernal, Francisco, rank of corporal."

"What's he like?" I asked the first sergeant.

"Don't know," the gray-haired man replied. "Too many young troops coming and going for me to keep track of them all."

"But that's your job," Ernie said.

"Screw you, Bascom."

"Save that for your troops," Ernie said.

I told the first sergeant we'd find our own way to the barracks. He didn't protest.

Outside, as our footsteps crunched across a field of gravel, I asked Ernie, "Why are you messing with him?"

Ernie shrugged. "Just in a good mood, I guess."

"But you're making life more difficult for us."

"I like flashing my badge and seeing first sergeants and field-grade officers squirm."

"We haven't even met Colonel Tidwell yet."

"We will."

He had that part right. And I wasn't looking forward to it. According to what I'd been told, Colonel Tidwell was about as grim and hard-assed as it's possible to be; which is very grim and hard-assed indeed when you're an intelligence officer in the U.S. Army.

The Twenty-one T Car barracks were Quonset huts, spray-painted green and hooked together by wooden passageways. We entered at the end of one Quonset hut and wound through a long maze of corridors, passing Korean houseboys in the latrine, standing in huge metal tubs, sloshing soap suds and laundry under their feet. Finally, we found Bernal's quarters, room 463-C. I tried to open it with the master key the first sergeant had provided. The lock clicked but the door remained secure.

"Barred from inside," Ernie said. He banged on the door with his fist. "Bernal! Open up!" No response. Ernie banged once more. When no one answered, he motioned for me to stand out of the way. I did. Ernie took a running start from the opposite side of the hallway and jammed his shoulder into the wooden door. It burst open and the two of us charged inside.

A dim bulb beneath a red lampshade illuminated a body laying in the bunk. A long slender body, glistening like polished ivory.

It definitely wasn't Corporal Bernal.

3

According to the Serious Incident Report, the G.I.s who knew Moretti well called him Flo. Back in those days, more than twenty years ago, the Broadway showman Flo Ziegfeld was still remembered so it wouldn't have seemed like such an odd name. The G.I.s who didn't know him well, and the business girls in Itaewon, called him Moretti or the Korean version: Mori Di. The MP investigator who typed out the report referred to him consistently as Moretti.

His height was given as five foot seven, his weight, 135 pounds, and there was a black-and-white photograph of him, the same one he would've had pasted onto his military ID card. His hair was dark, a little long by today's military standards, greased and combed into a slight wave at front. His lips were tight in the photograph, his brown eyes focused straight ahead, as if he were braced—physically and mentally—for the rigors of military life. I imagined him with a woolen cowl over his head, like an ascetic monk from the Middle Ages. But he wasn't a monk, he was an American G.I. who'd arrived in Korea while the war still raged and he was fortunate enough to be alive when the cease-fire was signed.

During the Korean War, air force pilots complained because all they were doing in their combat sorties was hitting targets that had already been hit. Making "rubble bounce on rubble," as they put it. Nothing was left in the city of Seoul. Moretti had been assigned to the 8th Army Civil Affairs Office and his job, according to the Serious Incident Report, was to rebuild the section of Seoul nearest the 8th Army headquarters, the area known as Itaewon.

The U.S. was funneling millions of dollars in military and economic reconstruction aid into Korea. Moretti had three two-and-a-half ton trucks at his disposal and three G.I. drivers. He also had access to U.S.-made building supplies being shipped into the Port of Inchon and the authority to hire and fire Korean construction crews. A lowly tech sergeant was given that much authority because things were nutso at the time, everything had to be done right now, and there weren't enough trained engineers to go around. The 8th Army Engineering staff did provide Moretti with blueprints and a list of approved Korean engineering firms to help him build and repair buildings. According to the report, Moretti set about reconstructing Itaewon with a zeal that few G.I.s exhibited. After the first brick hut was built, he moved out to Itaewon and supervised reconstruction work twenty-four hours a day.

Meanwhile, the Korean people were desperate for shelter. Shacks made of scrap metal and charred lumber went up overnight. Some of them were used as bars, more of them as brothels, catering to American G.I.s—the only people in the country at the time with disposable income. Itaewon was put off limits by 8th Army health authorities because of the lack of sanitation and the fear of communicable diseases such as tuberculosis and, of course, syphilis and gonorrhea. But that didn't stop G.I.s from sneaking out there. Eighth Army headquarters was only a half mile away. A short walk down the MSR and a G.I. would be in paradise. For a few black-market items, like cigarettes or soap or shoe polish, he could take his pick from amongst a small sea of destitute young women. The MPs did their best to enforce the off-limits restrictions but no one could stop the G.I.s from reaching

Itaewon. As the buildings started to be rebuilt and plumbing and sanitation and electricity gradually began to be restored, the 8th Army health authorities put certain facilities back "on-limits." G.I.s could go there without fear of being arrested by MP patrols.

Most of the buildings approved to be put back on limits were buildings built by Technical Sergeant Flo Moretti.

There was plenty of opportunity for Moretti to line his pockets. The MP investigator checked to see if Moretti had bought money orders from the one approved bank at 8th Army headquarters. This would've been the easiest way to send money home, but there was no record of Moretti ever making such a purchase. He was honest. And he was doing his best to reconstruct the country he'd been ordered to rebuild.

But then Moretti did something stunning. He decided to erect an orphanage, smack dab in the middle of the red-light district of Itaewon. The streets of Seoul were littered with children who, in the madness of war, were either orphaned or abandoned by their parents. The investigator mentioned this project above all the others that Moretti had going at that time because, he believed, this orphanage had led to Moretti's death.

Or supposed death. There were questions.

The MP investigator identified himself in the upper left corner of all his documents as Cort. That's it, just Cort. Cort interviewed everyone Moretti had known, including workmen who had to lay down their picks and shovels while a ROK Army MP translated his questions. Although he used precise, direct, and unemotional language in his report, Cort had been caught up in this investigation. The portrait he painted was of an honest man struggling to stay afloat in a swirling sea of corruption, doing his best to provide shelter for people who were desperately in need.

Cort was particularly meticulous in his reconstruction of the assault on Moretti. He interviewed everyone who'd been there, he took samples of the blood spatters and compared them to Moretti's blood type, and he searched long and hard for the weapons used.

But when the body stayed missing, I believe Cort went a little nuts.

* * *

The ivory body before us was topped by a tangled mass of thick red hair.

She wore sheer black panties and matching brassiere and lay sprawled on the twisted sheets of Corporal Francisco Bernal's unmade bunk. Her tongue lolled pink across rouged lips. Ernie checked her pulse, staring all the while at the voluptuous curves of her freckled flesh.

Ernie dropped her wrist. "Heart's still pumping. Looks like Corporal Bernal had himself a truly fine evening."

"With stolen money," I said.

The redhead shook her curly locks. They rustled past pink ears and then her eyes opened. Blazing green. She sat up suddenly, her breasts swinging wildly with the movement.

"What are you doing here?" she asked.

Ernie crowbarred a grin. "Good morning. Let me guess. You must be Miss Motor Pool of 1973."

The redhead's eyes darted around the room. "Where's Paco?"

Ernie gazed at me blankly.

"Paco's short for Francisco," I said.

Ernie nodded; his smile broadened once again and he turned back to the redhead.

"That's what we were going to ask you. Seems there's been a theft at Colonel Tidwell's residence."

She snorted. A dainty yet dismissive sound. Then she bent over and started groping for something, shoving her clothes out of the way. "Where are my cigarettes?"

Her tone was impatient, as if she were dealing with incompetent servants who weren't responding fast enough.

Ernie grabbed a small black purse off a scratched footlocker and rummaged inside. He found a pack of Kools and tossed them to her along with a lighter. While she fumbled with her cigarette, Ernie searched through the contents of the purse and pulled out a military dependent ID card. He studied it for a moment, his eyes growing wider, and then he whistled softly.

The redhead ignored him, apparently accustomed to people being impressed by her pedigree.

Ernie tossed the card to me.

I snatched it out of the air. Still watching the redhead, I tilted the laminated surface toward the dim light of the floor lamp.

Her name was Tidwell, Jessica H.

Paco—Corporal Francisco Bernal—was preparing himself for a world of hurt. Regardless of who had actually stolen the thousand dollars, Paco would be blamed, as the instigator. And from the evidence I could see in front of me, he'd also be charged with statutory rape.

I gazed at seventeen-year-old Jessica. She was still bleary eyed but sitting on the edge of the bunk now, sucking on her cancer stick, puffing smoke into the air in a way that she must have imagined appeared sophisticated. She wasn't concerned with being half naked and having two army cops leering at her. She had to have copied the safe combination from the slip of paper hidden in her father's wallet and sneaked the key to his home office. But I started questioning her from a different angle.

"Why did Paco take the money?" I asked.

She stared at me through a puff of smoke, not shocked by my question but thinking things through. "He didn't take the money," she said. "He *borrowed* it."

Ernie crossed his arms and leaned against a rickety chest of drawers, keeping his grin firmly in place, enjoying the show. One question had saved us a lot of work.

"Only a loan?" I asked.

She dimpled her cheeks and crossed her eyes, letting me know that she was pleased that the moron had understood.

"When does Paco plan to pay this thousand dollars back?" I asked.

Jessica let out a sigh of exasperation. "Before the end of the week. He needs it for an investment."

"What type of investment?"

Suddenly Jessica realized that she'd said too much. She inhaled nervously.

When she didn't answer, Ernie spoke up. "Maybe buying and selling a little weed? Or some hash? Something that the kids at the high school need?"

She lowered her glowing cigarette. "Paco's not a pusher."

"But he *is* a dealer," I said.

She didn't answer but looked away and continued to smoke.

A photo atop a footlocker showed Corporal Paco Bernal in green uniform and garrison cap. He was a full-cheeked Hispanic man. Dark. Handsome. A smile that could break teenage hearts.

I knew him. Of fifteen hundred enlisted men assigned to 8th Army headquarters, only two of us were Chicanos from East L.A., Paco and myself. I didn't know him well. We'd had only one or two casual conversations, asking one another if we had mutual acquaintances back in the barrio. We didn't. My cop instincts had picked up a devious side to Paco Bernal but I never thought he'd go as far as this. A thief and a defiler of young women, he was shaming the Latino world.

"By the way," Ernie asked, "where is the dear boy?"

Unconsciously, Jessica patted the sheet beneath her and gazed down.

"I don't know," she said.

"But he was here last night when you fell asleep?"

She raised the cigarette to her lips and nodded slowly, lost in thought. "Are you his only girlfriend?" Ernie asked.

Instead of growing angry she said, "I don't know. Why would I care about that?"

Ernie persuaded Jessica Tidwell to put on her clothes. After finishing her cigarette, she combed her hair and pulled herself together.

Ernie and I interviewed some of the other guys in the barracks. A few of them had seen Paco come in last night with Jessica. She was drunk and stumbling but Paco appeared sober. None of them had seen him leave. His full issue of uniforms was still hanging in his wall locker, so he must've been wearing civvies when he left. And his little traveling bag was still there, so he probably left wearing only the clothes on his back—with a thousand stolen dollars tucked safely in his pocket. One item was missing from his field gear, his bayonet.

After we notified CID headquarters about the incident, the search for Paco Bernal began. Despite a military police all-points bulletin, no trace of him was found on base, so we expanded our search to include Seoul's international airport at Kimpo. No Francisco Bernal on any of the manifests. We also checked the military embarkation point at Osan Air Force Base. Again, no sign of Paco. There are only a half-dozen international embarkation points from South Korea. We contacted them all. While conducting these checks, we passed along an edict from the 8th Army commander: If found, Corporal Francisco Bernal was to be arrested and detained.

Jessica Tidwell was whisked away to the 121st Evacuation Hospital for an examination in the emergency room. Her mother met her there. Colonel Tidwell, we were told, was still conducting business as usual in the J-2 office at the opulent headquarters of the 8th United States Army. He didn't call and ask us any questions or order us in for an interview but we knew he'd read our blotter report.

Back at the CID office, I started typing up that blotter report, trying to keep it as neutral sounding as possible. I figured the Tidwell family had suffered enough embarrassment. Word of the latest Jessica Tidwell incident spread through the 8th Army headquarters complex like wildfire. I heard words like "goddamn Mexicans" and "beaners" and "greasers" and did my best to keep my temper in check. Paco had placed Chicanos at the forefront of bigotry. I cursed him silently and swore that I'd find the son of a bitch. Which exactly matched the sentiments of Colonel Brace, the 8th Army provost marshal.

Ernie and I stood in front of his desk at the position of attention.

"You two are off the black-market detail until further notice. Understood?" We nodded. "I want this Corporal Bernal found and I want him found now. Any questions?"

Neither Ernie nor I had any. We saluted and left.

Just before we exited the building, the cannon went off signifying the end of the duty day. We waited until the last notes of the retreat bugles sounded and then jogged across the small parking lot to Ernie's jeep. We didn't have to talk about where we were going. Both of us knew. The same place either one of us would go if we'd just stolen a thousand dollars.

Itaewon.

Ernie and I hit Itaewon fast and hard.

Our plan was to start our search with the brothels and business-girl hooches farthest away from the main drag, the ones most well hidden, where a G.I. who'd just stolen a thousand dollars worth of greenbacks might feel safe.

Itaewon was somewhat more cosmopolitan than the other G.I. villages in Korea. That is, neither the 21st Transportation Company nor the 121st Evac nor the 8th Army Honor Guard had their own nightclub or bar staked out for them and them alone. G.I.s from various units mingled freely, if not always harmoniously, and unlike the compounds out at Kunsan or up north at Tonduchon or just south of the DMZ at Munsan, the various infantry or artillery or combat engineer units didn't have their own little enclaves. So Corporal Paco Bernal could be anywhere in Itaewon. Our strategy was simple: cover as much ground as possible before Paco Bernal became aware that we were in the village looking for him.

Of course, our entire search could be futile. Paco Bernal could be halfway to Pusan by now. But I was betting that he'd stay on familiar ground. Not only to be near his home turf and contacts— and to make whatever deal he'd planned—but also because G.I.s, although they won't admit it, are afraid of traveling in Korea. For the most part they don't speak Korean and don't understand Korean customs and can't read the street signs and when they wander too far from military compounds, they feel lost. So I believed that Paco Bernal was here in Itaewon—somewhere.

Itaewon was alive at this hour, preparing industriously for the busy evening to come. The front gates of the courtyards were mostly open; business girls coming and going from the local bathhouses or gathering around a low table in the mama-san's hooch, chatting, chopsticks flashing, stuffing rice and vegetables into their mouths as sustenance for the long night's work ahead. The smell of fermented kimchee and soap suds and hairspray was everywhere: in the open hooches, wafting from the balconies of upstairs apartments, and emerging from behind the sliding wooden doors of closetlike rooms. When Ernie and I approached the business girls, it was the same story: headshakes, denials that they knew Paco Bernal after gawking at the black-and-white photo from his personnel records that I held in front of their curious eyes.

Had they seen him before? Yes, around the village.

Did he have a girlfriend out here? Not that they were aware of.

Did they know where he was now? Heads shook vehemently. They hadn't a clue.

Ernie and I kept prowling through the back alleys of Itaewon, down narrow pedestrian lanes, around sharp corners defined by ten-foot-high brick and stone walls. The sun started to go down. Sodium streetlamps, spaced every twenty yards or so, switched on. Still, no sign of Paco Bernal.

Finally, at one hooch, a business girl stood up from scrubbing her face above a metal pan beneath a running faucet in the middle of a stone-paved courtyard. She turned to us and said, "You looking for Paco?"

"Yeah," Ernie replied. "You seen him?"

"No, but anybody say. Two MP in Itaewon lookey-lookey every-where for some G.I. called Paco. We hear. Anybody know."

She squatted back down and resumed scrubbing her face.

Ernie stuck another stick of ginseng gum in his mouth and chomped viciously. "So much for the element of surprise," he said.

The bars and brothels and nightclubs of Itaewon—and the peo-ple who work in them—have an intelligence system that beats 8th Army's hands down. Once word of our quest leaked out, it spread and kept spreading until the news was traveling so fast through the village that Ernie and I could not possibly hope to keep up. Paco Bernal, wherever he was, would be alerted—if he hadn't been already—and he'd probably *kara chogi*, take off. *Bali bali*, quickly.

The sun was completely down now and along the main drag, neon flashed to life.

Ernie took defeat stoically. "He'll show up eventually. Where the hell's he going to go?"

For a wanted G.I., there's no escape from the Korean Peninsula. Not with Communist North Korea guarding the DMZ to the north and the South Koreans guarding every port of international embar-kation. Ernie figured Paco would squander the thousand bucks he'd stumbled into and then, after a few days, come crawling back to the army compound begging for mercy. We'd seen it happen before;

G.I.s committing a crime, living big in the village, and then—when the money ran out—finally coming to their senses. And probably that's what would happen to Paco. Maybe. But one thing worried me. Why had he taken his bayonet—eight inches of sharpened steel—off compound with him?

What was Paco Bernal afraid of?

Now that we'd searched for Paco above and beyond the call of duty, Ernie wanted to find booze, broads, and excitement—not necessarily in that order. I agreed. There was no point in searching any further. Paco Bernal, wherever he was, would have been alerted. The better strategy now was to prowl the village and wait, like two coyotes watching a rabbit hole. We sauntered downhill toward the nightclub district.

Itaewon on this winter evening fairly sparkled with neon: red, blue, yellow, and green. Some of it spinning, some of it flashing, but all of it calling sweetly to the young American G.I., like the song of an ancient siren, beseeching him to enter an abode of pleasure, to spend his money, to enjoy the secret delights that make the nerve endings of a young man's skin tingle, like slender fingers with long red nails scratching gently across his chest.

Business girls stood in the shadows, shivering in skimpy dresses and short skirts, their eyes lined with black, their red lips pouting, calling to every man who passed; they stood in shoes with platforms so high that you were worried they'd fall over, their faces seeking, always seeking, for some strange creature to rescue them from the frigid night.

I wanted to find someone who'd been here in Itaewon back in the winter of 1953, someone who'd lived through the events recorded in Cort's Serious Incident Report, and maybe, with luck, someone who'd actually known Mori Di, the G.I. who ended up in the bed—at least spiritually—of a lovely Korean fortune teller by the name of Auntie Mee.

I mentioned my thoughts to Ernie. He chomped pensively on his ginseng gum. "Who in the hell's been here in Itaewon long enough to know about all that Mori Di stuff? It's been twenty years, ancient times."

"The winter of 1953," I said. "Not so ancient."

"Ancient enough."

Ernie waved to some of the business girls who giggled madly in response.

I thought about his question. Who *had* been here in Itaewon for twenty years or more? Certainly some of the club owners must've been here that long. And even a few of their employees: night managers, cashiers. But all the young waitresses and bartenders and pimps and whores came and went; they turned over regularly, every few months, if not every few weeks. None of them had been here that long ago. In the winter of 1953, many of them hadn't even been born.

Had any cops been here that long? No, the KNPs rotated assignments from station to station regularly; the military government of President Pak Chung-hee didn't want any one group staying together long enough to form a cohesive power base.

How about G.I.s? There were a few old military retirees around and most of them were veterans of the Korean War. But according to the stories I'd been told at tedious length, they hadn't been in Itaewon at the time. They'd been assigned to combat units up north near the DMZ, or on the road to the Yalu, or fighting Joe Chink at the Chosin Reservoir. Nobody admitted to being a rear-echelon support troop. Every veteran I'd ever talked to had been only one combat operation short of forcing Hollywood to forget about Audie Murphy.

So who had been living here in Itaewon twenty years ago? There must be somebody. The only way to find out would be to start asking questions. One person would lead to another person and eventually we'd find somebody who'd been witness to the events of 1953. But that might take a while. I needed to find some way to short-circuit the operation.

We stopped in front of the King Club, staring down the main drag of Itaewon at the Seven Club and the Lucky Seven Club and the UN Club. Ernie winked at the business girls who squealed and waved, and then he said, "How about Two Bellies?"

He was right. I hadn't thought about her. Two Bellies was plenty old enough. She'd lived and worked in Itaewon for as far back as anyone remembered, at least anyone I knew. And at this time of night we could guess, pretty reliably, where we'd be able to find her.

"We ain't there yet?" I asked.

We turned and trudged up the hill. Beyond the neon, at the darkest alley, we turned left into the night.

According to the testimony of Auntie Mee's spirit lover, the body of Mori Di was buried somewhere in Itaewon. Koreans believe that the remains of the dead should be buried with proper Confucian ceremony and then periodically honored so the ancestors can rest peacefully in heaven. Mori Di was not being so honored. A restless spirit can cause problems for those in the neighborhood who are still living and Auntie Mee, whether she was delusional or not, had problems. I saw it as just insomnia or nightmares brought on by stress but, in her mind, she was being haunted by a dead G.I. Finding Mori Di's Serious Incident Report hadn't been so difficult. Finding his burial place would be more challenging.

According to Cort, there'd been what amounted to a gang war in Itaewon in the winter of 1953. Moretti, and the Koreans who supported him, had been forced to defend themselves against organized toughs who were claiming the entire red-light district of Itaewon as their own. This gang—led by a group of hooligans with exotic names like Snake, Horsehead, and Dragon's Claw Number One—were extorting money from the prostitutes and black-marketeers who huddled in makeshift tents and lean-tos made of scrap metal and rotted boards. They called themselves the Seven Dragons.

As Moretti constructed new buildings and turned them over to the Ministry of the Interior, the buildings were occupied by legitimate investors. However, within hours, the gang of hoodlums known as the Itaewon *Chil Yong*, the Seven Dragons, would become, through extortion and coercion, the true power behind these legitimate businesses.

Cort reserved bitter words for the Korean National Police who were blind to this activity. He'd not only accused them of being corrupt but, in effect, part of the gang. And this criminal activity was far from benign. Cort mentioned one young woman who had been bought by a procurer and trafficked into Itaewon about two days before the end-of-month G.I. payday. Cort wasn't sure of her age but he estimated her to be either fourteen or fifteen. Sixteen tops. After being raped by all the gangsters, on G.I. payday they put her out for sale, cheap, to the droves of American G.I.s flooding into the ville. She suffered bleeding and internal damage and within a week she was dead. Cort wasn't sure what happened to her body. It probably was buried in a pauper's grave. Her family out in the countryside would've only known she was dead when the money stopped arriving.

But despite all the corruption and suffering that swirled around him, Moretti managed to keep his bearings. He was no chump. He and the three truck-driver G.I.s living with him in the ville saw what was going on. Instead of turning over buildings to the Ministry of the Interior, they switched their efforts to smaller projects. They started building on land already occupied by squatters. If someone was selling warm chestnuts from a shack made of scrap lumber, Moretti laid a cement foundation, built walls, and slapped on a roof. He classified this in his records as "repairs and upkeep" rather than as new construction. Therefore, he didn't have to turn it over to the Ministry of the Interior. As a tactic it had been worth a try but the Seven Dragons hadn't been fooled. As soon as a business started to prosper—and in this world "prosperity" meant a shop owner was able to feed his family—the Seven Dragons demanded their cut.

It was the orphanage that brought Moretti and the Seven Dragons into direct conflict. It was the biggest building in Itaewon, four stories high. When it was finished, Moretti commandeered the first floor of the building as his own headquarters. This meant that, technically, the building was under the jurisdiction of the 8th United States Army and, therefore, Moretti didn't have to turn it over to the corrupt ROK government. In the upper three stories, he allowed a group of Buddhist nuns to provide food and shelter for homeless children. The 8th Army Corps of Engineers backed Moretti on this and, in recompense, promised the Ministry of the Interior that the next three buildings constructed would be theirs. But the gangsters didn't want an orphanage in their midst. The Buddhist nuns were revered by the destitute business girls and soon the nuns were coun-seling them and even feeding them and encouraging them to return to their families. After praying at the little temple that was set up on a hill behind the ville, some of the girls ran away, breaking their contracts with the mama-sans who were their procurers. They stopped producing income, most of which would've gone to the Seven Dragons of Itaewon.

Moretti hustled a deal with 8th Army's Ration Breakdown Point, procuring a daily allotment of army chow for himself and his three troops. After the honcho at the breakdown point heard what Moretti was trying to do, he supplemented the daily ration with enough food to feed the entire orphanage. This wasn't as much chow as one might assume since both the orphans and the nuns ate like birds, mostly grain and green vegetables. Later, the 8th Army honchos signed off on yet another 30 percent supplement to Moretti's food allocation because he'd set up a soup kitchen that began operating out of the back door of the building. Soon he was feeding over a hundred people a day; just rice gruel and beans and sliced turnip but it was enough to keep them alive. And the people of Itaewon started to feel better about themselves, more confident about the future. And people who are well fed are less vulnerable to the demands of petty tyrants like the Seven Dragons of Itaewon.

This was too much. According to testimony Cort had gathered, Snake, Horsehead, and Dragon's Claw Number One called a confab of the Seven Dragons and after much cursing and posturing, they did what they'd been wanting to do for quite a while.

They declared war on Mori Di.

"Wei kurei, nonun?" What is it with you?

Two Bellies looked up from the *huatu*, flower cards, she was slapping on the warm vinyl floor, clearly wishing that Ernie and I would go away. She sat with her legs folded beneath her, at the edge of an army blanket which was piled in the middle with brass coins and the hard rectangular plastic flower cards. A half dozen other women sat around the same blanket. All of them rotund, all of them wearing loose housedresses, the skin sagging beneath their cheeks. They were maids or mama-sans for the business girls.

The open oil-papered door faced a dark courtyard surrounded by more hooches, all locked and silent. They were rented by the business girls who were now at the nightclubs or walking the streets.

At this hour, the old women who were the mentors to these mostly teenagers, finally were allowed a few minutes of peace and quiet that would be disrupted as soon as the midnight curfew approached and the girls started dragging half-drunk American G.I.s home with them. Then for a while, until everyone passed out, there'd be enough noise and drama to provide plots for twenty daytime soap operas.

I told Two Bellies what we wanted.

"How much you pay?" she asked.

"No pay," Ernie said. "If you don't help, we'll check your hooch and bust you for black-market."

That's how these women made the bulk of their income. By purchasing the American-made PX goods that the G.I.s brought out to the ville. It was a good deal all around. For the few dollars the G.I. spent on imported scotch or American cigarettes, he was able to spend the night with a beautiful young woman. The woman was reimbursed by Two Bellies in hard cash and Two Bellies kept the overage that she made on the black-market.

"What you wanna know?" she asked.

I mentioned the name Mori Di.

All of the card players stopped what they were doing and stared up at me, open mouthed.

"You know Mori Di?" Two Bellies asked.

I hesitated before answering. It wouldn't be a good idea to tell them that, according to Auntie Mee, Mori Di's spirit had returned to Itaewon. These women were superstitious enough to actually believe the story and then be too frightened to get involved. Instead, I shrugged and said, "I've heard of him. People say he was a good man. I want you to show me what the village was like back then, when Mori Di was alive."

Two Bellies pondered our proposition, cursed beneath her breath, but finally slammed her cards on the vinyl floor. She rose to her feet, stepped out of the hooch, slipped on her sandals, and led us across the courtyard to her room.

"*Yogi,*" Two Bellies said. Here.

We were outside, in the street. She pointed at the big cement three-story building known as the King Club. "That first one. Only building that time." She waved a flabby arm to indicate the entire panorama of Itaewon. "Everything mud, everything wood hooch, everything shit that time. Anybody cold. Anybody hungry. Only this building have. Mori Di build."

"You knew him?"

Two Bellies placed a hand on her hip, canted her rotund figure, and said, "Two Bellies know *anybody* that time." She pointed to the center of her chest. "But that time I no have two bellies." She grabbed her paunch. "Two Bellies look number *hana.*" Number one. "Better than any girl in Itaewon."

And it was true. Before we'd left her hooch, Two Bellies insisted we look at her photo album. It was filled with old black-and-white snapshots of a slender young woman with long legs and lovely breasts, always heavily made up, her jet black hair coiffed into expensive-looking hairdos, and wearing silk dresses that clung to her curvaceous figure.

"This me during war," she said. "This me after war."

While virtually everyone around her suffered, the woman we knew as Two Bellies had prospered.

"Lotta G.I.s," she said. "Lotta officers. Not all American. Many countries. How you say? England. Ethiopia. Swiss. Some have *taaksan* money." A lot of money. "Me, everybody call Miss Pak that time, not Two Bellies. Miss Pak number one girl. All man gotta be nice to Miss Pak. Miss Pak make a lot of money."

"What'd you do with all that money?" Ernie asked.

"You know," she said, flipping her wrist in the air. "Spend."

And now she was pointing at the King Club, inviting us to picture it standing alone like a shining beacon amidst a sea of shanties and suffering. Back when she had been the Empress of Itaewon. All of the photos in her album were of either herself posing alone or with one or two girlfriends. Invariably, she was in the center of the photograph. They were records of her sexiness. As if she was saying,*This is how I looked once. Eat your heart out.*

"Before," Two Bellies continued, "I have many picture with G.I. Many boyfriend, many different country. I takey all that kind picture, throw out." She mimicked ripping photographs into thin shreds.

"They all lie to Miss Pak. But Mori Di picture, I no have. He number one G.I. If I have picture of Mori Di, I no tear up."

"Were you his *yobo?*" Ernie asked.

"No. Mori Di no have girlfriend. He all the time work."

"With all the women around Itaewon," Ernie persisted, "he must've had some girlfriend."

"Maybe." Two Bellies shrugged. "I busy that time, work night-club. Mori Di, he no come inside nightclub. He all the time work."

Two Bellies paraded down the street, her posture erect, leaning back slightly, as if to show off the paunch for which she was named. Her cotton print dress clung to a figure that now resembled a soft melon. Like a proud tour guide, she pointed out the Seven Club, built by Moretti; the Lucky Seven Club, also built by Moretti; and finally, where the Itaewon main drag meets the Main Supply Route, the UN Club, also built by Moretti. Down the MSR, about one long block away, sat the 007 Club. Up the hill behind that sat the Grand Ole Opry Club. Those clubs plus the King Club—and the Yobo Club which had since been torn down—made seven major buildings constructed by Moretti and his three assistants. Not bad work in the middle of a country ravaged by war.

"Which one was the orphanage?" I asked.

Two Bellies eyes widened. "How you know?"

I shook my head. I wasn't going to tell her. "I know," I said.

"Come on," she said. "I show."

The Grand Ole Opry Club sat halfway up Hooker Hill. The narrow road was darker than most of the pedestrian pathways in Itaewon, the only neon to be found flashed right in front of the Grand Ole Opry Club. The gaggles of business girls who stared at us from shadowed doorways didn't bother to come out and clutch at our sleeves and coo and cajole as they usually did. Having Two Bellies with us was like a free pass. They knew we were up to something and, whatever it was, we weren't looking for women, so we weren't accosted. For an American G.I., walking up Hooker Hill could be a trial. The girls poured out at you like spiders from a trapdoor. Then, once you were surrounded, you had to gently unfold the pincerlike grips on your forearm, keep shaking your head no, and keep apologizing for not being more interested in the young woman's charms, making excuses, telling the girls you had to meet someone in one of the cubbyhole barrooms up the hill. It was a relief not to have to go through all that. I'm not sure Ernie felt the same way.

The Grand Ole Opry Club was a country-western bar, and one of the less frequented haunts in Itaewon. Still, the building was impressive. Four stories. The lowest housed the nightclub. In the three stories above it were small cubicles occupied by business girls. At least they had previously been occupied by business girls. In recent months, because of the burgeoning population in Seoul and the resulting housing shortage, families had started to move into even these quarters. I saw them in the morning: fresh-faced children wearing their tattered school uniforms—the girls with hair bobbed short, the boys with dark caps pulled down low on their foreheads— hoisting their backpacks on the way to catch the bus to school. Luckily, at that hour, the business girls were fast asleep and the G.I.s had scurried back to compound for morning formation. But when the kids came home at night, after extracurricular activities that most of the hardworking Korean students participated in, they had to wend their way through groups of rowdy G.I.s playing grab-ass with the now wide awake business girls of Itaewon. I never felt good about that. I wondered, once they grew up, what memories these kids would have of Americans.

Desultory crooning drifted out of the front door of the Grand Ole Opry Club. I recognized the voice: Buck Owens, in stereo.

"How about the Grand Ole Opry Club owner?" I asked Two Bellies. "Did he know Mori Di?'

Two Bellies shook her head vehemently. "No. Woman own now. Her daddy long time ago own bar. Long time ago, he die. Now she run place."

"How about the other owners of the other nightclubs?" Ernie said. "Did they know Mori Di?"

"Of course they know. They all know."

The nightclub owners Ernie was referring to were stalwarts of the local community. Whenever they were seen inside their own nightclubs—which was seldom—they were close shaved, slickly coifed, and clad in a suit and tie. They had formed an important organization with much influence here in the southern Yongsan District of Seoul: the Itaewon Club Owners' Association. And they had influence at 8th Army. More than once I'd seen one owner or another glad-handing with the brass at the 8th Army Officers' Club or shooting a round of golf at the 8th Army golf course.

"Who was Snake?" I asked.

Two Bellies eyes widened. "How you know?"

"Never mind. Who was he?"

"I no talk."

"Why? What are you afraid of?"

Two Bellies took a step backwards. Ernie positioned himself to grab her but I waved him off.

"How about Horsehead?" I asked. "Or Dragon's Claw Number One?"

Two Bellies's eyes glistened in the neon glow. She began stepping backward, stumbled, and then righted herself, waggling her forefinger at us.

"You no talk Two Bellies. You no tell nobody Two Bellies talk to you."

As if realizing suddenly that she stood in a public alleyway, Two Bellies glanced at the wary eyes lining the road. None of the business girls made a move. Two Bellies hugged herself over her ample paunch, turned, and started click-clacking her way down the cobbled road.

I shouted a question. "What about the night Mori Di was murdered? Were you there?"

She kept walking, waving her hand in the air. "Two Bellies no know nothing."

"Should I stop her?" Ernie asked.

I thought about it. We could stop her halfway down Hooker Hill. Embarrass her. Maybe get a little more information but we'd probably get even more information if we waited until we could catch her alone.

"No," I said finally. "Let her go. She told me plenty."

We turned and gazed up at the Grand Ole Opry Club.

"So what's next?" Ernie asked. "We roust the Club Owners' Association?"

Ernie was always in favor of direct action.

"Maybe. But not yet. First, let's take a look inside the Grand Ole Opry."

"You've seen it before."

"Only the bar. I want to inspect the entire building, from top to bottom."

Ernie rolled his eyes. "All you're going to find is business girls and booze."

We climbed the cement steps of the Grand Ole Opry Club.

As I pulled open one of the double doors and turned to let Ernie enter first, one of the shadows across the street shifted suddenly. The shadow had been tall, like a G.I. I looked again. Three business girls who'd been standing there were now gone.

Many American G.I.s are ashamed to let people know that they frequent Hooker Hill, so they lurk in the back alleys, bashful about emerging into the neon-spangled light of the nightclub district. Sometimes they're ashamed because they're in a position of authority, officers or senior NCOs. Other times its because they're married and have a photograph of their wife and children hanging in their wall locker or displayed prominently on their desk at work.

But this shadow had moved fast. Too fast.

I skipped down the cement steps and sprinted across the road.

A wooden gate started to swing shut. I shoved it open. A business girl fell backwards on her butt. I didn't wait to ask her questions. I ran across the courtyard and sidled down a narrow slit between the hooch and a cement-block wall. For a moment I was blind. But finally, moonlight revealed that another gate, in the wall behind the hooch, was open. I went through it.

Behind me, footsteps pounded. Ernie. He almost plowed into me.

"What is it?" he asked.

"Movement," I replied. "Too quick to be just somebody worried about being embarrassed."

We stared down the dark cobbled lane. Liquid trickled through an open drain, reeking of ammonia. Ernie ran one way, I ran the other. More intersections, more narrow pathways. Lights peeped out from homes behind high walls. Pots and pans clanged; radios blared; children laughed. Charcoal smoke wafted out of underground flues, irritating me like smelling salts up the nose. Periodically, I stopped and listened. No sound. No footsteps.

Finally, I returned to the hooch across from the Grand Ole

Opry. Ernie was waiting. Moonlight glistened off the perspiration on his forehead.

"Paco?" he asked.

"Maybe."

The frightened business girls didn't know the G.I.'s name but said he was dark, like me, except darker. We showed them the photo. Curled fingers rose to trembling lips. They were afraid they'd be in big trouble. I told them to relax.

Did they know where he was now?

They shook their heads negatively.

Did they know his name?

No.

Had they ever seen him before?

Again they shook their heads.

How long had he been watching us?

Since we'd arrived with Two Bellies.

Ernie and I weren't new to Itaewon. We knew a lot of people and were aware of the obvious hiding places. G.I.s had tried to hide from us before and hadn't been able to pull it off. Yet, after three hours of searching, we hadn't found Paco Bernal. Most likely, someone was helping him. Someone who had the means and connections to keep him hidden from us and that someone, almost certainly, was a Korean.

Ernie and I returned to the Grand Ole Opry to check it out.

It was like most of the nightclubs in Itaewon except not quite so rowdy. Most of the customers were older G.I.s, career noncommissioned officers: lifers. When Ernie and I were sitting at the bar, I heard a lot of words dragged out in slow country drawls.

"This place is dead," Ernie said. He swiveled on his barstool, stared at the half-empty ballroom in disgust, and tossed back some more suds from his brown beer bottle.

The business girls who occupied the rooms upstairs worked in the more lively nightclubs along the strip—the nightclubs that specialized in live bands and rock and roll and go-go girls. None of which could be found here at the Grand Ole Opry Club.

Surreptitiously, Ernie and I slipped into the back hallway, past the latrines, and climbed the cement stairs. Although we received some surprised looks from the occasional startled resident, we searched the building from top to bottom. Afterward, we examined the other clubs: The King Club, the Seven Club, the Lucky Seven, the UN, and the 007. I wasn't sure what I was looking for exactly; I was just looking.

Two hours before the midnight curfew, we climbed the highest hill overlooking Itaewon. A full moon rose red into a black sky. According to the lunar calendar, this was the time of year the Koreans call *Sohan*, the small cold. A storm cloud crossed the moon. A few splats of snow fell on the ground and then a few more on my forehead. At the top of the hill, we reached a small Buddhist shrine that had been here as long as anyone remembered, since before the Korean War, since the ancient days when the village of Itaewon had been nothing more than cultivated fields of rice and cabbage and turnip. A tile roof, upturned at the eaves, sheltered a bronze bell. I switched on my flashlight and examined the shrine, the stone foundation, and even the raked gravel surrounding it. With bent knuckles, Ernie bonged the bell.

"What the hell we doing up here, Sueño?"

"Looking for likely burial spots," I said.

"Like a needle in a freaking haystack?"

"Maybe not."

"I don't have time for this. I have people to see and things to do."

Ernie started walking down the hill, away from the temple.

I watched him go. It wasn't like him to leave while we were in the middle of an investigation but this wasn't an official investigation—not yet—so I couldn't really blame him.

"Stay out of trouble," I shouted after him.

Without looking back, Ernie waved his hand in the air. As if on cue, snowflakes began to pelt the roof above me; I turned back to my work.

After searching the temple and finding nothing, I started back down the hill toward the bright lights of Itaewon proper. The snow was falling a little thicker now and started to stick in the mud beneath my feet, creating a sheet of white lace. In two weeks we'd experience *Daehan*, the big cold; traditionally, the coldest day of the winter. So far this year, the weather had been unseasonably warm. It looked like that was about to change.

4

I sat in front of Doc Yong's desk, a warm earthenware cup of barley tea in my hands. She stared at me with a black-eyed intensity that I found so enticing.

"What have you found?" she asked.

She wore a white lab coat and a stethoscope hung from her neck. Outside in the waiting room a few pregnant women and a half-dozen business girls waited patiently for her attention. Each month, the business girls of Itaewon invaded Doc Yong's clinic to be inspected for venereal disease and, if they passed, their "VD card" was stamped with red ink and they were good for another month. The clinic was mostly funded by American dollars, which was why Doc Yong cooperated so closely with 8th Army health officials.

"Why is it so important to you, Doc," I asked, "this business about Mori Di? Sure, Auntie Mee helps you with the girls. Helps them keep a positive outlook on life. I understand that. But you know and I know that Auntie Mee hasn't been visited by the ghost of Mori Di nor by the ghost of anybody. She wants me to find his bones because she's nuts. But you're not. So why are you backing her up?"

Doctor Yong In-ja studied me as if I were a patient with curious symptoms. I loved the square shape of her face, the high cheekbones, the unblemished skin. But mostly I loved the full richness of her lips. Unrouged. No slime slathered on her face. Just flesh. Just woman.

She must've read my thoughts for her eyes shifted. She took her elbows off her desk and sat back in her wooden chair.

"I understand your concern," she said. She thought for a moment, composing herself, and then started once again. "The women I work with, especially the business girls, are mostly uneducated and mostly from rural areas. If Auntie Mee says she's being bothered by the ghost of a dead American, the word spreads quickly and, in no time, they believe it. And they all believe that this ghost will cause trouble in Itaewon. Bad luck. That adds to their depression. Depression leads to despair. Despair leads to illness or, worse, suicide. As a physician, I must try to prevent that."

Suicide was a fairly common event amongst the business girls of Itaewon. The Korean government didn't allow Doc Yong, or anybody, to keep statistics—not officially. But those of us who worked out here knew that at least three or four girls per year died by their own hands.

"But even if I locate the bones of Mori Di," I said, "and have them shipped back to the States, the business girls and Auntie Mee will just find something more to be depressed about."

"Yes. Of course. It's always something." She leaned toward me. "Someone's been complaining about Miss Kwon," Doc Yong continued. "An American G.I."

"A G.I. complaining about Miss Kwon?"

"Yes."

I was flabbergasted. Even before Doc Yong introduced me to Miss Kwon, I'd taken note of her while Ernie and I worked our regular rounds. She was a hostess at the King Club: a small, cute, country girl with chubby cheeks who kept to herself. Why would any G.I. complain about her?

"What sort of complaint?" I asked.

"I'm not sure. But the owner is concerned and there's even talk that Miss Kwon might lose her job. Not that losing *that* kind of work would be bad for her but I know the pressure these girls are under. She needs the money. Otherwise, where will she go? What will she do?" Doc Yong shook her head. "You can't believe what these girls go through. Many of them are the sole support of their families, putting their younger brothers and sisters through school."

Yes, I could imagine what they went through but I didn't interrupt.

Doc Yong stared into my eyes. "Will you look into it?"

How could I say no? I nodded. She smiled, reached out, and squeezed my hand.

On the way out of the clinic, the women in the waiting room stared at me. But all I could feel was the warmth where Doc Yong's hand had touched mine.

Although I'd questioned Doc Yong's motives for searching for the remains of Technical Sergeant Flo Moretti, I was beginning to develop motives of my own. Moretti had been murdered. Cort, the on-the-scene investigator, had strong suspicions as to who had murdered him but the body had gone missing and, after that, Cort had been hampered by both the Korean and the 8th Army powers that be. At the time, right after the war, Korea was still in turmoil. There was even talk that the Communists might make a comeback. In fact, the starving Korean populace would've followed just about anyone who promised to put food in their bellies and into those of their children. So the South Korean government and 8th Army wanted to squash, as quickly as possible, any sort of incident that portended discord between the U.S. and Korea, including the incident known as the Itaewon Massacre.

But those days were long gone and Ernie and I were new to the case—fresh eyes looking at the evidence. I was beginning to wonder if, in addition to finding his bones, we couldn't breathe life back into the search for the killer of Mori Di.

After all, Moretti had been a man of principle. A man who'd traveled thousands of miles from his hometown in New Jersey to a country on the far side of the world. He'd put everything on the line, including his life, to help people he didn't know. And, as Ernie said so succinctly, Tech Sergeant Moretti had been a fellow G.I.

That, in itself, was enough to keep us investigating.

Starting on the morning after the assault on Moretti, Cort had interviewed everybody he could find—both G.I.s and Koreans—who'd been present the night of the Itaewon Massacre. The evening had started routinely enough. The Buddhist nuns fed about a hundred people—men, women, children, and old folks—from the soup kitchen set up behind Moretti's headquarters building. Moretti had overseen the food preparation, taken inventory personally, and prepared the next day's ration order for the driver whose turn it was to make the pickup. Then he'd listened while the nuns told him about the various things that were needed for the orphans, including more diapers, soap, and textbooks for the older children who would be starting school as soon as the first one in the area reopened in February.

Where Moretti planned to find this stuff, Cort didn't know but he'd found entries concerning these items in Moretti's loose-leaf notebook.

What changed Moretti's routine that night was a group of business girls banging on the front door of his headquarters. According to their breathless report, another business girl, a friend of theirs, had been beaten up. She was laying in an alley just off the main drag, bleeding profusely.

As of yet, there wasn't an emergency medical service set up in the city of Seoul. And even the phone lines, what there were of them, were constantly overloaded and not much use when you had to get through to an ambulance. So, Moretti grabbed his army-issue first-aid kit and followed the business girls outside into the cold night.

He'd done this before, Cort found out. And when first aid had not been enough, he'd arranged for one of his trucks to transport a sick or injured person to the one functioning Korean hospital about four miles away in downtown Seoul.

On the way to the scene, Moretti was informed by the babbling women that a policeman had beaten the girl for nonpayment of the commission she owed to the Seven Dragons on a particularly large windfall—twenty dollars, they said—which the girl had earned in a secret assignation with some big-shot American. Moretti asked the girls who the American was but they claimed they didn't know. At the scene, Moretti used his army-issue flashlight and determined that the girl had been beaten badly but the external bleeding was not arterial. He cleaned and stanched the various flows as best he could but whether or not she had internal bleeding, only time would tell. The girl was conscious now and Moretti asked her who'd done this to her. She wouldn't talk. And then Moretti realized that the girls who'd brought him here had disappeared. The injured girl's eyes widened as she stared at the village's one streetlamp casting its amber glow on the main drag. Moretti turned. Approaching him were seven men, all of them wielding clubs.

Words were exchanged. The men told Moretti that the girl was their property and ordered him to stand away from her. Moretti refused. Within seconds, they were at it. Moretti threw his metal first-aid kit at them, kicking, punching, and clawing for his life. Other residents of Itaewon alerted the three G.I. truck drivers and they ran to the scene to join the melee, trying to pull Moretti to safety.

MPs were alerted. After a few minutes they arrived, sirens blaring, along with the Korean National Police. According to the first MP on the scene, seven men, just dark shadows, fled the moment their jeep rounded the corner. The MPs gave chase but lost them in the maze of dark passageways behind the main drag of Itaewon.

The three truck drivers had been hacked and stabbed and pummeled and sawed and beaten until there would've been nothing left to save if the MPs hadn't arrived when they did. They were lucky to be alive. The injured truck drivers were driven back to Yongsan Compound and checked into the emergency room of the 121 Evacuation Hospital.

But Moretti was missing. The seven thugs had taken him with them.

That night, the MPs started kicking doors in.

The KNPs protested. Eighth Army law enforcement had only limited jurisdiction in Itaewon; they could arrest G.I.s only. But by now dozens of MPs had seen how badly the three G.I. truck drivers had been beaten and they were enraged. And they knew who they were looking for: the Itaewon *Chil Yong*.

The MPs forced their way into all the usual haunts that the Seven Dragons frequented: nightclubs, bars, brothels, the black-market warehouses. But Snake, Horsehead, and Dragon's Claw Number One, along with their four brethren, were nowhere to be found.

Neither was Moretti.

Judging by the shape they'd found the three truck drivers in, the MPs thought that Moretti was probably dead. The Seven Dragons must have taken his body because they wanted to eliminate all evidence of the crime. Without a body to prove that a murder had been committed, and without weapons to prove how the murder had been perpetrated, the likelihood of the Seven Dragons being indicted— much less convicted—was virtually nil.

The reaction at 8th Army headquarters was outrage. Not at the men who'd perpetrated this crime but at the MPs who'd gone on their midnight rampage in search of Mori Di. The Korean newspapers were flooded with reports of Korean citizens being ripped cruelly from their homes in the middle of the night, of innocent black-market entrepreneurs being interrogated and slapped around by long-nosed foreigners, and of the Korean National Police being shamed in their own precincts by burly American MPs who showed no regard for the sanctity of Korean law.

All of the responding MPs were brought up on charges.

The civil affairs operation that Moretti had run in Itaewon was curtailed. His headquarters building was decommissioned by 8th Army and turned over to the ROK Ministry of the Interior. Construction operations, financed by American money, were no longer run by 8th Army Engineering but shifted to Korean subcontractors approved by the ROK government. This was supposed to help strengthen the Korean economy. But the real reason was to insure that there was not another Itaewon Massacre.

After a hearing conducted by the judge advocate general, the MPs who responded to Moretti's distress call that night were formally reprimanded though not brought up on court-martial charges, and all of them were shipped back to the States.

When the dust settled, the hunt for Moretti had been forgotten. As was the hunt for the seven men who had assaulted him. Forgotten by everybody, that is, except for an MP investigator named Cort.

The progress report I turned into Staff Sergeant Riley at the 8th Army CID office indicated that our search of Itaewon the previous night for Corporal Paco Bernal had turned up negative results.

"You mean he's not there?" Riley asked us.

I shrugged. Ernie was busy fixing himself a cup of coffee poured from the big silver urn behind Miss Kim's desk.

"I can't tell the first sergeant this shit," Riley said, "that you didn't find nothing."

"Why not? That's what happened."

"So you don't have any leads on the whereabouts of this guy?"

I shrugged again. "We're working on it," I said.

"The provost marshal wants positive, measurable progress," Riley said. "Estimates of when a goal will be attained. Not just 'we didn't find nothing.'"

"If they want positive," I said, "they'll just have to wait."

"No, they won't," Riley said, grabbing a pencil. He spoke as he wrote. "Ongoing searches of the areas the suspect was known to frequent are expected to turn up results prior to the next reporting period."

"Bullshit."

Riley looked up from his work. "What do you think we do here?"

Ernie finished his coffee.

The two of us left the CID office and drove over to the barracks at the 21 T Car motor pool. According to the head houseboy, Paco Bernal had not returned to his room. A couple of the G.I.s who knew him couldn't provide any new information and, moreover, they didn't seem concerned about Paco's fate.

As we walked back to the jeep, Ernie said, "They really watch out for one another in this unit, don't they?"

As we left 21 T Car and drove out Gate 9, heading toward Itaewon, I surprised Ernie by telling him to turn left on the road leading toward Namsan Tunnel.

He swiveled his head and asked, "We going downtown?"

I nodded.

"What the hell for?"

"You'll see."

I'm not sure why I hadn't told Riley that we had thought we had actually seen Paco Bernal—although only fleetingly. Something told me it wasn't going to be easy to catch Paco until he wanted to be caught.

At the tollbooth I tossed a hundred *won* into the tin basket. Ernie gunned the jeep's engine and slid through the milling field of kimchee cabs. *Namsan* means literally "South Mountain" and it hovers on the southern edge of Seoul like a sentinel monitoring the life of the entire city. The tunnel that was recently carved through it is the technological pride of the country. It's open mouth loomed before us.

We cruised into its cold depths.

Ernie and I must have been the only *Miguks* to enter the big cement block building of Seoul City Hall in quite a while judging by the stares we received. None of the signs were in English and some of the Korean was beyond my capacity so I ended up stopping men in suits carrying briefcases and asking them tomfool questions. Since I didn't know the technical jargon, I described what I needed in broad terms. Cute young secretaries stared at Ernie and me as if we were animals escaped from the zoo. Ernie grows antsy in these situations and I was worried he'd do something ill-considered. After we were directed to the third wrong office in a row, a kindly elderly woman finally directed us to what I later found out was the Office of Building Plans for the Southern Districts of Seoul.

The original plans to the seven buildings Moretti had built were still on file. Not blueprints. Nobody had time for something so time consuming after the war. Buildings had to be built and they had to be built now. Most of the plans were nothing more, really, than glorified sketches done on pulp paper with pencil and ruler, notations in Korean and English made in the margins. Then, after a number of erasures, the broad outlines of the structure had been recopied, right over the pencil lines, in blue ink.

I paid for photocopies to be made of each set of plans. I counted out the *won* and the grim-faced clerk handed me the plans in a brown envelope along with a receipt. Ernie and I walked back out into the broad hallway.

"What are you going to do with these things?" Ernie asked.

"Some comparison shopping."

"You really are nuts, Sueño."

Across the street from city hall, we found a teahouse with waitresses wearing blue uniforms and white gloves. Ernie convinced one of the girls to slip off her gloves and started fondling her fingers, all the while—supposedly—teaching her how to count in English. While the waitresses giggled, I sipped on ginseng tea and studied the plans, comparing them to what I'd seen in Itaewon last night.

There had been a lot of changes made since the buildings were originally erected. Rooms added, walls torn down, electrical wiring installed. And, of course, the Yobo Club had been completely demolished and replaced by a brand new structure, not a nightclub but a shopping emporium: trinkets, T-shirts, sporting equipment.

After the Itaewon Massacre, the ROK Army and the Korean National Police had clamped down on the entire area. For the better part of a month, Itaewon had been put off-limits to all civilians. The only people allowed to enter were those who could prove, by the address on their national identity card, that they were residents. All vehicles leaving the village were searched, either by the ROK Army at roadblocks or by the KNPs. Cort searched Itaewon himself, assisted by two armed MPs. They concentrated on the bars and brothels controlled by the Seven Dragons and any places likely to hide a corpse, including icehouses and electrical refrigeration units. They came up with nothing.

The Han River was about two miles away but the KNP roadblocks had been slapped on so fast after the fight that it was unlikely the killers could have made it out of there in time to dump the body. And even if they had, the corpse probably would've been spotted when it rose to the surface a few miles downstream near the Han River Estuary.

Of course, the Seven Dragons could've buried Moretti's body in an empty field. But the southern edge of Seoul—and, indeed, the entire city—was so crammed with refugees after the war that there weren't any empty fields to be found. Squatters were everywhere. Someone would've spotted men burying a corpse. The squatters would have been afraid to report it to the KNPs. Still, rumors would've spread. Someone would've heard something. And no such rumor had ever come to light.

Maybe the Seven Dragons had chopped up Moretti's body and disposed of it. This was a possibility so grim I didn't like to think about it. As vicious as the Seven Dragons were, they had never been known to resort to anything quite so macabre, according to Cort. The Seven Dragons would have been subject to the same superstitions as other Koreans and chopping up someone's body is the perfect way to insure that their spirit will come back to haunt you.

In fact, when no sign of Moretti's corpse surfaced, Investigator Cort started to suspect—or maybe hope—that Technical Sergeant Flo Moretti was still alive.

5

That night, Ernie and I caught a kimchee cab out to the ville and then entered into the den of iniquity known as the King Club. We were wearing our running-the-ville outfits: blue jeans, sneakers, sports shirts and nylon jackets with fire-breathing dragons embroidered on the back. In other words, we looked like two typical G.I.s out to spend a mindless evening of drinking beer and playing pinch-butt with as many Korean business girls as we could get our hands on.

During the duty day, Ernie and I are required to wear a white shirt with a tie and a sports jacket. Not uniforms. That getup, coupled with our short haircuts, fairly screams that the two guys you're looking at are 8th Army CID agents. But that's the military mind. They want us in civilian clothes in order to blend in with the civilian population but they don't want us wearing the clothes that civilians actually wear.

At least now, after work, we could dress like two regular G.I.s. Not that we were fooling many people. Itaewon is a small village and most everybody knew who we were.

Miss Kwon hadn't arrived at work yet and the all-Korean rock-and-roll band on the stage was still tuning up so I started talking to the middle-aged woman behind the bar, Mrs. Bei. She managed the place for the real owner.

"Who's the G.I. who complained about Miss Kwon?" I asked.

Mrs. Bei frowned. She didn't know his name. She only knew that he was a black man, that he wasn't a youngster, and then she held her splayed fingers at the side of her head to show me that his hair stuck out farther than army regulation allowed.

There are over 1,500 American G.I.s stationed at 8th Army headquarters on Yongsan Compound. After you've been here awhile, and especially when you're in my line of work, you get to know quite a few of them. In fact, 8th Army is much like a small town, full of gossip and backbiting, and everyone knows all about everyone else's business.

Back at my barstool, I told Ernie what Mrs. Bei had said.

Without hesitating, Ernie said, "Hilliard."

He was referring to Sergeant First Class Quinton A. Hilliard, the NCO-in-charge of the 8th Army EEO Office. Equal Employment Opportunity.

I agreed. It sounded like Hilliard.

After the "race riot" in Itaewon in 1972, the 8th Army honchos finally acquiesced to setting up what other government agencies already had: a staff to monitor race relations within the command. Prior to 1972, Itaewon had been segregated. White soldiers, and other "honorary" whites like Chicanos and Asians, frequented the red-light village of Itaewon. The black soldiers had their own smaller ville on the other side of Yongsan Compound, in a district of Seoul called Samgakji. Samgakji is still there, and still thriving, but now black soldiers can venture into Itaewon without fear of reprisal, for the most part. However, when Ernie and I had occasionally gone to Samgakji on an investigation, we'd never once seen a white G.I.

Ernie and I ordered beers and sat through the rock band's first set. After a half hour, when the club was almost full, Miss Kwon still hadn't shown up. We decided to look for her. I asked around amongst the business girls and received directions to her hooch which was, as I suspected, located in the maze of dark alleys behind the nightclub district. We pushed through the double doors of the King Club and stepped out into the street. After some searching through narrow pedestrian lanes and knocking on doors, we found the hooch the King Club business girls had described. It was a three-story building behind a high brick wall.

I pounded on the wooden gate. When a cleaning woman opened up, I explained who we were and who we wanted to talk to. The bent-over old woman nodded and shuffled off slowly and led us to Miss Kwon's hooch on the top floor. She slid open the oiled-paper door. Darkness. Ernie stepped into the room and switched on the single naked bulb hanging from the ceiling.

The room was just a ten-foot-by-twelve-foot square with flowered paper peeling off the walls and yellow vinyl pasted to the floor, empty except for a few scraps of newspaper crumpled at the bottom of a plastic armoire.

"*Domang kasso,*" the cleaning woman said. Miss Kwon had run away.

I was happy for the shy young woman. Maybe she could escape from this life, escape from doing things that she hated to do.

Ernie was less optimistic. "She'll be back," he said.

Cort was reassigned to other investigations; the usual ones that came up back in those days, thievery—of heating oil, food, medical supplies—anything that could alleviate the unrelenting poverty the Koreans were living in, being the most prevalent. At that time G.I.s weren't allowed to wear civilian clothes. They were ordered to be in uniform at all times, on and off compound. In spring and summer, they wore puke green army fatigues. But in the autumn, when the leaves turned red and yellow and brown and the nights became longer and colder, G.I.s started to wear their woolen winter fatigues. The tailor shops in Itaewon specialized in sewing a silk lining inside them and, if a G.I. popped for the money, he enjoyed the luxury of wearing a very comfortable set of clothes—smooth on the inside, warm on the outside.

That was the type of uniform Moretti was wearing on the night of the Itaewon Massacre.

During his off-duty time, Cort searched the Korean open-air markets looking for Moretti's uniform. It was a long shot, he knew, but what Cort was counting on was that in Korea at that time, nothing was wasted, not even a wool uniform stolen from a dead G.I.

Cort knew Moretti's uniform size and, of course, Moretti would've had his name tag sewn onto the front of his fatigue blouse but that could've easily been removed. But what might've been overlooked by the person selling the garment would be the laundry tag, a strip of white cloth with the G.I.'s initials written on it, attached to every piece of clothing a G.I. owned so that during the massive laundry operation conducted each morning in the 8th Army barracks, each item could be identified. Even socks.

The old women dealing in salvaged clothing at the canvas lean-to stalls in the Itaewon Market must've thought Cort was a very careful shopper. In the weeks following the Itaewon massacre, Cort sorted through mountains of used clothing. Finally, his diligence paid off. He found a pair of wool pants with the silk lining ripped out, but with a small white patch sewn on the inside of the left cuff bearing the initials FRM.

Three spots of crusted blood had dried into the material.

Cort made a show of bargaining with the proprietress. In the end he paid too much for the garment but he didn't mind. He immediately had the blood tested at the 121 Evacuation Hospital. The result was O-positive, the same blood type as Moretti. That didn't prove it was his, not for sure, but it was indicative.

Cort indicated in his notes that this discovery gave him a certain sense of accomplishment. It also gave him a sense of sadness. Now hope of finding Moretti alive was all but gone.

Based on the new evidence, Cort asked for permission to upgrade the Moretti case from absent without leave to murder. Eighth Army thought it over but without a body, they wouldn't upgrade the case. And furthermore, Cort was ordered to lay off. If he didn't, his investigative specialty would be pulled from his personnel records and he'd be sent back to where he came from. The infantry. That meant walking the DMZ in three feet of snow in the freezing Korean winter.

In his notes, Cort speculated as to why 8th Army had refused.

To him, the answer was obvious. For public relations reasons they wished the Itaewon Massacre had never happened. And if they ignored it, it would go away.

Cort saluted, said nothing, and, on his own time, continued to investigate the death of Technical Sergeant Flo Moretti.

The next morning, I sat in a teahouse in the Namyong-dong district of Seoul and watched as Doctor Yong In-ja studied the copies of the building plans I'd purchased from Seoul City Hall. She immediately absorbed the meaning of what I was trying to do.

"You compare these," she said, pointing to the short stack of papers, "to the buildings today and see if you can find some place where they might have, a long time ago, buried Mori Di."

"Exactly."

"But they might've buried the body some other place."

"Maybe not," I said. I explained my theories of how crowded Seoul was in those days—and still is—and how digging a grave and dropping a body in it wouldn't likely go unnoticed. And the culprits couldn't take the chance that someone might spot them, report them, and an honest cop might be called. Or at least a cop who would then blackmail them for more money than they wanted to pay.

Doc Yong frowned at my implication that the Korean cops in those days were corrupt.

"Everybody was poor at that time," she said.

I nodded in agreement. People were poor now too but, thankfully, not as desperate as they were then.

"Maybe they took the body to mountain," Doc Yong said. By "mountain" she meant the countryside. Korea is a mountainous country and every square inch of arable land is either cultivated or used for human habitation. So when Koreans refer to the wilderness they often use the word *mountain* because only on craggy peaks does any sort of wilderness still remain.

"There were too many roadblocks in those days," I replied. "Some by the Korean army, some by the American army. Everybody was looking for North Korean Communist agents. It would be too dangerous for the killers to rent a truck and take the body out of Seoul. If they were stopped by 8th Army MPs, they'd be toast."

"Toast?"

"It means they'd be burned, like a slice of bread."

She nodded, not quite sure what I meant. I also explained why I didn't believe the Han River was a good place to dispose of a body. And no unidentified G.I. bodies, floating or otherwise, had been reported any time after the Itaewon Massacre. Cort had checked.

"So they bury him someplace safe," she said.

"Exactly."

"In the buildings they own."

"They didn't own the buildings on paper but they controlled them."

"Same-same," she said.

I agreed. "Same-same."

In her agitation, Doc Yong was stooping to using business-girl slang. It figured she'd pick some up, working with them all the time. Probably she had picked it up unconsciously, what with the empathy she felt for those downtrodden women.

I'd already told Doc Yong about Miss Kwon packing up and leaving Itaewon. She took the news stoically but asked me to continue to check out the details of the complaint that had been filed against the young woman. I promised her I would.

She riffled through the photocopies of the old building plans, as if airing them out, and then slid the pile back to me.

"So where are you going to look?"

"Moretti's headquarters," I said, pointing on the drawing to the southwest corner of what is now the basement of the Grand Ole Opry Club. "Here. In the basement, where they make the beer deliveries."

I looked into her black eyes. I longed to reach out and take her hand in mine but that would be inappropriate in this formal setting. Instead, I cleared my throat and said, "On your day off, when you're not working, can I see you? We could go somewhere. We could talk."

At first Doc Yong seemed puzzled, as if she was having trouble translating my words, mentally, from English into Korean. And then, once my full meaning sank in, she looked alarmed. Regaining control of herself, she smiled.

"That's very nice of you," she replied. "But I've been very busy."

"We can go where you feel comfortable," I said. "On the compound, if you like."

I knew that being seen in public with a foreigner was not what most respectable Korean women wanted. On 8th Army compound we'd be away, if not from all gossips, at least from the Korean ones. She hesitated, thinking things over.

"Maybe some day," she said finally. "But not now. Many things are happening."

The disappointment knotted in my gut. I hoped my face showed nothing.

"When things quiet down," she said, smiling.

But we both knew that in Itaewon things never quiet down.

The Yongsan Compound Facilities Command is located in a cement-walled building with Roman pillars out front that looks vaguely like the home of an old southern cotton plantation owner. However, it was built by the Japanese Imperial Army during the three-and-a-half decades after 1910 when they forcibly colonized what had been the Kingdom of Korea. The 8th Army Equal Employment Opportunity Office was one of the many bureaucracies housed here.

When Ernie and I walked into the EEO Office, a black female soldier at the front studying some paperwork didn't bother to look up to greet us and ask, "Can I help you?" She kept her eyes glued to the paperwork.

She was an attractive young woman, a private first class. Her name tag said WALLINGS. Her shoulders were tense and she clutched the paperwork as if she were afraid it might make a break for freedom.

"Is Sergeant Hilliard in?" I asked.

She didn't look up. Instead she said, "Who wants to know?" Racial tension was high in the early seventies in the army just as it was throughout American society.

I pulled out my CID badge, opened it, and lowered it until it was between her nose and the paperwork she was still reading. She snorted, twisted her face, but still didn't look up at us. "You gonna have to wait," she said.

Ernie'd had enough. He slammed his open palm down on her desk. "Hilliard!" he said. "Now!"

The young woman rose from her desk and started cursing. Ernie cursed back. While they shouted at one another, I walked back toward a room with a nameplate that said: Sergeant First Class Quinton A. Hilliard, 8th Army EEO NCO-in-charge.

PFC Wallings shouted at me. "Get your ass back here, damn you!"

I went through the door to Sergeant Hilliard's office. He was on his feet—Afro a little too wide for his head, green fatigues neatly pressed, a belly just slightly protruding over his highly polished brass belt buckle.

"Why you messing with my secretary?" he shouted. He rushed past me out into the front room and pointed a finger at Ernie. "You keep your damn white-ass hands to yourself."

Ernie hadn't touched anyone, not yet, and he told Hilliard to get bent.

Hilliard stepped toward Ernie and I rushed forward and placed my body between them. PFC Wallings was still shouting and waggling her finger, her pretty face contorted in rage. Suddenly, from down the hallway, about a half-dozen more people joined us. One of them was a second lieutenant, a white female with short-cropped blonde hair, doing her best to be heard amidst the yelling, beseeching Sergeant Hilliard to calm down, asking PFC Wallings to take her seat behind her desk.

Ernie had vented as much as he wanted to and now he was grinning, arms crossed. I kept my face straight, standing protectively in front of Ernie, not because I was worried that either Wallings or Hilliard would hurt him but because I was worried that they might try and then Ernie would be in trouble for knocking them out.

The second lieutenant rushed back and forth between Wallings and Hilliard, pleading for calm. Hilliard never would've confronted Ernie like this out in the ville. Only here where he felt safe, with plenty of witnesses and plenty of co-workers to protect him, was he a tiger. PFC Wallings, however, was truly angry—and ready to fight. A real hellion, with pent-up anger, the cause of which I could only begin to imagine. The young lieutenant, whose name tag said Beresford, kept most of her attention on Wallings. Smart girl.

Finally, Lieutenant Beresford convinced PFC Wallings to stop shouting and take her seat.

Whatever happened to giving orders? Second Lieutenant Beresford was acting more like a social worker than a commanding officer. A young female lieutenant, that's why she'd been assigned to this office. EEO had no real power in 8th Army except the power to occasionally embarrass the command. No officer who was ambitious would accept an assignment to EEO. Beresford was either too naïve to realize that or, more likely, she had no plans to make the military her career.

When things calmed down, Lieutenant Beresford turned to Ernie and me and asked to see our credentials. We flashed our CID badges.

"Is this an official visit?" she asked.

"That's the only reason we'd be here," Ernie replied.

Hilliard glowered at him.

I spit out what we were after, mentioning the King Club and Miss Kwon's name.

"Yes," Beresford said. "I remember that one. We have a copy of the complaint here, don't we Sergeant Hilliard?"

"We gonna turn it over to *them*?"

"Why not?"

"Don't they have to subpoena it or something?"

"I don't think that's necessary. They just want to look at it. Isn't that so, Agent Sueño?"

"Yes, ma'am."

Hilliard crossed his arms. "Well, I don't like it."

Beresford looked dismayed and her face reddened. Her complexion was pocked from teenage acne and she wore thick-lensed glasses. She seemed like a nice woman; probably recently graduated from college, she was trying to do her best here although, with our long history of racial tension at 8th Army, I believed she was in over her head. Fights between black and white soldiers were common, hard feelings ubiquitous.

"Well, I ain't giving them nothing," Hilliard told Lieutenant Beresford, "If you want to turn one of our reports over to them, that's your lookout. I'm leaving." Hilliard grabbed his garrison cap and stormed toward the exit. "Hold my calls," he told PFC Wallings on the way out. It didn't make any sense but I suppose he thought it sounded good.

Ernie grinned again. "On his way over to the NCO Club for a shot and a beer."

Lieutenant Beresford's face turned even redder. Misconduct on duty reflected poorly on a soldier's immediate supervisor. Or at least it should.

"What was the name again?" Beresford asked.

"Miss Kwon," I replied. "At the King Club."

PFC Wallings sat at the front desk, her back to us, fuming. Lieutenant Beresford didn't ask her to retrieve the file. Instead, she walked over to a row of gray metal filing cabinets, rummaged through the green folders inside until she found what she was looking for. The complaint was a typed, onionskin sheet, three pages long. She disappeared down the hallway and two minutes later she returned with a photocopy.

"Here you are," she said.

We thanked her. PFC Wallings was so angry that she rapped the heels of her combat boots rhythmically on the floor

Once we were outside the building, Ernie said, "Nuthouse."

I didn't argue.

In the Serious Incident Report concerning the Itaewon Massacre, Cort never revealed his thoughts on what might've happened to Moretti's body. But despite being taken off the case, he continued to interview everyone he could locate with knowledge of the incident. Even the Buddhist nuns.

Once the Seven Dragons took over as the new landlords, the Buddhist nuns, and the orphans, were run out of Itaewon. Someone had written, in Korean, the name of the Buddhist order that the nuns belonged to. The same person also had written down the area of Kyongki Province where their nunnery was located. I could tell it was the same person because the note was still in the file and the handwriting matched perfectly. On a Sunday afternoon about a month after the Itaewon Massacre, Cort signed out a jeep from the

21 T Car motor pool, filled it with mogas and, using an army-issue map, drove out to a Buddhist temple known as the Temple of Constant Truth.

When the nuns greeted him, they were confused at first as to why a G.I. had driven all the way up to the slopes of Yongmun Mountain. Then, Cort showed them the black-and-white photograph he had retrieved from Moretti's military personnel file. They understood immediately and soon Cort was sitting cross-legged on a warm floor drinking tea with a half-dozen, bald-headed female Buddhist nuns. He came to understand through sign language and some broken English that these nuns had been the cadre assigned to operate the Itaewon orphanage and take care of the children.

Cort asked them where the children were.

The nuns didn't want to talk about it but some of them started crying and then apologized for their unseemly display of emotion. Cort assumed that because of lack of funds, the nuns had been forced to turn the kids over to one of the many international organizations which were actively saving children all over South Korea. Being a polite kind of guy, Cort didn't press the issue. Instead, he sipped on his tea and waited for them to calm down.

Then Cort asked them about the night of the Itaewon Massacre.

6

We found Sergeant First Class Hilliard at the 8th Army NCO Club, sipping on a bourbon and Seven and dropping coins into a pinball machine. In the cocktail lounge, a Korean go-go girl danced on a well-lit stage to music blaring from a jukebox. G.I.s ate their lunch and drank beer, mostly ignoring her. As soon as Hilliard sensed our presence, he took his hands off the machine and turned slowly.

"Didn't you get everything you want?"

"Not everything. I wanted to talk to you about this report." I waved the copy of the three typed pages in front of him.

"Nothing to talk about," Hilliard replied.

He turned back to the pinball machine and launched a metal ball into play. Lights lit up and bells clanged as the tiny silver sphere bounced back and forth. Finally, the ball slipped past Hilliard's flippers and dropped, exhausted, into a dark hole. Hilliard was ready to launch another ball when Ernie placed his hand over Hilliard's knuckles.

"Talk to the man, Sarge," Ernie said, leaning close. Then he grinned.

Hilliard turned again, anger flaring in his eyes. "I told you, there ain't nothing to talk about."

"You're the one who filed this complaint," I said.

"Yes. I filed it but on behalf of the brothers."

"It's your name as complainant."

"Only because I was there at the time. They be racist out there at the King Club. They discriminate. When a black soldier want to talk to a woman, want to get to know her, she move away from you fast. Just 'cause you black. They be racist out there because the white G.I. *taught* the Korean woman how to be racist." Now he was waggling his forefinger at us, preaching. "It ain't enough that you racist yourself but you have to export it to every country you go to."

Ernie rolled his eyes.

I kept my face impassive. Koreans are smart enough to form their own opinions about people and they don't need any help from American G.I.s. Instead of arguing with him, I pointed at the report. "It says here that you requested Miss Kwon's company and she refused. When you asked her why, she told you that it was because you were black."

Hilliard thrust his shoulders back. "That's what she said."

I shook my head.

"Why you shaking your head?" Hilliard asked. "You calling me a liar?"

"Miss Kwon," I replied, "doesn't speak English."

"How you know? You the one taught her to be racist?"

"I didn't teach her nothing. She's shy, just in from the country, she's afraid of G.I.s. All G.I.s. Black or white."

"She friendly enough with the white ones."

Now we were getting down to it. Hilliard was jealous that Miss Kwon had been going with other G.I.s but not with him.

"Maybe they were kind to her," I said. "Maybe they took it slow and easy."

"Maybe they be white and maybe they told her if they saw her with a black man, they wouldn't talk to her no more."

"Maybe," I said. He seemed surprised at me agreeing with him. I continued. "But maybe she's also just a frightened young girl from the countryside and it takes time for her to get to know someone."

"You trying to make this complaint go away. Well, it ain't going to happen. Black G.I.s got a *right* to be treated like anybody else. Whether it be here on compound or out there in Itaewon. And the King Club is racist. Whites only. They might as well put up a sign. And this Miss Kwon, she going along with the program." He crossed his arms, thinking it over. Then he said, "What makes the CID so interested in all this anyway?"

"I'm worried about putting Miss Kwon under too much pressure. Her family's poor, she needs the job. She's just trying to get by."

Hilliard's eyes narrowed. "Snake sent you, didn't he?"

"Snake?" The name electrified me.

"Don't pretend you don't know. You kissing his butt." Hilliard was smiling now, sure he was on to something. "He sent you out here to make sure that my complaint don't go through. To make sure that the King Club ain't put off-limits for being racist."

Hilliard slugged down the last of his bourbon and Seven, checked the coin return of the pinball machine to make sure he hadn't forgotten anything, and then pulled his cap from his belt.

"You can tell Snake," he said, "that if he wants this complaint pulled, he gonna have to deal with Q himself." Q for Quinton, Hilliard's first name. "And tell Snake not to send out anymore whitey CID agents to try to push *this* black man around."

"You're a moron, Hilliard," Ernie said.

Once again, Hilliard waggled his forefinger at Ernie's nose. "You mess with Q, you find out who be a moron."

Ernie slapped his hand.

The motion was so fast and the crack of flesh on flesh so loud, that for a moment Hilliard just stood there, stunned. Then he said, "You keep your hands off me, you understand? You keep your damn hands off me!"

But he was no longer waggling his forefinger.

The morning after the Itaewon Massacre the nuns searched the ville.

"We want to prepare his body," they told Cort. "For cremation or for return to America."

"Why did you think he was dead?"

"Everybody say."

They used their contacts in the ville, which were extensive, to ask questions. Most of the business girls were Buddhists and virtually all of them prayed and burned incense at the shrine atop the hill overlooking Itaewon. Many of them were there that morning, praying for the soul of Mori Di.

Rumors were flying. Most of them centered around Mori Di's condition after his beating. Some said he was already dead when the Seven Dragons took him away, others said he was still breathing but just barely. No one had any doubt about why the Seven Dragons had absconded with the corpse. They wanted to avoid a criminal prosecution.

In addition to being concerned about Mori Di's welfare, many of the families in Itaewon were concerned about Mori Di's bank. *Unheing* is the word the nuns used. Literally, "silver storage."

Cort was taken aback by this, suddenly on the alert for an illegal activity that Moretti might have been conducting. Was he changing money from *won* to U.S. currency? Possession of greenbacks was illegal both for G.I.s and Korean civilians and yet U.S. currency was highly prized and worth much more than either the G.I. Military Payment Certificates or the struggling Korean *won*. A healthy profit could be made on such transactions. Or was Moretti being paid by desperate Koreans to buy U.S. postal money orders on compound and mail them off to some relative living overseas? Also illegal, but profitable.

As it turned out, Mori Di's silver storage was none of these things.

"Everybody robbed all the time in Itaewon," was the way one of the nuns put it to Cort. There was no security. War refugees, of which there were millions, had long since taken to carrying their most precious possessions on their persons. But this was cumbersome. Especially once a family had stopped in Itaewon, set up a ramshackle home and maybe opened some sort of business. They couldn't keep family heirlooms tied around their waist or taped to an inner thigh forever. So when people saw a trustworthy man like Mori Di, living in a solid building protected by himself and Buddhist nuns and three G.I. truck drivers, they started to ask him to store their valuables.

At first Moretti hesitated. He already had too many responsibilities: the construction operations, the orphanage, and the soup kitchen. He had more than enough to do. But people kept begging him and, finally, he set up a system whereby people could turn over family heirlooms to him, have them boxed up and numbered and a receipt would be provided. After that, Moretti stashed them somewhere, presumably in his headquarters building.

"Seven Dragons kick us out," one of the nuns told Cort. "All orphans outside too. Winter that time. Cold. We have no money, no food. Seven Dragons no care. We take children, beg money, beg food, and ride on bus, train, whatever we can find and walk back up here in mountains to Temple of Constant Truth."

Cort waited for what he knew would come next.

"After leave Itaewon, five children die. Two lose foot. One lose hand."

Despite these hardships, the rest of the children, and all the nuns, arrived safely at the temple.

"The families," Cort asked, "that left valuables with Moretti, what did they do?"

"They fight," one of the nuns replied. "Nobody see. No American MPs, no Korean police. Only poor people of Itaewon and Seven Dragons."

Then she raised her forefinger to her neck and sliced it across her neck.

"*Chukin-da,*" she said. Kill.

I explained to Ernie the options the Seven Dragons had when deciding how to dispose of Tech Sergeant Moretti's body. Their ability to cover things up only extended to the cops the Seven Dragons had on their payroll in and around Itaewon; it didn't extend to a mobile ROK Army surveillance patrol. Cort monitored U.S. and ROK Army blotter reports every morning but nothing had been reported. The remains of Technical Sergeant Flo Moretti had vanished. They might be interred in one of the buildings.

"Do you think there might still be old treasures there?" Ernie asked. "Family heirlooms, things like that."

"No. I'm sure that's all long gone. But the body is different. Nobody would want to touch that. As long as it was well hidden, they'd leave it where it was. I believe that it's right here."

I pointed to a spot on the building plans. Ernie studied the sketch.

Two Bellies had told us that within days of the Seven Dragons kicking out the nuns and orphans, Mori Di's headquarters had been transformed into a bar and brothel. And since at least one of the Seven Dragons seemed to like American country-western music, they'd renamed the place The Grand Ole Opry Club.

"They slicky beer," Two Bellies told me. Slicky, G.I. slang for steal.

Military two-and-a-half-ton trucks, laden with pallets of American-made beer, had backed down the alley behind the Grand Ole Opry Club. They unloaded case after case of beer, all of it imported at U.S. taxpayer expense and pilfered directly from the PX supply line. To streamline the delivery process, the Seven Dragons knocked a hole in the wall through which they shoved a ramp and slid the cases down from the back of the trucks into the basement for storage. The work had been expertly done. Bricks lined the delivery chute. To support the ramp, a portion of the wall had been extended out, forming a narrow room with an angled roof. There was no opening into that room. It had been walled-in using bricks. The entire construction had been the first modification made to the original building, the plans of which Ernie stared at intently.

"You think Moretti's in there," he said, pointing to the angled space beneath the loading ramp.

"I think it's possible. It would make sense for the Seven Dragons to hide him there. It would be safe, away from prying eyes, and they wouldn't have to take the chance of transporting the corpse out of Seoul."

"Wouldn't it stink?"

I shrugged. "Not so much. Not sealed behind brick."

I imagined a desiccated corpse, sitting in the darkness, fading away to bones.

Then Ernie looked up at me. "Oh, no. I know what you're thinking."

We had no jurisdiction in Itaewon. Officially, everything we did had to be done with the approval of the Korean government. Years ago an agreement had been signed so American MPs could police the ville but our jurisdiction extended only to our own personnel: G.I.s, the occasional American dependent, or U.S. civilian workers who happened to wander out there. But we couldn't promulgate our own search warrant.

"You're nuts, Sueño," Ernie said.

"It could be done."

One thing I'd learned here at 8th Army is that if you really want to do something, don't ask for permission. If we presented a proposal to search the Grand Ole Opry Club to the provost marshal he would almost certainly say no. If we went ahead anyway, we'd be not only searching without a warrant but we'd also be directly violating an order. If, on the other hand, the PMO liked the idea of us searching the Grand Ole Opry Club, he would forward our request up the chain of command. There, it would be staffed to the ROK–U.S. governmental affairs committee, reports would be filed, questions answered, and great minds would cogitate. After a few weeks, if we were lucky, we'd receive an answer. Almost certainly no. But if by some chance the answer were yes, it would already be too late. By then, the rumors about a pending search of the Grand Ole Opry would have leaked out of 8th Army headquarters like rice wine from a broken *soju* bottle. Nobody keeps a secret for long in 8th Army headquarters. And if any hint reached Itaewon concerning a search, what we sought would either be moved or, more likely, destroyed.

Ernie kept staring at me. "You're nuts," he said again. "This is just a hunch. You don't know for sure there's anything there."

"You're right. But it makes sense, you have to admit that."

"Maybe." Ernie kept shaking his head, jiggling the copies of the building plans. And then he began to laugh. "Sueño, you never cease to amaze me. Why can't you just worry about getting your twenty years in like everybody else?"

"Moretti," I told Ernie, "didn't get the chance to retire."

Ernie shook his head, a sardonic smile on his chops, knowing I was putting all the pressure on him I could. Finally, he set the paperwork down.

"Sueño, do you have any idea how embarrassing this is going to be if you're wrong? A couple of Eighth Army CID agents knocking down walls, looking for old bones?"

I nodded.

"We could end up on the DMZ, trudging through snow in the middle of the night, searching for North Korean infiltrators."

I nodded again.

Ernie rolled his eyes, rubbed the back of his neck, and said, "How would we pull it off?"

I told him.

The members of about a dozen families—men, women, and even children—stood in front of the building that had once been Mori Di's headquarters but now belonged to the gang of criminals known as the Seven Dragons. Wind laced with stray flakes of snow blew down the narrow Itaewon roadway, a roadway that would later become known by G.I.s as "Hooker Hill." It was the middle of the morning, about nine or ten, and what had started with a small group of men loudly complaining to one another had grown into a crowd that the nuns estimated at a hundred people.

The ragamuffin Korean civilians wielded clubs and hoes and sickles and broom handles and any sort of weapon they could get their hands on. All of them were screaming, blood in their eyes. In most cases, every bit of wealth that their family retained, whether in the form of gold or jewelry or ancient artwork, had been entrusted to Technical Sergeant Flo Moretti. And with him gone, along with their wealth, and with no economic prospects in sight, all these Korean families could forget about any chance of a future, of education for their children or of being able to afford to set up a business. Instead, they faced poverty, misery, and—possibly—slow and agonizing starvation.

Every person in the mob was prepared to fight to the death.

When faced with this band of desperate people, the Seven Dragons were, at first, caught off guard. Within minutes, they regrouped. By now, the Seven Dragons had attracted dozens of shiftless young men to their ranks. Once these men realized what was going on, they armed themselves with knives and cudgels and prepared to attack.

While this fight was brewing in the middle of Itaewon the American MPs were back on the compound. Since most G.I.s work during the day outside of Itaewon, the MPs didn't bother to patrol the ville until after regular duty hours. The KNPs were in Itaewon but not where the crowd was gathering. They were at their comfortable heated police station, staying put. The Seven Dragons must have warned them off. They'd known this fight with the families who'd entrusted their wealth to Mori Di was inevitable and wanted it to end quickly and decisively.

The nuns told Cort that the Seven Dragons envisioned a shining era of postwar corruption opening before them. They had money; they had power; they had influence and they didn't want a lot of whining men, women, and children yapping at their heels, threatening their corrupt empire. They wanted to settle the issue now—in blood.

The families threw themselves at the front door of the Grand Ole Opry Club. Using improvised battering rams, they knocked it down. But the Seven Dragons were ready for them. As the mob poured in, from the wooden rafters above, men rained bricks down upon their heads. Still the crowd surged forward. At the far end of the open room, the Seven Dragons had locked the big double doors and barred them with metal rods. The crowd surged up against the doors, pushed against them, but could go no further. In confusion, the crowd turned back on itself but by now more people had pushed into the huge room and were milling around like cattle. Bricks kept falling.

Then a phalanx of Seven Dragon punks rushed down the stairs. Another group attacked through the side door that led into the kitchen. The crowd fought back on both fronts but that's exactly what the Seven Dragons wanted. Upon a shouted order, the two groups of Seven Dragon fighters pulled back. Small groups of enraged men fighting for their families last possessions followed in small groups, pushed forward by the mob. They found themselves outnumbered by the Seven Dragon minions. One by one, the rioters were ground into mush.

The main body of rioters realized things were not going their way. More and more people had crumpled to their knees, victims of the vicious rain of bricks that had never relented. The bravest men, the ones who had taken the lead, had been knocked back down the stairs or had entered the double door of the kitchen never to return. Panicked, the crowd started surging back toward the front door.

A third squad of Seven Dragon lackeys, all holding sharpened broom handles, were waiting for them. The first rioters out the door tried to stop but they were pushed forward by the rushing mob and fell down the steep cement stairs. Many were impaled on the sharply pointed tips of the waiting broom handles. More screams. More blood. More panic. And then the Seven Dragons ordered their men on the stairs and in the kitchen to charge into the main room. They did and now the rioters were set upon from all sides.

Once the mob had been totally routed, the Seven Dragons and their vicious auxiliaries waded through the blood and the bodies. Some of the women, especially those with children, had not charged into the building but had waited outside. Now, the Seven Dragons' lackeys turned on them. The women screamed and attempted to run away, children clinging to their skirts. The women were attacked from behind, clubbed, stabbed, and knocked down. Some of them were murdered immediately. Others were dragged into side alleys and gang-raped. Children wandered through the gore and the screaming crowd, crying and calling for their mothers.

The Seven Dragons laid out the unconscious and bloodied attackers in a huge pile in the street. Then the Seven Dragons ordered gasoline poured atop the bodies. Amidst the screams of the few relatives cowering in the distance, one of the men struck a wooden match, watched it sizzle, and then tossed it onto the pile. As the bodies began to smolder and then burn, some of the rioters actually roused themselves and stumbled away from the growing conflagration. Children dragged their fathers out of the pile. The bravest bystanders pulled bodies away from the flames but they were quickly beaten back. In the end, the children and the few still-conscious women managed to save only a handful of men from the fire.

Not a single Korean National Policeman appeared.

7

Cort was appalled. He'd been monitoring blotter reports every day since he'd been in country and he'd never heard of any such incident. He asked a question to make sure he understood correctly what the nuns told him.

"The Korean police did nothing?"

The nuns nodded their bald heads. Yes. Nothing.

How many people died?

More than a dozen. Many others were wounded and scarred for life.

Did anyone retrieve their valuables?

No one.

Does anyone know what the Seven Dragons did with those valuables?

Shrugs all around. But the nuns did know that soon after, Itaewon began to explode in a riot of bright lights and fancy nightclubs.

Cort spent the night with the nuns because there was too much snow outside to drive home safely. In the morning he fastened chains to the back tires of his jeep, ate a warming breakfast of hot rice gruel and dried turnip, thanked the nuns, and left.

Upon his return to 8th Army, he checked with the MPs who'd been on duty during the day of the bonfire. There were only two of them. One of the MPs, a guy name Smith, told Cort that he and his partner had been aware of the fire.

"The KNPs told us they were taking care of it," he said. "Only Korean nationals were involved and they didn't want us there."

"You weren't curious?" Cort asked.

"I've seen fires before."

"Did the KNPs tell you that there'd been a fight before the fire and that during the fire people were injured?"

"They said something about it. Told us it was Reds agitating."

That would explain 8th Army's indifference. Any action taken against Communists would have been condoned. If there had been violence, the honchos of 8th Army would just as soon not know.

Cort thanked the MP named Smith and asked him to write out a report. The young man agreed, according to Cort, but something must've gone wrong. A copy of Smith's statement was never included in the SIR.

Tonight the Grand Ole Opry was jumping.

The Kimchee Kowboys, the most popular band on the G.I. circuit, was performing. Only two days had passed since the end-of-month military payday and so, by the time Ernie and I arrived that evening, the place was packed. And noisy. It was the noise I was counting on.

We entered the club at different times. I melted into the crowd for a while but instead of joining in the frivolities, as soon as I figured no one was watching, I made my way to the back steps behind the latrines. While I waited, I checked the tools I'd stuffed inside my winter coat: a wooden mallet and a chisel. All I figured I'd need. As soon as Ernie joined me, he started mumbling. "You're nuts, Sueño. Really nuts."

I ignored him. Together, we sneaked down the back stairs.

A faint green glow from fluorescent bulbs followed us down the cement steps. At the bottom, the door leading to the storeroom was padlocked. While I shone the beam from my flashlight on the lock, Ernie stepped forward and, using the small crowbar he had stuffed under his jacket, he popped open the lock. I picked up the broken lock and dropped it in my pocket. I closed the storeroom door behind us and switched on the overhead bulb.

Pallets of OB Beer, product of the Oriental Brewery, in brown bottles and wooden crates, Korean-made, met our eyes. The days of pilfering American beer from the PX supply lines were over. But judging from the crowd upstairs, and their general state of inebriation, the Grand Ole Opry was still selling plenty of suds. And making a hell of a profit.

The Kimchee Kowboys clanged determinedly into a new song, the heels of their boots pounding on the wooden stage. The bass player and the drummer set up a driving rhythm. They were a hell of a sight, five Korean musicians wearing sequined cowboy outfits and broad-brimmed hats. I wished I could go upstairs and drink beer and enjoy the show but no time for that now.

"Come on," I told Ernie. "Over here."

We took off our jackets and started heaving crates of beer away from under the delivery ramp. It was cold down here, though not refrigerated. The howling wind outside kept the temperature close to freezing. Clouds of our breath billowed in front of us yet within minutes we'd both worked up a sweat.

"How much beer do these lifers drink?" Ernie asked.

"Enough to float the Seventh Fleet," I replied.

Finally, the brick wall of the angle-roofed room was revealed. We stood back and looked at it.

"Maybe nothing's in there," Ernie said.

"Maybe."

But there was only one way to find out. I knelt in front of the wall and poked the tip of the iron chisel into the mortar between bricks. I pulled the wooden mallet out of my pocket and, keeping time with the rhythm of the Kimchee Kowboys' latest, I started to pound. Dust flew. The chisel slid, held, and then gradually started to edge deeper into the crusted mortar.

Ernie knelt a few feet away from me, pulled out his own mallet and chisel, and began hammering to the same driving rhythm. When the song stopped, we stopped. After a few seconds, a new song— this one having something to do with mom and trains and prison— started up. Ernie and I, like two convicts making a break for freedom, resumed our rhythmic labors.

Cort did his best to convince the honchos of 8th Army that the Seven Dragons were a menace. He also promised that, given enough resources and enough search warrants, he could find Mori Di's remains and put the Seven Dragons out of business. But 8th Army didn't want to hear it. Already, Itaewon was the wonder of the country. Nightclubs, lit up and operating seven nights a week, offered such amenities as cold beer and cocktails and shaved ice in every drink along with gorgeous women to serve those drinks and entertainers on wooden stages and the best musicians in the country. The 8th Army G.I.s, who were Itaewon's only customers, were happy. And if the G.I.s were happy, and there were no major incidents in the ville, and there was no hint of any Commie activity, the honchos of 8th Army were happy.

The Seven Dragons provided order. Maybe not law, but order. And in a country recovering from chaos, that was considered to be a good thing. And with their newfound wealth, the Seven Dragons soon made friends in high places. First within the Korean government and, before long, at 8th Army itself. Charities were contributed to, transportation and free food and free beer were provided to officers for their promotion or retirement parties. And with the money the Seven Dragons made from the girls and the booze and the debauchery of Itaewon, they expanded their operations into construction, Moretti's old bailiwick. The only organizations with enough money to order new construction projects were, coincidentally enough, the Korean government and the 8th United State Army. The Seven Dragons became richer and more influential every day.

And Cort became a pest. People groaned when they saw him coming and rolled their eyes after he left. But for a while he convinced his superiors to keep Moretti's SIR open. And on his own time he kept adding to it, although less often than before.

* * *

A door slammed above us.

Ernie stopped hammering. So did I.

A small pile of gray powder lay on the floor beneath me but I still had not managed to pull even one brick out of the wall.

Footsteps.

Ernie stood and switched off the overhead light. We crouched in darkness, hidden behind a wall of stacked cases of beer.

Someone entered, mumbling to himself, cursing *"Miguk-nom"*—loutish Americans—and switched on the overhead light. He grabbed what I believed was a case of Seven Star soda water, and carried it outside. After setting it down, he returned, switched the light off again and carried the tinkling bottles upstairs.

Without speaking, Ernie and I returned to our labors.

The reports in the SIR became fewer and Cort only bothered to write one up once or twice a month. He was using his own time to investigate because the provost marshal had long ago pulled him off the Moretti case and assigned him to new duties, mostly involving the accountability of 8th Army supply lines. Since the end of the war, these lines had been porous. They had started prosecuting G.I.s for diverting supplies and selling them on the black-market. Their Korean co-conspirators were occasionally rounded up by the Korean National Police for dealing in contraband but keeping tabs on the millions of dollars in military supplies arriving in Korea was a project that would keep the MPs busy for years. Ernie and I, on the black-market detail, were still fighting that battle, however reluctantly.

Cort wrote a personal memorandum that he left in the SIR file. He didn't mention names but someone in his chain of command had once again ordered him to lay off the Moretti case. It was over, ancient history, don't stir it up now! But it wasn't over for Cort. He kept working, gathering data, trying to figure a way to assault the impregnable fortress that now surrounded the Seven Dragons.

And every day the walls of that fortress grew higher.

* * *

Ernie was the first to pull a brick free. I stuck my nose into the opening and inhaled. There was a musty odor but nothing else in particular, other than dust. I shone the flashlight and looked inside. An open space stared back at me, about the same length as my elbow to my fingertip. How high this opening went I didn't know but probably up to the angled ramp. Whatever we were looking for, however, would probably be resting on the dirt floor beneath, a floor that I couldn't see.

We kept hammering.

When the Kimchee Kowboys took a break, we took a break. While we sat in the darkness, listening to the conversation and drunken laughter upstairs, someone clomped down the steps. Two people this time. When they switched on the light they were cursing and laughing. They grabbed crates of beer and carried them upstairs, making two trips, and then they switched off the light and left us alone in the dark. Evidently, they weren't concerned about the padlock and they made no effort to lock the outside door. It figured that on a busy night they'd just as soon leave the door open. When the Kimchee Kowboys started up again, Ernie and I resumed hammering.

After a few minutes, the opening wasn't quite as large as I wanted but it was large enough. Besides, we were both tired of this bone-jarring work. Ernie switched on his flashlight and pointed it into the hole. With his open palm, he invited me to enter. I stuck my head in as far as I could, twisting my neck as I did so. My shoulders stopped my progress.

"Twist the flashlight over here," I said.

Ernie tried but I could only make out the wall on the far end of the narrow opening. Nothing to be seen. I needed more room to maneuver.

We started hammering again. After three more songs, we'd removed four more bricks and I tried again. This time, I could just barely squeeze my shoulders in. Ernie stuck his forearm in beneath my chest and twisted his flashlight around at my command.

"Hold it there," I said. He did. "Twist it down farther." Ernie complied. The light swept slowly across ancient dust.

That's when I saw him. A scream started in my throat but somehow, before it erupted, I held it back. I pulled my head out of the opening, breathing heavily.

"What's wrong?" Ernie asked.

I just pointed my thumb at the wall. He leaned past me and stuck his head inside all the way up to his shoulders. Within seconds, he'd pulled out again too.

Not talking, we loosened a few more bricks. Then, with enough space to stick my upper torso in and my forearm, I made a more careful examination and then grabbed what I wanted. I held it in my open palm. In the light of the flashlight, Ernie squinted, reading the embossed print. Tears came to his eyes. It was the first time I'd ever seen Ernie weep—about anything. Angrily, with dirty knuckles, he rubbed the moisture out of his eyes.

It was a dog tag. The metal had rusted a reddish brown but the imprinted name was clear enough: MORETTI, FLORENCIO R. The blood type too: O-POSITIVE. And the religious preference: ROMAN CATHOLIC.

As I'd promised Aunite Mee and Miss Kwon and Doc Yong, I'd found Mori Di.

I was sure it was him. The tattered remains of a uniform and even combat boots lay near the skeleton. The garment Cort had bought over twenty years ago in the Itaewon Market must have been amongst Moretti's extra clothing stuffed into his duffle bag, not the uniform he was wearing. Whoever had done this hadn't stripped him. Circling the still intact neck bones was a stainless steel chain looped through one dog tag and a smaller chain looped through a second dog tag. There was a reason for this duplication. The dog tag on the big chain, according to army policy, would be left with the corpse. The other dog tag, the one on the smaller chain, would be collected by soldiers of the body recovery unit to make a complete accounting of casualties. That's the one I unfastened, the small chain, the one the body recovery unit normally would collect when cleaning up after a battle.

All the while, Technical Sergeant Flo Moretti was grinning at me. At least his skull was. It sat in the dust as if it had been waiting a long time and now it was happy that someone had finally stumbled into this tiny brick ossuary. By the light of Ernie's flashlight, I studied the bones. I even reached in and touched one of them, turning it this way and that in the harsh beam of the flashlight, making sure that I wasn't imagining what had jumped out at me when I first saw the skeleton.

The bones had been sliced with what appeared to be a sharp-edged knife. Not everywhere. Only on the fingers and the toes, as if someone had purposely tormented Moretti while he was still alive. One of the fingers, the large middle finger, was not only sliced but it had been forced backward so far that it had finally snapped between the big middle knuckle and the joint where the finger joined the hand. Even now, gazing at the wound some twenty years after the fact, I winced.

And then I studied the tip of another finger. It appeared discolored. I lifted the bone into the beam of the flashlight. No doubt. The tip of the bone was darker than the rest of the skeleton, as if it had been singed by fire. The fingertips are the most sensitive parts of the human body. Moretti's fingertip, at least one of them, had been burnt off.

When the Seven Dragons spirited him away from the scene of the original attack on the night of the Itaewon Massacre, they'd hidden him from the American MPs and later nursed him back to—if not health—consciousness. Then they'd begun questioning Moretti as to the whereabouts of the gold and silver and ancient family heirlooms that the residents of Itaewon had left in his safekeeping. Maybe Moretti thought the MPs would rescue him any minute. Maybe he thought that the Seven Dragons were a bunch of punks and he could bluff them. Whatever he thought, he resisted. And when the answers weren't forthcoming, the Seven Dragons had tortured him. How long had it lasted? How long had it taken for Mori Di to break? I would estimate quite a while. Maybe even a few days. But as bad as the torture was, there was something else that bothered me even more.

Handcuffs, laying in the dirt near Moretti's hands. G.I. issue. I recognized them because exactly the same type of metal cuffs were still in use today. And near his neck, dried wads of cotton and a narrow cloth sash. A gag.

Why would anyone gag a dead man?

The answer: they wouldn't.

My conclusion seemed inescapable. So far, I hadn't discussed it, even with Ernie, but all the evidence pointed toward one thing. Once the Seven Dragons tortured Moretti and he'd either told him where he'd hidden the valuables—or the Seven Dragons had discovered the hiding place on their own—they had no further use for Technical Sergeant Flo Moretti. He was a liability. They couldn't let him go free. And it wouldn't have been easy to transport him anywhere, not in a city swarming with military patrols. So they decided to hide him in the basement of the Grand Ole Opry Club. In this narrow opening not much larger than a coffin. And once they had him inside, handcuffed and gagged, they bricked the opening closed.

Technical Sergeant Flo Moretti, a man who'd tried to help the impoverished people of Itaewon, had watched the Seven Dragons do their work. He'd watched a gang of punk gangsters wall him up, brick by brick, until the final glimmer of light was covered by mortar.

He could scream inside his little brick tomb but no one could've heard those screams, except himself.

When I marched alone into the main ballroom of the Grand Ole Opry Club, I still wore my winter jacket with the tools stuck into the inner pockets, making me feel twenty pounds heavier than I actually was. I received some funny looks from the old retirees. It was the Korean employees I was most worried about. But none of them, neither bartenders nor waitresses, stopped their work to pay any attention to me.

I headed straight for the door and pushed through out into the fresh air of the cold Korean night.

A few minutes later, Ernie popped out after me. We hurried down the street.

We'd replaced all the bricks and repositioned the stacked cases of beer in the basement as best we could, to camouflage our activities. I hoped this would give us a couple of days before someone discovered what we'd done. Once someone took the time to look, it would be obvious as to what had happened. Would one of the Korean employees investigate? I was hoping that, what with the place being frantically busy, they wouldn't notice the two guys who'd walked in, disappeared for an hour and a half or so, and then walked back out. That they'd just write off our behavior as the weirdness that they were used to in American G.I.s.

Still, we didn't have much time until someone discovered that we'd broken through the brick wall in the storeroom. Before then, somehow, I had to convince 8th Army to wrangle us a search warrant so we could take full advantage of the evidence we'd discovered. We needed it to make our activities retrospectively legal.

I was filthy. So was Ernie. Brick dust salted my hair. It was still early, only half past eight, so we headed toward the far side of the nightclub district and entered an alley near the open-air Itaewon Market. The stalls were dark and shuttered at this hour, canvas flapping in the cold evening breeze. Hidden in a dark alley, lit only by a half-dozen green bulbs, lurked the last Korean bathhouse still open. At the entranceway, I plopped down a five thousand *won* note—about ten bucks—and the proprietress smiled a toothy grin, happy for the unexpected business.

The middle-aged woman assigned to scrub my hair clawed with the ferociousness of a lioness. Then she slipped her hand into a coarse red mitten and started in on my back. It felt as if she were systematically peeling my flesh. Oily pellets of black dirt emerged from every pore of my skin, like tiny insects searching for light. By the time she was done, I felt completely clean but my skin flamed red. She rinsed me off, dried me, and then oiled me with some sort of lotion. After slipping my clothes back on, I sat in the waiting room chatting with the bathhouse women, sipping on a can of cold guava juice. Ernie took a lot longer than I did. More than an hour longer. When he finally emerged he looked, for once in his life, subdued. And as limp as a freshly washed rag.

There was less than an hour left until the midnight curfew. We made our way back to the Grand Ole Opry Club and waited out front, watching as the band loaded their equipment onto a flatbed truck.

Kimchee Kitty, the lead singer for the Kimchee Kowboys emerged. Her lush hair was piled high atop her head and she was wrapped in a long cloth coat with a fur collar that she held tightly beneath the soft flesh of her face. Our eyes met and she smiled at me. I almost asked for her autograph but decided at the last minute not to. Too shy.

Ernie mingled with the half-looped retirees in the street who'd stayed until the end of the show. I sauntered around inside and casually listened to the conversations of the bartender and the waitresses. There was no indication that anyone had noticed the hole Ernie and I had knocked in the brick wall of the basement. This was good. It meant we'd have time to obtain our search warrant and retrieve the bones of Mori Di and any still existing evidence of who had murdered him.

The truck carrying the Kimchee Kowboys had departed and most of the customers had left when I emerged from the club. A couple of business girls were tugging on Ernie's sleeve. They weren't propositioning him, not this time. Instead there was terror in their eyes.

One of them said, "You CID, right?"

"Right," he answered. No sense trying to keep it a secret. Everyone in the ville knew anyway.

"You go King Club," she said. *"Bali bali."* Quickly.

"Why?" Ernie asked.

"You look at roof. Some *yoboseiyo* up there."

In Korean, *yoboseiyo* means "hello." In G.I. slang, it means a person, usually a Korean person.

Ernie didn't bother to question them further. He started to run, swerving left on Hooker Hill, heading for the King Club. I followed him.

A crowd had gathered in front of the King Club.

People were looking up, pointing, and that's when I saw her. She wore a short skirt, its hemline above her knees and I noticed that her calves were round and sturdy. Her hair was cropped short, like a middle-school girl's but shaggier. This was a common cut amongst the business girls of Itaewon since many of them had left school only weeks—or days—before starting work here.

Her blouse, long-sleeved and white, was made of a flimsy material that billowed in the cold wind blowing across the roof of the King Club. She had already climbed over the parapet and stood with the heels of her flat shoes dug into a ledge that was only three or four inches wide. Her arms were spread-eagled, holding onto drainpipes on either side of her.

"It's Miss Kwon," I said to Ernie.

"Who?" Ernie had never met her.

"The one Hilliard complained about."

Ernie's head swiveled. "I thought she went home."

"Apparently," I said, "she's back."

I ran through the entryway of the King Club, still clutching my winter jacket tightly around my waist, wishing like hell I didn't have a mallet and chisel stuck inside my belt. The main ballroom was empty, no band, no G.I.s, no business girls. They were all out on the street gawking up at the suicidal Miss Kwon. Some of the G.I.s were already chanting, "Jump!" in mocking voices as if they were kidding. But I knew they weren't kidding. That's what they wanted her to do.

I shoved through the back door, found the steps, and climbed. Ernie was right behind me. We reached the top floor and spotted a wooden ladder at the end of the hall that had been pulled down from the roof. We climbed as fast as we could. On the roof I found Mrs. Bei, the manager of the King Club. Standing near her was a young man in black slacks, white shirt and bow tie—her bartender—and three or four waitresses. They all clutched the edge of the parapet, looking down, shouting at the person who clung to the outside of the wall. One elderly man, the janitor, stood farther away, leaning over the edge of the roof, staring at Miss Kwon with an embarrassed smile on his face.

I took off my jacket, dropped the chisel and mallet atop it, and peered over the edge of the roof.

I was only ten feet from Miss Kwon but she wasn't looking my way. She was staring down at the street below, perspiration pouring off the soft cheeks of her sweet face. I turned and grabbed Mrs. Bei.

"She come back," Mrs Bei said in English. "Family no want. They need money. Snake say she gotta sleep with any G.I. She no want."

Ordering Miss Kwon to spend the night with Hilliard was the only way for Snake, the owner of the King Club, to avoid having Hilliard press his complaint. Since the race riot out here less than two years ago—white American G.I.s fighting black American G.I.s—8th Army was phobic about even the slightest appearance of racial conflict. That riot had hit the Stateside newspapers and caused the 8th Army commander to be relieved. The current commander wanted no repeat. To keep Hilliard from raising a stink there was an even chance that the 8th Army honchos would put Snake's nightclub off-limits. Fifty-fifty wasn't good enough odds for Miss Kwon to maintain her personal moral standards. She had to give it up.

Ernie was ready to climb over the parapet.

"Hold it," I told him. "Even if you grab her, she could fall and pull you over with her."

"We gotta do something."

That was Ernie. Without thinking, he'd already decided that somebody he didn't know had to be saved, even at the risk of his own life. But Agent Ernie Bascom never calculated risk. He just did what seemed right at the time.

I thought of speaking to Miss Kwon in Korean, but I was worried that just the voice of an American G.I. might cause her to jump. Mrs. Bei kept up a steady, soothing, harangue and it must've been doing some good because Miss Kwon hadn't jumped yet.

Finally, four stories below us, two uniformed Korean cops made their way through the crowd. They looked up, saw Miss Kwon on the edge of the roof of the King Club and spoke together rapidly. One of them took off in the direction of the KNP station. The other moved the crowd back, away from Miss Kwon's probable point of impact.

Mrs. Bei said something about respecting one's parents.

This made Miss Kwon look away from the street below. She stared directly at us. "My parents want me to make money," she said in Korean. "That's all I'm good for. No better than a cow. They hate me."

"They don't hate you," Mrs. Bei replied. "They are poor. They have no choice."

"*Narul miyo!*" Miss Kwon shouted. They hate me!

Instinctively, Mrs. Bei reached out to the girl and Miss Kwon flinched. One of her heels slipped off the ledge. She started to fall forward but her grip on the drainpipes held her back. Still, within seconds, the added weight made one of the pipes groan and then bend. Miss Kwon's right hand lost its grip.

With one heel still on the ledge and her left hand still gripping one of the drainpipes, Miss Kwon's right foot swung out into the open air in a wide arc. The movement was slow and graceful and as she rotated, the crowd below, involuntarily, let out a loud gasp. The gasp coincided with Miss Kwon's pirouette and then stopped abruptly when Miss Kwon slammed face first into the wall to her left. Scrabbling with her right foot, she managed to gain another toehold and with her right hand she clutched an outcropping of brick. Now she clung to the wall, facing dirty mortar, looking as if she were hugging the indifferent brick edifice.

I moved to my left and stared down at her.

Her soft cheek was pressed up against the wall. The cheek was wet with moisture. I could see her features clearly because directly below red and blue neon flickered: the King Club sign. Beyond the glow, I spotted a familiar figure shoving her way through the gawking crowd.

"*Jom kanman*," I told Miss Kwon in Korean. Wait a moment. "A friend of yours is on the way." She seemed to be listening, so I continued. "Doctor Yong In-ja. She'll be here any second."

Miss Kwon hugged the building tighter.

Doc Yong reached the roof and approached me as if swimming through moonlight. Her face was contorted in rage, her white coat flailing at her side.

"Her parents sent her back," she said in English.

I nodded.

"And now the owners here want her to sleep with that old G.I."

I nodded again.

Doc Yong stepped up to the roof, placed her hands flat on the parapet, and looked down. She gasped, held the sudden intake of breath, and managed to calm herself.

"Kwon," she said, leaning forward. "I am here."

Ernie motioned for everyone else to back away from the ledge.

Doc Yong continued to speak. Miss Kwon, face still pushed up against the cold brick wall, was crying profusely. Doc Yong kept telling her that she understood, that she knew that Miss Kwon had dreams to make something of herself, of getting an education, of some day marrying a man of her own choosing, of having a family, of seeing her children grow, of watching her own sons and daughters marry, and of one day becoming—herself—an honored grandmother. All these things were understandable, Doc Yong continued. And laudable. And they were still possible. Difficult, surely, but possible. But they would only be possible if Miss Kwon decided that she wanted to live. If Miss Kwon decided that she wanted to fight against her troubles. If Miss Kwon decided that no matter how many problems were hurled at her by life that she would stand up and stare those problems in their evil eyes and she would fight back. That somehow, some way, she would make something of herself.

Miss Kwon was nodding now, still crying, but nodding.

Now, Doc Yong said, give me your hand and me and my friend—she meant me—will help pull you up.

Miss Kwon hesitated.

Doc Yong stood silent, holding her breath. She knew that this was the moment in which Miss Kwon had to make her decision. Should she live or should she die? And on that roof in Itaewon, staring down at this teenage girl who'd only recently left school, I watched her choose between life and death.

Without thinking, Doc Yong and I clasped each other's hands and squeezed.

The cold wind gusted and the moron G.I.s below continued with their mocking chants: "Jump!" Then shameful laughter. Thankfully, I don't think Miss Kwon heard.

She stared up at us, eyes flooding. Then she smiled bravely and held out her left hand.

Doc Yong reached for it and grabbed it. I leaned over the ledge and I felt Ernie wrap his arms around my waist, leaning back, ready to brace me as I reached for Miss Kwon's other arm.

But when Doc Yong's hand touched Miss Kwon's, Miss Kwon leaned back, putting too much of her weight on the doctor's grasp. Doc Yong tried but she couldn't hold on and Miss Kwon teetered backward, panic suffusing her moist face. I lunged forward, trying to grab a handhold, but all I touched was hair. My fingertips brushed the top of her skull and then she tilted farther back, her arms flailing, and her face showing complete panic. From behind Mrs. Bei, the bartender grabbed Doc Yong and held onto her to keep her from plunging over the ledge too. And then Miss Kwon had gone too far, too far for anyone to believe she could be saved. And then her feet left the toehold and she was floating free in space, her sweet face looking not panicked but confused.

Something had gone wrong and she wasn't quite sure what.

And she fell. And the G.I. voices below were silent but the Korean women started to scream. So shrilly that when Ernie jerked me back over the ledge I rolled onto the dirty cement of the flat roof, pounding my fists against my ears, trying to force the screaming to stop. And then we heard a crash, a whining squeal, as if lines of metal and copper wire were being ripped out of their moorings and, finally, something much more awful.

A thud.

Doc Yong, Ernie, and I bounded down the inner stairwell of the King Club.

On the way, I remembered Auntie Mee's curse. She said if I didn't find the bones of Mori Di, Miss Kwon would meet an unpleasant fate. Most likely, she'd die. But now, after we'd found the bones, in complete contravention of the fortune teller's foolish prediction, Miss Kwon had met that unpleasant fate.

Miss Kwon lay in a mangled mess of wire and neon in the street. On the way down, she'd slammed back first onto the King Club's flashing sign. She'd done everything she could to break her fall— grabbed at support cables, flashing tubes, metal brace work to slow her downward progress. Wrapped, now, sinuously around her body, live electrical wires sputtered angrily into the cold night air.

Ernie reached her first and, with no thought to his own safety, stepped gingerly over the juice still surging through hot lines. He bent over, reached beneath Miss Kwon's limp body, and lifted her up and away from the sparking mess. Doc Yong and I helped untangle her arms and legs. She was groaning when we carried her away and laid her on dirty cement, groaning and still breathing.

A squad of uniformed KNPs arrived. Doc Yong identified herself and tried to ward them off but, using their nightsticks, they shoved us away from Miss Kwon. Ernie shoved back. One of the cops screamed at Ernie and pulled his .38. Before Ernie could do something truly stupid, I stepped between the two men. We stood that way for a moment, curses flying back and forth in English and Korean. The sergeant-in-charge finally shouted an order. He recognized Ernie and me from the many times we'd worked out here in Itaewon with the KNPs. He told his man that we were cops and to lay off. The officer took a step backwards and reholstered his weapon.

By now the KNPs had Miss Kwon completely surrounded. She had, technically, committed a crime: attempted suicide. Still, Doc Yong was doing her best to convince the sergeant-in-charge not to take Miss Kwon into custody. A Korean ambulance arrived. White-clad paramedics emerged but they didn't bother to pull a stretcher out of the back of the ambulance. Instead, they grabbed Miss Kwon's legs and her shoulders and, carrying her like a sack of spring rice, tossed her into the back of the small white van. Doc Yong assisted the paramedics, trying to keep Miss Kwon's back as straight as possible. Then she hopped into the back of the emergency van, squatted next to Miss Kwon, and spoke soothing words. Just before the medics slammed the door, Doc Yong glanced up at me, gave me a half smile, and waved.

I waved back.

The next morning at the 8th Army CID office, our goal was to obtain an official search warrant and obtain it fast. If the employees of the Grand Ole Opry discovered that we'd busted a hole in the wall of Mori Di's crypt, it wouldn't take long for the Seven Dragons to find out. They'd destroy all the evidence fast.

Colonel Brace, the 8th Army provost marshal, stared at the rusted dog tag laying in the center of his highly polished mahogany desk.

"They buried him?" he asked.

Ernie and I nodded.

"Alive?"

We nodded again.

"After torturing him?"

This time we didn't move.

The colonel shook his head, sighed, and continued to stare at the dog tag. He hadn't asked us how we'd gotten it. He didn't want to know. Finally, he looked up at the first sergeant who was standing beside his desk.

"Top, how soon can we obtain a search warrant from the KNP Liaison Office?"

The first sergeant shrugged. "This morning, if they get up off their butts."

"Make sure they do," the colonel replied. "Tell them the Eighth Army PMO considers it top priority."

"They'll want to know why, sir."

"Tell them it's a suspected black-market cache."

The first sergeant saluted and left the office. The colonel turned back to us.

"I'm going to keep this," he said, picking up the dog tag. "I'll show it to the CG during this morning's briefing."

Neither Ernie nor I had any objection to that, as long as we got our hands on a search warrant.

Then Colonel Brace clutched the dog tag in his hand. And squeezed.

It was hard to tell which report was Cort's last entry. Someone had gone through the SIR some time after his last entry and jumbled the order of the papers. Unfortunately, many of the second and third pages of the various entries weren't properly numbered and dated. Cort might've been a hell of an investigator but he wasn't a hell of a clerk. So I had to read through them all and try to figure which one went with which starting page based on content. All the reports had been knocked out on what seemed to be the same manual type-writer. Probably an old Remington, one of the army's favorite brands at that time. I could see where the ink had faded and the ribbon had been replaced. That too, helped me place the pages in the correct order.

Cort had never given up, even after he'd been officially assigned to other duties. He'd kept trying to make a case concerning Moretti's death until the day he left country. I stacked up the pages and was about to tie the SIR with the knotted string I'd found it in, when I noticed a clump of sheets that had slipped down into the sleeve of one of the brown folders. It was as if they'd purposely been hidden. I pulled them out and unfolded the brittle sheets until they were flat on the table. They were new to me. I hadn't read them before. The subject title was *Provisional Inventory*.

I began to read.

It was an inventory of all the valuables that Moretti held for safekeeping for the refugee families of Itaewon. How Cort had obtained such an inventory I couldn't be sure. Maybe the nuns had given it to him or maybe one of the G.I. truck drivers who'd worked with Moretti. However he'd gotten it, this list of riches explained where the Seven Dragons had found the capital to construct the glittering red-light district of Itaewon.

There were names in one column, first written in Korean in varying hands, and then spelled out in English. The English handwriting was consistently the same. Probably Moretti's. And if the variability of the *hangul* writing was any indication, the Koreans had written their own names on the sheet as they'd turned in their valuables to him. Some had even written their names in Japanese. For much of the thirty-five-year occupation of Korea, from 1910 to 1945, the ancient Korean language had not been taught in Korean schools, only Japanese, so the Koreans would become dedicated subjects of Emperor Hirohito. It hadn't worked. Through it all, the Koreans held steadfast to their own culture and their own national identity.

After the names were written, a description of the item and quantity or approximate size was provided. First in Korean in the varying hands, and then again in English in the script that I could only assume belonged to Moretti. Finally, a date of receipt and then two signatures: first the Korean's and then a set of initials, FRM. Florencio R. Moretti.

All very official looking. Probably Moretti had given the depositor a scrap of paper with the same information written on it. But I was only guessing because I searched and no receipts were to be found in the pockets of the various folders that comprised the Mori Di Serious Incident Report.

The inventory read like a museum catalog. There were tiaras from the Yi Dynasty; porcelain from an earlier Korean dynasty known as Koryo; gold necklaces imported from Burma; jade pendants shipped in from the Chinese province of Fujian; antler horn from Manchuria; a Buddhist codex from Tibet; and a number of paintings and calligraphy scrolls from all over the Far East. Of course there were the more mundane items, like small bricks of silver bullion, gold coins minted in Mexico, and even a few spirit tablets recorded with the names written in Chinese characters, of revered ancestors.

These treasures must have been sold on the black-market by the Seven Dragons. Of course, they might have retained some of the precious objects. Yes, I decided it was possible. That might be important evidence in building a case against them. Yes. That is why, instead of returning the Serious Incident Report and the inventory to the SIR warehouse, I locked the entire sheaf of folders in the safe in the Administration Office of the 8th Army Criminal Investigation Detachment.

Staff Sergeant Riley helped me make an inventory, for the record, on an 8th Army hand receipt. Just to be thorough, he kept one onionskin copy, I kept the other. Folding it neatly, I stuffed it in my wallet, just in case I encountered any of these precious objects on my sojourns through the ville. I'd seldom seen anything as valuable as these artifacts—not, at least, outside of museums—but soon I'd be entering the offices and dens of the inner sanctum of the Seven Dragons and who knew what riches I'd find there?

Maybe gold bullion. Maybe ancient tiaras. And maybe more evidence leading to the death of the man who the Koreans called Mori Di.

Ernie and I didn't make it out to the Grand Ole Opry Club until late afternoon.

The KNP liaison officer had been dragging his feet all day, seeking clearance for the search warrant from his superiors who were supposedly indisposed or locked in high-level governmental meetings or on distant journeys that made it impossible to contact them. Finally, the 8th Army commanding general stepped in. His adjutant called the assistant to the KNP commander in Seoul and, within ten minutes, we had our search warrant.

Moretti's dog tag was working its magic.

This time Ernie and I didn't have to disguise our intentions. Neither did the four uniformed 8th Army MPs who tagged along with us. The owner of the Grand Ole Opry was a tall, slender Korean woman who the G.I. customers called Olive. Perspiration showed on Olive's forehead and her straight black hair was in disarray. She accepted our warrant without complaint and seemed completely relaxed, claiming that she knew she didn't have any black-market activities going on in her club. In fact she was chatty, in English, and told us that her father, who was now deceased, bought the Grand Ole Opry from the original owner, a Mr. Ju, who was also now deceased. Mr. Ju, I'd been led to understand by Two Bellies, was one of the original Seven Dragons. Six of them were still alive and, supposedly, still pulling the strings here in Itaewon—and elsewhere.

Olive led us downstairs. Had she been down here at all today? I asked. No, she always had her employees restock at night, after closing, so the club would be ready to open at four in the afternoon, just before the 8th Army G.I.s got off work and started to make their way out to Itaewon.

"You don't unlock the storeroom before that?" I asked.

"No. I opened the front door about two this afternoon and let my janitor in. We've been cleaning in the main bar ever since."

The time was now fifteen hundred hours so that meant that she'd opened about an hour ago. Olive switched on the overhead fluorescent light in the hallway and stopped at the entrance to the storeroom. She stared at the broken padlock dangling from the hasp.

"*Isang hei,*" Olive said. Strange.

Olive frowned. She entered the storeroom first and switched on the overhead bulb. Trash was piled by the rear door, ready to be taken out.

The 8th Army KNP liaison officer, Lieutenant Pong, had also tagged along. Since the commanding general of the 8th United States Army had shown such an interest in this case, KNP headquarters in downtown Seoul wanted a full report. He stood back, out of the way, and crossed his arms.

At Ernie's instruction, the four burly MPs started hoisting crates of beer. Soon the brick wall was exposed. So were the piles of dried mortar on the floor and the loose bricks that Ernie and I had stuck back into the wall.

Olive gasped. "Who do?" she asked, pointing.

I shook my head and didn't answer. Then Ernie and I knelt on the floor and started pulling the bricks out. Even before we were finished, I could smell it. A fleshy smell, as if someone had been sitting in a sauna bath too long.

What the hell was this all about? I hadn't noticed any such odor last night. Or had I just been too nervous?

When the opening in the brick wall was large enough, I switched on my flashlight and poked my nose in. This time I couldn't hold back.

I screamed.

While waiting for the KNP Liaison Office to come up with our search warrant, Ernie and I drove downtown to the Beikhua Hospital. Doc Yong was there, in a room with Miss Kwon. The little chipmunk-looking erstwhile business girl was snoring heavily. Doc Yong gave us a wan smile and bade us to sit down next to her on wooden stools.

I figured she'd paid for Miss Kwon's medical care, in advance, which is the way Korean hospitals usually want it. And, judging by her disheveled appearance, the good doctor had probably been here all night. I sat down next to her and took her hand. To my surprise, she squeezed my palm.

"Thank you," she said, to both Ernie and me, "for helping last night."

"We weren't much help," Ernie said, nodding toward Miss Kwon.

"You tried," Doc Yong answered, "and we're lucky she's not dead."

She described the prognosis. Not bad, considering. The doctors speculated that Miss Kwon's wild flailing, grabbing instinctively onto anything that would break her fall, had, in fact, saved her life. Miss Kwon had no internal injuries. That was the important thing. Her left ankle had been sprained badly but not broken and the only other injuries were a pomegranate-sized lump on her noggin and scratches and bruises both on her legs and on her hands, fingers, and forearms, where she'd tried so desperately to slow her plunge to the dirty pavement. After internal injuries, what the doctors were most worried about was concussion but she seemed to be in the clear. Now, after being heavily sedated, all she'd need was rest and recuperation. Not something Itaewon business girls were usually allowed.

"You need rest too," I told Doc Yong.

She nodded her head slowly. "And the clinic—"

"The clinic can wait," I said.

I pulled her to her feet, guided her out to the jeep, and Ernie and I drove her home.

It was the first time I'd seen where she lived. It was a small room, she told us, on the third floor of a rundown apartment building, shoved into a crowded slot in a tightly packed neighborhood known as Oksu-dong. She left me at the first floor and, although I offered to help her to her door, she shook her head negatively and trudged alone up the squeaking wooden stairs.

When I poked my head through the hole in the brick wall of the basement of the Grand Ole Opry Club, I normally would've been embarrassed about screaming except that all the MPs—and Ernie too—were as scared shitless as I was. Especially when they took their turns peering inside. Even Lieutenant Pong, who normally had a ferocious expression on his face, appeared a little green around the gills.

We had to pull the body out from behind the wall because it was no longer a skeleton. It was a big, fleshy corpse, full of blood and mucous and other bodily fluids, and it was wrapped in a flowery pink dress and its dyed black hair was damp and strung around its ears and neck like snakes uncoiling from the skull of Medusa.

Once we dragged her through the hole and plopped her on the floor and searched back inside the opening, we discovered that the bones of Mori Di, every last one, were now gone. Along with the tattered uniform and the combat boots and the rusty old pair of handcuffs and the cotton swabs and the woolen gag. Mori Di had once again been spirited away—to points unknown, by person or persons unknown. And in his place had been left the rotund, no longer breathing body of Two Bellies.

Her mouth was open in horror. Her throat cut. Blood covered everything.

One of the MPs vomited. Then the rest of us did. Olive ran for a mop. Lieutenant Pong disappeared into the back alley.

8

The Korean National Police insisted on taking over the investigation into the death of Two Bellies. We tried to retain jurisdiction but they wouldn't hear of it. She was a Korean citizen, murdered on Korean soil and, at this point, there was no reason to believe that an American had been involved. That is until they interrogated the night bartender, and the other employees who'd been working the late shift at the Grand Ole Opry.

Lieutenant Pong was assigned to the case, personally, which surprised everybody because his job at 8th Army as the ROK–U.S. liaison officer centered around the political and diplomatic rather than the investigative. But once he sank his teeth into police work he was thorough. Maybe that was because he wanted to prove that he was a real cop and not just a paper pusher. He even interviewed Kimchee Kitty, the beautiful female lead singer of the Kimchee Kowboys and I was flattered that she'd noticed me—but not Ernie—entering and leaving the club. I was further flattered that she watched me proceed to the back hallway that led to the latrines and she noticed that even after her third number, I had not emerged. During the second set of the evening, while she was backstage, she peered through the curtains to watch the crowd and saw me emerge from the latrine area and leave the club. My winter jacket was still wrapped around me, she told Lieutenant Pong, and my short hair was moist and in disarray, as if I'd been working. And there appeared to be smudges on my knees and the sides of my blue jeans from dirt or dust of some sort.

Had I known Kimchee Kitty was watching me that closely, I would've asked her for a date a long time ago.

Ernie, for his part, was slightly offended that she hadn't noticed him. But the bartender had and so had a couple of the other employees. And at least one of them, the bartender, had noticed that during the entire time we'd been in the Grand Ole Opry Club, we hadn't bought a drink.

Unusual for us.

The evidence recovery team working in the basement discovered some threads that appeared to come from American-made blue jeans. They also searched the crypt where Two Bellies's body had been found and discovered that the dirt below had been thoroughly sifted. They found no combat boots, no dog tags, no bones, no tattered remnants of a twenty-year-old U.S. Army uniform. In short, they found nothing that would indicate the presence of Technical Sergeant Flo Moretti's remains. They did find Two Bellies. And they found that her throat had been slashed with a very sharp knife; so sharp that she probably didn't have time to whistle, much less scream, before her windpipe was severed. And Lieutenant Pong also discovered that we'd been seen around Itaewon with Two Bellies a couple of nights before her death, having her show us the sights.

The result of this evidence was that, instead of recovering the twenty-year-old remains of Tech Sergeant Flo Moretti, Ernie and I were taken into custody by the Korean National Police. All this happened quickly. Before the midnight curfew, Ernie and I were downtown, under harsh lights, being sweated.

The interrogation wasn't as bad as I feared. No bamboo shoots up the fingernails or acetylene torches singeing my private parts. Maybe the KNPs were saving all that for later. Mainly, the interrogation consisted of Lieutenant Pong trying to trick me into admitting that I'd somehow sneaked Two Bellies into the basement of the Grand Ole

Opry and, while down there, I'd slit her throat.

"If I did that," I asked him, "why would I request a search warrant to go back to the scene of the crime?"

He had no answer for that. Despite his scowl, he didn't believe for a minute that Ernie or I had murdered Two Bellies. This was all a sham. He knew it, I knew it, but of course he'd never admit it. The point was to cast suspicion on Ernie and me and then, if the real killer of Two Bellies turned out to be someone important, Ernie and I could be charged in order to protect the powerful.

I was in a dangerous position and I knew it. Some sort of chess game was being played behind the scenes and Ernie and I had been turned into pawns. What had triggered the start of the game? Our inquiries into the death of Mori Di. Who was behind these machinations? Probably the Seven Dragons but could someone else be involved? And what were the stakes? Old grudges? Or something more?

Ernie and I had probably been watched all along. Maybe from when we first talked to Two Bellies. Maybe earlier. Whoever had taken Two Bellies down there and slit her throat was demonstrating to us how much power they had. Enough power to make anything, no matter how improbable, happen. And there was nothing that Ernie or I could do about it.

Lieutenant Pong kept hammering away at the time I'd spent with Two Bellies. Trying to build a timeline to be able to show that if nothing else I'd had the opportunity to murder her if I'd wanted to. I answered his questions honestly, knowing that Ernie would too. Being near somebody, talking to them, is not a crime. I knew that even though Lieutenant Pong might be able to establish the means and opportunity for murder, he'd never be able to establish a motive. Neither Ernie nor I had any reason to kill Two Bellies. In fact, I pitied the old gal, lying there in that brick-lined pit. Whoever had done that to her had dispatched her without remorse. A blade sliced expertly through her throat—a lot of blood, a little twitching—and *fini.* No more Two Bellies.

Lieutenant Pong was intelligent enough to know that Ernie and I had no possible reason to murder Two Bellies but, apparently, his bosses wanted him to build as much of a case against us as he could.

And build a case he would.

* * *

The provost marshal's reaction was not good. He'd authorized a search warrant, expecting to recover the remains of a long-dead American G.I. and instead he was told that we'd stumbled onto the freshly slaughtered corpse of an overweight, middle-aged ex-prostitute with the charming name of Two Bellies. He was embarrassed. So was the entire command.

The next morning, as he sat on a short wooden stool outside my cell in the third-level subbasement of the Korean National Police headquarters in downtown Seoul, the first sergeant of the Criminal Investigation Detachment took great delight in telling me all this.

"You're on the shit list," he said.

"How's Ernie?" I asked.

The first sergeant looked up toward a ceiling of jagged rock. "He's on the second level. Beat up pretty bad. He shouldn't have resisted."

"Resisted when?"

"During the interrogation. He punched Lieutenant Pong."

I sighed. "They had no call to take us in," I said.

The first sergeant's eyes widened. "You led them to a basement claiming ancient remains would be found and the night before you were mucking around in the selfsame basement with no legal authorization whatsoever. And then a body is found. And you'd been seen on the street, repeatedly, with the victim. What the hell else were they going to do?"

"Question us, sure," I replied. "But they didn't have to handcuff us and take us downtown."

The first sergeant thought about that one. "Yes, they did. You're the logical suspects. Besides, the KNPs are being careful. As long as they're tough with you, they're more likely to save face no matter how this turns out."

Reluctantly, I decided that the first sergeant was probably right. If the Seven Dragons were behind the murder of Two Bellies—and I had every reason to believe they were—then they'd be pulling strings at the top levels of the ROK government to make sure the blame was diverted elsewhere. Like towards Ernie and me. Furthermore, whoever murdered Two Bellies had gone to great lengths to abscond, once again, with the remains of Mori Di. Finding those remains now would be impossible, unless I acted quickly.

"I have to get out of here," I said.

"You and everyone else."

Down the hallway, men groaned. Curses were shouted. Mostly in Korean. One or two in broken English, as if trying to get our attention.

"What's JAG say?" I meant the military lawyers at 8th Army's Judge Advocate General's Office.

"They're working on it," Top replied. "The SOFA committee is holding an emergency meeting this afternoon."

Under the Status of Forces Agreement between the ROK and U.S. governments, the joint U.S.–ROK steering committee decides who takes jurisdiction over cases involving American servicemen and Korean civilians. And, more important to me at the moment, they decide who—the Americans or the Koreans—should have physical custody of prisoners.

"The good news," Top said, "is that the ROKs haven't charged you with murder. Not yet."

"When will I know?"

"I'll be back tomorrow morning. First thing."

He stood and left. I watched him walk down the long corridor and step through a thick wooden door opened by an armed Korean cop. When the door slammed shut, the voices around me howled even louder. I squatted on the stone floor, listening to the words being shouted, trying to decipher them. Pain and agony is all they said, although I doubted that my Korean-English dictionary would explain them quite that way, or even contain them, for that matter.

A half hour after Top left, four Korean cops approached my cell, rattled keys, and popped the door open. They motioned for me to join them in the hallway. I did. Then they grabbed me by the arms and shoved me down the corridor toward the main holding cell. It was an enormous cage made of metal bars; there must've been thirty men inside. I hesitated. Americans, according to the SOFA agreement, are supposed to be kept segregated from the general prison population. It seemed these cops hadn't read the agreement. They pushed me roughly forward, opened the door of the main cell and shoved me inside. I stood staring at over thirty Korean prisoners from teenage hoodlums to old papa-san reprobates and every age of scoundrel in between. I was frightened, of course, but did my best not to show it. Still, I felt as if I were a side of meat flopped down in front of hungry wolves. As if to confirm my fears, some of the prisoners surrounding me, literally, began to howl.

The big holding cell had a cement slab floor and raised above it about two feet was a rickety wooden platform upon which the prisoners lived and slept. A huge metal tub sat near the front door, reeking of filth. No flush toilet here.

All the men stared at me—silent now after the initial howling— studying this strange foreign fish shoved into their midst. Every square inch of the wooden platform was occupied. There was no place for me to sit. I felt awkward, not knowing what to do with my body, so I stood and stared back at the men, trying to keep my face impassive, keep my body still, and fake bravery. Life had taught me that if you can fake bravery—even when you're scared shitless—you can go a long way toward protecting yourself. Finally, one of the men rose to his feet, stepped into rubber slippers, and hobbled toward me. His face was scarred, square, weather beaten. I loomed over him by a full foot but he seemed not one whit afraid of me.

He squinted up at me and said, "You got cigarette, G.I.?"

I shook my head negatively, not trusting myself to speak.

He frowned and cursed.

"They take from you?" His head gestured toward the cops down the hallway.

I shook my head again. "No. I don't smoke."

"No smokey?" He started to laugh. Actually, it sounded more like a rasping cough. Then he turned back to the men behind him and repeated what I'd said in Korean. They laughed again. He turned back to me and said, "You cherry boy?"

I didn't bother to answer. I just stared at him. The smile left his face.

"You lie to Charley Lee?"

Again, I didn't answer. I'd been through this kind of interrogation before, on the streets and playgrounds of East L.A. The bully will ask you questions that befuddle you and he'll keep asking questions until eventually the questions become impossible to answer.

The best thing to do, usually, is stare him down and not answer his questions and start the fight as soon as possible. It's inevitable anyway. Might as well get it over with.

Charley Lee started cursing in Korean. It was a long diatribe and he kept looking me up and down as he spoke. I didn't understand most of it but I understood enough. He was insulting me, questioning my manhood, talking about how useless and soft Americans were. All the while the men behind him were smiling, enjoying the spectacle. Most of them, anyway. A few looked away, uncomfortable about what was going on but powerless to do anything about it.

I waited for the right moment and then I shouted, *"Shikuro!"* Shut up!

Charley Lee stared at me, his eyes wide, and behind him all the men held their breath. His face became inflamed with anger. He stepped closer to me, so close that I could feel his hot, fetid breath rising up my chest until, like a clammy hand, it caressed my chin and poked its dirty fingers into my nostrils. Now he was shouting so loud that spittle splashed on my neck. In one quick move, I shoved him backwards.

The crowd exploded in outrage. Like a Siberian tiger, Charley Lee regained his balance and sprang at me. Other men joined him. I landed a solid left to Charley Lee's skull and as I did so I backed up to the metal bars behind me. As the men came in, I winged punches to my right and left. A few landed but within seconds I was being pummeled from all sides and I found myself kneeling on the floor. Someone was down there with me. I couldn't be sure but I believe it was Charley Lee. His arm was wrapped around my neck and his mouth pressed against my ear.

"Chil Yong," he said, "say hello." Then he punched me in the gut.

A herd of footsteps pounded down the hallway. The front door clanged open and men began shoving and shouting. I stayed kneeling on the cement floor, curled up, doing my best to protect my head and other sensitive body parts.

Charley Lee rolled away and within seconds Korean cops were grabbing my shoulders and pulling me backward toward the door. I kicked out as best I could and then I was on my feet and outside of the cell, my vision blurred by blood. A few seconds later I was in some sort of dispensary, being washed and tended by a male nurse. Patched up, I was returned to my cell.

Alone this time.

I groaned, held my stomach, and tried to sleep on the cold cement floor.

If the Seven Dragons wanted to send me a message, they could've used Western Union.

When the first sergeant returned the next morning, and the door to my cell was opened, his eyes widened.

"What the hell happened to you?"

I shrugged. "Walked into a door."

"The door to a meat grinder?" When I didn't answer he said, "Do you want to put in a complaint?"

"Have I been released?"

"Yeah. To the custody of Eighth Army."

"Then I don't need to complain." Ernie was released too, although he was in somewhat better shape than I was.

Silently, we all rode back to Yongsan Compound in the first sergeant's green sedan. He didn't ask us any questions. And we didn't feel like answering any.

The first thing the provost marshal did was take us off the case.

The KNPs warned 8th Army that, pending further investigation into the murder of the woman known as Two Bellies, we might be formally charged at any time. Therefore, Colonel Brace had no option but to suspend us from all law enforcement duties. We were reduced to being put under the supervision of Staff Sergeant Riley and he had us sitting in his office, catching up with some clerical duties that had backlogged over the months.

Miss Lee, the statuesque secretary of the Admin office, seemed bemused by this turn of events because it had been some weeks since she and Ernie had last gone out on a date. But Ernie was on his best behavior and she was adapting well. He even brought her a fresh flower in the morning to replace the old one in the little glass vase on her desk. She accepted it with a snort. But really, as hard to figure as women are, my guess was that she was pleased.

Corporal Paco Bernal hadn't been caught yet. And since the regular MP patrols out in Itaewon hadn't uncovered any hint of him, it was assumed that he'd moved on elsewhere in country. He was still on the watch list at all international points of embarkation and every military law enforcement officer in the country—from Munsan to Pusan—was keeping an eye out for him.

The most important thing, as far as Ernie and I were concerned, was that we weren't restricted to compound. Once the flag was lowered and the cannon went off at the end of the duty day—as it did every day at seventeen hundred hours with military precision—we were free to do whatever we wanted to do. And what we wanted to do, more than anything else, was head out to the ville.

I was asleep in my bunk when the MP desk sergeant shook me awake. I shielded my eyes from the glare of his flashlight.

"You Sueño?"

"Yeah. What happened?"

"The J-2's daughter escaped."

"Huh?"

"Colonel Tidwell. His daughter, Jessica, she escaped."

I shoved the army blanket away and sat up. "What do you mean 'escaped'?"

"She climbed out of the window of her bedroom at Colonel Tidwell's quarters and made her way to the main gate. A guard there spotted her leaving the compound but he was too stupid to stop her. He did see her waving down a kimchee cab. She headed toward Itaewon."

"And the provost marshal wants me to get out of bed and look for her, is that it?"

"That's it. You and your partner, what's his name."

"Did you wake up what's his name yet?"

"Yeah. He took a swing at me when I did. Good thing he missed. Otherwise I'd have written him up on charges."

At least I could be sure that he'd woken up the right guy.

I climbed out of my bunk, opened my wall locker, and started putting on my clothes. The beam from the MP desk sergeant's flashlight disappeared down the hallway.

9

It was oh-dark-thirty, right smack dab in the middle of the midnight-to-four curfew, when Ernie and I arrived back in the red-light district of Itaewon.

"Seems like we just left," Ernie said.

"Yeah."

Itaewon was a different world. A dark world, all the flashing lights shut off, windows shuttered tight, swinging double doors padlocked and barred from the inside. Unlit neon drooped from dirty brick walls like cheap earrings dangling from a prostitute's ear.

Only law enforcement personnel and emergency vehicles are allowed to operate during the midnight-to-four curfew. A couple of times "white mice"—the white-clad curfew-enforcement police—stopped us and inspected our CID badges. Each time I spoke in Korean and asked if they'd seen a young American woman in the area. They shook their heads.

Jessica Tidwell had arrived in Itaewon just before the midnight-to-four curfew took effect.

"We're not going to find her out here now," Ernie said.

"Maybe not," I answered. "If you were her, where would you go?"

Ernie thought about it. "To see Paco."

"Right," I said. "That's what I thought to. So maybe Paco Bernal didn't leave Itaewon after all. Maybe he's been hiding here the last few days and maybe he found a way to get word to Jessica Tidwell."

"And as soon as she had a chance, she flew the coop."

"Right again."

"So they're together. And Paco found a hideout in or near Itaewon that we haven't been able to snoop out. A lot of good that does us. We still don't know where they are."

"There's one other thing."

"What?" Ernie asked.

"Paco has some business to conduct, remember? With that thousand dollars."

"Sure," Ernie said. "he was going to buy some drugs in bulk, move them quickly, make a profit, and return the thousand dollars to Colonel Tidwell's safe."

"Maybe."

"No maybe about it. The perfect plan, other than a few minor factors. He didn't know that when Jessica stole the money she'd leave the safe unlocked and the door to her father's den open just to piss off her mom. Only thing he hadn't counted on, the dumb shit. But other than drugs, what else could he buy and make a quick profit? Had to be drugs."

Paco could have bought expensive items at the PX—like imported cameras or stereo equipment—to sell at a profit. The problem was that all such items are recorded by 8th Army Data Processing and at the end of each G.I.'s tour you have to either produce the item or, more often, produce a receipt that it is being shipped back to the States in your hold baggage. Paco would want something untraceable. Therefore it had to be something illicit, like drugs.

"So if he were going to do that," I said, "in Itaewon, who would he see?"

Ernie thought about it a moment. "Nobody deals drugs in the open in Itaewon. Not if we're talking something other than marijuana."

In Korea, the penalty for dealing in hard drugs—heroin or

cocaine—is death. And it's strictly enforced. More than one culprit, foreign and Korean, had been hanged for the offense. The military government of Pak Chung-hee was trying, by force of will, to pull Korea out of poverty and they weren't going to allow drug dealers to corrupt its youth and thereby hold the country back.

"So if Paco'd set up some sort of exchange," I said, "it was probably a one shot deal with somebody who was willing to take a big chance. Who would that be?"

"Somebody desperate," Ernie said.

"Which, in Itaewon, doesn't narrow it down much."

"No."

"So when it comes to money, who knows everything that goes on in Itaewon?"

Ernie thought about it a moment. "Haggler Lee." Then he smiled and said, "We ain't there yet?"

An alley not much wider than the width of my shoulders led up a steep hill. We followed it and took a right and then a left and another left. No electric lights shone behind the ten-foot-high stone and brick walls that lined the narrow lane. Orienting ourselves by moonlight, we finally stopped and pounded on an ancient wood-plank door.

We kept pounding for ten minutes, taking turns when our knuckles grew raw. After another five minutes, the big door squeaked open.

An old woman wearing a traditional Korean dress bowed to us and motioned for us to follow her across the narrow courtyard. She shoved open a heavy wooden door that squeaked on rusty wheels and then closed it behind us. Ernie and I entered a vast, two-story-high warehouse. In the center of the warehouse, guttering like a fading ghost, flame flickered from a fat wax candle.

Haggler Lee sat cross-legged on a *kang*, a platform raised about two feet off the floor and covered with thickly layered oil paper. After wending our way around mountains of crated goods, Ernie and I took off our shoes, stepped up onto the platform, and sat across from Haggler Lee. Between us stood a foot-high round table with mother-of-pearl dragons inlaid in its black lacquer surface.

Haggler Lee smiled.

Two teeth poked out of red gums, both of them brown. Haggler Lee had been a youngish-looking man, probably in his mid to late forties, but lately he'd been sick. In the flickering candlelight, his skin looked yellow, shading toward orange. Nobody knew exactly what disease he was suffering from but my guess was something endemic to Korea, like hepatitis.

"Paco Bernal," Haggler Lee said, without any hint of weariness in his voice. "He's a good boy."

I did my best not to show surprise. But when I thought about it, I shouldn't have been startled that Haggler Lee already knew why we were here. People watch everything G.I.s do in Itaewon, especially two G.I.s who happen to be agents for 8th Army's Criminal Investigation Division. Through his black-market business, Haggler Lee would have dealings with business girls and cocktail waitresses and bartenders and just about everyone else who keeps the nightclub district of Itaewon humming. What else did Haggler Lee know? Did he know about Colonel Tidwell and Jessica? I'd soon find out.

"Does Paco work for you?" Ernie asked.

"He run errand sometimes."

"What kind of errands?"

"On compound." Haggler Lee shrugged his narrow shoulders. The hand-stitched white cranes embroidered onto his silk tunic made a rustling sound, as if flapping feathered wings. "Deliveries," Lee said.

"Of dope?"

The flushed skin of Haggler Lee's face grimaced in pain. "Not dope. Only natural product."

"Like marijuana?"

"What grows from the earth no can hurt body."

Also, it can't get you in trouble with the Korean National Police. The Korean authorities are much more tolerant about mildly hallu-cinogenic plants that grow from the soil. Korea is an ancient agricul-tural country. Farmers need to supplement their income between harvests. If G.I.s want to smoke some weed, what harm could it do?

I pushed the candle-holder forward, trying to throw more light on Haggler Lee's face. "Did Paco make a big buy recently?" I asked. "Like a thousand bucks?"

Haggler Lee looked pained again, as if his small stomach were churning razor blades.

"Paco has some problems," Haggler Lee replied.

That was the understatement of the week.

"What kind of problems?"

"Like bad people hear about thousand dollars stolen on compound," Lee said. "Same bad people also hear that good boy, Paco, he the one stole thousand dollars."

"So Paco's money is gone," I said, "stolen by hoodlums. And he never had a chance to make the deal he was going to make."

Haggler Lee splayed his bony hands. "So sad story."

"Yes," I answered. "So sad story."

"Where is Paco now?" Ernie asked.

"He run away. With that American girl. She come to get him tonight. She have some more money so Paco can hide."

"Where'd they go?"

Haggler Lee breathed deeply and then let the air out slowly between clenched teeth, a traditional sign of painful indecision. When he didn't answer, Ernie rapped his knuckles on the inlaid mother-of-pearl table.

"What do you want, Lee?" he asked.

Haggler Lee's eyes shone. "Who on black-market detail now?"

"Burrows and Slabem," Ernie answered.

Jake Burrows and Felix Slabem, our fellow agents at 8th Army CID, not friends of ours.

"Can you make sure," Haggler Lee asked, "that they no visit me tomorrow?"

Although they had no direct jurisdiction over Haggler Lee, Agents Burrows and Slabem routinely showed up to scare G.I.s away and disrupt Lee's black-market operation, costing him money. Ernie and I seldom did. He was too valuable a source of information.

"What time?" Ernie asked.

"Noontime until four o'clock."

"We'll make something up," Ernie said. "Our case is top priority. We'll tell the first sergeant we need their help to research something."

Lee nodded in agreement. "Good. Then I tell you where Paco

and colonel's daughter go." He clawed his long fingernails on the edge of the small table. "But you no like."

"We like, no like. No make difference," Ernie said. He was beginning to sound like a Korean himself.

"Paco Bernal go someplace hide. Nobody know where. But before he go, colonel's daughter say goodbye to Paco. Say she go back to American compound. But she no go compound. She go Golden Dragon Travel Agency."

"To buy tickets to leave the country?" I asked.

"No." Lee said. "To earn one thousand dollars. To give back to her father. To get Paco out of trouble."

Ernie's eyes widened. "How in the hell is she going to make a thousand bucks at a travel agency?"

Lee waited for us to figure it out. I already had. A few seconds later, so did Ernie.

"Japanese tourists," he said.

Lee nodded. The pain in his stomach must've hurt something fierce. His wrinkled face twisted in anguish.

"Not good," Lee said. "Eighth Army, any honcho, my friend. They loose face, Haggler Lee loose face."

I believed he meant it. Haggler Lee had grown rich off of the 8th United States Army and anything that cut them down a notch, cut him down a notch too.

My gut wasn't feeling too good at this news. If something awful happened to Jessica Tidwell, if she wasn't saved from hurting herself, the lowest-ranking enlisted men standing near the disaster would be blamed. In this case, that would be myself and Agent Ernie Bascom.

I asked Haggler Lee about Two Bellies. He recoiled at the name and claimed he knew nothing about her murder. Ernie started to ask follow-up questions but within seconds the maid came back in and the candle was snuffed out. By the light of a flashlight, we were ushered out of the warehouse.

We could've raised hell, tried to force more information out of him, but I knew from experience that Haggler Lee, despite his frail appearance, couldn't be intimidated. But if you remained on his good side, and played the game the way he expected it to be played, he'd parcel out information the same way he parceled out money: one coin at a time.

With nothing more to go on, Ernie and I returned to the MP Station on Yongsan Compound and reported that, so far, we'd been unable to find Jessica Tidwell. I did my best to catch a couple of hours sleep before reveille.

Shortly after the morning bugle sounded, Ernie and I were up, hunched over our favorite table at the 8th Army snack bar, slurping on bitter coffee and munching bacon, lettuce, and tomato sandwiches. The big question we faced was whether or not to report what we'd learned from Haggler Lee up the chain of command. Plenty of waste had already hit the fan but now even more of that waste was liable to splatter back on us.

"Before I report anything," I said, "we should talk to Jesssica's mom."

"Her *mom?*" Ernie said. "What about the colonel?"

"First, we start with his wife," I said. "The *real* power in 8th Army."

"No way," Ernie replied. "Not yet. She'll have a conniption fit and be all over us like a she-cat."

Ernie was right. Once Mrs. Tidwell knew what her daughter might be facing, she'd demand that all the resources of 8th Army be diverted to save her precious offspring. The first sergeant, or more likely the provost marshal, would be directing our every move. In some ways, that would get us off the hook. If something went wrong—and it most likely would—the blame would be shared. But Ernie just thought of solving things and for him the direct way was the best way.

But there was one other thing Mrs. Tidwell might be able to do for us. So far, Ernie and I were still stripped of our investigative powers. If Mrs. Tidwell demanded that we be fully reinstated, it would probably happen. Then, in addition to searching for the precious Jessica Tidwell, Ernie and I would be in a better position to investigate the death of Mori Di and, just as importantly, the recent brutal murder of Two Bellies.

"We need to get our butts out to this Golden Dragon Travel Agency," Ernie said. "Find Jessica, and drag her ass home."

Something told me it wouldn't be that easy. Still, it was worth a try.

After finishing our sumptuous 8th Army repast, we walked up the hill to the CID Admin Office where I used the Korean phone book to look up the number and address of the Golden Dragon Travel Agency. I called but there was no answer. At this time of the morning, it figured. Travel agencies in Korea are full service affairs—not just shops that sell airplane tickets—and they do most of their business late in the day and especially at night. The Golden Dragon Travel Agency might not even open its doors until noon. Still, it wouldn't do for Ernie and me to sit around the office waiting to be harangued by questions and giving every little Napoleon a chance to instruct us as to what action to take.

I left a note for Staff Sergeant Riley telling him that Ernie and I would be in Itaewon, searching for Jessica Tidwell.

We took some time gassing up Ernie's jeep and having some maintenance done on it, so it was almost noon by the time we found the right neighborhood. Ernie stood in front of an open-fronted store that sold Korean fast-food items: packaged dried noodles, discs of puffed rice, canned guava juice, and the corpses of dried cuttlefish nailed to a wooden rafter. Ernie had loaded up on two double packs of ginseng gum and offered me a stick. For once I took one, unwrapped it, and stuck it in my mouth. The stuff tasted bitter, like a powder of dried aspirin, but was sweetened by some sort of sugary mint flavor. All in all, nauseating. But "good for the metabolism" as Ernie was fond of saying.

Why he felt he needed something to fire up his metabolism, I never did figure out.

He said, "What's the address of that Golden Dragon Travel Agency?"

"One-two-five *dong*, three-six-four *ho*, in Hannam-dong," I replied. "That's it across the street."

Ernie wasn't able to read the sign but he was able to make out the sinuous dragon painted gold and red.

"We ain't there yet?"

We crossed the street, ducked through the open door, and breezed past the secretary. At the back office we pushed open the door. A plaque in front of his desk said his name was Kim. When Ernie pulled his .45 and shoved the barrel up into Mr. Kim's nostril, the middle-aged travel agent couldn't talk fast enough.

Unfolded on his desk was a huge album featuring wallet-sized snapshots of dozens of Korean women. His sales portfolio. Japanese businessmen arrived in country in organized junkets, usually paid for by the company they worked for. Before they left their home country, each participant had already picked out a Korean girl to act as his "hostess" upon arrival.

I didn't see Jessica's photo but when I mentioned her name he knew who she was quick enough.

"She go with Mr. Fukushima."

"Fuku-whatta?" Ernie asked.

"Ondo Fukushima. Very powerful man."

"How powerful?" I asked.

The manager of the Golden Dragon Travel Agency stared into the barrel of Ernie's .45 and swallowed. "Yakuza," he said.

The Japanese mafia.

"What hotel is he staying at?"

"Not there yet. He arrive airport in Pusan one hour ago. Has many business meetings in many places: Kuangju, Taegu, Taejon. I don't know where."

Ernie punched him. The travel agent howled in pain. I checked to make sure that his secretary hadn't reached for the telephone. She hadn't. She sat at her desk, hands flat on the lacquered wooden desk in front of her, shaking like a frightened rabbit. I felt bad about this treatment, but we had no choice but to scare the hell out of them. If I'd asked Mr. Kim questions without using intimidation, he would've either told me to take a hike or stalled and demanded money. Neither of which I had time for. Would he turn us in to the Korean National Police for using threats and intimidation? Probably not. Because that's what the KNPs use themselves. In Korea, it's an unofficial—but accepted—law-enforcement technique. I assuaged my guilt by reminding myself that many of the women in Mr. Kim's portfolio— the lost young faces staring out at me—were forced into prostitution by threats and intimidation. This was a nice office, and Mr. Kim wore a clean pressed suit, but from wall to wall the place stank.

"I don't *know* where Mr. Fukushima go," Kim said. "Yakuza don't write down . . . how you say?"

"Itinerary," I told him.

He nodded. "Yes. Itinerary."

"Is Jessica with him now?"

"Not yet. His driver pick her up this morning, take her some-place south. She will greet Mr. Fukushima tomorrow morning and stay with him during all meetings. Tomorrow night, maybe late, they come back Seoul."

That was unusual. Usually the Japanese sex tourists hide their girls in their hotel rooms. Sometimes they take them to the casinos or the nightclubs, but that's about it. Never to official business meetings.

Kim responded to my questioning look. "Fukushima get good *face*," he said. "He want everybody see American girl. Daughter of G.I. honcho. He show her to everybody."

"How much is he paying her?" I asked.

"One thousand dollars. For whole weekend."

"What does she have to do?"

Kim's eyes widened. "What you mean?"

"What service does she have to perform for the thousand dollars?"

A look of confusion clouded Kim's face.

"Does she have to sleep with him?" I asked.

Then he understood. "Of course," he answered. "She woman. He man."

Ernie slapped him. Not hard. Just with his left hand.

"When he arrives in Seoul," Ernie asked, "what hotel will he be staying at?"

"White Crane Hotel," Kim answered. "New one. Best in Seoul."

Kim didn't know what time they'd be arriving at the hotel. Like he said, a yakuza doesn't advertise his itinerary. But late, he figured. Late tomorrow night.

Before we left, Ernie pointed his .45 once more between Kim's eyes.

"No phone calls," Ernie said, "to this yakuza or to any of his buddies. Or to the police. You got that?"

Kim nodded frantically.

"If you forget," Ernie said, "I'll be back."

Kim sat frozen as we left. The secretary was still shaking.

Korean television news broadcasts use language that is too difficult for me to understand. The stories are read by a dignified-looking Korean man in a well-pressed suit who alternates with a gorgeous Korean woman wearing an expensive Western-style dress. As they drone on, I can pick out a few words and phrases but one thing I've noticed in the months I've been in Korea is that they seldom report on the 50,000 American soldiers stationed in their country. When they do, it is only with footage of big ROK–U.S. joint maneuvers showing ships and planes and tanks moving over hilly countryside. They never show individual G.I.s close up. And they certainly never report on American soldiers tearing through their towns and villages, drunk, on a Saturday night. So I knew that the indiscretions of Jessica Tidwell, no matter how egregious, would never be allowed to be aired on a Korean television news broadcast or on the radio or even in a newspaper. But nevertheless people would know. Everyone at 8th Army, all the thousands of members of the Korean National Police, and most importantly, officials at the top levels of the U.S. and South Korean governments; they would all know. The embarrassment would be massive: the daughter of the 8th Army J-2 selling herself to a Japanese mobster. Colonel Tidwell would lose his job, Mrs. Tidwell would never be able to show her face at the Officers' Wives' Club again, and the entire family would probably be run out of the country.

"So what do you care about them?" Ernie asked. "What have they ever done for you?"

We were in Ernie's jeep now, heading back toward Yongsan Compound.

"They deserve to know," I replied. "At least Mrs. Tidwell does."

"Before we report it up the chain of command, you mean?"

"Exactly."

Ernie shrugged. "What difference does it make? We'll have to report it eventually."

"Not necessarily."

"What the hell do you mean?"

"If we take Jessica away from this Fukushima, return her to her mom, then nobody needs to know. But if we make it official, Eighth Army's going to lose face."

"Are you nuts, Sueño?"

"Eighth Army's done a lot of good in this country," I said, "despite the crime we see every day. Look at what Moretti did twenty years ago, built an orphanage, fed people who were starving. Eighth Army has built roads and aqueducts and—"

"And we saved the south from the horrors of Communism," Ernie said, "just like we're going to do in Vietnam."

"That too," I replied.

Ernie sighed. "So you want to keep this quiet?"

"Why not?"

"Because it could be dangerous, that's why not. If Jessica Tidwell gets seriously hurt, or disappears, it'll be on us. The provost marshal will come down on us with both feet."

"A little danger never bothered you before."

That challenge finally brought Ernie Bascom over. "If you're game, so am I," he replied.

"I'm game."

When we reached Yongsan Compound, Ernie turned left into Gate Number 9, the easternmost entrance to 8th Army South Post. As we approached Colonel Tidwell's quarters, Mrs. Tidwell stood at her front door, arms crossed.

"Apparently," I told Mrs. Tidwell, "Jessica believes that if she can raise the thousand dollars and return it to your husband's safe, he will drop the charges against Corporal Bernal."

Ernie and I sat on a leather sofa in the front room, two cups of hot black coffee in front of us on a glass-topped table. Mrs. Tidwell sat on a straight-backed chair opposite, her manicured fingers folded on her lap. Her hair was combed, her face made up, and she wore a blue print dress that lay across her knees in stiff pleats.

Mrs. Tidwell rose, turned away form us, and strode toward a plate-glass window that looked out over a row of tightly pruned cherry trees.

"Jessica might be right," Mrs. Tidwell said. "My husband brought the charges against Corporal Bernal. He can also drop the charges."

What she was telling us, I believed, was that if Jessica raised the money she would make sure her husband dropped the charges. Good. But what she needed to know now was how Jessica planned to raise the money.

Ernie glanced at me. I swallowed and opened my mouth.

"I think you'll agree, Mrs. Tidwell," I said, "that Jessica's plan to raise the money is not a wise one."

Mrs. Tidwell turned away from the garden scene outside, returned, and sat down facing me.

"Just what is her plan?"

I spread my fingers. "According to the information we've uncovered, Jessica plans to engage in a business deal sponsored by the Golden Dragon Travel Agency."

Mrs. Tidwell stared at me blankly.

"To be frank, ma'am," I continued, "their practices are somewhat unsavory. Trips arranged for wealthy Japanese businessmen. Introductions made."

Her eyes widened. "Sex tours," she said.

"Not always," I answered. "Sometimes the women act as escorts only."

Mrs. Tidwell kept her green eyes on me, allowing the heat of her stare to linger on my face. "Don't lie to me," she said.

I didn't answer.

"This Golden Dragon Travel Agency is going to set Jessica up with some rich Japanese businessman here in Seoul?" Mrs. Tidwell leaned forward, intent. Somehow, the tiny muscles in her face hardened. "What fun for him," she said. "A beautiful redheaded American girl. Only seventeen. And what good face for him. The daughter of the intelligence chief of the 8th United States Army."

She glared at me as if I were Jessica Tidwell's pimp. Ernie studied the floor, not breathing.

"That's why we came to you first," I said, stammering. "Before reporting anything . . . officially."

She sat back, breathed deeply, and turned her head as if seeing the intricately designed wallpaper for the first time. Then she snapped her attention back to me.

"Can you find her?"

"With the help of the Korean National Police and possibly with the—"

"Not with them. Alone."

"It would be difficult."

"But not impossible?"

"No," I answered, "not impossible." I spread my fingers again. "But we'd need to be reinstated back to our full investigative status."

"Reinstated?"

I explained to her what had happened, about our search for the bones of Mori Di and about the unexpected discovery of the death of Two Bellies. I left out a lot of the details.

"So the ROKs think you murdered this overage prostitute?" Mrs. Tidwell said.

"They know we didn't," Ernie replied. "They're just keeping the charges open to keep pressure on Eighth Army."

"And to save face," she said, getting the picture immediately.

I nodded.

"Who's your boss?" she asked.

"Colonel Brace," I told her. "The provost marshal."

When she rose again, she walked over to the mantelpiece. Atop it sat pictures of Jessica: when she was a baby, on a Girl Scout camping trip, laughing with other teenage girls and waving pompoms.

"We've spoiled her," Mrs. Tidwell said. "You know that."

Neither Ernie nor I answered. Instead, we stared into our cold coffee.

"If we make Jessica's . . . uh . . . indiscretions official," Mrs. Tidwell said, "my husband would be embarrassed. The Korean government would know of our shame, and eventually the U.S. ambassador. My husband might even have to resign from his position as J-2 for 8th Army." She shook her head. "That would kill him. The thought that every Korean policeman in the country would know that my daughter planned to sell herself to a rich Japanese, is not tolerable."

She walked quickly across the thick carpet, entered the den, and slid the door shut behind her.

"What's she doing?" Ernie asked.

"Probably making a phone call."

"To who?"

"Not to her husband, you can count on that."

Five minutes later she returned.

"I just talked to Meg Waldron," she said. "Do you know who she is?"

I nodded. "The wife of the CG."

The wife of the commanding general of the 8th United States Army. Also the president of the Officers' Wives' Club.

"She says that she'll put a call in to Colonel Brace immediately. Consider yourselves reinstated. And she says that if you rescue Jessica, there is no way that the U.S. or Korean authorities are going to touch you in any way." Mrs. Tidwell strode forward and sat back down in front of us. "You must find Jessica. You must find her right away, before she does this horrible thing. Meg Waldron and I and all the women of the Officers' Wives' Club will be here to protect you."

I believed that she meant it. But I didn't believe it would do us much good. If somebody got hurt—really hurt—the situation would be beyond her control.

Ernie and I rose from the sofa. She shook my hand.

"And one more thing," she said. "When you find Paco, don't hurt him. Jessica would never forgive me."

"We'll try not to hurt anybody, ma'am," I said.

We walked down the long driveway to Ernie's jeep. Mrs. Tidwell stood at the huge entranceway to the J-2's quarters and watched until we drove away.

Ernie glanced at me as he rounded a corner. "Sticking our necks out for the brass. I'm not sure I like it."

"I figure we're doing it for Eighth Army."

Ernie raised one eyebrow and asked again. "What has Eighth Army ever done for you?"

We were just leaving Yongsan Compound South Post and crossing the MSR, the Main Supply Route. I waved my hand toward Itaewon.

"Eighth Army's given me all this," I said. "And this." I plucked the front of my white shirt and tie.

Ernie grunted and wheeled the jeep between the barricade that led to main post.

At the Yongsan Compound Military Police Arms Room, Staff Sergeant Palinki, the Unit Armorer, presented me with a well-oiled .45 automatic and matching shoulder holster. Ernie was already carrying. He was supposed to have turned the weapon in when we were stripped of our investigative duties but he hadn't bothered. Ernie handed over his weapon and allowed Palinki to perform a quick maintenance check and cleaning.

"Bad boys," Palinki said. "This will make them think twice before messing with you two."

"Nobody messes with us, Palinki," Ernie said.

"Nobody. Sure, boss. Nobody mess with Sueño and Bascom. In case they do though . . . " He pointed a big finger at the business end of the .45. "This is the part you point at them, brother. Make them think twice. If they don't be good boys, you blow their fucking heads off, OK brother?"

Ernie offered Palinki a stick of ginseng gum. The big man took two. He chomped on them both and grinned as we slipped into our leather straps, holstered the .45s with the grips pointing out, and then put on our jackets over them.

"Nobody know you packing," Palinki said.

Nobody except somebody who might wonder why we had two-inch-wide bulges under our armpits.

We saluted Sergeant Palinki and left.

10

I was the only CID agent—or MP for that matter—in the entire Republic of Korea who could speak Korean. Not that I received any credit for having slaved in night classes. On the contrary, I was most often accused of being "too close to the Koreans." The honchos wouldn't admit that actually talking to the people you're investigating can sometimes help.

Ernie, on the other hand, could move in any low-life circles. Whether the G.I.s off post were druggies or criminals or perverts on the prowl for unmentionable delights, Ernie could gain their confidence. Probably it was Vietnam that had done it to him. He spent two tours there. On the first he'd bought marijuana and hashish like most G.I.s but on his second tour all the marijuana and hash had disappeared, replaced now by vials of pure China White. A plan encouraged by the North Vietnamese to incapacitate American soldiers, he thought. Upon returning to the States, Ernie found the willpower to lay off drugs. He switched to booze, a perfectly acceptable alternative as far as the United States Army is concerned. I admired him for his strength of will and his ability to move chameleon-like from one world to the other.

But what ultimately forced the provost marshal and the other honchos at 8th Army to tolerate George Sueño and Ernie Bascom was that Ernie and I were the only investigators in country willing and able to waltz right into any G.I. village and come back with the goods. The other CID agents were tight-asses. They didn't know how to conduct themselves in nightclubs or bars or brothels and they froze up, acting stilted and embarrassed. And, of course, none of them could speak the language. Neither the language of the people of Korea nor the language of the night.

Eighth Army needed Ernie and me. And because there was a lot more G.I. crime off compound than 8th Army liked to admit—which was the reason they kept the SIRs under lock and key—the skills of George Sueño and Ernie Bascom were, if not prized, at least tolerated. But you wouldn't have known it by the scowling countenances of the CID first sergeant and the 8th Army Provost Marshal, Colonel Brace.

"You went over my head," Colonel Brace told us.

Ernie and I kept quiet.

"Out of nowhere," Colonel Brace continued, "the CG's chief of staff calls me and says that I'm to reinstate your full investigative powers and to hell with what the Korean National Police might think. And, furthermore, I'm to let you concentrate full time on the Jessica Tidwell case."

Ernie and I hadn't been asked a question, so we didn't respond.

"Don't you have anything to say for yourselves?" Colonel Brace asked.

"The KNPs are just playing games," Ernie replied, "embarrassed that we're digging up old, and not-so-old, skeletons in their closets. They're using the murder of Two Bellies to badger us into dropping the investigation."

This seemed to make Colonel Brace even angrier.

"I don't give a damn about this Two Bellies. But I do give a damn about unidentified G.I. bones. You keep looking for them and to hell with the ROKs." Now Colonel Brace jabbed his forefinger at us. "And by god you'd better find Jessica Tidwell and find her fast before something happens to her. You got that?"

What he was so angrily telling us to do was exactly what the chief of staff had just ordered him to do. Pretending you're a tough guy while slavishly following orders is an excellent way to enhance your career in the United States Army.

Ernie and I nodded.

Once Colonel Brace dismissed us, we saluted and walked back through the CID Admin Office. Both Staff Sergeant Riley and Miss Kim sat at their desks, pretending to be engrossed in their work. Neither one of them looked up at us.

Out in the parking lot, Ernie said with exasperation in his voice, "Lifer bullshit."

Huatu, Korean flower cards, is played with twelve suits that are identified by vegetation. The suits follow the seasonal progressions. The first suit is January and features the evergreen pine; the next suit is February and is symbolized by brightly splashed paintings of purple plum flowers. The suit representing March is festooned with red cherry blossoms opening in early spring. Colorful stuff. Idyllic. But in contrast, actually gambling with *huatu* is a ferocious exercise.

The friends of the late Two Bellies surrounded the tattered old army blanket and took turns slapping the tough little plastic cards atop a pile of bronze coins, all the while cursing, grabbing money, and surveying every move as the next player took her turn. If a player stuck her hand into the center at the wrong time, one of the flying cards would have sliced off a finger.

When Ernie and I stepped onto the creaking wooden floorboards outside the hooch, the group of women stopped their game and gazed up at us.

"We know nothing," one of them said.

Each of the retired business girls—women who were so aggressive only seconds ago—now seemed frozen in fear.

"Who killed Two Bellies?" Ernie asked.

No answer.

"Was it the Seven Dragons?"

Still no answer.

Ernie stepped past the open sliding door, grabbed the edge of the army blanket, and in one deft movement swept it off the floor. Flower cards and coins and ashtrays and lit cigarettes flew everywhere. Strangely, none of the women screamed. They merely scooted back on the warm vinyl floor until their backs were protected. Some of them covered their knees with their arms and looked down. Others glared at us directly.

"She was your friend," Ernie said.

Finally, a woman spoke. "She dead. She help you so she dead. You no protect her. You no help Two Bellies."

What she said was true but it just made Ernie angry. He wadded up the army blanket and tossed it at them in disgust.

I crouched down so I was at eye level with the women. "The night she died, where did she go? Who was she going to see?" No answer. "Did somebody come here and meet her or did she go out on her own?"

Still no answer.

"I'm going to find the man who killed her," I said. "Whoever that is, he will be punished. But I need your help."

After a long silence, one of the *huatu* players said, "That night, Two Bellies go out, nobody know where go but she dress up like she got big business. You know, important business. She no tell us what kind business she got."

"Do you know where she went?" I asked.

"Itaewon, somewhere. She no take handbag. If she gotta go long way, she take handbag."

So that was something. The night of her death, Two Bellies was operating close to home. I had another question for them but I had to phrase it delicately.

"That night, when Two Bellies went out," I said, "do you think she was going out to have fun? Or was she going out, somewhere, to make money?"

The talkative woman barked a sardonic laugh. "Two Bellies never go anywhere have fun. She only go out make money."

"Did she go alone?" Ernie asked.

The women stared at him warily for a moment. Finally, one of them said, "She say somebody follow her all the time. She no like."

"Who?" I asked.

The women shrugged. I studied the circle. Nothing but blank faces.

"So someone had been following her," I said. "A man or a woman?"

They all laughed. I wasn't sure what I'd said that was so funny. Finally, the talkative one spoke up again. "If it man," she said, "then Two Bellies no mind. She likey."

The women cackled with glee. I figured it was best to leave them laughing. At least we'd learned something. Not much, but something.

We retreated back across the courtyard and ducked through the small gate out into the Itaewon street.

Doc Yong helped me research the Golden Dragon Travel Agency. From her clinic she made a few phone calls for me, received a few evasive answers, and eventually we formed the same working hypothesis: The Golden Dragon Travel Agency was owned, or at least controlled, by the Seven Dragons. A few of the women who'd been treated in her clinic freelanced part time for Japanese sex tours. She gave me their names and addresses and Ernie and I wandered around the village searching for them.

The day was overcast, the wind growing colder by the minute but still, in this late afternoon, dozens of young women were parading back and forth to the bathhouses in the Itaewon area: cleanliness was a virtue close to the Korean heart. Their straight black hair was tied up over their heads with brightly colored yarn or metal clasps and against their hips they held plastic pans filled with soap and scrubbing implements and skin lotion and shampoo. Most of them wore only shorts and T-shirts and their goose-pimpled flesh and shapely figures were on display.

The girl we finally found was called Ahn Un-ja. She was slender, probably weighing in at less than ninety-five pounds, and she was frank with us, saying that many of the Japanese businessmen liked diminutive girls like herself. We asked her about the Golden Dragon Travel Agency and she admitted that she sometimes worked for them but she was afraid to say more. Ernie kept wheedling for more information and finally she told us why she was so frightened.

"Horsehead get angry," she said.

We thanked her, promised we wouldn't mention her name to anyone, and left.

Sergeant First Class Quinton Hilliard, the man who liked to call himself Q, was holding court at the King Club. This time he was complaining to a few of the cocktail waitresses, who were hovering around him, that the band never played any soul music. The band was a group of teenage Korean rock musicians who probably knew five chords and six songs between them but that didn't seem to matter to Hilliard. If they weren't up on the latest James Brown or Marvin Gaye, he considered their lack of knowledge to be a personal affront.

We were leaning against the bar. Ernie hadn't taken his eyes off Hilliard since we walked in.

The young cocktail waitresses were all smiling and cooing around Hilliard. For his part, he sat at his table like the godfather of Itaewon, lapping up the phony adulation.

"Ignore him," I said. "We have more important things to do."

Ernie grunted before saying, "How's Miss Kwon doing?"

"Doc Yong says better."

"That son of a bitch likes to throw his weight around." Ernie glared at Hilliard. "Everybody knows the club owners have to kiss his ass. Otherwise he'll sic Eighth Army EEO on them. That's why the waitresses are treating him like that. If he accepts one free drink," Ernie said, "I'm busting him."

Accepting gratuities for performing—or not performing—your military duties is against the Uniform Code of Military Justice. However, it's a difficult charge to prove. If I could prove it, I'd be able to bring half the honchos at 8th Army up on charges.

"Forget it, Ernie." I dragged him out of the King Club.

Once we were out on the street, Ernie said, "All right," and shrugged my grip off his elbow. "Where to now?"

"Mrs. Bei told me that Jimmy Pak was in his office tonight." Mrs. Bei was the manager behind the bar at the King Club and was tuned into the scuttlebutt that pulsed through Itaewon. Also, she was grateful to Ernie and me for having tried to save Miss Kwon.

The attempted suicide had caused the local KNPs to blame Mrs. Bei for Miss Kwon's ill-considered act; they were threatening her with charges and fines for not properly counseling the "hostesses" who plied their trade in the King Club. So far, Mrs. Bei confided in me, she'd had to shell out over 30,000 *won*, more than sixty bucks. If the girl had died, the King Club would've been closed by the Korean authorities and it would've cost her ten times that much to re-open.

I would've preferred to talk to Horsehead but I had no idea where to find him. We settled for another charter member of the Seven Dragons. Jimmy Pak was the long time owner of the UN Club, probably the classiest club in Itaewon. It sat right on the corner of the Itaewon main drag and the MSR and was always busy, filled with some of the most gorgeous women Itaewon had to offer. Civilian tourists, diplomats, and foreign businessmen who occasionally found their way to Itaewon, usually ended up partying in the UN Club.

Neon glittered brightly in the dark night. Korean business girls and American G.I.s jostled one another in the busy pedestrian thoroughfare. The wind had picked up and flakes of snow swirled haphazardly through the crowds, landing on brick walls and cement steps and cobbled lanes and beginning to stick, to form drifts in the midwinter cold. If the Armed Forces Korea Network weather report was accurate, we could expect more precipitation moving south down the peninsula, out of Manchuria, closing in on Seoul.

As we shoved through the double doors of the UN Club, a boy in black slacks, white shirt, and bow tie bowed to us and said, "*Oso-oseiyo*." Please come in.

The place was packed and there were no empty tables but we didn't muscle our way to the bar as we usually did. Instead, we walked up narrow varnished steps that led to a chophouse upstairs. The joint served hamburgers with oddly flavored meat patties and fat french fries and sliced cucumbers instead of pickles. The menu also featured other delicacies such as *ohmu* rice—steamed rice wrapped in an omelet—which the G.I.s considered to be Korean food but which was actually viewed by the Koreans as a form of *yang sik*, foreign food.

Western influence, Japanese influence, Chinese influence and the Korean ability to adapt in order to survive; all these factors made it difficult for me to look back in time and discern which parts of the culture that swirled around me were authentic Korean and which parts had been tacked on recently. I worked at it, constantly. But the Koreans were a puzzle to me. Who they were. What they wanted. And although I discovered and snapped into place a new piece of the puzzle every day, I felt sometimes that the picture was becoming more blurry. Maybe I was doomed to be confused. Maybe a foreigner can never understand Asia or the Asian mind. But I'd keep trying. Especially now. For Moretti's sake, so we could find his bones and return them to his family. And for Ernie's sake and my own sake. So we'd have a shot at not having to return to a Korean jail. Which would be good.

Ernie and I didn't enter the chophouse. Instead, we turned left and walked down a short hallway that led to a door marked *sammusil*. Office. I started to knock but Ernie stepped past me, twisted the handle, and shoved.

It was locked.

There was a lot of banging behind the door to Jimmy Pak's office. It sounded like furniture being moved around and there was whispering, of the urgent type. Finally, the handle of the door turned and the door began to open. A beautiful pagoda of black hair peeked out.

I recognized her right away. Miss Liu, a waitress here at the UN Club. She had long legs and a gorgeous smile and beautiful black hair that she piled atop her head into a structure like a temple from a Chinese fairy tale. She peered out at us from behind the door, smiled and bowed and then, holding her silver cocktail tray under her arm, minced her way out into the hallway. She was wearing the high-heeled shoes she usually wore and her legs were smooth and unsheathed. Something about her short blue dress seemed slightly askew, as if it had been twisted over her torso too quickly. Miss Liu kept her head down as she left the office and slouched past us. Ernie and I both watched as she sashayed down the hallway and tiptoed down the steps.

Inside the office, a green fluorescent light flickered to life.

Behind his desk, Jimmy Pak was on his feet, smiling, slipping on his neatly pressed white shirt, tucking the starched tails into his trousers.

"Agent Ernie," he said. "And Geogi. Welcome. Come in. Have a seat."

He motioned with his open palm to the chairs on the far side of his desk. Then he lifted his telephone. "Would either of you gentlemen care for a drink?"

I shook my head.

Ernie said, "I'll take a scotch and soda."

When someone answered, Jimmy said in English, "Two scotch and sodas for my important friends. *Allaso*, Mr. Jin?" Do you understand, Mr. Jin?

The response must have been positive because Jimmy Pak smiled more broadly and hung up the phone.

"Sit, sit," he said. Then he retied his tie and slipped on his jacket and placed himself behind his desk in his comfortable leather swivel chair. He folded his pudgy hands on the blotter in front of him and said, "Now, gentlemen, how can I help you?"

Before we could answer, someone knocked discreetly on the office door.

"*Entrez-vous*," Jimmy shouted.

Another waitress, this one less statuesque than Miss Liu, entered with two drinks on her tray and plopped one each in front of Ernie and me. She asked if Jimmy wanted anything but he waved her away. After she left, he reached inside his desk drawer, pulled out a crystal tumbler and a small bottle of ginseng liqueur. He poured himself a thimbleful and said, "For my tummy." He patted his ample paunch. Then he raised the glass, and said, "Bottoms up!"

We all drank. Ernie downed his entire drink. I sipped mine.

"Now," Jimmy said. "To what do I owe this pleasant surprise?"

"That Miss Liu," Ernie said, "she's not bad."

"No. Not bad at all," Jimmy replied. Gold lined the edge of one of his front teeth but on him it looked good, accentuating his constant smile.

Ernie rattled the ice in his glass. "How long have you owned this club, Jimmy?"

"Oh. Many, many years. Why do you ask?"

"You're the coolest owner. The only bar owner in Itaewon who speaks English really well and who mingles with the G.I.s. Why? Why don't you pull away from the day-to-day operations like the other owners?"

Jimmy spread his arms. "Because I love people. Especially my American friends."

He was smiling as broadly as an evangelist in a pulpit, welcoming new souls into the kingdom of heaven.

"You love people," Ernie said, "but you're also one of the gangsters who used to be called the Seven Dragons."

Jimmy looked surprised. "The who?"

"Don't pretend you don't know. You were here in Itaewon right after the war. You helped build this place and the entire village of Itaewon."

Jimmy kept smiling. "You flatter me."

"And you did it," Ernie continued, "by stealing money from the poor refugees who flooded down here from North Korea."

"Steal? Me?" Jimmy Pak's face was suffused with mirth. "My friend, you have such a vivid imagination. These 'Seven Dragons' as you call them. Such an exotic name. No doubt some mysterious Oriental organization designed to do evil in the world. But don't you see, I'm nothing but a harmless businessman."

"Not so harmless," Ernie said. "At least Two Bellies doesn't think so."

The smile disappeared from Jimmy Pak's face. "Such a terrible thing."

Ernie's fist tightened around his empty glass. I was worried he might throw it at Jimmy. I spoke up.

"Don't give us your shit, Jimmy," I told him. "Just listen to the facts. We know what you did to Mori Di, Sergeant Flo Moretti, and we know where you hid his body. And we know that you stole a lot of money from people and sent a passel of Buddhist nuns and orphans out into the snow to die. But they didn't die. They lived, most of them, and reached a nunnery and most of those kids are alive now and well, although probably not living in Korea. So you're a legitimate businessman these days. You don't want people poking into your past. And when Ernie and I went looking for Moretti's remains, you removed the remains from their resting place and replaced them with the corpse of Two Bellies, to warn off anybody else who tries to help us."

"Me?" Jimmy asked.

"Yes, you," Ernie growled. "Maybe you didn't do the dirty work yourself, you didn't actually slice Two Bellies's throat, but you know who did because you're the one who paid for the job."

Jimmy Pak smiled indulgently.

"So I'm willing to make a deal," I said. "I want the remains of Moretti. Somebody's got to return those remains to his family in the States. They've been waiting over twenty years. You give us that—his dog tags, his uniform, his bones, everything—and then we lay off. No more prying into the people who were hurt in the past or the antiques and family heirlooms and the gold bullion that was stolen."

Jimmy looked suddenly serious. "And Two Bellies?" he asked.

Ernie and I glanced at one another. I spoke. "The Korean cops are responsible for her."

Jimmy leaned back in his chair, his fingers steepled in front of him. "You want another drink?" he asked.

Ernie shook his head.

"Your proposal is interesting," he said. "It has nothing to do with me, of course, but I'll pass it along. Maybe someone, somewhere, will be interested in what you have to say."

"We want the remains," Ernie said. "And we want them now."

Jimmy Pak smiled.

We were halfway down the narrow stairwell when a big man bumped into me. He was Korean but hefty. Over six feet tall with broad shoulders and thick forearms and fists like mallets.

"*Weikurei?*" he said. What's wrong with you?

I knew who he was. *Maldeigari*, the Koreans called him. Horsehead. What a coincidence.

I considered asking Horsehead right there and then about the whereabouts of Jessica Tidwell. If the information I'd been gathering the last few days was correct, Horsehead and his minions at the Golden Dragon Travel Agency had made it possible for Jessica Tidwell to set up a thousand-dollar deal with a Japanese gangster. Certainly, Horsehead was taking a cut from this transaction. And maybe Horsehead was even more deeply involved in the drama of Paco Bernal and Jessica Tidwell than I yet knew.

I thought of laying my cards on the table, seeing what he had to say, but decided against it. Tomorrow morning, Jessica Tidwell was scheduled to meet up with the Japanese gangster, Ondo Fukushima, somewhere many miles south of here. And after spending the day with him, she would be returning to Seoul to the White Crane Hotel. I didn't want Horsehead to know that I'd be there, ready to pounce, or the venue would be changed and then it would be much more difficult to find Jessica.

But there was another reason I decided not to discuss things with Horsehead: I was angry.

Being pushed around was becoming a little old. I didn't like the Seven Dragons. And I particularly didn't like this tough guy Horsehead, with his three or four henchmen standing behind him and his too-expensive suit and his gaudy jewelry and his ill-gotten money and his attitude that he could bump into me and intimidate me into standing out of his way.

I bumped him back.

He reached out and shoved me and actually I was glad he did. I was released from the restraint of being a good cop. Now I could say I was defending myself. Maybe Horsehead saw the look in my eyes and maybe he realized that, if he was going to go up against me, he needed solid footing. He retreated down the steps.

When I reached the ground floor he popped a right at my nose. I dodged it, hooked him in the ribcage, and then we were wrestling back the few feet toward the bar. A waitress was in the way and we bumped into her tray of drinks and the glassware and ice flew straight up in the air and then crashed to the floor; women screamed. Ernie jumped past me and started pummeling Horsehead's pals because Horsehead didn't travel alone. They, in turn, started pummeling Ernie. Other G.I.s jumped in. Waitresses, swearing their allegiance to Korea, bonged stainless steel cocktail trays on the heads of the G.I.s, trying to get them off of Horsehead. Horsehead, for his part, seemed to be having a wonderful time, punching and wrestling and kicking and spitting.

And then the boy at the door started screaming.

"MP!" he shouted. "MP coming!"

I had backed up to the safety of the bar and Ernie was still jostling with Horsehead but most of the customers pushed past us like a horde of panicked cattle, everybody heading for the front door. Horsehead staggered backward, cursing.

By now his men had surrounded him. He pointed a thick finger at me.

"You, Sueño!" he said. *"Chukiyo ra!"*

I stepped forward but Horsehead's men grabbed him and pulled him through the front door of the UN Club.

By now, the police whistles were shrill and we could hear their boots pounding on the pavement outside. Ernie dragged me through the back storage room and out into the street. Neither Horsehead nor his boys followed.

"Asshole," Ernie said. "What did he say?"

"He said he's going to kill me." By now we had emerged through an alley onto the main drag. "But never mind about that. Look up the street, at the King Club."

There was a much larger fight going on up there and that's where a half dozen MPs were headed, nightsticks drawn.

"Riot."

He was right. Even from this distance we could tell that the men fighting one another were American G.I.s—about half of them white, half of them black.

"That damn Hilliard," Ernie said.

And then we were running toward the center of the fray.

Less than ten minutes remained until the midnight curfew and Ernie and I were becoming more nervous by the second. Maybe the bartender had slipped out the front door. But that seemed unlikely because I knew from previously casing the Grand Ole Opry Club that they barred the front door from inside at night. It made sense for the employees, after cleaning up, to leave via the back door and emerge into this dark alley lined with trash cans and wooden crates of empty brown beer bottles. But if the bartender had gone out the front door, Ernie and I were wasting our time. I shivered in the cold night air. A few more wisps of snow swirled in front of my nose, falling to the ground and mostly melting away, except for clumps that collected in corners and on the edges of brick walls.

I wanted to talk to the Grand Ole Opry Club bartender because on the night Ernie and I found Moretti's remains, he would've been the man in charge. Someone in Itaewon—maybe the Seven Dragons—had been aware of what Ernie and I were up to. After we left that night they sent someone down there to see what we'd discovered. Sometime during the night they cleared out Mori Di's remains, brought Two Bellies down there, and executed her. The bartender, the man on the scene, must have some knowledge of what happened. Probably he'd been paid, or more likely intimidated, into keeping his mouth shut. The statement he made to the KNPs was innocuous: he claimed he locked up that night, went home, and saw nothing. The strange part is that the KNPs let him get away with that statement. They didn't arrest him, they didn't lock him up in a cell, they didn't sweat information from him with hours of brutal interrogation. Instead, they took his statement and thanked him and sent him on his way.

They were happy to let the suspicion linger that Ernie and I had taken Two Bellies down there and executed her. Of course they knew it was ridiculous but it served the vital purpose of deflecting attention away from the "person or persons unknown" who'd gone to all the trouble of removing Mori Di's remains. The person who'd been vindictive enough to murder Two Bellies for having talked to us.

The KNPs seemed satisfied to let this case drift. Why were they completely unconcerned about finding the people who'd really murdered Two Bellies? The answer that seemed most likely was not an answer I was happy with. The local KNPs were under the thumb, and probably in the employ, of the syndicate known as the Seven Dragons.

While we shivered, waiting in the cold night for the bartender to appear, I thought about the fight we'd just witnessed outside the

King Club. It had been predictable enough. As more black soldiers arrived at the King Club, Sergeant First Class Hilliard's harangue took effect. Some of the black G.I.s demanded that the Korean rock band play soul music: Curtis Mayfield, Jackie Wilson, the Temptations. But the little band's repertoire included only a handful of songs and all of them were either rock or country-western. When they launched into them, Hilliard complained bitterly and the black G.I.s started hooting at the hapless band and some of the white G.I.s told them to lay off and then the insults started being hurled. Before long everyone was out in the street hurling knuckles.

The MPs broke up the fight and ferried a couple of the guys who needed stitches back to the compound, but they didn't arrest anybody. They shooed everyone off the street and it was pretty close to the midnight curfew by the time the situation returned to normal.

The MPs didn't arrest anybody because the desk sergeant who was communicating with the MP patrols by radio from the station back on Yongsan Compound didn't want to have to write up a racial incident. All hell would break loose—bureaucratically anyway—and everyone involved would have to be interviewed formally, under oath, and the reports would have to be filed in triplicate and be staffed up the chain of command and those reports would be personally reviewed by the 8th Army judge advocate general and eventually by the commanding general himself.

In other words, 8th Army was making it so cumbersome to report a racial incident that it was unlikely anyone would actually go to the trouble of doing so. Good for the stats. Then the honchos could claim that there were no racial incidents in their command.

Sergeant Hilliard was the joker in the deck. While fists had been flying, he'd been nowhere to be found. I know because I looked. And he's lucky Ernie didn't find him. But the big question was, would Hilliard raise hell tomorrow morning at 8th Army? Would he file a complaint and accuse the MPs of a cover-up?

I didn't believe that there were no racial problems in 8th Army. I'd been in the service long enough to know that black soldiers were discriminated against. I'd seen it happen with my own eyes; racist sergeants whispering about who would get the shit detail or miscreant officers scratching out the names of black soldiers when it came time for promotion. As a Mexican-American myself, I knew that sometimes those whisperings were directed at me. So the problems were real, the solutions elusive. But what I disliked about Sergeant First Class Hilliard was that he wasn't really searching for solutions. Rather he was using racial tensions to elevate himself above the crowd and stroke his own ego. And, not incidentally, to wriggle his way into the panties of a certain teenage business girl by the name of Miss Kwon.

The back door of the Grand Ole Opry Club creaked open and a sliver of light bit into the dirty darkness of the narrow alleyway. A figure emerged. A young Korean man, wrapped in a heavy coat, a white shirt and a bow tie barely visible beneath it. He stepped out into the alley and slammed the door behind him. Ernie and I hid in the shadows—he on one side of the alley, me on the other—holding our breath. Without looking to either side, the bartender marched past us, hands shoved deep into his pockets. At the end of the alleyway, he turned a corner and Ernie and I emerged from the shadows.

Following.

Itaewon is an endless maze.

Narrow pedestrian lanes zigzag every which way because the homes and hooches and stores and brothels were plopped down every which way. So now, with frigid moonlight shining down and the midnight curfew finally upon us, Ernie and I were having trouble keeping up with the young bartender. We couldn't run or he'd hear our footsteps. Periodically, we had to stop and listen for his. But he kept turning this way and that, like a very intelligent rat winding his way through a maze. Finally, headlights flashed against a wall. Ernie and I ducked into darkness—a recessed wooden gate in a cement brick wall.

"White mice," Ernie said. The curfew cops. Their jeeps were painted white and their uniforms were white, supposedly so they wouldn't be mistaken, after curfew, for North Korean intruders and be shot by their fellow cops. Ernie and I were not dressed in white and therefore were subject to being shot. Few people were actually gunned down for a curfew violation. Usually, what happened was that the white mice took the violator into custody, locked him or her up overnight at the local police station, and in the morning a relative came by to vouch for them and profusely apologize to the cops for having caused them any inconvenience. Of course, they also had to pay a fine. G.I.s would be similarly detained, but the MPs would be called and their transgressions would end up on the 8th Army blotter report.

Ernie and I were protected by our CID badges which allowed us to be out after curfew. Still, we didn't want to talk to the white mice because we didn't particularly want anyone taking note of our stalking the Grand Ole Opry bartender. Another reason we hid from the white mice was because it was always possible that the curfew cops would make a mistake—or be having a bad day—and we would be shot on sight. Perfectly permissible in a country trying to protect itself from 700,000 half-crazed Communist soldiers stationed just thirty miles north of their capital city.

We stayed hidden and when the beam of the headlights passed on, we breathed a sigh of relief. We resumed following the young bartender. Ernie ran to the intersection where we had last spotted him and stopped; we both listened. Pots and pans clanged. A stray voice shouted in the distance. Far away, a dog barked.

No footsteps.

We stood listening for a long time. Perspiration ran down my forehead. I wiped it out of my eyes.

Nothing. No sound.

I checked one intersection, Ernie checked another. Then we returned to where we had started.

"Shit," Ernie said finally.

My sentiments exactly. We'd lost him.

Ernie snorted.

Using back alleys, we made our way the mile or so to Yongsan Compound. At the main gate, I talked to the MP and, citing law enforcement solidarity, I asked him not to write us up for having returned to compound after curfew. Even though CID agents were allowed to be out after curfew, the gate guards were supposed to make a record of our return, but I didn't need grief from the first sergeant.

The MP listened—at this late hour no honchos were around anyway—and he finally agreed. Ernie promised to buy him a drink at the NCO Club. But since the MP didn't drink, Ernie was at a loss as to how to reward him.

I just said thank you.

11

The next morning, Doc Yong pulled me out of her office and into the back hallway. "No time now, Geogi," she said. "Too many girls sick."

Influenza was storming its way through Itaewon. G.I.s on compound were coming down with it too, especially the ones who had avoided taking the mandatory annual vaccination. So far, neither Ernie nor I had any symptoms; we'd taken our shots.

Doc Yong waited for me to say what I'd come to say. I asked her about health certificates. Specifically, the one belonging to the Grand Ole Opry bartender.

Of course, he had one. Everyone who worked in a food or beverage establishment was required to be checked for communicable diseases, particularly tuberculosis, a scourge that ran rampant after the Korean War. She looked it up in her files. His name was Noh Bang-ok. Then she gave me his local address here in Itaewon and his home of record, an address in Mapo. Next, I asked if Horsehead had a county health certificate.

Doc Yong stared at me, her eyes wide. She knew something, I'm not sure what. Maybe she'd heard of our altercation last night. While she stared, I studied her soft flesh and hungered for its touch.

"Horsehead doesn't need a health certificate," she finally said.

"Why not?"

She looked at me as if I were dumb.

"He own Itaewon," she said. "Owner don't need nothing."

She was busy and exasperated with me and exhausted by the full waiting room in her little clinic. That's why her English was deteriorating.

"How's Miss Kwon?" I asked.

"Better." Then she shook her head. "Everywhere hurt but anyway she start work last night."

"Still at the King Club?"

She nodded.

I wondered if Miss Kwon had been involved in the white-on-black fighting last night. I hoped not. I thanked Doc Yong for the information and started to leave. She grabbed my elbow. I was surprised at how cool her fingertips felt on my skin.

"Last night," she said, "everybody say Horsehead punch you."

I nodded. He did more than that. He also threatened my life but I didn't tell her that.

"*Chosim,*" she said. Be careful.

Once again, I nodded, almost a bow this time, and left.

As I made my way through the waiting room, business girls, their puffy faces splotched and naked, stared at me. I wondered why but probably they'd heard of Horsehead's threats too. Maybe they were studying someone who they expected, any minute now, would be dead.

Ernie and I checked the bartender's address in Itaewon. His landlord told us that early this morning he'd packed his few belongings and moved on. No, he hadn't left a forwarding address. I had to believe that Noh Bang-ok was a clever young man. He'd spotted us last night, following him, and he'd taken evasive maneuvers. He'd also realized that from here on out things were going to get rough. We'd want to interview him and whoever was behind the murder of Two Bellies might decide that he knew too much to be allowed to go on living. Whatever his motivation, there was no doubt he was scared. Nobody in this country leaves a good paying job on a lark. Noh Bang-ok was running. To where? I could only hope he'd act like most frightened people and return to the place where he felt safest. In this case, his hometown of Mapo.

We returned to Yongsan Compound, gassed up the jeep, and then drove over to the CID office. I told Staff Sergeant Riley where we were going.

"All the way to Mapo? he asked. "What the hell for?"

"This guy ran," I replied. "That means he knows something that he doesn't want to tell us."

"What about the Tidwell girl?"

"Don't tell Top anything, or the provost marshal, but we might have a lead on her tonight."

"And you'll be back in time to follow it up?"

"Sure."

"You been listening to the weather report?"

"Not lately."

"Maybe you'd better."

The Armed Forces Korea Network is a television station that broadcasts from a small hill in the center of Yongsan Compound. During duty hours there is no programming but at night they broadcast reruns of Stateside shows, whatever they can buy cheaply.

AFKN also, of course, does plenty of news and weather. The news show comes on in black-and-white and is pretty bland. A couple of uniformed G.I.s sit behind desks and read wire service reports. Things pick up when the weatherman comes on. He's a zoomie, a sergeant in the air force, and as such he's zany—at least when compared to the army automatons who read the regular news. He points at a huge map of Korea and moves cutouts around the board representing a shining sun or a storm cloud or wind blowing in the shape of an arrow.

Exciting stuff.

But hold on to your hat because next comes sports, the only part of the news that G.I.s pay attention to. It doesn't matter how monotonously the latest sports statistics are droned out, G.I.s focus all of their attention on such things as batting averages and yardage gained and historical rates of fielding errors. This information is reported in minute detail and soldiers absorb these facts with the intense concentration of actuarial accountants.

But for the last few days the air force weatherman had been in his glory, outshining even the sports announcer. According to his map of Korea, a huge front was bubbling out of Manchuria, from deep within unclimbed mountains and uncharted forests. The front had begun rolling south down the Korean Peninsula. Pyongyang, in North Korea, had already been swallowed up by every storm cloud cutout the airman had. And he kept shoving those storm clouds south, in a jumble that looked like an invasion of chubby snowmen. But the report was no joke. Barometric pressure was dropping, the temperature was dropping, precipitation was increasing, and within the next twenty-four to forty-eight hours the capital city of Seoul could expect anywhere from six to fifteen inches of precipitation, in the form of thick, slushy snow.

The worst storm the republic had experienced in over ten years.

Electricity would go out, roads would be closed, tree branches would snap, power lines would be sheathed in tubes of ice, heating fuel would become difficult if not impossible to obtain, and water pipes would most likely freeze. Finally, once the storm hit full force, food shipments would stop.

The airman predicted the cold front would linger over the peninsula for three to four days before it moved slowly out to sea. And then he grinned a big toothy grin and pulled out a fur-lined cap and slipped it on over his head.

"Gonna be cold, folks," he said into the microphone.

Off-camera, a stagehand barked a laugh.

Military humor.

What the airman hadn't mentioned was that the last time a cold front of this size moved in from Manchuria over three hundred people, most of them elderly citizens or children not yet in school, had died within the city limits of Seoul. Despite the attempt at levity, a few score people were now marked for death—in Seoul, in Itaewon, and throughout the country.

The only question was who, when, and how painfully.

* * *

We were making good time. The engine of Ernie's jeep purred like the well-oiled machine it was and the little heater under the metal dashboard was churning out a steady flow of warm air. I sat in the passenger seat, my nose pressed against the plastic window in the jeep's canvas canopy, watching rice paddies roll by. Out here, most of the farmhouses were thatched in straw. President Pak Chung-hee's New Village Movement had yet to provide tile roofs for all the families that tilled the soil.

"What if we don't find him?" Ernie said. "We could get stuck out here." Snow covered the countryside like a sheet of white silk.

"Not if we hurry," I said. "The zoomie on AFKN claims that the worst of the storm won't hit until tomorrow morning."

Ernie snorted. AFKN weather reports were notoriously wrong. When we'd departed through the main gate of Yongsan Compound, the MP shack had already taken down the yellow placard, meaning "caution, dangerous road conditions" and replaced it with red for "emergency vehicles only."

Luckily, our CID Dispatch qualified us as an emergency vehicle. Or maybe not so luckily, depending on how you looked at it.

"Maybe he's not even here," Ernie said.

I didn't bother to reply. Ernie was becoming increasingly morose. Maybe it was the fact that the KNPs still considered us to be suspects in the murder of Two Bellies. Whatever the reason, I figured it would be best to get our business over with and return to Seoul as quickly as possible.

On the outskirts of Mapo, a policeman in a yellow rain slicker stood on a circular platform directing traffic. Ernie pulled the jeep right up next to him and I climbed out and showed him my badge. Then I asked him in Korean if he could guide us to the address Doc Yong had provided.

He crinkled his nose, giving it some thought. Then he pointed with his gloved hand and told me, "The Small Stream District is on the northern edge of town, near the Gold Mountain Temple."

That was as close as he could come.

We drove on. I glanced back at the young cop and pitied him, standing there exposed to the elements, snowflakes drifting down on his slickly clad shoulders.

Gold Mountain Temple was easy enough to find, an old stone edifice dedicated to Buddha. Once there, I stopped a couple of housewives on their way back from the open-air Mapo Market and showed them the address I'd written in *hangul*. They conferred for a moment and pointed me toward an alley that led up a hill behind the temple. Ernie locked the jeep and together we trudged up the steep lane.

At the top of the hill, I asked a man working inside a bicycle repair shop if he could direct me to the address and this time he was even more specific.

"The next alley," he told me. "Turn left. About twenty paces beyond."

The bicycle shop guy stared after us, as did everyone we met here in the Small Steam District of Mapo. There were no American military compounds within thirty miles and this was a working-class agrarian area. No reason for foreigners to come out here. Judging by the stares directed our way, you would've thought Ernie and I were two men from Mars. And at the moment, that was exactly how we felt.

I knocked on the front gate. The wood was rotted and old. The brick wall also appeared to be ancient but it had been built solidly. No answer to my knock. I pounded again. Finally, from the other side of the wall, plastic sandals slapped against cement. The small door in the wooden gate creaked open. A face peeked out. The face of an elderly woman. Her eyes widened so much that the creases on her forehead scrunched up like an accordion.

I said the bartenders name. "Noh Bang-ok *isso-yo?*" Is he here?

The old woman screamed.

Ernie figured that must mean we had the right address so he barged through the open door. The courtyard was small and barren except for a row of earthenware kimchee pots lining the inside of the brick wall. Footsteps pounded from within the darkened hooch.

"*Nugu siyo?*" a man's voice said. Who is it? Then, wearing a sleeveless T-shirt and pajama bottoms, he appeared at the open sliding door of the hooch. Ernie and I both recognized him immediately, the bartender from the Grand Ole Opry, sans white shirt and bow tie. At first, he flinched, as if preparing to run. But Ernie was across the courtyard

GOD LOVES YOU

(A) For God so loved the world that he gave his only begotten Son, that whosoever believeth in him should not perish, but have everlasting life. (John 3:16)

(B) All ARE SINNERS: (Sin is breaking God's law). For all have sinned, and come short of the glory of God. (Romans 3:23)

(C) GOD'S REMEDY FOR SIN: For the wages of sin is death; but the gift of God is eternal life through Jesus Christ our Lord. (Romans 6:23) →

(D) RECEIVE CHRIST: That if you will confess with your mouth the Lord Jesus Christ, and will believe in your heart that God has raised him from the dead, you will be saved. (Romans 10:9) If you honestly believe Jesus died for you sins and arose the third day, then Praise God, you are now a Christian!

HOW TO BECOME A GOOD CHRISTIAN
(E) Start with studying the New Testament and attend a good bible believing church.
(F) Keep the two great commandments.(Matthew 22:37-)
Remember, Christians aren't perfect, just forgiven.

in three steps and Noh must've realized the futility of trying to flee. Instead, his shoulders slumped and then he squatted on his haunches, staring at us thoughtfully, wondering what he was in for.

When the bartender realized who we were and why we were there, it was as if he'd resigned himself to some horrible fate. He didn't invite us in and so I started questioning him on the low porch that ran along the front edge of the hooch. What had he seen on the night Ernie and I sneaked into the basement of the Grand Ole Opry? Had he discovered the hole we'd made in the wall? Did he look inside and see the bones of Mori Di? Who'd come in that night and taken those bones and then replaced them with the corpse of Two Bellies? Had she been alive when she'd been brought in? Who, exactly, had done the killing?

He didn't answer any of my questions, not at first, but he promised that he would, just as soon as he changed clothes. As Noh Bang-ok rose to his feet, I asked him why he'd left Itaewon. His eyes widened, making his forehead wrinkle much as the old woman's forehead had.

"Because," he replied, as if talking to a child, "I was afraid."

He turned and walked back into the hooch. Ernie and I stood in the courtyard. With my eyes, I motioned for Ernie to go around back to make sure that the bartender didn't try to slip away from us.

Then the old woman, still looking worried, slipped off her shoes, climbed up on the wooden platform and entered the hooch. She waddled back into the darkness and seconds later she screamed again.

Ernie and I were inside the hooch before the sound faded. He entered through the back door, me through the front. In a small bedroom we saw the bartender kneeling on the vinyl-covered floor. The old woman was clutching him, still screaming. Blood poured from the young man's wrist. He held his arm up for us to see. A huge gash leered at us.

I applied first aid as best I could and soon a neighbor who owned a cab was helping us bundle the young bartender into the back seat and telling me in Korean that he was taking him to the big hospital downtown. Ernie and I ran back to the jeep parked in front of the Gold Mountain Temple and managed to follow the cab across slippery, snow-covered roads to the hospital.

By the time the bartender had been checked in and attended to by a physician, Ernie and I were surrounded by angry relatives. Apparently, he was part of a large clan here in Mapo. The snow outside was falling faster and we weren't about to obtain any useful information from him now.

I knew the wound was superficial, inflicted to avoid being taken to the KNP station. Noh Bang-ok would live. But Ernie and I didn't contact the local Korean cops and have him arrested because they would contact the Itaewon cops and something told me that the Itaewon cops weren't too interested in investigating the murder of Two Bellies. KNPs have a habit of sticking together. If we talked to the local cops, they might end up arresting us instead of the Grand Ole Opry bartender, on trumped-up charges like hounding him and forcing him to become distressed and attempting to commit suicide. Best for us to say goodbye to Mapo.

Ernie and I fought our way outside. Ernie fired up the jeep and we wound through the narrow streets of the city of Mapo until we reached the main highway. A wooden sign pointed toward Seoul.

Ernie bulled his way into the flow of traffic and stepped on the gas.

The lobby of the White Crane Hotel was almost as big as an airplane hangar. The floor was carpeted in a red design that spread from the long sleek front desk toward a mock waterfall and a circular stairway leading up to chic restaurants and boutiques with French names. A European pianist wearing a tuxedo with tails tinkled out soft tunes on an enormous grand piano.

"This joint stinks," Ernie said.

He was referring to the scent of roses permeating the air.

G.I.s weren't welcome. I felt as out of place as a gorilla shuffling through a fashion show.

All the customers were Asian: a few Chinese from Hong Kong but mostly whole regiments of Japanese tourists. The not-so-rich Japanese tended to migrate in herds, arriving in heated buses. The rich ones traveled in sleek black sedans with white upholstery driven by white-gloved chauffeurs.

"I thought America ruled the world," Ernie said.

"Americans only *think* they rule the world," I answered.

We sat on frail metal chairs in a tea shop with a clear view of the entrance to the hotel. Flurries of snow drifted by sporadically—not enough to clog traffic. Not yet. When we first arrived from Mapo, we cased the joint, tipping a bellhop to find out if Mr. Ondo Fukushima had checked in. The bellhop said his suite was ready but he had not yet arrived. Then we ate chow in a workingman's chophouse across the street and returned to wait.

"Where do you think she met him?" Ernie asked. He was referring to Jessica Tidwell.

"Probably somewhere south of Seoul," I answered, "in Suwon or Taejon. The driver takes her down there, hooks her up with Fukushima and together they attend a few afternoon meetings, maybe a formal dinner, and then they drive up to Seoul."

"Or check into a hotel down there and don't bother to come out for a couple of days."

I shrugged. "Anyway, this is the only lead we have. We wait here until they arrive."

"Terrific," Ernie said. He shifted his butt on the tiny chair and sipped unhappily on scented oolong tea.

It was almost midnight now. If Ondo Fukushima and Jessica Tidwell didn't show up soon, they wouldn't at all.

Ernie elbowed me. "Check out the armored battalion."

A line of five black sedans pulled up outside the plate glass entranceway of the hotel. The liveried doormen scurried up and down the row, swinging doors open. Burly Japanese men in expensive suits and highly polished shoes emerged first. Their hair was slicked back, and if communication devices had been plugged into their ears, I would've thought they were Secret Service. One of them barked an all clear, and from the central sedan a diminutive Japanese man emerged wearing a pin-striped suit in a shade of green so dark that it glowed.

"The head honcho," Ernie said.

As he strode through the door, his immaculately coiffed body-guards arrayed themselves around him like a phalanx of ancient Greek warriors protecting their king.

Behind them, high heels clicked on marble.

Jessica Tidwell wore the same skimpy blue dress that had been crumpled on the floor of Paco Bernal's room, but it was cleaned and pressed now. The freckled flesh of her décolletage peeked over the silk material like the prow of a sailing ship. Jessica scurried behind the formation of men, keeping her head down, ignored but never-theless making it clear that she was a woman following her master.

Ernie snorted in derision.

"Come on," he said. "Enough of this freaking tea. It's showtime."

Ernie and I had discussed how we'd approach Jessica. Our fondest hope was that the yakuza chief would treat her like a worthless woman and make her follow far behind. He hadn't let us down. If we could, we'd move her away quietly, out the door, and into the army-issue jeep waiting around the corner.

At least that's how I hoped things would turn out.

Instead, as soon as I moved forward and put my hand on Jessica's elbow, two of Ondo Fukushima's thugs stopped in their tracks and turned on us. Ernie slipped his hand beneath his coat, not pulling his .45 but making it clear to the men he was armed. I tugged on Jessica's elbow.

"Let me go," she said.

"Don't make trouble," I told her. "We're taking you home."

"Like hell." With her free hand she reached inside the purse strapped to her shoulder. She pulled out a wad of blue bills, ten-thousand yen notes. "*This* is what he paid me," she said. "More than a thousand bucks." In a falsetto voice, she said, "*You change money, G.I.?*" Then she reverted to her regular voice. "But I have to stay with him for the whole weekend."

"Is it worth it?"

"If it saves Paco, yes."

"Why don't you just ask your father to drop the charges?"

The smooth flesh of her face crinkled. "I wouldn't ask him for anything! Especially something that would embarrass the great J-2. When he gets his money back, he'll *have* to drop the charges."

That wasn't strictly true, but this was no time to argue the intricacies of the Uniform Code of Military Justice. I tugged on her arm again. The two thugs closed in. Ernie stepped closer and pulled the .45 from his holster.

The Japanese gangsters froze.

The yakuza have influence in Korea but gun control is absolute here, only military and law-enforcement personnel are allowed to carry weapons. The yakuza can't bring weapons into the country. Still, the well-muscled men spaced themselves around the lobby, ready to pounce. I had no doubt that each one of them was an expert in one of the martial arts.

Ondo Fukushima turned. He approached slowly, surveying the situation. Gradually, his face achieved an expression as fierce as a carved mask. I worked at not letting it effect me, but it did. My gut froze into a fist-sized chunk of dry ice.

Jessica took advantage of my hesitation. She twisted quickly and kicked my knee, at the same time ripping her elbow out of my grasp. But instead of running toward her Japanese benefactor, she staggered backward toward the waterfall.

By now the tuxedoed pianist had stopped playing and around the lounge everyone had stopped moving. Behind the front desk, fingers tapped out a phone number.

If Ernie and I were ever going to be able to keep Jessica's indiscretion quiet, we had to drag her out of here before the Korean cops arrived.

Two more of the Japanese thugs glided toward me. I pulled out my .45. They stopped. But a half dozen of them had surrounded us now, waiting for a single mistake.

"Steady, Ernie," I said. "Don't fire unless you have to."

"What are you *doing?*"

The voice roared out from the center of the Japanese thugs. And then I realized that the enormous sound had erupted from the small man in the glowing green suit: Ondo Fukushima.

I kept my voice steady. "She's coming with us," I said.

"She's *mine*," he bellowed. "I paid for her." He jammed his thumb into his puffed-out chest. "Me. Ondo Fukushima. A boy who used to steal from your American compounds. I bought and paid for the daughter of one of your 8th Army generals. You're not going to take her away from me now."

His English was almost perfect; he had only a slight accent. Jessica Tidwell's father was a colonel, not a general, but I didn't bother to correct him. Ondo Fukushima was the right age to have picked up the language—and his familiarity with military ranks—as a hustler outside the American bases during the occupation at the end of World War II.

"We're taking her," Ernie shot back.

"You have no right," Fukushima said.

Ernie waved the barrel of his .45. "This says we have the right."

The Japanese thugs inched closer. Ernie and I couldn't possibly take all of them on hand-to-hand. Our only chance was to fire. But killing men here in the middle of Seoul?

Ondo Fukushima could smell our indecision. Before he could make his move, flesh slapped on flesh, ringing through the silent lobby like the sharp peeling of a bell.

"*Cabrona!*" I understood the Spanish curse word.

I turned to look, still keeping my pistol pointed at the Japanese mobsters.

Corporal Paco Bernal, wearing an ill-fitting black suit, had pulled Jessica away from us, right up to the edge of the waterfall. He slapped her again.

"You would go with *him?*"

Jessica pawed at his chest. "It was for you, Paco." She pointed at the bills sticking out of her purse. "See? I have enough yen here to cover the thousand dollars we stole. My dad will drop the charges. He'll have to. We'll be OK."

Paco Bernal looked like one of those heartthrobs I used to see in the corny old Mexican movies we used to watch in East L.A. when I was a kid. In the suit, with his hair slicked back, all he needed was a pencil-thin mustache to complete the picture. At the moment, he didn't care about us. He didn't care about the Japanese gangsters. All he cared about is what he perceived as Jessica Tidwell's betrayal.

Ondo Fukushima turned his scowling face toward Paco. His lips were pursed so tight that I thought his face would burst.

Behind the counter, hotel employees whispered the word *kyongchal*. Police.

Now it was Fukushima's turn to wrestle with indecision. Time was running out. If he were to pull Jessica away from her lover just as the police arrived on the scene, he'd be arrested, and the whole world would know what happened here tonight. Not that he'd do any prison time. His money and his attorneys would see to that. But more important, much more important, he'd lose face. He'd be seen as the old man in a love triangle with two good-looking young foreigners.

The thugs were no longer planning to pounce. They seemed to sense their boss's thoughts.

In the distance, a siren wailed.

Fukushima made his decision. He barked something in guttural Japanese.

As if their batteries had been turned off, the Japanese thugs relaxed. Moving like one organism, they backed away from us, surrounded their boss, and headed at a brisk pace toward the executive elevator.

Ernie turned his .45 toward Paco.

"Move away from the girl, Paco. Assume the position against the wall. You must be familiar with it."

As if waking from a nightmare, Paco seemed to see us clearly for the first time. Instead of pushing Jessica away, he hugged her closer and then, moving so quickly that she couldn't react, he twirled her around, forcing his forearm up under her neck. From his pocket a gleaming blade of steel appeared.

The bayonet that had been missing from his field gear.

He pressed the tip of it lightly into Jessica's neck.

"Paco?" she asked.

"Shut up!" He turned his attention to me and Ernie. "If you come any closer, I'll slice her. I swear I will."

Instead, Ernie moved to his side. Paco jabbed the bayonet a little farther into Jessica's throat, warning me off. I lowered my .45.

"You're a smart man, Paco," I said. "Up to now you're only facing a theft charge. It's only money. Nobody's going to come down too hard on you. But if you hurt Jessica . . ." I let the thought hang.

While Paco stared at me, Ernie inched a little closer. I knew he'd take a shot at Paco's head if he got a clear one. He had to. An innocent person's life was in danger. And there was no way I could stop him.

Paco kept his eyes on me, pondering my words. A moment of clarity washed over his face. His anger at Jessica faded. He was starting to see the enormity of the mistake he'd made.

"Put down the bayonet, Paco," I said.

At the same time, Jessica seemed to realize that she'd also made an error. Her big green eyes stared down at the glistening bayonet. But she wasn't going to go down without a fight.

The sirens grew louder. Ernie inched even closer, keeping his .45 pointed at Paco's head. That's when I saw the decision in Jessica's eyes. She raised her high-heeled shoe. I knew what she was going to do. I wanted to stop her. I wanted to cry out but no sound came out of my throat. She lifted her heel and stomped it down on Paco Bernal's toe. Paco jerked back. Ernie lowered his .45 and charged, ramming his shoulder into Paco's side.

Paco spun away from the rock waterfall, kept his balance, and grabbed the collar of Ernie's coat. With his free hand he raised the bayonet in the air.

I jerked my .45 up in front of me, flexed my knees, and shouted, "No!"

Jessica dropped to the floor. Before Paco could chop the blade down on Ernie, the cold steel in my hand bucked and an enormous blast filled my ears and then the odor of burnt cordite billowed in the air.

Jessica screamed. A red hole burst open in Paco Bernal's side. He reeled backwards toward the rock retaining wall of the waterfall like a yo-yo bouncing on a string.

More sirens, louder now, screamed behind me; car doors slammed. Ernie was up, crouching over Paco. Jessica had stopped screaming but her eyes were flooded with tears. She shoved Ernie out of the way, reaching for Paco. Ernie shoved her back.

She stumbled, rose to her feet, and charged at me. I was still holding the smoking .45 pointed directly at her. She knocked it out of the way and rammed both of her small fists into my chest.

"What have you done? Why'd you shoot him?"

She punched me two more times, in the face. I held my .45 pointed at the floor and didn't resist. Suddenly, she kicked off her high heels, and ran in her bare feet back to Paco.

Ernie was trying to stop the bleeding that pulsed from Paco's chest. He looked around for a compress, noticed the wad of bills sticking out of Jessica's purse. He snatched them. "Here," he told her. "Press these down on the wound. Press hard! So the bleeding will stop."

Jessica knelt on the bloody floor and did as she was told. Ernie hurried over to me, grabbed my shoulders, and gazed into my eyes; he didn't like what he saw. He moved me over to an upholstered bench against the wall, sat me down, and pried the .45 out of my fist. He took out the clip, stuck it in his jacket pocket, and put the empty weapon back into my shoulder holster.

"Don't move, Sueño," he said. "You stay right here."

Then he returned to Jessica.

Even from this distance I could see the blood seeping past Jessica's splayed fingers and dripping down Paco's side.

The next morning, veins not only protruded from the first sergeant's neck but they also pulsed beneath the skin of his forehead.

"You didn't report it?" he asked. "The daughter of the Eighth Army J-2 is being held by a Japanese mobster and you decide it's not important enough to let anyone know?"

Ernie shrugged. "You guys would've just got in the way."

"Got in the way?" The first sergeant gets like that when he's angry; he keeps repeating whatever you say. He raised his forefinger and pointed it at me and then at Ernie. "You not only botch the operation but you end up shooting a suspect and then, to top it off, the J-2's daughter ends up disappearing all over again!"

"We'll find her," Ernie said. "Piece of cake."

We were in the CID Admin Office, taking our ass-chewing—a serious one this time. So far, no one had questioned my decision to pop a round into Corporal Paco Bernal. In the KNP report a number of witnesses testified that he had been about to stab Ernie with his bayonet. I acted to protect a fellow CID agent and everyone agreed I had no choice. Even I agreed, I think.

Staff Sergeant Riley sat at his desk, head bobbing over a stack of paperwork, attempting to stay removed from this conversation. As soon as the first sergeant raised his voice, Miss Kim disappeared down the hallway. She hadn't returned yet.

"The provost marshal has gone ballistic," the first sergeant continued. "He has to report to the CG and Colonel Tidwell, and tell them that two of his investigators didn't let him know they had a lead on the whereabouts of Jessica Tidwell and then, on their own, they shot an Eighth Army G.I. and allowed Jessica Tidwell to escape again."

Ernie didn't say anything this time. I hadn't said anything since the first sergeant started screaming. Actually, I didn't feel as bad as when I thought that Paco Bernal would die from the bullet I'd blasted into him. As it was, Paco was currently in the Intensive Care Unit of the 121 Evacuation Hospital. Prognosis: guarded. Which, although not good, is better than dead. He'd lose a couple of ribs but the bullet hadn't passed through any vital organs.

At the White Crane Hotel, seconds after Ernie sat me down on that bench, the KNPs swarmed in and took charge of the crime scene. An ambulance arrived and carted Paco away. The head KNP investigator requested an interview with Ondo Fukushima and after a few minutes, he was allowed an audience with the great man. In the opulence of Fukushima's suite, the KNP investigator determined that the Japanese yakuza wasn't involved in the shooting and, in fact, this entire mess was an American-style soap opera— not Korean or Japanese.

I sat pretty much stunned by what I had done—shot a man— and rejoiced inwardly when the ambulance took him away and it was reported that Paco Bernal was still breathing. Ernie, as usual, started in with the KNPs and there was a scuffle and finally a half-dozen of them cornered him on one of the couches in the lobby and questioned him without letting him go check on me.

Meanwhile, no one was paying much attention to Jessica Tidwell. I pieced it together later, mostly by talking to the bellhops and the doormen outside.

A Korean man, a large Korean man, had shown up shortly after the arrival of the KNPs. He seemed to know some of the KNP investigators but stayed studiously out of their way and finally, when he had a chance, he approached Jessica Tidwell. They seemed to know each other. He lit a cigarette for her and while she smoked and nodded he whispered in her ear. Jessica kept nodding in an absent-minded sort of way. After the paramedics took Paco away, she left with the tall Korean man.

I asked the KNPs why they'd allowed her to leave. They told me the name of the man she had left with: Son Ryu-jon. I didn't recognize it. And then, in response to my blank stare, one of the KNPs finally relented and explained, "Everybody call him *Maldeigari.*"

Horsehead. His influence was such that no one had stopped them.

The first sergeant still hadn't finished our ass-chewing. "They're saying it's your fault that Jessica is running wild," he told us.

"Who's saying?" Ernie asked.

"Colonel Tidwell, the CG, even the Officers' Wives' Club," the first sergeant answered. "They're saying if you had done your jobs and picked up Jessica, none of this would've happened."

"Maybe it's their fault," Ernie said, "for raising her like they did."

The first sergeant pointed his finger at Ernie's nose. "Don't you be showing disrespect to your superior officers, Bascom."

Before Ernie could reply, I said, "We'll find her, Top."

Our ace in the hole was that, despite everything that had happened, Ernie and I were still the only 8th Army CID agents who had any contacts whatsoever in Itaewon.

The phone rang. It was for the first sergeant. He said, "Yes, sir" and then "Yes, sir" again and again. About a half-dozen times. He hung up the phone and looked at us.

"That was the duty officer over at the 121 Evac. A redhead in a short skirt was spotted in the intensive care unit, hanging around Paco. A medic tried to shoo her out. She threw a tantrum, told him to go to hell."

"Sounds like Jessica," I said, standing up from my chair. "Did she leave?"

"Not until he threatened to call the MPs."

We ran outside and jumped in Ernie's jeep. After he started the engine, Ernie turned to me and said, "You OK?"

I nodded. "I'm OK. And I'll stay OK as long as Paco Bernal keeps breathing."

Ernie jammed the jeep in gear and roared off towards the 121 Evacuation Hospital.

When we arrived, the redhead in the ICU had already left. I asked the medic how long ago she'd left and he said about ten minutes.

In front of the main entrance to the 121 was a PX hot dog stand and a turnaround for the big black Ford Granada PX taxis. I spoke to one of the drivers and he used the radio bolted beneath his dashboard and called dispatch. The driver and the dispatcher chatted for a while in Korean and the dispatcher contacted other units, eventually locating a driver who had picked up Jessica Tidwell. I took the mic and spoke to him, surprising everyone by using Korean. This driver said the woman he picked up in front of the 121 wore a short blue dress and had been quite agitated. She'd ordered him to take her to Itaewon. He let her off on the MSR across from the UN Club, at the front entrance to the Hamilton Hotel.

Had she entered the hotel? I asked.

No. She took off on foot, heading north.

Then I asked another question, still in Korean. What currency had she used to pay him? That was another odd thing, the driver replied. Although she was an American, she had insisted on paying her fare in Japanese yen. In fact, he told me that he was holding the thousand yen note in his hand right now and he wasn't even sure how much it was worth. Another thing was odd. There was a brown smudge on the edge of the bill and it looked, almost, like dried blood.

Paco was still comatose. When I asked the nurse in the intensive care unit how he was doing, she stared at me with sad eyes and shook her head.

"You don't think he'll pull through?" I asked.

"He might," she replied. She gazed in his direction. "Yes, probably. But he will never be the man he once was."

Ernie patted me on the shoulder.

On our way out, the phone rang behind the emergency room

counter. A medic picked it up and then called us over. "You guys Sweeno and Bascom?"

"That's us," Ernie replied.

"Somebody wants to talk to you."

I took the call. It was Riley. He started talking without preamble.

"Do either of you guys know somebody named Mel Gardi?" he asked.

"Who?"

"Mel Gardi," he repeated.

My eyes widened. "You mean '*Maldeigari.*'"

"Whatever."

"That's Horsehead," I said. "What about him?"

"You better get your butts out to Itaewon."

"Why? What's up?"

"I ain't repeating this shit," Riley said.

I pulled out my notebook and jotted down directions: a block and a half up the hill from the Dingy Dingy Pool Hall.

"This is in Itaewon?" I asked.

"That's what they tell me. Not far from the Hamilton Hotel."

The front entrance to the Hamilton Hotel was the only authorized PX taxi stand in Itaewon.

"What about Horsehead?" I asked again. "Did something happen to him?"

"Go look!" Riley shouted and hung up.

"What is it?" Ernie asked.

I told him.

We ran outside of the 121 Evac, jumped in his jeep, and laid rubber halfway out the gate.

12

Horsehead had fought back.

The rope around his wrists was frayed and bit sharply into the flesh of his forearm. He'd tried to rip himself free. Instead, he'd managed only to tear great gaps in his skin. Blood had flowed down his wrist and his hands and onto the small of his back where his wrists were tied. He'd kicked against the wall of the little hooch, too, despite the fact that his ankles—like his wrists—were bound together with rope that had been laced in intricate knots.

And he'd been gagged. With a wool scarf and cotton stuffed into his mouth.

Like Moretti.

Maybe the similarities were coincidental. Maybe the Seven Dragons had nothing to do with this crime. Maybe. I knelt next to Horsehead's body. The single bare bulb overhead had been switched on but I needed more illumination. I used my army-issue flashlight.

Last night, Horsehead had been spotted at the White Crane Hotel, policing up Jessica Tidwell. Then he had ended up here, in this dark and crowded neighborhood of Itaewon, in this tiny hooch rented by the hour, face down in his own vomit, his hands and feet bound, his body stabbed so many times that he looked like pulverized goose liver.

And where was Jessica Tidwell?

The old woman who owned the hooch was in tears. A gaggle of KNPs surrounded her, shooting questions at her. Her wrinkled face was smeared with moisture, and she kept repeating over and over again. *"Na moolah. Chinja moolah."* I don't know. I really don't know.

What the old woman didn't know was who the people were who'd brought in Horsehead.

"He was drunk," she'd told us through sobs. "Two men were carrying him. They said they wanted a room so he could sleep it off. They paid me in advance and carried him to the room and laid him down and left him there. They said some women would be along to check on him and make him comfortable and I should let them in and they'd take care of him."

She hadn't recognized the men, had never seen them before. But they were Korean men, well into middle age, and they wore workingmen's clothes as if they'd just come from some sort of job in a warehouse or a factory. And the women had shuffled in immediately after the men left. The landlady hadn't paid much attention because by then she was watching *Chonwon Diary,* a popular prime-time soap opera. Her favorite show, she added. But there were three women and each wore some sort of jacket or shawl with a hood; she hadn't seen their faces.

"Did they carry weapons?" one of the cops asked.

She didn't know. She hadn't looked. If they did they weren't carrying them in their hands where she could see.

"Was there much noise?"

Not much. Some moaning. But she'd had drunks sleep it off in the rooms she rented before and they were never quiet, so she hadn't paid attention. Except for the pounding on the wall. For a second there, she thought the drunken man was going to kick the house down but the women managed to get him under control.

"When did the women leave?"

She wasn't sure. After her program was over she realized that all was quiet down the hall. But she hadn't gone to look. It was late so she locked the outer gate and went to sleep. She believed the women had already left because she didn't hear any footsteps pounding down the hallway during the night and no one had called for her to unlock the front gate.

"When did you discover the body?"

In the morning, while she was scrubbing the central hallway with a moist rag. The sun had been up for over an hour and she hadn't heard any sound coming from the room. All her other guests—mostly business girls and American G.I.s—were up before dawn and had already left. When she reached the door to Horsehead's room, she paused for a moment, listening. When she heard nothing, she knocked on the latticework door and called out. No answer. Finally, she peeked in.

Then the old woman sobbed again.

"Terrible," she said, covering her eyes.

She ran next door to a neighbor who had a telephone and they'd called the police.

The KNPs notified 8th Army and now here we were. Ernie and I looked down on the remains of a man who, only hours before, had been wealthy and confident, abrasive and full of life. He liked to fight. I suppose, somewhere deep in Horsehead's fevered mind, fighting had made him feel alive.

He'd lived. That was for sure. A full life. Maybe not a good life but an active life and now he was nothing more than chopped meat.

Ernie glanced at me, shook his head. I suppose we were both thinking the same thing. Who were the men who'd brought him here? And even more importantly, who were the women? Who could systematically chop a living, breathing human being to death? There must've been a hundred entry wounds in Horsehead's body. Even without measuring them I could see that they were from different sized cutting implements. Three sizes, I thought. Probably knives. And that matched what the landlady had told us. Three women.

Had they been hired by a rival gang? Or had they been sent by one of the other Seven Dragons? Or were they just women who harbored a grudge against Horsehead? And who were their two male helpers? None of it made sense. People who murder don't operate in groups. Not unless they're professionals and they're hired and well paid. But if they were professionals, why hadn't they tried to hide their crime? Why hadn't they hidden the corpse?

The coroner's van from downtown Seoul pulled up and after a few more minutes of collecting evidence, the paramedics were allowed to hoist up the body and cart it away. The KNPs didn't want us there anymore. It was their case. Ernie and I staggered away from the crime scene and then found ourselves wandering aimlessly through a maze of alleys.

The sky was as gray as my mood. It was still only fifteen hundred hours but I wanted a drink more than I'd wanted one in a long time. The nightclubs along the main drag of Itaewon were shuttered. All the neon was switched off and the signs looked sad and dusty in the dull afternoon light.

Very little of last night's snow had stuck but a few drifts still clung to roofs and the tops of walls. The temperature had dropped noticeably. It was as if a new, cleaner brand of air had invaded Itaewon, air that was filtered by acres of mountainous pines and cedars. Air that was indifferent to the suffering of mere mortals.

The Sexy Lady Club was open. Ernie and I pushed through a beaded curtain. The joint was dark, only the red and green lights of the jukebox twinkled. The air in here reeked of ammonia and sliced lemon. Behind the bar a gal with long straight black hair came toward us. We stared at her a while, blankly, and then ordered two straight shots of brandy. Doubles. Chased by beer.

She plunked them down on the bar, took our money, and stared at us impassively. Her complexion was smooth, soft, sweet looking.

"You see Horsehead?" she asked.

We nodded.

She shrugged her narrow shoulders, turned, and sashayed her cute little butt back to the cash register.

Night had fallen. In the Sexy Lady Club, Ernie and I had talked and a mutual resolve had started to take hold. We were through pussyfooting around with the Seven Dragons. Two Bellies had told us that Snake was their head honcho. We'd already talked to Jimmy Pak and gotten nowhere. Horsehead was dead. Now it was time to talk to the head man himself: the man called Snake. If Jessica wanted to hide she'd stay hidden. We decided to bust things wide open.

Ernie sprinted up the stairwell that led to the Seven Club, taking the steps three at a time. He didn't pause at the second-story landing that led into the nightclub but kept going up to the third floor. That's where Snake's offices were.

Snake's real name was Lim, his family name, and Americans referred to him as Mr. Lim. I'd met him a few times, mostly when he was hobnobbing with 8th Army officers—either invited to a formal function or hosting a retirement party for one of them at the 8th Army golf club. The honchos at 8th Army loved him. Snake was always smiling and he laughed at their jokes and his English was impeccable. Not to mention that he had connections with the big-money corporations that were lining up for the neverending flow of multimillion dollar U.S. military construction projects. Gifts, parties, social events, award ceremonies, these were the places where Mr. Lim could be found. Shaking hands, bowing, being a good chum to American officers who saw him as the perfect example of the modern Korean entrepreneur. And the perfect avatar of the republic's bright future.

He was a slender man, almost willowy, and his smile had a certain reptilian cast. But maybe I saw him differently than the officers at 8th Army saw him. Snake didn't do any favors for *me*. I only knew him from the people who worked in his various operations: his nightclubs, his bars, and his apartment buildings, which were nothing more than brothels. I knew how the country girls suffered. Sometimes physically but if not physically always through shame.

But once you have money, no matter how it is come by, you are seen by everyone—or at least by everyone who matters—as a wonderful guy. That was Snake. A wonderful, generous guy.

The door to his office was locked. Ernie pounded on it. No answer. He pounded again and when it still didn't open, he backed down the hallway, took a running start and plowed into the door shoulder first. It burst inward.

Nobody home. But we both took an involuntary gasp at the opulence of the furnishings. Even a couple of lowlifes like us could tell that everything from the leather upholstered chairs to the mahogany desk to the handcrafted porcelain was expensive.

A bronze effigy of a youthful, narrow-waisted Buddha sat in its own shrine in the corner. The smiling god held one palm facing to the sky and the fingers of his other hand formed a circle near his ear. I turned my flashlight on the statuette and studied it. What surprised me was that this was the same Buddha embossed onto the surface of the bronze bell in the temple on the hill overlooking Itaewon.

Footsteps clattered up the stairwell. High heels. We turned and a statuesque woman entered the room. She wore a tight-fitting black cocktail dress, low cut to accentuate her décolletage and it seemed that her legs were longer and straighter than those of any Korean woman I'd ever seen. She was a gorgeous woman, like a fashion model, with a curly shag hairdo and more makeup than a dozen circus clowns.

"Weikurei nonun?" What is it with you? And not spoken politely, either.

I flashed my badge at her. "Where's Snake?"

"Who?"

"Mr. Lim."

"He's out." She waved her left arm at the broken door. "What are you doing?"

"Who the hell are you?" Ernie asked.

"Jibei-in," she said in Korean. And then remembered to speak English. "I'm the manager."

"Then you can open the safe," Ernie said, pointing at the squat black iron block behind Snake's mahogany desk.

"No," she said, shaking her elegant head. "Only Snake . . . I mean Mr. Lim can open the safe."

"What's in there?" Ernie asked.

The woman's eyes widened. "How I know?"

"Snake must have you up here when he counts his money. You're the manager, aren't you?"

She laughed. "He no keep money there."

"Then what does he keep there? Antiques?" Ernie pointed again at the safe.

"I don't know." The woman thrust back her shoulders. "He no tell me." Then she pointed toward the door. "Get out. You two must get out. Not your office."

We took our time, gazing at the antiques and the art objects, wondering if any of them had been amongst the stash that Technical Sergeant Flo Moretti had stored for the refugees that flooded into Itaewon at the end of the Korean War.

"Out," the woman said. "I call KNPs."

"No you won't," Ernie replied. He walked up close to her.

"Why not?" she asked.

"Because if you do, after I bust Snake, I'm coming after you."

This seemed to unnerve the woman. She'd seen my badge and in Korea, law enforcement personnel have tremendous power, often much more power than they're granted by law. Still, she held her ground.

"Out," she said.

I discovered later that her name was Miss Park. She'd been the manager here at the Seven Club for over a month. I admired her spunk. We did what she said: we left Snake's office. And she didn't call the KNPs.

We stopped at the bar inside the main ballroom of the Seven Club, just to make sure that Snake wasn't on the premises. Ernie ordered a beer but before it arrived, something in the crowded room caught his attention.

"Look," he said.

American G.I.s and Korean business girls sat at every table, many of them lazing about in the aisles, and dozens of them jammed onto the dance floor. The Korean band was playing some schmaltzy ballad and the big G.I.s were hunched over the small Asian women, their eyes closed, lost in erotic ecstasy. Most of the Korean women, however, kept their eyes open, studying the crowd, blasé expressions on their round faces, jaws chomping on chewing gum.

I followed Ernie's nose and spotted the couple he was staring at.

Sergeant First Class Quinton "Q" Hilliard was grinding away in time with the music with the full-cheeked little Miss Kwon enveloped in his bearlike embrace.

The power cables that radiated from the side of the King Club had saved Miss Kwon during her fall. After she leaped from the roof, she plowed into a heavy cable which snapped beneath her weight but slowed her enough that she landed atop the neon sign with a jarring thud that was enough to knock the wind out of her but not enough to snap her spine. From there, instinct took over and she'd grabbed onto the sparking neon tubes and although she'd suffered burned fingers and a huge lump on the back of her head and her ankle was viciously sprained, she was fundamentally in good shape. Doc Yong attributed her good fortune to her youth and her round-ness. She landed, bounced, and survived. A plastic cast was clipped around Miss Kwon's left ankle, a white patch had been taped over her left eye, and three of the fingers of her right hand were tightly bandaged. Still, she was back at work, dancing with the man who'd been her tormentor, Sergeant First Class Quinton Hilliard.

Maybe they were at the Seven Club because her main employer, Mrs. Bei at the King Club, would've nagged her to go home and recuperate rather than immediately return to the money-making grind. Hilliard had her waist pulled in tightly and her legs spread so he could shove his knee up into her. He was almost lifting her off the ground. Control. That's what this was all about. So Hilliard could show anyone who cared to watch that Miss Kwon, bandages and all, was his and he could do anything he wanted to do with her. For her part, Miss Kwon's uncovered eye was closed tight, her teeth clenched. I couldn't be sure from this distance but my guess was that tears were seeping out of her eyes. She was suffering pain, from Hilliard's grinding knee, and humiliation, from being manhandled like this in public. But she kept her eyes shut and did her best to bear this, the fate that poverty had thrust upon her.

"That son of a bitch," Ernie said.

At that moment I knew Ernie was gone. There was no stopping him.

Before I could reach out and make the attempt to reason with him, he was shoving his way through the crowd, ignoring the out-raged rebukes of G.I.s and business girls alike. Within seconds, he'd grabbed Hilliard by the shoulders and spun him around. Hilliard let go of Miss Kwon and Miss Kwon's good eye popped open in sur-prise. And then the left jab shot out and the right and Hilliard stag-gered back, falling against cocktail tables, flailing wildly with his arms, knocking over glassware and beer bottles and magnums of cheap sparkling wine. Women screamed. G.I.s cursed.

Hilliard was back on his feet now, pointing at Ernie, shouting "Racist attack!"

Like a leopard, Ernie pounced on him and began pummeling away and Hilliard did his best to cover himself. By the time I fought my way through the screaming crowd, a few of Hilliard's soul brothers had joined the fray. One of them punched Ernie in the back. I pulled the guy away and, keeping his body's momentum going, twirled him into a fallen cocktail table. While I did this, another friend of Hilliard's punched me in the side of the head. I crouched, swiveled, and caught him with a left cross as he came in. Breath erupted out of his mouth, he curled over, and I slammed him with a right to the head. He went down.

The place was madness now; everyone was punching everyone else. Even some of the business girls were duking it out with G.I.s, releasing frustrations that had been pent up for years. I found Ernie and pulled him toward the door.

On our way out, Miss Park pointed her finger at me and screamed. What she was saying, I couldn't hear but it had something to do with "Snake."

Outside, snow swirled through the air. Ernie and I ran on the slick surface through an alley that led toward the Itaewon Market. The open wooden stalls were deserted. In the morning, farmers would arrive with cabbages and oversized turnips and fist-sized scallions and before dawn the market would be bustling with buyers and sellers. But two hours before the midnight curfew, we stood under a flapping canvas roof, listening to MP sirens howl and the pounding footsteps of squads of KNPs as they made their way toward the melee at the Seven Club.

"What in the hell's the matter with you?" I said.

"He deserved it," Ernie replied. "That little girl was just out of the hospital and Hilliard forces her, immediately, to become his sex slave."

"How do you know she's his sex slave?"

"Did you see the way he was grinding on her? The way he had his hands on her butt?"

"Hey, Ernie," I said, "take a deep breath."

He did. Then he let his shoulders slump.

"You can't save the world," I said.

"Maybe not." Ernie rubbed his knuckles. "But I can pop one son of a bitch upside the head."

"You did that," I said. "Royally. But we're in trouble again," I continued. "Hilliard's certain to lodge an EEO complaint."

"Let him. No jury in the world would convict me."

I wasn't so sure about that but, at the moment, we had other things to worry about, like how to find out who murdered Two Bellies, and Horsehead, and where to find Jessica Tidwell. And Snake.

Down the alleyway, a stick tapped and then something thumped. Ernie and I stepped back into the shadows. Behind the turnip stall was another, larger canvas lean-to. This one contained bamboo animal pens. Dark splotches stained the ground and the odor of raw pig flesh suffused my sinuses. The sound grew louder: a rhythmic series of one tap and then one thump. Whoever was coming down the alleyway was making slow progress.

Flickering neon from the main drag illuminated the alleyway. When her silhouette came into view I realized that whoever was approaching was somewhat shorter than your average Korean woman. She couldn't see us but I could see her. Perspiration streamed off her face and her eyes darted around as if looking for something. She was balancing herself with one crutch, her left foot encumbered by a white cast. Miss Kwon.

She stopped and peered into the canvas-covered darkness, looking right at us as if she could see us but she couldn't. I was sure of that. It was too dark back here. But somehow, she'd known where we'd hide.

Ernie and I stepped out of the shadows.

After an involuntary intake of breath, Miss Kwon said, "Geogi, I look for you."

Her English was improving.

I nodded. Ernie offered her a stick of ginseng gum. She declined. *"Yong Uisa kidariyo,"* she said. Doctor Yong is waiting for you.

"Why?" I asked.

Miss Kwon shrugged her shoulders. "Come," she said. "I show."

With grim determination, Miss Kwon turned around on her crutches and then started her slow progress back up the alley. I followed, Ernie right behind me, but Miss Kwon stopped and said. "Him, no."

"Doc Yong doesn't want to talk to Ernie?"

"No." Miss Kwon shook her head vehemently. "You." She pointed at me.

"Must be something personal," Ernie said. I glared at him. He shrugged and said, "I'll see you in the morning."

I nodded and followed Miss Kwon as she struggled through the darkness.

Doc Yong was waiting for us outside her clinic. A white light from inside lit the narrow alleyway. She was dressed for an outing in blue jeans, a warm sweater, and a bright red cap pulled down over her black hair. Her round nose was flushed from the cold and her glasses were fogged and I thought she was just about the cutest pixie I'd ever seen. She thanked Miss Kwon for bringing me. Miss Kwon paused for a second, facing Doc Yong. Then, as best she could while still holding on to her crutch, she bowed at the waist. Then she turned and hobbled her way back toward the sparkling lights of Itaewon.

When she was gone, I turned to Doc Yong and said, "What is it?"

Doc Yong shook her head. "Not good."

"What's not good?"

"No talk now. Come."

She crossed her arms over her chest, hunched her shoulders slightly, and marched off into the darkness of Itaewon. I followed.

She seemed to know exactly where she was going but after five minutes, I was totally lost. Korean society isn't built around the car. Many pathways are only wide enough for pedestrians to pass, maybe two abreast, sometimes only single file. And people are used to walking long distances, carrying heavy loads, climbing up steep and slippery inclines, or gingerly stepping down precipitous slopes.

Dark ice patches covered many surfaces so we had to watch our step over the haphazardly cobbled pathways. A light snow continued to fall. I pulled my jacket tighter around my chest and wished I'd brought the long heavy overcoat the army issues. The lanes became gradually narrower and there was less sound in the hooches behind the high brick walls. I started to realize where we were going. Approaching from this direction I hadn't been sure at first but now I was. Within ten minutes, we stood in front of the rotted wooden gate that led into the home of Auntie Mee, the fortune teller.

Everything was quiet except for the tiny bells tinkling and the red spirit flags flapping in the late-night breeze. Doc Yong didn't bother to knock. She pushed open the wooden doorway in the gate and the rusted hinges groaned, like a ghost being called from the dead.

I hesitated for a second, knowing from Doc Yong's grim expression and from the silence that surrounded us like a shroud, that something was desperately wrong. I crouched, stepped through the little gate, and entered the darkness of the quiet courtyard.

My mother died before I even started school. My father, the coward that he was, shrugged off his responsibility toward me and took off back to Mexico. That left me, U.S. citizen George Sueño, alone in the world. Growing up as a foster child in East L.A. was difficult but what kept me going through all of it was what my mother had told me before she died. "Be good, Jorge *mío*," she said. "Never betray those you love."

The problem was that, so far, I'd never found anyone to love. I wasn't even sure, exactly, what the word meant. Were they talking about the feelings I had toward my mom? Or where they talking about new feelings I would develop some day as I matured, feelings that I would have toward a young woman closer to my own age?

I knew about lust. That feeling was quite familiar to me. In fact, lust was an enemy that never let me rest. Visions of sex exploded in my brain night and day and from what I could tell of other young G.I.s, I wasn't alone. But love, I suspected, was something else entirely.

I watched Doc Yong walking in front of me, arms crossed on her chest, her head down, straight black hair sticking out beneath the edge of her red cap. What was most astonishing about her was her relentless desire to help the business girls of Itaewon. To offer them a hand. To pull them out of the mire in which they were so securely stuck. Doc Yong was almost thirty so she was older than me. I didn't believe the age difference mattered and so far she had treated me strictly as a colleague. Sort of her own personal U.S. Army liaison officer. A job she needed done because the Korean business girls who swamped her clinic had so many interactions, most of them unpleasant, with 8th Army G.I.s and there always seemed to be something that needed to be worked out with military officialdom. I was happy to perform the role and the closer I was to her the better I felt.

Tonight, I sensed, was a turning point for us. She was taking me somewhere, preparing to show me something that would take us beyond our workday acquaintance stage. Something told me that what I was about to see would be horrible beyond belief. And I believed that this horrible event, whatever it was, would either bring Doc Yong and me closer together or it would split us apart forever. I didn't know which.

So I was braced not just for blood but for heartache. Either or both, would not be new to me. I could handle anything, or at least that's what I thought at the time.

Auntie Mee's hooch was silent and completely dark. I took a few tentative steps across the varnished wooden floor. Silvery moonlight filtered through a back window. A shadow moved through the moonbeams. Doc Yong. She had crouched in front of a wooden cabinet and was fumbling around, looking for something. Finally, she found it. Cardboard scratched on cardboard and then a match scraped and hissed. A tiny fire erupted and I turned my head away from the sudden glow. Deft hands lit two candles. Doc Yong handed one to me.

"Come," she said.

We walked toward the moonglow. Wind rustled silk curtains. In the distance a dog howled. There weren't many howling dogs in Korea. People lived too close together and they worked too hard to allow their sleep to be disrupted by some canine barking at the moon. So a noisy pooch was seldom tolerated. But for some reason, tonight, a dog howled. Maybe it wasn't a dog. Maybe it was something else. I pushed such superstitious thoughts out of my mind. Instead, I searched the shadows.

They looked back at me.

13

Auntie Mee's hooch hadn't been trashed. In all my years in law enforcement I'd never seen anyone break into a house and be so respectful of the furniture and the artifacts and the personal possessions within. Nothing seemed to have been disturbed. Nothing, that is, except for Auntie Mee.

She was still wearing her silk robes. She had been kneeling in front of the small table upon which lay her ancient codex. It was open to an astrological entry. I held my candle closer to examine the script. Chinese. Although I recognized a few characters—like those for sun and moon and the autumn season—I couldn't read enough to make any sense of it. Doc Yong knelt next to me.

"The rites of burial," she said. "How to honor a dead person, how to prepare their grave, how to place them in it, what rituals to perform to assuage their spirit and make sure that they continue to receive honor from their living descendents and therefore will be allowed to take their rightful place in heaven."

"All that here," I said, pointing at the long rows of script.

"Yes." Doc Yong flipped the thick page. "And on further. We Koreans have no end of instructions when it comes to honoring the dead."

"And she was studying this," I said, "just before her murderer showed up?"

"Maybe after," Doc Yong replied.

"After?"

I thought about it. It made sense. Auntie Mee seemed so composed in death. Her corpse lay back on the wood-slat floor, her knees curled in front of her, as if she'd been kneeling in front of this *cheiksang*, book table, just prior to death. And she'd purposely opened her codex to the rites for the dead, leaving instructions to whoever found her as to the proper method of her burial. So she'd known someone was going to kill her. Possibly they'd talked. Possibly, Auntie Mee had slipped on the same long silk robe in which she gave psychic readings so she'd be presentable in death. But who would do that? Who would face their murderer calmly and quietly and accept their fate? Why hadn't she tried to run? Why hadn't she screamed? Why hadn't she put up a fight?

It only made sense if Auntie Mee knew that there was no place for her to run to. If she knew that whoever was here to kill her—or whoever had ordered her to be killed—was too powerful to resist. Auntie Mee's only source of income was fortune-telling and psychic readings. If she couldn't do that, then she couldn't live. And if the person who wanted her killed was powerful enough to hunt her down, to find her wherever she happened to set up shop, then she might've decided that there was no use trying to run. That there was no use trying to fight. Better to accept her fate gracefully. To go out in style, wearing her best silk robes and leaving instructions for her burial so the rites performed after her death would bring honor to her memory and give her prestige on her journey to join her ancestors.

"She didn't fight," I told Doc Yong.

"No."

The cause of death was strangulation. Her neck was bruised and her jaw was cracked open; her tongue lolled out purple and bloated. She'd bitten her own tongue and lips while trying to gasp for breath and she must've lost her resolve to die peacefully because she had scratched at her neck with her own fingernails. Long red welts ran down the smooth flesh. A silk rope lay next to her corpse, a few strands of Auntie Mee's long black hair entertwined with it. The rope was composed of at least a half-dozen plies of silk strips braided together and then tied into thick knots at the ends. There was little bleeding. Only what Auntie Mee's frantic scratching had caused on her own neck. Her body looked frail and helpless now in death. But calm. Acceptant.

"Who told you she was dead?" I asked.

"One of the business girls. She came here to ask Auntie Mee to read her fortune. The front gate was open. When there was no answer she came inside, found Auntie Mee like this."

"And she came straight to you?"

"Yes."

"Who was it?"

"Miss Kwon."

Again, Miss Kwon. She seemed to be everywhere at all times.

"She recovered quickly from her accident," I said.

"Very quickly."

"And she's determined."

Doc Yong nodded. What, I thought, was Miss Kwon so determined about? Even if she couldn't afford to stay in the hospital, certainly Doc Yong would've loaned her enough money to enable her to eat and to rest a few days. Instead, Miss Kwon had gone right back to work. In fact, she'd become a busybody. What was the purpose of all this determination? Or was I becoming paranoid? I said, "And after telling you about the body, Miss Kwon went to the Seven Club to meet Hilliard?"

Doc Yong shrugged. "She has to live."

"But just a few days ago, she tried to kill herself."

"That was then. Now she wants to live."

Yes. She did. Even to the point of putting up with Sergeant First Class Quinton Hilliard. But life, even a life of shame, is preferable to death. That's what I thought at the moment, with the reek of lifeless flesh filling my nostrils.

A fly buzzed our heads and landed on the edge of Auntie Mee's smooth jawline. I waved it away.

"Come on," I said. "Let's go."

"I want to pray first."

And then, reading from the codex, Doc Yong instructed me in how to assist her in lining up candles and igniting incense in a bronze burner and reciting chants in a language so ancient I couldn't understand it. We spent the better part of an hour doing this, she instructing me carefully in the arcane rites of the dead. Meanwhile, outside, the silent storm brewed. And when we were finally done, Doc Yong gently closed Auntie Mee's eyes.

"Goodbye, my friend," she said.

We stayed still, kneeling, for a long time.

When we emerged from that place of horror, the outside world had been transformed into a universe of darkness and swirling snow. The electricity had gone out and the glow of the moon and the stars were just a memory. I knew we'd never find our way back to Doc Yong's clinic, not while we groped blindly through this endless maze of narrow pathways. And the thought of reaching her apartment or the front gate of 8th Army compound was completely out of the question. They were much too far away. Meanwhile, the city of Seoul, blasted by the Manchurian weather, had shut down. Anyone with any sense had long ago taken shelter. There were no taxis roaming the streets, no buses; even the white mice curfew police had given up trying to find North Korean infiltrators and had taken shelter somewhere, probably in an igloo.

With a gloved finger, Doc Yong pointed ahead.

A plastic sign. Unlit. I could barely make it out in the darkness but the sign said *yoguan*. Literally, mattress hall. A traditional Korean inn. After staggering a few more steps, I pounded on the double wooden doors. They were locked tight and there seemed to be no life within. Still, I kept pounding. We either found shelter here or we lay down in one of the snowdrifts behind us and when the storm finally subsided the local residents would find us, frozen stiff. After every major snowstorm in Seoul, dozens of people are found dead on the streets the following day. The city fathers don't like to advertise this fact but it's true. In Korea, poverty is rampant but being homeless is rare. Most everyone has somewhere to go. But for those few who don't, life is short.

Doc Yong started pulling on my elbow, ready to give up and move on but I resisted. Instead, I continued hammering my fist on the unmoving wooden door. After ten more minutes even I was about to call it quits but just before I did, metal creaked loudly behind the door. It wedged open, crusted snow falling everywhere, and then finally, with a sigh of warm air, the door opened.

A woman wrapped in a cloth overcoat motioned for us to enter. "*Bali,*" she said. "*Chuyo.*" Hurry. It's cold.

Doc Yong and I rushed in, stamping our feet on a flagstone walkway. The woman slammed the door shut behind us and without saying a word, scurried back toward the warmth of the two story building. Before entering, Doc Yong and I brushed as much snow as possible off our outer coats and then, in the foyer, we slipped off our shoes and stepped up on the raised lacquered floor.

"*Aigu,*" the woman said, "*wei pakei naggaso?*" Why did you go outside?

"We made a mistake," Doc Yong replied in Korean. Then she asked if we could rent a room. The woman nodded and led us down a hallway. There was no light in the building but the owner provided us with a candle. It was an *ondol* room, meaning it was heated by charcoal gas running through ducts below the floorboards. This meant that even though the electricity was out, the room was warm and cozy. The owner arranged the *yo,* the sleeping mats, and opened a cabinet that held silk-covered comforters. She showed us where the outside *byonso* was located and later she came into the room carrying a tray with two cups and a thermos of warm barley tea.

I paid her and after she left, Doc Yong and I took off most of our clothes, grabbed the comforters, and lay down on the warm sleeping mattress on the floor. Within seconds we were clutching one another, strictly for warmth. We were both exhausted and after a few minutes our mutual body heat and the warm floor below finally allowed us to thaw out. And then I was kissing her and she was kissing me back.

Maybe it was the death we'd seen in Auntie Mee's hooch. The horrible death and the horrible pain. It made life, every second of it, seem more important. And then I was slipping the last of Doc Yong's clothes off and she was slipping off the last of mine. We found a joy in one another, a joy that people rarely find, both of us becoming rabid with our desire to touch one another and suddenly, and completely, embrace life.

When we woke up on the mattresses in the *yoguan*, we didn't talk to one another.

Gray sunlight filtered through the oil-papered windows and I tried to speak but Doc Yong shrugged me off, not making eye contact, acting as if I'd committed a great sin. I wasn't sure what to say, so I said nothing. Maybe she needed time; time to deal with what we'd done last night. I didn't need any time myself. I felt great. But I had no idea what feelings she was dealing with so I left her alone. She didn't even use the *byonso* but started to leave before I was half dressed.

"Wait," I said. "I'll go with you."

"*No.*" It was a shout. Too loud. And then she realized that she was showing panic and she took a deep breath. "Better," she said, holding out her hand in a halting gesture, "if I go first. Anyway, I must go to the clinic and you must go to your compound."

I nodded, not trusting myself to speak. She was ashamed of me. Ashamed to be seen on the street with a big-nosed foreigner. But I didn't blame her. All the Koreans would look at her with amused smiles on their faces and later they would talk about her. Relentlessly. "*Yang kalbo,*" they'd whisper. Foreign whore.

I longed to step toward her and take her hand and tell her I understood. That she didn't have to be seen on the street with me if she found it embarrassing. But she looked so skittish, like a yearling ready to bolt, that I didn't dare. Instead, I stayed where I was and just nodded. Dumbly.

She said, "OK," and walked out and closed the door behind her.

I listened to her footsteps retreat down the hallway.

The provost marshal was about to pop a blood vessel.

"You did what?"

Ernie stood in front of Colonel Brace at the position of attention, his jaw thrust out, his lips set into a grim sneer. "I punched his lights out." Then he said, "sir."

"Oh, I see. You punched his lights out. Any particular reason why you punched his lights out?"

"He had it coming. He was manhandling a business girl on the dance floor of the Seven Club."

The provost marshal crinkled his nose in confusion and glanced at the first sergeant and then at me. You could almost hear his thoughts: *Manhandling a business girl? That's a crime?* He glanced at the paperwork on his desk. "Hilliard said it was a racist attack."

"Not so, sir. I would've been happy to punch his lights out regardless of his color."

The provost marshal rolled his eyes and lifted both hands to the side of his head and rubbed his temples. He was through talking to Ernie. Instead, he talked to the first sergeant.

"We'll have to answer this, Top. See if you can write up a statement that makes sense and before you send it out, run it by the JAG Office to see what they think."

"Yes, sir."

"Meanwhile, Bascom, you and your partner here are liable to come up on EEO charges."

The colonel was about to go on but Ernie interrupted him.

"Sueño had nothing to do with it, sir. In fact, he tried to stop me."

"Well he wasn't very effective, was he?"

"I was too quick for him, sir," Ernie continued. "I'll accept the punishment but Sueño's innocent."

"Not according to the KNPs."

The Korean National Police had not yet cleared Ernie and me of suspicion concerning the death of Two Bellies.

"That's bull, sir. You know it. That's their way of deflecting blame from any Korean who might have power. A safety valve. So in case they find that whoever murdered Two Bellies has money and influence, they can pretend that they suspect us."

Colonel Brace didn't respond to that. But he didn't contradict Ernie either.

"All right," he said, looking back and forth between us. "You two are about to lose your ratings as criminal investigation agents and, if you keep pissing off the power structure here at Eighth Army, you're about to get court-martialed or even booted out of the army." Colonel Brace held up his hand, not allowing us to respond.

"Bascom, you're restricted to compound. No, no argument. At least until this discrimination charge blows over. Sueño, find Jessica Tidwell," he said. "And then, once she's safe, find the bones of that G.I. who was murdered twenty years ago. That will redeem you. That and only that. Am I understood?"

We both nodded.

Colonel Brace further told the first sergeant that he wanted extra MP patrols in Itaewon tonight, searching for Jessica Tidwell.

Colonel Brace hadn't even mentioned the murder of Horsehead, nor the murder of Auntie Mee. And he'd only mentioned Two Bellies because Ernie and I had been falsely charged by the KNPs, thereby embarrassing the command. To the 8th Army honchos, the murder of Koreans was an abstract concept. Even the village of Itaewon itself, where the single G.I.s went, was not anything more than something to be snickered at during polite conversation at the Officers' Club cocktail hour.

But I'd seen the blood. I'd touched it and smelled it. And my cop instincts told me that it wouldn't be long until a G.I. was involved in some way with the mayhem that was going on in Itaewon. I didn't know who was behind this madness or what it was all about but I believed that at it's source, somehow, was Technical Sergeant Flo Moretti.

The fluorescent light above the provost marshal's desk flickered and went out.

"Shit," he said. "There goes the juice. Top, see if you can get the engineers to start up the generator."

"Will do, sir."

Outside, snow continued to fall in steady sheets. The first sergeant left the room. The provost marshal glanced at us. "Why are you still here?"

We didn't reply. Instead, we saluted, performed a smart about-face, and left the room.

Jimmy Pak was looking for me. At least a half dozen business girls had relayed the message. The communications apparatus in

Itaewon—word of mouth—may be ancient but it's efficient. Once one of the Seven Dragons issues a summons, in short order the entire village knows about it.

I could've gone over to the UN Club to see what the hell he wanted but I was in no hurry. Maybe I didn't feel comfortable about walking into his place of business without Ernie to back me up. But I didn't think that was it. If Jimmy Pak, or any of the Seven Dragons, were out to get me they wouldn't make it public knowledge that they wanted to see me. If they were out to get me, the attack would happen in a dark alley, when no one was looking and when I least expected it. As had happened to Mori Di.

I was more curious at the moment, about the Korean police reaction to the murder of Auntie Mee.

When the cannon fired on Yongsan Compound, signifying the end of 8th Army's workday, I marched up to the mess hall, ate some chow, and then took a shower and changed into my running-the-ville outfit.

I gazed at my bunk longingly. I hadn't been getting much sleep lately, ever since I'd first heard about Mori Di. And I'd gotten virtually no sleep with Doc Yong last night. My crotch was sore. But I couldn't afford the luxury of letting down. Two Bellies had trusted me and she'd been killed. The remains of Tech Sergeant Flo Moretti were still missing. A harmless fortune teller had been brutally murdered and Horsehead, one of the Seven Dragons, had been hacked to death by a group of women covered in dark hoods. Ernie and I had vowed to get to Snake. Now it was all up to me.

Captain Kim was overjoyed to see me.

His cheeks sagged and his eyes took on a deathly stillness that would've made a mafia godfather look like a cheerleader at a high school football game. He didn't even ask me what I wanted. He just stared.

"*Anyonghaseiyo?*" I said cheerfully. Are you at peace?

He didn't answer. His head was square, his short black hair combed straight back, and the collar of his sharply pressed khaki uniform gleamed with three canted rectangles of polished gold. He didn't smoke. Unusual for a mature Korean man, so I didn't bother to offer him a cigarette. I didn't smoke either but sometimes, when visiting Korean officialdom, I carried a pack of American-made cancer sticks, more as a peace offering than anything else.

I started with Horsehead.

"Important man," I said. "Dead. Maybe the Seven Dragons are *taaksan* pissed off."

Captain Kim shrugged. Not a syllable left his thick lips.

"And Two Bellies," I continued. "She die same-same."

The murder weapon had been similar. A knife. But instead of a thousand cuts, Two Bellies was killed by one quick slice through the throat.

"And now Auntie Mee," I said, and mimed a hand around a throat. This seemed to pique Captain Kim's interest.

"How you know?" he asked.

I shrugged. "Everybody say."

Captain Kim glared at me.

We often spoke this pigeon English to one another. He didn't like it when I spoke Korean. It made him uncomfortable to hear Korean sounds coming out of a foreign face. No matter what I said to him in Korean, he insisted on answering me in English. A lot of Koreans did this. The younger ones because they didn't want to pass up an opportunity to practice their English. The older ones because they didn't want a foreigner mangling their ancient language—a language that to them was sacred.

"You know a lot," Captain Kim said.

"Because I'm a cop," I said.

He studied me. The unspoken statement being, "Is that the only reason?"

Captain Kim knew as well as I did that I hadn't murdered anyone. Still, if the higher-ups told him to charge me, he'd do it *and* watch me go to prison for that matter. Life is cheap here in Korea and had been since, at least, the Korean War. Nobody knows exactly how many civilians were killed in the war. Estimates vary from two to three million. After something like that happens to a society, death doesn't seem so unusual. And hardship and injustice become merely routine. Even to a cop. Especially to a cop.

"So, who killed Auntie Mee?" I asked.

Captain Kim shrugged and glanced at the paperwork in front of him. I answered my own question.

"Maybe someone who had power over her," I said.

He glanced up at me. "Everybody have power over her."

"The Seven Dragons," I said.

He glanced back down at the paperwork. It was a stack of handwritten notes on cheap brown pulp paper. The Korean police can't afford the expensive white vellum that the U.S. Army uses. Nor could they afford typewriters, except for a handful at police headquarters. But one thing I'll say for the Korean police force, there's no shortage of excellent typists to choose from. Each and every typewriter at KNP headquarters was staffed by a gorgeous young female police officer.

"Are you going to do anything about it?" I asked.

"What you mean?"

"About Auntie Mee's death? About finding out who killed her?"

He shrugged again, more elaborately this time. "If we find up."

He meant, if we discover who murdered her.

"Any evidence so far?"

"No. Same-same Two Bellies. They no leave nothing. Except for one thing." He stared straight at me. "Somebody light candles, burn incense, perform ceremony of the dead."

That would've been me and Doc Yong but I wasn't about to tell him. I changed the subject.

"How about the bones of Mori Di?" I asked.

"That G.I. business. Not my business."

And finding the remains of Tech Sergeant Flo Moretti wouldn't become his business unless Korean officialdom ordered him to make it his business. Evidently, the higher-ups in the ROK government, despite 8th Army's messages of concern, had not ordered the KNPs to find Moretti's bones. Maybe because they didn't want them found. Or somebody who had influence had decided that they didn't want them found.

A young Korean patrolman ran into the office so fast that he practically skidded to a halt in front of Captain Kim's desk. His face was flushed red and when he saw me it became even redder.

"Officer Jiang reporting," he said in Korean and saluted.

Captain Kim stared at him with a look of resigned expectation. "What is it?"

The patrolman glanced at me again, hesitating to speak.

Gruffly, Captain Kim said, *"Iyaggi hei!"* Speak!

The patrolman chattered away, speaking so quickly that I had trouble following the convoluted Korean sentences but I caught a few of them and some words and phrases. He was talking about the Lucky Lady Club and blood and women who were hysterical and Captain Kim was on his feet, reaching behind his desk for his cap. I stood, and although Captain Kim stared at me morosely, I followed. We ran out the front door of the Itaewon Police Station, turned the corner, and sprinted up the ice-covered road. A road that despite mounds of drifted snow, glittered with sparkling neon overhead and fancy women hidden in recessed doorways.

14

This time it happened more publicly.

Two Korean men had been in the office of Mr. Sung, also known as *Mulkei*. *Mulkei*, literally translated, means "water dog." Its dictionary meaning though is "fur seal" or "otter." Sung was a small man, full of pep, and years ago some G.I. had mistranslated his Korean nickname and started calling him "Water Doggy." The name stuck and that's what Sung had been called ever since, by both Koreans and Americans. The two visitors had come to see him supposedly about a rewiring project they were going to undertake on the building adjacent to the Lucky Lady Club. They told some of the other employees that they wanted Water Doggy to be aware that construction would be going on and they were hoping to make arrangements that would not be disruptive to the operations of the Lucky Lady Club. The club was one of the biggest money-makers in Itaewon. While the two men discussed the construction project with Water Doggy, three women entered the club. They weren't your regular Lucky Lady customers. They were not young prostitutes because they were dressed in thick-soled shoes and trousers and heavy jackets as protection from the frigid winter weather outside. When one of the waitresses asked politely what she could do for them, the lead woman merely pointed to the back office and kept walking, averting her face and keeping her hood pulled over her head.

The waitresses hadn't seen the faces of any of the women. They had purposely kept their features concealed.

Seconds later, voices were raised in the office. The cocktail waitresses weren't unduly alarmed. Water Doggy argued with any number of people. Besides, they were paid to look nice and wait tables, not interfere with business dealings. Just as quickly as the voices had been raised, the office went quiet. Minutes later the two impostor electrical contractors and the three hooded women emerged. No one thought anything about it.

G.I.s were off duty now and even though they had to brave snowdrifts and icy roads, they were gradually beginning to arrive in Itaewon. Groups of them, mostly regulars, were entering the Lucky Lady Club, doffing their hats and coats, dusting off snowflakes, taking their seats and ordering the Korean-made Oscar sparkling wine or brown bottles of OB Beer. The cocktail waitresses were flirting with them, the band was mangling some monotonous rock tune, and the business girls were lurking in the shadows waiting for the alcohol to take effect on their G.I. prey.

Everything was normal at the Lucky Lady Club. And elsewhere in Itaewon. The power outages had been fixed, the snow had stopped falling—at least for the moment—and, as yet, word of the murder of Auntie Mee had not spread to the general population.

Everything was normal, that is, except for in the office of the Lucky Lady Club.

On her way to the women's latrine, one of the waitresses noticed something in the dim light of the hallway: a dark liquid seeping from beneath Water Doggy's closed office. She walked past it at first, finished her business in the bathroom and then, upon returning, knelt to take a closer look at the liquid. At first, she thought Water Doggy had spilled coffee or broken a bottle of liquor. But as she leaned closer, the meaty odor of the fluid filled the air and she realized that it was thick and not flowing quickly and when the rotating glass bulb hanging above the dance floor finally cast a beam of pure white light on the floor in front of her, she realized the true color of the liquid. Red.

She screamed. At first, no one heard her scream above the din of the rock and roll so she kept screaming and soon the cashier and the bartender shoved her aside and kicked in the office door and found, crumpled atop his desk, the mangled and slashed body of *Mulkei*, the man G.I.s called Water Doggy.

Captain Kim surveyed the murder scene with all the grim concentration of a demon evaluating an invoice from Beelzebub.

"Same-same Horsehead," I said.

Captain Kim grunted but did not answer.

There were numerous stab wounds on the body of Water Doggy. Three different implements had been employed was my guess but I couldn't be sure without actually touching the wounds and measuring their width and depth. But that wasn't my job. As usual, I was here simply as an observer for 8th Army, at the tolerance of Captain Kim. Just the fact that he allowed me to observe the murder scene told me that he didn't believe for a minute the charges that Lieutenant Pong from the 8th Army KNP liaison officer had leveled against Ernie and me. There were factions within the Korean National Police, many of them, and my experience with Captain Kim was that he was so stubborn and opinionated and protective of his Itaewon turf that he formed a major faction of the KNPs all by himself.

Lights were brought in to illuminate the scene for the evidence gathering team. They weren't an independent group because Captain Kim hovered over them, barking orders. After a couple of hours he left one of his lieutenants in charge of the crime scene and made the trip that no cop anywhere in the world wants to make: to the home of the victim, in order to officially notify Water Doggy's wife and his family of what had happened. He didn't ask me to go along and I certainly didn't volunteer. Regardless of what type of dissolute life Water Doggy had led, regardless of what crimes he'd committed, and regardless of what his wife might've put up with while living with him, telling her that he was dead was not going to be easy.

Water Doggy's office didn't tell us much. There didn't seem to be anything missing. A cashbox in the bottom drawer of his desk was unmolested. The furnishings in his office weren't nearly as elaborate as in the office of Snake, or even Jimmy Pak. What Water Doggy had that his fellow Seven Dragons did not have was a long leather couch across from his desk. Plenty long enough for the diminutive Water Doggy to lie down on and still have enough room for one of the leggy cocktail waitresses to join him. Or at least that's what I imagined but that's the way my thoughts were going since I'd spent the night with Doctor Yong In-ja.

The effect of Water Doggy's demise on the waitresses and bartenders and the cashier of the Lucky Lady Club was devastating. They stopped working and huddled in front of the bar, hugging one another, whispering and staring at the cops and medical personnel entering and exiting Water Doggy's office. The band packed up its instruments and left. The G.I. customers hung around for a while until the novelty of being near a crime scene wore off. And then the word of Water Doggy's brutal murder began to spread throughout Itaewon.

When I walked outside, I paused on the cement porch of the Lucky Lady Club and surveyed the street. The snow had stopped falling but still lay in drifts against brick walls topped with rusty barbed wire. Neon still flashed up the strip but in the dark environs of Hooker Hill the women stood in front of their little wooden gates, concerned faces lit by dim streetlamps. In front of the nightclubs, G.I.s and business girls huddled in groups, talking and occasionally glancing in the direction of the Lucky Lady Club. Beneath the floodlamps at the entrances to the Seven Club and the King Club, groups of uniformed waitresses, canting round cocktail trays against their hips, gossiped and nodded their heads and twitched their necks spasmodically in the direction of the Lucky Lady Club.

When I stepped off the porch and started walking forward, people backed away as if I were contaminated with some hideous communicable disease.

"Water Doggy," they whispered. Or "Horsehead" or "Two Bellies." And now, finally, I was hearing them whisper the name "Auntie Mee." Some of them cried, their eyes riveted on me as if searching for an answer. I didn't have one. The only thing I knew for sure was that the village of Itaewon was cursed. Not by the supernatural, as the late Auntie Mee had claimed, but by people who were filled with a murderous rage. And by gauging the looks of the business girls and G.I.s and cocktail waitresses all around me, the village of Itaewon was about to reach the stage of full-fledged panic.

I stood at a wooden counter alone, slurping down a cold mug of beer at a new joint on the edge of Itaewon called the OB Stand Bar. I wanted to be alone, away from G.I.s, away for a while even from the English language. I wanted time to think. The OB Stand Bar stood near a major bus terminal and, as such, commuters came in here for a quick drink. There were no chairs, just tall tables for standing and a long counter that ran around the edge of the rectangular shaped room. Most of the customers were either reading Korean newspapers or staring into space. A few talked quietly with friends but there were no Americans here. Only Koreans. And as I was the only American, I was left alone. Nobody interrupted me and I had, at last, some time to ponder the madness I'd seen in the last few days.

I wanted to think about the evidence I'd seen, about the crime scenes, about who would have the motive to murder four people. Instead, what I thought about was Doc Yong. About the night we'd spent together. About the subtle, soft curves of her body. About her smooth fresh skin. About the moonlight illuminating her face as she leaned back, eyes closed, concentrating on ecstasy. I had to get her out of my mind, at least long enough to think about what was going on here in Itaewon.

With an effort of will, I did.

Four murders. All of them had started when Ernie and I uncovered the bones of Technical Sergeant Flo Moretti. It was as if by pulling out those bricks and making a hole in that wall, I'd not only unleashed twenty-year-old air, I'd also unleashed the spirit of Mori Di himself. A spirit that was insisting on revenge. Of course that was silly but the fact was undeniable that exposing the bones of Moretti to this new era had set off a chain of events that resulted in multiple deaths: Two Bellies, Horsehead, Auntie Mee, Water Doggy. And a trio of hooded women assisted by two men had committed at least two of the murders. Were both murders committed by the same two men and the same three women? I had to assume so. The method of operation in both instances was the same: brutal, efficient, and full of rage. The two men, Horsehead and Water Doggy, had been hacked to death and if their bodies had been chopped up any more they would've fallen apart like so many chunks of pulverized meat. But what of Two Bellies? No chopping there, just a single slice through the throat and gradual exsanguination as the victim gasped unsuccessfully for air. An ugly way to go. Maybe worse than being hacked to death. The victim is aware, probably, that there's no hope but can look around, wishing that he could breathe, wishing that there wasn't a huge gash in his neck. Staring, probably, at the person who'd just slashed him. It was those few seconds while he was still alive that frightened me.

Two Bellies didn't struggle with her executioner. Or at least there was no evidence that she had. And neither had Auntie Mee, although she'd been slowly strangled. Both women had accepted their fates. There was no escape. And since both of the women lived their lives at the bottom, or very near the bottom, of a strict Confucian hierarchy, they allowed the sentence of death to be carried out.

Two types of killing, two types of victims. Unlike Auntie Mee and Two Bellies, the other two victims were men who'd grabbed life by the throat, shaken it, and demanded money, power, and prestige. Neither Horsehead nor Water Doggy had acquiesced in their deaths. Horsehead had been either drugged or extremely drunk—or both—and he'd been tied up. Water Doggy was a small man and had shouted and fought, but had been overwhelmed by the two men and three women crowded into his office.

Men like Horsehead and Water Doggy had made many enemies in their lives. Was it a coincidence that these two men and three women were seeking revenge at the same time that Ernie and I had uncovered the bones of Technical Sergeant Flo Moretti?

Something about all this bothered me but I hadn't quite put my finger on what it was when I realized that someone was tugging on my sleeve. I set my beer mug down and turned around.

Miss Kwon stared up at me.

She still had the crutch beneath her left arm and her ankle was still enveloped by a plastic brace and a gauze patch still covered her left eye. But she seemed alert and concerned and busy.

"You come," she said.

"How'd you find me?" I asked.

She waved her right hand in the air and twirled it slightly. "This Itaewon. Everybody see everybody. *Bali bali* you come." Come quickly.

"Why?"

"Jimmy Pak. He want talk to you."

I sipped on my beer. "Are you working for Jimmy Pak these days?"

"Yes." Miss Kwon pulled a wadded bill out of the pocket of her skirt. Five thousand *won*, about ten bucks. "He pay me *taaksan* money find you. Now you come."

"Maybe I don't want to see him."

"You have to," she said, staring at me with her moist brown eyes as if I were an idiot to whom everything had to be carefully explained. "He know about bones."

I sat up straighter on my stool. "He told you that?"

She nodded vehemently.

"Where are they?" I asked.

She looked disappointed. "I don't know. You talk Jimmy Pak. He tell."

"OK," I said. "Did you see Doctor Yong today?"

"No time," she said. "I have to workey."

She'd made a remarkable recovery. I was starting to wonder if the suicide attempt had been sincere or if it had been merely a ploy to attract attention. I took her shoulders in my hands and stared directly into her eyes.

"And how are *you?*" I asked.

She shrugged. "OK. No more jump off King Club." She shook her head vehemently. "No more. Now I make money." She pointed her forefinger at the tip of her nose. "Now I take care of Miss Kwon. Make money. Pretty soon, I be happy."

Miss Kwon said all this with a determination that seemed laughable, as if happiness were a thing she could construct. But I knew better than to smile as she said these things. Instead, I watched her. She stared back at me with an intensity that, for a moment, I found disconcerting.

"Nobody help Miss Kwon," she said, "but I help Miss Kwon." Then she turned and hobbled out of the OB Beer Stand.

I studied the waddling little rear of this serious young woman, glad—I think—that she'd overcome her despair. Then I chugalugged the rest of my beer and followed her out into the street.

I said goodbye to Miss Kwon, not wanting her to struggle alongside me on her single crutch. At one of the dark pedestrian lanes I told her she could return to the Seven Club now; I would go on to the UN Club to meet Jimmy Pak. But after I said goodbye to her and rounded the corner of the next dimly lit intersection I saw Jimmy Pak standing beneath a streetlamp, smiling.

Two bodyguards stood next to him. Not burly men, although the contours of muscles showed through their jackets. I saw it in their eyes and in the walnut-sized calluses on their knuckles: martial arts experts. Probably skilled in tae kwon do, the indigenous Korean form of karate, meaning "the path of kicking and punching." Some young men had turned themselves into awesome physical machines designed to do just that: kick and punch.

Jimmy smiled even more broadly and opened his arms as if to hug me.

"Geogi," he said. "My friend. How are you?"

"OK, Jimmy." I didn't step forward into his embrace.

He lowered his arms but his smile never faltered.

"We must talk," he said.

"I thought you wanted to talk to me at the UN Club."

"Right here is good, too."

Jimmy Pak's smile faded and I saw an expression I'd never seen on his face before: a frown. It made him look like a different man, a very frightening man.

"Mori Di," he said. "You uncovered his bones. This cause much trouble in Itaewon."

The two bodyguards were starting to step slightly away from Jimmy, as if to improve their angle of attack.

"What do you want, Jimmy?" I said.

"It's not me," Jimmy said. "It's Snake. He wants to talk to you."

"And I want to talk to him," I said.

"Good. We go now."

"Not now," I said. "I'm busy." I wasn't happy with these conditions. No one, except Miss Kwon, would know my whereabouts. And she would know that I'd talked to Jimmy Pak, but not about Snake. "Give me a time and place."

"The time is now," Jimmy said. "And we'll show you the place."

"No. Make an appointment."

I started to walk away. The two men scurried forward. I turned and reached inside my jacket, touching the hilt of my .45, letting my jacket fall open. They stopped.

"If Snake wants to talk, all he has to do is give me a time and place," I said.

Once again, Jimmy Pak smiled.

"You're right, Geogi. I apologize. We're just so anxious because so many things have been going wrong. How about tonight, at midnight?"

"Where?"

"My club."

I thought about it. Then I said, "I'll be there."

And I'd notify Ernie and the desk sergeant at the Yongsan MP Station as to where I'd be and who I'd be talking to. I turned and walked down the alley. Jimmy's two bodyguards went the other way. I heard them conferring with their boss as their voices faded.

I was about to step out of the narrow lane into the light of the Itaewon main drag when I saw Miss Kwon, standing in an alley, a worried expression on her face. I stopped, and was about to speak to her when something heavy cracked the back of my skull.

It didn't hurt at that moment; it would later. The world started to spin, lights flashed, brightly at first, and then, as if someone was turning them off one by one, they began to fade. I felt my knees melting, and then a feeling like flying and then the world, spinning around, faded into darkness. Nothing but darkness. Complete and total.

15

When I was a kid in East L.A., schoolyard fights were a regular occurrence. But it wasn't those fights I was afraid of. Invariably, even when we became teenagers, they would be broken up by someone in authority. A teacher or, in the case of full-fledged melees, by a group of male gym teachers wielding wooden paddles. So, in general, on school grounds, you were safe.

It was between home and school that things were dicey. Not so much on the way to school in the mornings. Mexican *vatos* and other gang members tend not be early risers. But by the time school let out, two or three in the afternoon, they were up, had already taken their first jolt of nicotine or uppers; they were ready to start their day's work, tormenting people weaker than they. Nobody had any plans for protecting children on their way home. From the edge of the schoolyard to the front door of your apartment or your house or your trailer, the good kids were like a migrating herd of caribou, fair game for whatever pack of predators happened to be prowling.

We scurried forward, our heads down, hoping that the punks

wouldn't pick us out of the crowd but it was never long, it seemed, before somebody picked me. I always dealt with it somehow, by fighting, by taking my lumps, and occasionally by running. But it was the smaller kids who bothered me. The ones who cried their eyes out after they'd been punched for no reason or had their glasses stomped or whose prized slide rule had been ripped out of their book bag and snapped in two. I didn't like seeing these things. They hurt me and I found it impossible to look away. It was, in many ways, worse than being tormented myself. Somehow, when watching one of these torture sessions, I'd find a way to screw up my courage and I'd tell the bad guys to leave the kid alone.

Leave the kid alone. That's all I'd said. But the *vatos* were astounded. You would've thought I'd defiled the holy sepulcher. The punks in the gangs considered it their sacred right to pick on kids weaker than themselves and not to countenance interference. When I rudely interrupted, all their wrath was turned on me. It got to the point that I didn't mind. The bumps and bruises and occasional kicks in the ribs I took were not as painful as watching a helpless kid being molested by a pack of bullies. And then a few boys started sticking close to me and then the girls. And after a while we were a pack that moved together, seeking safety as we approached the homes of our various members. And one by one each child would peel off and run pell-mell to the front door of an apartment or trailer and then wave goodbye as the rest of us continued to move toward home. I felt good about doing this. About protecting the other kids. Until one day when the *vatos* caught me alone.

I was hospitalized. And when the cop from juvenile hall asked me who'd done this to me, I told him I'd fallen down a flight of steps. He spat in disgust, considering me a coward. But I wasn't a coward, only a realist. There was nothing he could do to protect me. He'd never be there for our midafternoon odysseys and we kids, like all people in the end, were on our own.

A report was made and a few days after my release from the hospital, the Supervisors of the County of Los Angeles moved me to another foster home. I don't know what happened to my flock. Although I thought of them often, I never saw them again.

* * *

Someone had tied me to a gurney. Leather straps held my arms and legs securely against a white linen sheet. My shirt had been taken off but my pants were still on and I could feel my wallet behind my butt and my keys and loose change in my front pocket. So I hadn't been robbed.

The light seemed too bright but I opened my eyes anyway. And then shut them, allowing my pupils to accommodate themselves to the bright bulb focused on me like the eye of a malevolent dragon. Somebody turned the bulb away. I chanced a peek. Gazing down at me, smiling, was the narrow face of the dark-complexioned Korean man known as Snake.

"You fight too much," he said.

"Let me up," I said.

"You need rest."

"I need to pop you in the jaw."

Snake turned back and said something to the men standing behind him. They laughed. Must've been about a half dozen of them. But what Snake said had been spoken too rapidly for me to understand.

Snake aimed the light back to my face. "Somebody kill Water Doggy," he said.

I squeezed my eyes shut.

"And before that," Snake continued, "somebody kill Horsehead."

"Maybe they had it coming," I said.

My eyes were becoming accustomed to the light.

Snake puffed on a cigarette in a black holder. "People who kill Horsehead," Snake said, "and people who kill Water Doggy. I think same-same."

I snorted. I wasn't going to give him my professional opinion while I was tied to a gurney.

"Maybe you find up," Snake said.

"The KNPs will find them," I replied. "They work for you, don't they?"

Snake smiled his slow smile, the one that spread across his narrow lips gradually, finally lifting slightly at the corners. "Some do," he said equitably. "Some KNP are like you. Stubborn. Anyway, they already try. No can find. Two men, three women. Seoul very big city. How they find up?"

"That's your problem," I said.

"No," Snake said patiently. "Your problem too. Anyway, you have SIR."

I was surprised that Snake knew the acronym. But I shouldn't have been. After more than two decades of working with the United States military, there were probably not many 8th Army acronyms that Snake didn't recognize.

"So I have the SIR," I said. "So what?"

"Cort was good man."

I tried to sit up but the leather straps held me firmly.

"That's right," Snake continued. "I knew Cort. He try very hard to find up who kill Mori Di," Snake shook his head woefully. "Good man, stubborn too. Like you."

Koreans have an odd national trait. They like perseverance. Even if you think or do things completely opposed to them, they will respect you if you stick to your principles. What Snake was referring to was the fact that Cort never gave up trying to find and bring to justice the men who had murdered Moretti. It was my opinion, as it was Cort's, that the killers had been the Seven Dragons, or at least they'd been the ones who'd ordered the killing. Still, after all these years, Snake was expressing admiration for the man who kept trying to charge him with murder.

Snake said, "You know what happen Cort?"

"What do you mean?" I asked. "He finished his tour in Korea, went back to the States."

Snake shook his head. "No. He no go back."

Now that I thought about it, there was nothing about Cort's post-investigation activities in the SIR. He merely stopped making entries. I tried not to show much interest. It was not wise to let Snake think that he had some information that I wanted.

"So what happened to him?" I asked.

"You go Eighth Army," Snake replied, pointing toward Yongsan Compound. "You find up there. Now, I want you find people who kill Horsehead, people who kill Water Doggy. KNPs they no can do. First, they stupid. Second, they fight now with Snake, with Jimmy Pak. They all the time want more money."

The KNPs were not stupid. That wasn't the reason they weren't solving the murders of Horsehead and Water Doggy. The reason was that they didn't, yet, have enough evidence to lead them to the killers. But the other thing that Snake said, about them wanting more money, that was a possibility. Maybe that's why there was a rift between Lieutenant Pong, the 8th Army KNP liaison officer, and Captain Kim, the commander of the Itaewon Police Station. Factions. Infighting. These were facts of life. Itaewon, and all its rich operations, represented a ripe plum full of juice, power, and money. A plum worth fighting over. Maybe someone was making a play for that ripe piece of fruit and thereby threatening the power of the Seven Dragons. And if that was true, maybe the KNPs were the ones who'd unleashed the people who murdered Horsehead and Water Doggy. Or, if they hadn't unleashed them, maybe they weren't in any big hurry to bring the culprits to justice. If this were true, Snake and Jimmy Pak and the other remaining members of the original Seven Dragons, were vulnerable.

Finally, I said, "You want me to save your skinny ass."

Snake shrugged. "You have SIR. You have good information."

"What information?" I asked.

"You look inside, you find. Many people there, they don't like Seven Dragons."

I'd never heard one of them use the term *Seven Dragons*. But there it was, an admission that the Seven Dragons actually existed. Snake was more than just vulnerable. If somebody in the KNPs was after him, he and the other surviving Seven Dragons were desperate. I wasn't sure what evidence the SIR contained that could lead me to the killers of Horsehead and Water Doggy but I knew that now was the time to drive a hard bargain, even though I was half naked, strapped to a gurney, and surrounded by a gaggle of Korean mobsters.

"If I do try to find out who murdered Horsehead and Water Doggy," I said, "I'm going to want something in return. I want you to release Miss Kwon from her contract. Give her money, enough to go to school and help her parents. Let her return to her hometown."

Snake puffed on his cigarette. "Why I do that?"

"If you want my help, you'll have to."

"Snake no have to do nothing."

"I have the SIR," I said. "It's back on the compound, somewhere safe where you can't get it." In Sergeant Riley's safe at the CID Admin Office to be exact. "And I also want the bones of Mori Di. I know you took them when you had Two Bellies murdered."

"Bones? Why I need bones?"

"You need them because the bones prove that you murdered Mori Di."

"How they do that?"

"Forensic evidence."

I could tell by the puzzled look on Snake's face that he didn't understand the word *forensic.* But anyway, I was bluffing. The bones of Mori Di might prove two things: one, that he'd been tortured before his death and, possibly two, that he'd been alive when his tormentors bricked him up in the basement of the Grand Ole Opry Club.

After thinking it over, the worry vanished from Snake's face and he laughed. For me, that cemented his guilt. He'd reviewed the crime scene mentally and decided there was no way—forensic science or not—that I could pin anything on him.

"Anyway, I got to go," Snake said. "You find up who killed Horsehead and Water Doggy. Then everything OK."

"Screw you, Snake," I said. "I want Miss Kwon set free and the bones of Mori Di delivered to me immediately. That's the deal."

Snake turned back to the gurney and leaned down. "You stupid?"

I didn't answer but waited.

"Why I bring you here?" Snake waved his arms around the clinic we were in. And then I realized where I was: Doc Yong's clinic, the Itaewon branch of the Yongsan County Public Health Clinic.

Snake leaned in closer. His hot breath, laced with the stink of nicotine, covered my face like a wet glove. "You think Snake come beg you do something?" he asked. "No way. Never *bachi.* I have something you want, Snake already got it, so you have to give me what I want. You find up who kill Horsehead and Water Doggy. After you find up, you tell Snake, then I take care everything. You *alla?*" You understand?

When I didn't reply, Snake went on. "Once Snake have what Snake want, then you get what you want."

He pulled something black and long out of his back pocket and tossed it atop my chest. I writhed in panic. For a second, I thought it was a snake; and then I relaxed. The metal disc at the end felt cold against my chest. It was a stethoscope.

"You *bali bali*," Snake said. You hurry. "She strong woman, stubborn too, like you. But if no eat, all the time have boom-boom, then pretty soon die.

The faceless men behind Snake started to laugh. Their laughter grew louder and then Snake left the room and his men followed. Even after the footsteps of Snake and his thugs faded, I could still hear them laughing.

What Snake had that I wanted was Doc Yong. "Boom-boom" is G.I. slang for having sex.

I strained at the leather straps that held me. They wouldn't budge.

I'm not sure how long I lay tied to the gurney. Maybe a couple of hours. I was dozing off again when I woke to the sound of someone fiddling with the door to the clinic. The door opened and amber light from a streetlamp streamed in. Then, whoever had entered, shut the door again. I strained to see but I was tied too flat to be able to get a good look.

Footsteps pounded toward me in an uneven rhythm: first a clump and then a step and then another clump.

A round face peered down at me. Miss Kwon. She placed her forefinger to her lips, warning me to be quiet. Then in the dim light she studied the leather straps that held me. With the hand that wasn't holding her crutch, she systematically released them. Finally, I could sit upright.

"How did you know I was here?" I asked.

"I watch," she said. "I see you talk Jimmy Pak. I see Jimmy Pak become *taaksan* angry." Very angry. "Then I see they follow you. I know something bad happen. When I no see you later, I come here find up."

"Thanks," I said.

Her English was improving. Most of the business girls, even the ones with only a middle-school education, studied English in school.

Once they arrive in Itaewon, they pick up the language fast as they gain the confidence to use what they already know.

"You gonna help Doc Yong?" Miss Kwon asked.

"How'd you know about that?"

"Anybody in village know already."

Maybe Snake hadn't been trying to keep it a secret.

I stood and found my shirt and jacket hanging on the back of a chair. My wallet was still in my pocket and none of my money or identification had been taken. My shoulder holster was there with the .45 untouched. Snake and his boys had wanted to communicate, not to rob me. My head pulsed with a dull ache that seemed to radiate from my skull, slice through gray mush, and finally stab into my spine.

I buttoned my shirt and asked Miss Kwon, "Where are you going now?"

"Back to hooch."

"To Hilliard?"

Her eyes crinkled in confusion.

"To Q?"

"Yeah," she said. "To Q."

She turned and hobbled out of the clinic.

I sat with my head on the front edge of the Admin sergeant's desk, snoozing a little, mostly suffering from nightmares. I must've dozed off into an even deeper sleep when suddenly a doorknob rattled, the overhead fluorescent lights blazed to life, and a voice barked out, "What the hell you doing here, Sueño?"

Staff Sergeant Riley strode toward me, his polished low quarters clattering on the wood-slat floor. I sat upright, rubbing my eyes.

"You're late," I said.

"The hell I'm late. I'm an hour early. What'd you do? Sleep here last night?"

"No sleep," I said. "I was reading this."

I pointed to the stacked files of the Moretti Serious Incident Report.

"You opened my safe?"

"Why not?"

"Because I have classified documents in there. That's why not."

"I'm not interested in those."

Besides, I'd relocked the safe. But I didn't bother to explain that to Riley. He was just being his usual self. He stepped past me to the service counter and busied himself making a four-gallon urn of over-strengthed java to jump-start the staff of the 8th Army Criminal Investigation Division at the beginning of their workday.

When he was finished and the coffee was perking, I said, "I need something from you, Riley."

He sat down behind his desk. "Will it get Mrs. Tidwell off our backs?"

"Not hardly."

"Then don't bother telling me. You ain't getting it."

I told him anyway. He listened, frowned, and the flesh of his narrow forehead wrinkled.

"How the hell am I going to find something like that?" he asked.

"You know everybody in the headquarters. Tell them to search their records."

"Christ, Sueño, what do you need this for?"

"To save a life."

I told him about Doc Yong. I told him about Snake.

"You mean Mr. Lim?" he asked. "The big construction honcho?"

"That's the one."

"You're out of your gourd, Sueño. The 8th Army commander thinks Lim walks on water."

"Well, he doesn't and I'm going to prove it."

Riley shook his head. "Is Bascom going to help you with this nonsense?"

"Of course," I said. "And so are you."

"What's this gal's name again?"

"Doctor Yong In-ja."

"And Mr. Lim's holding her?"

"That's right. But in the ville they call him Snake."

"'Snake,'" Riley repeated. "And the guy you want me to find out about is called Cort?"

I nodded.

"Didn't he put his full name in the SIR?"

"No," I replied. "Just Cort."

Riley shook his head. "Sloppy work." Then he picked up the big black telephone on his desk. "Maybe Smitty's in early."

While Riley called, I continued to study the SIR. Snake said that in the SIR I'd find some clue as to who had murdered Horsehead and Water Doggy. How he knew that, I had no idea. Maybe he was just making it up, trying to get me to try all angles to solve the case. Or maybe there was something here. I went over the notes I'd made during the hours that I'd pored through the multiple folders and stacks of papers that constituted the Moretti SIR.

After helping myself to a cup of Riley's coffee, I concluded that there was only one item in the SIR that might have a bearing on the murders of Horsehead and Water Doggy: the list of valuables that had been turned over by the refugee families to Mori Di for safekeeping. The names on the list were the names of aggrieved people who'd been robbed and—in some cases— killed in the Itaewon Massacre. People who had every reason to seek revenge on Horsehead and Water Doggy and on the Seven Dragons in general. But many of these people had either been slain in the massacre or had passed away from natural causes in the intervening two decades.

And then it dawned on me. Most likely, few of these people were still alive. But what of their children? They had been taken to an orphanage in the mountains. According to Cort, he'd traveled to the Buddhist temple there to interview the nuns who'd saved them. Maybe, if I compared the list of orphans with the list of people whose valuables had been stolen, I'd come up with a lead. Even if I didn't, it would be something to show to Snake. Something that, just maybe, I could use to run a bluff. But I had to work fast. As soon as Ernie walked in, I told him what we had to do.

"But I'm restricted to compound," Ernie said.

In the excitement, I'd forgotten about that. "This is an emergency," I replied. "Staff Sergeant Riley will authorize it."

Riley, mumbling to himself and cursing, was still working the telephone and waved us away, not hearing a word we'd said. We ran outside to the jeep. I noticed a bandage on Ernie's hand. "What the hell happened to you?"

"I've taken up competitive needlepoint."

After we pulled out the main gate and turned east on the MSR, another thought struck me. Even if I obtained the information I needed, once I went up against Snake and his thugs, I was going to need backup. But 8th Army wasn't going to deploy a squad of MPs to go after their top civilian contractor. He didn't even fall under 8th Army jurisdiction. I was going to need help from someone. I told Ernie to pull over and let me out in front of the Itaewon Police Station. He waited outside, engine running.

When I marched into his office and sat down and told him what I wanted, Captain Kim looked at me as if I were mad.

"I need a search warrant," he replied.

"So get one."

"From who?"

"From a judge."

His eyes narrowed. "You gonna tell judge, say Snake slicky Korean woman?"

"Yes."

"Say Snake slicky Korean woman doctor and you think he gonna believe you after Snake already told judge he didn't slicky Korean woman doctor?"

"Snake already told him?"

"He will. Who you think work for Snake?"

I knew the business girls did, and the bartenders and the waitresses. The owners of the small record shops and sports equipment outlets and food stands in the environs of Itaewon had to cough up a tribute to the honcho of the Seven Dragons. But judges, too? Clearly, Snake's influence was more pervasive than I thought.

"How about you?" I asked.

It was a risky thing to say but I was desperate. Captain Kim's entire body tensed. I was sure he was going to spring at me from across his desk and I prepared to pop him with a left while he was still on the fly.

Instead of attacking, he took a deep breath. Slowly, he relaxed.

"You don't know," he said finally. "Americans don't know. Here, everybody gotta make money. Extra money. If don't make extra money then can't buy house, can't send children to school, after too old to work, no have nothing. Everybody gotta do. So, I make money too."

Captain Kim stared at me defiantly. I knew that the salaries of Korean cops—and the salaries of most civil servants—were miserably low. And the ROK government, and even the Korean taxpayer, winked at the fact that the cops and other people in government were expected to supplement their income by doing favors for people, like busting them for some small infraction and then collecting the fine on the spot or expediting paperwork that had mysteriously become stuck in bureaucratic channels. They were expected to do those things—everyone was allowed to make a living—but they were also expected to act in a humane way, a way that wouldn't cause innocent people to suffer unduly. But the rich received their due. In Korea, as everywhere else, money talked. But loud enough to suppress a kidnapping accusation?

"If I go talk to Snake now," Captain Kim said, "he hide woman, we never find. But, if you do what he tell you to do, bow low to him, do everything he say, then he relax."

Captain Kim stared into my eyes, wondering if I understood. I did. No official action could be taken. Not without a judge's order and since Snake was involved, a judge's order was unobtainable.

"Then I'll do what he says," I told Captain Kim. "Quickly. And then I'll present him with what I've found. Then I'll make my move."

"When people fighting," Captain Kim said, "I don't need judge."

He meant that if there was an altercation at Snake's mansion, or anywhere else in Itaewon, he could order his cops to move in without a search warrant.

A great boxer works best in close. He can lean in on his opponent and hammer him with hooks and methodically batter his ribs and his torso. But in order to get in close, I had to offer Snake something he wanted, the identity of the people who'd murdered Horsehead and Water Doggy, or at least some sort of credible evidence pointing in that direction.

And Captain Kim, in his own oblique way, was offering to help. Or at least I hoped he was.

* * *

Ernie's jeep purred down the two-lane highway lined on either side with frost-covered rice paddies. Kids in black school uniforms skated on patches of water frozen between ancient mud berms. In the distance, straw-thatched farmhouses, smoke rising from narrow chimneys, stood in cozy clumps. Behind them rows of hills rose blue in the distance, capped with white, everything shrouded in a shawl of gray mist.

"Why don't we just check out a couple of shotguns from the arms room?" Ernie asked. "Then we kick Snake's door in, shove both barrels up his nose, and let him know we mean business instead of going to all this trouble."

I'd already thought of that option and I'd rejected it. First, it would be a pretty difficult door to kick in. His home was situated atop a row of hills between Itaewon and the gently flowing Han River. There were mansions up there, all of them surrounded by ten-foot-high granite walls topped with shards of broken glass embedded in mortar. In addition to those routine security precautions, Snake also had a small army protecting his household. So kicking his door in, as Ernie suggested, would require the backup of your average-sized infantry battalion. I didn't even bother to float the idea past the provost marshal. I knew what he'd say: The alleged kidnapping of one Korean national by another Korean national was clearly a problem for the Korean National Police. Who would he refer the information to? Lieutenant Pong, the KNP liaison officer at 8th Army, one of the men who, I suspected, was involved in the power struggle now playing itself out in the barrooms and back alleys of Itaewon. And the man who still hoped to charge Ernie and me with the murder of Two Bellies.

We were some twenty-five miles due east of Seoul now, heading for a mountain called Yongmun-san. Ernie downshifted through a patch of black ice. Either side of the road was lined with country folk waiting at the first bus stop we'd seen in over a mile. Some of the women balanced bundles of laundry atop their heads, others carried packages wrapped in red bandannas. The men wore sports coats without ties or, if they were older, the traditional silk vest and pantaloons of a retired Korean scholar, although I doubted there were many scholars out here. Everyone worked on the land.

I pulled an old map out of one of the folders in the SIR. It was dated September 24, 1952, issued by the Army Corps of Engineers, and stamped FOR OFFICIAL USE ONLY. An inverted swastika, the symbol for a Buddhist temple, was stenciled in blue ink on the side of Yongmun Mountain. In the past twenty years, the mountain hadn't changed, neither had the location of the Temple of Constant Truth, but the roads had altered considerably. Where there had been none, two-lane highways ran; where there had been only a dashed line on the map twenty years ago, indicating a gravel-topped path, there was now a modern four-lane paved thoroughfare. U.S. tax dollars at work so men and equipment could be quickly transported where needed in case of a resumed attack on the Republic of Korea by the forces of the Communist North.

It took a few wrong turns and a lot of questions shouted at startled farmers before Ernie and I found the narrow road that wound up the side of Yongmun Mountain to the nunnery. About halfway up to the craggy peak, we came to a halt in front of a walled fortress that seemed to have been transported here from out of the middle ages. Crows fluttered amongst stone ramparts. A wooden-slat bridge crossed a gully through which a half-frozen stream trickled and beyond that loomed a gate hewn from oak. Both massive doors stood wide open.

"A castle with a moat," Ernie said, climbing out of the jeep.

I imagined that twenty years ago, to a band of frightened and half-starved orphans, this nunnery must've looked like a fairy castle. We waited out front, at the edge of the bridge, until finally someone came out to greet us. She was a shriveled Buddhist nun, bald, wrapped in gray robes. She bowed to us and I bowed back and then I told her in Korean about the orphans who'd come here twenty years ago and about Cort and about the reason we'd come.

When I finished my long speech in my rudimentary Korean, the wrinkled woman stared at me calmly and said in English, "Why don't you come in and have a cup of tea?"

Ernie and I glanced at one another, grinned, and accepted gladly.

* * *

During and after the Korean War, hundreds of thousands, maybe millions, of Korean orphans were adopted by families overseas. Even years after the war the practice was still going on. Unwanted children were left at the doorsteps of churches or temples, transferred to adoption agencies, and sent overseas to grow up speaking English or Dutch or German or French. But the old nun told us that they had kept the children who'd been dumped on their doorstep after the Itaewon Massacre and raised them right here at the Temple of the Constant Truth, raised them as Koreans and sent them to the public school in the village in the valley below Yongmun Mountain. And when they'd come of age, they'd been told the full story of how they'd been brought to the nunnery. Of course, some of them had been old enough at the time to remember but some had to be schooled as to what had happened to their parents.

The nuns had taught them not to be angry, that when you resent the actions of others, they own you; they own the most important part of you, your soul. But if you eliminate need, especially the need for revenge, then you are free. At least that's what I think she told them. When she explained it to us over tea, Ernie and I had some trouble following her. Not only was the Buddhist philosophy itself hard to follow but she spoke English with the perfect syntax of a woman who'd been highly educated in the language but hadn't had the opportunity to actually speak it in years, if not decades. Still, throughout the entire dissertation, Ernie and I sipped on our tea and smiled and nodded our heads.

Ernie wanted to know where those orphans were now. Did she have a list of names? he asked. She did. She had a few current addresses, those of the ones who wrote occasionally. The children had left, found jobs, married, and started families of their own.

"Did any of them stay here?" I asked.

The nun shook her head sadly. None.

Staring at the damp gray walls that surrounded us, that didn't seem surprising.

We told the nun about the murders. She seemed shocked. It seemed to me that some of the children might have wanted to take revenge despite the nuns' instructions. How could they stand by and watch the Seven Dragons strut around Seoul as rich men, knowing that they'd robbed and murdered their parents.

The nun had pulled out a photo and presented it to me with a flourish. It had taken me a moment to focus. It showed two adults. One a handsome Korean woman with high cheekbones and a square face, wearing a long Western-style dress. But what shocked me was the man standing next to her. I recognized the old uniform: khaki pants, short fatigue jacket, overseas cap cocked to the side, curly brown hair that would nowadays be too long for a regulation army haircut. The rank insignia on the sleeve was for technical sergeant but the lettering on the name tag was too small to read. I studied the photo for a while.

"Mori Di," the nun said.

"This is him?" I'd handed the photo to Ernie. The nun nodded her head. "How'd you get it?" I asked.

"One of the children bring," she said.

"Mori Di had a child?"

"No." The nun shook her bald head vehemently. "The child was the daughter of this woman." She pointed to the woman standing next to Technical Sergeant Flo Moretti. "Her daddy Korean, already dead in war."

"So her mom moved in with Moretti," I said.

The nun nodded her head. "And when Moretti was killed, this woman was probably killed also and her daughter kept this photograph and brought it here with her."

"Yes."

The nun showed me on the list the name of the little girl who'd brought the photo of Mori Di. Min-ju was her name. Family name Shin. She'd been about ten years old when she'd arrived and after middle school, she'd been sent to Seoul to complete her education.

"Do you have her current address?"

"No. After she leave, she never write."

Ernie handed the photo back to the nun. "Why did she leave this photograph here?" he asked. "She couldn't have too many photos of her mom."

"She tough woman," the nun told us. "She and her mom. That's why her mom not afraid to live with American G.I. even though everybody talk, call her bad name. She did it to save her daughter. And when Min-ju leave, she say she don't want nothing from the past. She only want future."

I resisted, because it seemed like such a precious heirloom, but before we left, the nun forced me to take the photo of Mori Di and his *yobo*. "Maybe you need," she told me.

I thanked her and slid the photo into my pocket.

We bowed to the nun and were heading back to the jeep when she stopped us and said, "You no see?"

"See?" Ernie asked.

"Him." The nun pointed through the gray mist and at first I thought she was pointing toward heaven. But then I realized that there was a bend in the road that continued up the mountain and on a granite outcropping overlooking a precipice, about three quarters of a mile above us as the crow flies, sat another Buddhist temple.

"Why two temples?" Ernie asked.

"Monks," the nun replied.

That's where the boys lived.

We asked her who it was we were supposed to see but she wouldn't answer. She just kept pointing, indicating that we should go there first before leaving Yongmun Mountain. When we finally complied and climbed in the jeep and Ernie started up the engine, the nun bowed deeply as we drove off and then stood and waved, American style.

It was quiet up here. Darker, too, because we were now on the shadowy side of Yongmun Mountain. The crows didn't flutter between ramparts but sat perched on brick ledges, staring down at us, wondering just as much as we were what the hell we were doing here. There was no movement inside the compound of wooden buildings; no gongs sounding; no chanting of ancient prayers; no susurrant sweeping of gravel courtyards, none of the noises that one would associate with a Buddhist monastery. But when I thought about it, maybe silence was the correct sound for a Buddhist monastery. The sound of people keeping quiet while they waited patiently, forever if necessary, to hear—just once—the lonely voice of god.

Ernie shifted his weight in the driver's seat of the jeep, crossed his arms, and frowned. He didn't like waiting any more than I did but we both figured that someone would come out to talk to us sooner or later.

It was sooner.

A thin monk hustled toward us, his blue robe flapping in the mountain breeze, leather sandals slapping on dirt.

"Irriwa," he said. Come.

We both hopped out of the jeep and followed him up a path that led toward a ridge on the northern side of the temple. Once we topped the ridge the monk stopped and pointed. There, in the distance, was a work shed and a storage area for grain and agricultural equipment. Men in broad straw hats worked amongst fields, not harvesting anything now in the middle of winter but puttering about near cylindrical greenhouses made of bamboo and plastic.

The monk, who I could see now was a very young man, pointed toward the shed and said, *"Chogi. Kidarriyo."* There. Wait.

He left us. Ernie and I glanced at one another, shrugged, and walked down the frozen pathway toward the shed. The accommodations weren't much. Just a couple of rough hewn benches. We sat, pulled our jackets tighter around our torsos and waited. For what I wasn't sure. The bald-headed nun had said we would want to talk to "him." A man. Who the man was I couldn't be sure. Probably the patriarch of this temple complex. Maybe he had more information for us. More likely, he just wanted to check us out and make sure we weren't going to cause him any headaches. Either way, Ernie and I resigned ourselves to waiting.

Of course, Ernie shouldn't have been here at all. Colonel Brace had ordered him restricted to compound. Staff Sergeant Riley wouldn't rat us out unless he was asked a direct question. And it was at least possible that Ernie and I could make it back to Seoul, and Ernie could resume his normal duties, before either the first sergeant or Colonel Brace noticed he was missing. Unlikely, but possible.

Still, if the provost marshal did find out that Ernie had violated his orders, I would say that for safety reasons I'd needed Ernie's backup. It's against 8th Army policy to come so far away from Seoul, so far from American MP protection, without backup. And I would say that due to the immediacy of the requirement I didn't have time to request someone else. Ernie was available, I used him. The ploy wouldn't work, of course. The provost marshal wouldn't buy it and we'd both be in hot water but at least it was some sort of excuse we could hang on to. But Ernie wasn't complaining. He knew that finding Moretti's remains and solving this twenty-year-old mystery was more important than any temporary discomfort we might suffer. And anyway we were used to being in hot water. We'd bathed in that tub before, so often our skin was wrinkled.

Dozens of tiny feet beat on dirt. Reedy voices bleated. Over a low ridge, furry creatures stampeded our way. Goats. Tiny ones. Cute, with little horns, like the small porcelain bulls they used to sell at curio shops in East L.A. But these hoofed animals were alive and covered with shaggy black fur. They floated toward us like a moving blanket. We stood and then a straw hat appeared over the ridge and beneath the hat, a man. He was tall, long-legged, gawky. His face was still in shadow but as he came toward us he waved a ten-foot-long staff back and forth in the air, gently tapping the tiny goats on their sides and hindquarters, keeping them moving forward in a loose formation. He reached a low fenced area twenty yards from the shed where we were waiting, opened the gate, and herded his charges inside. Once the last reluctant kid was induced to enter the pen, he latched it shut, and stood for a moment staring down at the ground, as if in prayer. Then he roused himself from his reverie and started toward us.

As he did so, the shadows lifted from his face. Gross features emerged. A long nose, full lips, bronze-fleshed cheeks that had to be shaved every day. Finally, Ernie and I were staring into a pair of deep-set blue eyes surrounded by a map of wrinkles. They were intelligent eyes, knowing, watchful.

I knew who he was.

"Cort," I said, stepping forward and holding out my hand.

16

Cort seemed unsurprised to see us. Although I couldn't say the same about Ernie and me, I realized now what had happened. Who was it who had told me earlier in the investigation that Cort never left? Whoever it was, they'd been right. Occasionally a G.I. will terminate his time in the service but not return to the States. It takes special permission from the military and, of course, the G.I. must obtain a passport from the State Department and some sort of visa from the host government. But if he accomplishes all that, he is not required to take the "Freedom Bird" back to the good old U.S.A. He can stay right here in Korea.

Apparently, that's what Cort had done.

And how had he made a living all these years? He'd become a monk.

Cort set his ten-foot staff aside, sat down on the wooden bench opposite us, and pulled off his straw hat. He was totally bald. And although his body looked strong, he was rail thin, probably from years of living on unhusked rice and fermented cabbage and boiled bean curd. He stared at us, a slightly amused smile on his lips, and then he said, "Tell me everything."

I started from the beginning, leaving nothing out. Cort listened patiently without interrupting. So patiently that I wondered if he was actually concentrating on what I was saying. There was a far-away look in his eye, a relaxed posture to his body, and a steady rhythm to his breathing. He was meditating, I finally realized. Something he probably did three or four times a day here.

I told Cort about my trip to Auntie Mee's home and her complaints about the spirit of Mori Di and her prediction about the fate of Miss Kwon if the bones weren't found soon. And then I told him about the new SIR warehouse on Yongsan compound and finding Moretti's Serious Incident Report and about everything that had happened since then: the murder of Two Bellies, the murder of Horsehead, the silken rope enveloping Auntie Mee's throat, and the chopped-up corpse of Water Doggy.

When I was through, Cort became alert and started asking questions. He picked apart our entire investigation. He trusted no one and questioned every assumption.

Ernie finally became angry. "You weren't there," he told Cort. "Why're you putting down everything my partner says?"

"Not putting it down," Cort replied. "Only plunging in. Searching for the deeper meaning."

Ernie snorted. "Snake offed Mori Di when he was first taking over Itaewon and to cover up his crime, twenty years later he murders Two Bellies and then Auntie Mee. A few of these orphans, meanwhile, take their revenge on Horsehead and Water Doggy. That's all there is to it."

"Maybe," Cort replied.

"No 'maybe' about it."

I knew what Ernie was doing. He was deliberately trying to throw Cort off stride and make him angry. Maybe in his anger he'd reveal something that he wouldn't otherwise disclose. But Cort remained calm. Maybe it was his Buddhist training, or the years of patiently herding goats on the side of Yongmun. If anything, he seemed vaguely amused.

Cort asked us if we'd interviewed every orphan on the list. "They

have a motive for murder," Cort agreed. We told him that there wasn't
time. He insisted that we should. He was certain that by interviewing
these people, putting pressure on them, leads would open up.

I told him again about Doc Yong and I explained that we didn't
have the time to track these people down and coax information out
of them.

Cort said, "Snake could cause much harm to the people on
that list."

"Yes," I said. "But I'll have to deal with that later, after Doc Yong
is free."

Cort asked if I'd looked at this case from a Buddhist perspective.
I said I hadn't. Cort explained that bricking up Moretti, while he was
still alive, was a very Buddhist thing to do. Not sanctioned by their
religious precepts, of course. But they're taught not to spill blood.
Butchers, for example, are looked down upon, eating meat is dis-
couraged, and a Buddhist criminal who wanted to rid himself of a
G.I. named Moretti might very well leave him gagged and bound in
a small room and then brick him up, alive, and leave him to die. That
way, there'd be no blood on his hands to stain his karma.

Ernie and I stared at Cort as if he were nuts. Maybe he'd been
here too long. But on the other hand, maybe he was right. A devout
Buddhist criminal was a possibility I hadn't considered.

"That would corroborate what you've already assumed," Cort
said. "That Snake or his thugs also murdered the woman you call
Auntie Mee. A very Buddhist type of killing. But it wouldn't explain
the murder of Two Bellies."

"Maybe they were in a hurry," Ernie said.

Cort looked at Ernie, who sat quiet and grim, and then back at
me. He said, "Try not to kill. You'll set yourselves back. That would
delay you from finally attaining nirvana."

Ernie rolled his eyes.

"You don't agree?" Cort asked.

"I attain nirvana," Ernie said, "almost every Saturday night."

As Ernie drove the jeep back to Seoul, I kept glancing at the photograph of the handsome Korean woman standing proudly beside

Moretti. The more I stared at her face—the high cheekbones, the full lips, the penetrating gaze—the more I was infatuated with her looks. Was she the reason Moretti had thrown in his lot with the impoverished refugees flooding into Itaewon? What had become of her? Maybe she was still alive somewhere, walking around, waiting for Ernie and me to find her and ask her the questions that she'd been longing to answer for twenty years.

I sat in the passenger's seat, comparing the family names on Mori Di's list of people who'd turned over heirlooms to the nun's list of orphans. Except for three, all the family names were the same. Only a half dozen of the thirty-six names were accompanied by addresses. Some of the addresses were fairly old, the nun had warned us, so they might not still be valid.

Modern Korea is a highly mobile society. People move from job to job and apartment to apartment. No longer is it a kingdom of villages where farm families can trace their roots back to before the founding of the Yi Dynasty. Two of the addresses were in Seoul, the other four were scattered down in the southern end of the country. I didn't see how we'd have time to talk to these people. Or for that matter, what good it would do? Two men and three women might be responsible for murdering Horsehead and Water Doggy, and they might be on this list. Finding them would be faster if I turned the lists over to Snake and let him and his people figure out if they were the killers. The problem was that the Seven Dragons might make a mistake. And they wouldn't be gentle in their investigation. Innocent people could get hurt. But what choice did I have? Doc Yong was being held hostage I needed this information to get close to Snake. Once on the inside, Ernie and I would attack. Our backup? Captain Kim.

Ernie crossed a ridge and the city of Seoul lay spread before us.

Far on the other side of the valley, beyond a range of hills, a red sun set slowly into the Yellow Sea. Seoul itself was bathed in a darkening blue light. Streetlights twinkled on, as did lamps in the windows of hotels and high rises downtown. And then, more abundantly, millions of small lights in homes and storefront businesses blinked to life and spread out like a great spangled fan radiating from Namsan Mountain in the middle of the shining city.

Even Ernie seemed impressed. And excited. Going downhill, he must've been exceeding the speed limit by about twenty kilometers.

A front moved in from the Yellow Sea, sliding over the red-tinged hills in the distance. Clouds of billowing gray enveloped the peaks and crept toward Seoul, like a great angry beast ready to devour everything in its path. Lightning flashed. Thunder cracked. Seoul shuddered beneath the onslaught.

Ernie chuckled to himself as he drove down the narrow highway.

"What's so funny?" I asked.

"Just thinking about somebody."

"Who?"

"Somebody sweet. Somebody I met last night."

"On compound?"

Ernie twisted his head slightly and gave me a sly look, as if to say, "Are you out of your mind?"

"You went off compound last night," I said.

Ernie shrugged and then smiled again. "Not to Itaewon," he told me. "I knew the place would be crawling with MP patrols."

It was.

"But I got to thinking about Jessica Tidwell."

Oh, oh. That's when I started holding my breath.

"I got to thinking," Ernie continued, "about the deal that Paco Bernal had set up. He had to be working with somebody powerful to come up with a thousand dollars worth of product, no matter what the product was. And then he has Jessica steal the greenbacks from her dad and Paco takes the money out to the ville and the first thing that happens to him is he's robbed."

I nodded. So far we knew all this.

"So I asked myself," Ernie said, "'how often are G.I.s robbed in Itaewon?' Not often. G.I.s might end up with no money but it's usually through trickery, or more often seduction. Not out-and-out robbery. The Koreans don't work that way. Not usually. Of course somebody must've known that Paco had that much money. We've been sort of assuming that he'd flashed the wad to a business girl or he'd bragged about the money to the wrong person but we don't

know for sure that's what happened. And I got to thinking that whoever helped Paco set up the deal in the first place was the most likely
candidate for knowing he had the cash and then sending some thugs
over to take it from him."

Ernie glanced over at me. I nodded and turned my eyes back to
an ox-drawn cart on the side of the highway. At the last moment,
Ernie swerved around it.

"So I thought," Ernie said, "'who's powerful enough to set all this
up?' Obviously, one of the Seven Dragons could pull it off. Which
one? Any of them, but do circumstances point to any one in particular? And then I remembered that it was Horsehead who'd shown up
Johnny-on-the-spot and whisked Jessica Tidwell away from the
White Crane Hotel."

I remembered, all too well.

"So," Ernie said, "I decided to do a little investigating. You
remember Jenny over at the 007 Club?"

I nodded. Ernie was referring to a cocktail waitresses he'd once
spent some time with.

"She works over at the Salon Bar in Myong-dong now so I
jumped in a cab and rode downtown to talk to her," Ernie told me.
"I remembered her telling me once about Horsehead's second wife."

His mistress.

"So I asked her how the second wife was doing now that
Horsehead was dead and Jenny told me that she was still working
over at the Tower Hotel nightclub. So I waved down another cab
and went over there."

During all this travel, Ernie would not have had to worry about
American MPs. They only patrol Itaewon and he was miles from there.

"Her name is Hei-myong," Ernie said, "and she was all teary-eyed
over Horsehead and asked me a lot of details about his death that she
claimed the Korean National Police were withholding information
from her. So I made a lot of stuff up, hoping I'd make her feel better."

I knew that over the next ridge of hills, we'd start to encounter
the heavier traffic leading into Seoul; I hoped Ernie would hurry up
with his story.

"Anyway," Ernie said, "she told me where I could find Jessica
Tidwell."

My jaw dropped. I stared at him.

"You talked to her?"

Ernie grinned and nodded his head.

He kept smiling and I said, "You son of a bitch."

He shrugged, still grinning.

"You didn't do anything you shouldn't, did you?"

Ernie looked offended. "Me?"

"Yeah, you."

"Of course not."

"So what did you do?"

"She had a room in one of those Western-style hotels in Hannam-dong that aren't fancy enough to be called 'tourist hotels' but are a step up from a *yoguan*." I knew the ones he meant; they were used mostly for sexual encounters. "Horsehead had set her up in a room but she was bored and tired of sitting there, and tired of smoking Turtleboat cigarettes." A Korean brand.

"So she was happy to see you?"

"Not hardly. She took the bayonet to me."

The same one Paco had almost killed Ernie with.

"Yeah. After I took it away from her and slapped her a couple of times, she settled down. We talked. She asked if I had any word on Paco and I told her that, as far as I knew, his condition hadn't changed since she'd made her visit to the 121." I waited while Ernie savored the memory. "So after letting her rant for a while, about you not having to shoot him and all, I told her she was under arrest."

"How'd she take it?"

"I reached around to lock a handcuff on one of her wrists but she stood up and turned toward me and leaned into me and then she started crying." Ernie shrugged. "You know, I sort of felt sorry for the kid and she was leaning into me and pressing her face against my chest and then she started breathing on my neck and . . ."

"You got a hard-on."

Ernie shrugged.

"She's just a kid," I told him. "Seventeen years old. Didn't your conscience bother you?"

"Seventeen years old but built like she's twenty-five. Even Jiminy Cricket would've had a woody."

"Oh, shit, Ernie," I said. "Statutory rape. Are you out of your mind?"

"I was at the time," he said, "until she was kind enough to bring me back to my senses."

"How'd she do that?"

"You're not going to tell anybody, are you?" Ernie was more embarrassed about whatever he was preparing to tell me than he was about admitting that he was fully prepared to have sexual relations with a minor.

"I won't tell anybody," I told him.

Ernie turned away, took a deep breath, and said, "She kneed me in the balls."

I groaned. "And while you were bent over, holding onto yourself, she ran."

"And a lot faster than I would've expected."

"She took the bayonet with her?"

"That and her purse. I think she had it all planned from the minute I walked in the door."

Back in Itaewon, Ernie and I didn't seek out Jimmy Pak right away. And we didn't leave word with the manager of the Seven Club or do any of the things that one would normally do when *requesting* an audience with Snake. At the Itaewon Police Station, Captain Kim was out but I wrote a short note in English, folded it over two times and left it with the desk sergeant. All I wrote was the day, the time, my name and *Going to see Snake.*

The desk sergeant took the note but he was distracted, ordering his cops to pull candles and flashlights and batteries out of the storage bin, expecting the usual power outage that strikes so often in Seoul during a sudden storm. I hoped he'd remember to give the note to Captain Kim. I had to believe he would. Then, we drove directly to Snake's home.

Snow was falling steadily now and Ernie had to bulldoze a three-foot-high drift out of the way to make a parking space next to the big stone walls in front of Snake's mansion. He waited in the jeep, alert.

I stood beneath the stone arch in the recessed entranceway, out of the way of the ice-laced wind, and buzzed the bell of the intercom repeatedly. No answer. Finally, I started kicking the bottom of the wooden gate. Ernie climbed out of the jeep and walked over.

"Nobody's home," he said.

Just then the intercom buzzed. A voice said. *"Nugu syo?"* Who is it.

"Sueño," I said. "Here to see Snake. Important. You *alla?* I have to see him *now!"*

The intercom buzzed off.

Ernie studied me, a little shocked by my impatience but I was thinking of Doc Yong. I hoped that Snake's taunts about her being subject to a lot of "boom-boom" were just that—taunts and nothing more. It was even possible that they didn't have her. Maybe she had left town for some reason of her own or they had frightened her away. I had to assume the worst until I knew for sure that she was OK.

Snake wouldn't risk hurting Ernie and me ordinarily. The 8th United States Army was his bread and butter. He wouldn't do anything to piss them off. Not unless he thought he could get away with it, that is. But at the moment no one at 8th Army knew we were here. In fact, we weren't supposed to be here. Snake might risk taking us out. After all, he had offed Moretti. But that had been a long time ago, before Snake became rich and controlled a myriad of business interests. Corruption had imposed certain rules, the purpose of which was to make the rich richer and the poor poorer. I was still hoping Snake would honor our deal. If he didn't, Ernie and I were armed and ready to fight.

As for the murder of Two Bellies and Auntie Mee, and locating the bones of Moretti, first things first. After I'd freed Doc Yong, I'd think about the next problem.

The door creaked open.

Ernie and I walked in.

Snake was wearing a papa-san outfit: turquoise blue silk vest, billowing white pantaloons tapered at the ankle, white socks, and slippers. He held a long-stemmed pipe to his mouth.

"Welcome," he said, smiling. "Sit, sit."

Snake pointed to a hand-carved mahogany divan with embroidered cushions. We were in a large traditional room whose floor was covered with tatami mats. In the corner a bronze Buddha was enshrined in front of paintings of silk-robed goddesses floating through billowing clouds and star-filled skies. Everything in the room—celadon vases, porcelain jars, bronze incense burners—appeared to be an antique and signified Snake's Buddhist faith. Ernie slapped snow off the shoulders of his jacket and stomped his feet. He didn't like the place. We both ignored Snake's invitation to sit.

"Where is she?" I asked.

Snake puffed on his pipe, still smiling, and a cloud of tobacco smoke floated in front of him. "First," he said. "What you got?"

"A list," I said, "right out of Cort's Serious Incident Report, of the families that left valuables with Moretti for safekeeping. And I've compared it with another list of every orphan that was taken from Itaewon after Moretti's murder."

As I said the word *murder* I stared into Snake's eyes, searching for a reaction. What I found was an amused smile. I continued.

"According to the Buddhist nuns at the Temple of Constant Truth, all of the children stayed here in Korea. None of them were adopted overseas. The list the nuns gave me is almost identical to Cort's. Only a few names differ."

I handed the copies to Snake. He shuffled through them.

"A lot of people here," he said. "So which one kill Horsehead? Which one kill Water Doggy?"

"There were two men," I said, "and three women. It figures that their names are on that list."

"But which ones? And where are they now? How I find up?"

I shrugged. "Send your boys out." There were about a dozen of them standing in the foyer behind us. "Put them to work instead of letting them stand around with their thumbs up their ass."

Ernie pulled a stick of ginseng gum out of his pocket, unwrapped it, and stuck it in his mouth. He chewed slowly and steadily. A sure sign that he was nervous but ready to fight.

"No way," Snake said. "You find up which ones on this list kill Horsehead. *Then* we talk." He handed the list back to me. Ernie tensed.

Slowly, I folded the paperwork and stuck it in my pocket. When my hand came back out of my jacket, I was holding my .45.

Ernie's had appeared in his hand as if by magic. He stepped quickly toward the foyer and trained his pistol on the thugs that were lurking about.

"*Umjiki-jima*," Ernie growled. Don't move.

Sometimes, when he has to, Ernie speaks enough Korean to surprise me.

"Where you think you go?" Snake said. "You think you can get away from Snake?

I stood next to him and pressed the business end of the .45 against his temple.

"Now!" I shouted. "Doc Yong. *Bali bali!*" Quickly.

Snake glanced at his men and nodded. One of them stepped forward, holding his hands at his side, palms out.

"He show you," Snake said.

"No. Not him. He stays here with Ernie and the rest of them. You show me."

Snake was starting to sweat. Maybe he knew that love can make an American G.I. act irrationally. Maybe he thought I really would shoot him.

I thought so too.

"Move!" I said.

Snake started moving.

Ernie motioned for the thugs to kneel on the floor. They did, still keeping their hands up.

Gun control is absolute in Korea. Only the police and the military are allowed to carry firearms. You could bet that Snake had a few weapons squirreled away somewhere but they were for emergency use only. To be seen carrying one or, worse yet, to use a gun in the commission of a crime would bring the wrath of Korean officialdom down on him. Connections or no, Snake was too smart to risk it. Therefore, for the moment, Ernie and I were holding all the firepower.

Snake and I waltzed down a long corridor lined with oil-papered sliding doors. At the end we turned down a varnished wooden stairwell that creaked beneath our feet. I held his frail left arm firmly in

my grip, keeping the .45 pointed at his head. He was sweating profusely now, and breathing rapidly.

We reached an underground stone-walled corridor that was
lined with barred wooden doors.

"Which one?" I asked.

Snake pointed to the third one down.

We moved down the damp corridor quickly and, still holding the
.45 to his head, I ordered Snake to open the door. He slid back a
metal rod and then pulled on a flat handle. The door creaked open.

Inside, a single naked bulb hung from a wire. There was a small
diesel space heater in the middle of the room and, on either side,
broad wooden benches. On one of them a woman sat. Her hands
were clasped over her knees. She wore blue jeans and sneakers and a
warm woolen jacket. She wore spectacles. Turning her head slowly,
as if disoriented, she gazed at me. And then she struggled to focus, as
if straining to see what stood there in front of her. She didn't smile,
she just stared.

Doc Yong.

"It's me," I said. "Geogi. Come to get you."

She continued to stare.

"Come on," I said. "No time."

Still, she stared. She didn't move. I started talking to her, jabber-
ing simply to try to coax her back to reality. She continued to stare
at us with a blank look on her face.

I shoved Snake against the stone wall. "What the hell did you do
to her?"

He didn't answer. I knew I didn't have much time. More of
Snake's thugs might arrive any minute, more than Ernie could handle.
Or one of the thugs downstairs might try something foolish. We had
to start moving but Doc Yong was immobile.

I pressed the .45 harder up against Snake's skull.

"You walk over to her," I said. "Slowly. You grab her by the arms
and pull her up and out into the corridor. You got that?"

Snake nodded.

"If you try anything, I'll blow that stupid smile off your face. You
alla?"

Snake nodded again.

I let go of his arm. He stepped forward, speaking soothingly to Doc Yong. When he stood next to her he patted her gently on the shoulder and continued to speak to her as if speaking to a child. Finally, he coaxed her to stand up. He patted her on the back as if she'd accomplished something momentous. Then, slipping his arm behind her, he turned her body and started to guide her toward the door.

Maybe I was studying her face too closely. Staring at the smooth complexion and the soft lips and the round tip of her nose. For however long my concentration wandered, it was long enough for Snake to slip his hand inside his blue silk vest and, faster than I could react, the hand was back out and a glimmering steel blade appeared at Doc Yong's throat.

"Freeze!" he said.

I did. But my .45 was still pointed at his head. Unfortunately, his head was mostly hidden behind hers.

"Drop it!" he said.

"Hell no."

"I'll slice her throat."

I gulped. "If you do, I'll blow your freaking head off!"

"Drop it."

"I ain't going to drop it. But I *will* blow your head off. You can count on it, Snake."

He shoved Doc Yong forward and followed her closely. Involuntarily, I stepped back. Shuffling like that, inch by inch—me still holding the .45 pointed at his narrow face and he still pressing the sharp edge of the daggerlike blade up against Doc Yong's throat—the three of us backed out of the small cell. In the hallway, Snake maneuvered himself closest to the stairwell and started inching backwards.

I knew I should shoot him now. If the bullet slammed into his eyeball it would penetrate his brain so fast that he would have no time to react. He wouldn't be able to harm Doc Yong. But if I missed—and .45s were notoriously inaccurate even at close range—he'd fall back and, even if he didn't intend to, he'd slice open Doc Yong's throat. Or worse, what if I missed Snake and hit Doc Yong? These thoughts flashed through my mind as we neared the stairwell. If I didn't stop him now Snake would start backing up the steps. He might cut Doc Yong and run. It was here I had to take him down. Now!

The .45 quivered in my grip. The barrel was aimed right at Snake but, involuntarily, the barrel bounced and pointed at Doc Yong.

She had become alert, and terrified, realizing now that her life was in danger.

I aimed the .45 and started to squeeze.

A huge bang lit up the world, so bright that I was blinded. Doc Yong screamed. So did I, I think. The electrical wires in the corridor sparked and then, as quickly as it had come, the bright light disappeared. I was still blinded. Seconds passed, no one moving, but then I heard thunder and when I opened my eyes again, everything was pitch black.

Upstairs, footsteps pounded and then I heard more screams and shots being fired. Ernie. At the same time, the stairwell creaked as someone ran up the ancient wooden steps.

I realized what must have happened. The eye of the Manchurian storm now hovered over Itaewon. Lightning had struck and the electricity in Snake's mansion had gone out.

I crouched and, with my free hand, touched the brick floor beneath me, orienting myself. Snake had fled. That meant that Doc Yong was still here.

"Yong-a," I said, calling her name. "Na yo." It's me.

No reply. The footsteps upstairs were treading every which way. Men were shouting. Glass, or porcelain was shattered. Men cursed in Korean. Someone shouted for lights.

I crawled forward, sweeping in front of me with my free hand, searching for her.

I touched something. A foot I think. Someone screeched and then a fist hit me on the side of my head. It was a small fist and it didn't hurt much. It told me where she was. I lunged forward, felt her arms, and then we were grappling with one another in the dark. I enveloped her in my arms. She struggled until she realized who I was. I lay atop her. Her arms found the back of my neck and hugged tightly.

She was safe. For the moment anyway.

17

A beam of light searched down the stairwell.

"Sueño? You down there?"

"Down here," I said.

"We have to un-ass the area, immediately if not sooner."

"Was it lightning?" I asked.

"Must be. Electricity's out in the whole area. Those assholes are regrouping out there. I heard them use the word *chung*." Gun.

Doc Yong would have a solid charge to file against Snake: false imprisonment, kidnapping, maybe worse. Snake couldn't allow that to happen. And the perfect time to make sure that it didn't happen was in the middle of the night while a Manchurian storm raged and the electricity was out in the entire village of Itaewon.

I listened for sirens. Nothing. No sign of Captain Kim and the Korean National Police. What with a power outage and a snowstorm, their hands were full. If Captain Kim came to check on Ernie and me, it would be too late.

Doc Yong was already moving toward the light. Ernie shifted the beam of the flashlight and we climbed the stairs to the first floor of Snake's mansion. Outside, more flashlights cast harsh rays on window panes. Shadows moved stealthily, whispering instructions to one another.

"This way," Ernie said.

We scurried through a kitchen. At the back door, Ernie paused, listened, and then unlatched the door and pushed it open. Someone shouted.

"Shit," Ernie said and relocked the door.

"Come on," I said. I had an idea.

The three of us hurried back into the house. I led Doc Yong and Ernie upstairs.

The house itself was two stories tall, with balconies, and on the east side of the building was a garage, the kind the Koreans build, a small cement-block enclosure, barely large enough to contain a car, with a metal pull-down grating in front that can be securely locked. No flimsy wooden outbuildings as found in the States. In Korea, cars are valuable commodities and their owners don't want them either stolen or exposed to the elements.

Attached to the garage was a party wall shared with Snake's neighbor. If we could make it there, unseen, we could escape. If we had to, Ernie and I could shoot it out with Snake and his boys. We were both armed but I hoped to avoid that type of bloodshed. There was no guarantee that Ernie and I would get the better of the exchange and I had Doc Yong's safety to think about.

Sneaking away seemed to be the best policy.

I climbed out of a bedroom window and onto the roof of the garage. I stayed low and moved toward the back of the mansion. There, where the neighbor's wall ended, was a ten-foot drop into a cul-de-sac surrounded by more granite walls. Snake and his boys would be cut off from us. I waved at Ernie to follow. He sent Doc Yong first. When she was halfway across the roof of the garage, Ernie climbed out after her. Then we heard a shot.

Ernie's military training had stood him in good stead during two tours in Vietnam and it stood him in good stead now. He flattened himself and as he did so a second gunshot erupted from the front of

Snake's mansion. The round winged through the air just a few feet above Ernie's head. He low-crawled across the roof.

I jumped down into the cul-de-sac first, then helped Doc Yong. Ernie followed. From the shouts in front of Snake's mansion, his men had realized where we'd gone. In seconds they'd be scurrying through connecting pathways, trying to cut us off.

We ran.

Itaewon is a maze of pedestrian walkways. All the twists and turns and dead ends and curving paths doubling back on themselves would baffle an Apache tracker, especially on a dark night with snow falling. But Ernie had a general rule: head toward booze. That is, keep yourself oriented on the two- and three-story buildings that rise along the edge of the strip that is the beating heart of the night-club district of Itaewon. The neon was not blinking because of the lateness of the hour—and the electricity outage. And the night sky with its overhanging snow clouds was pitch black. Only the occasional flicker from indoor candlelight or the flame of a charcoal stove illuminated a small portion of the world. Despite these handicaps, Ernie somehow kept us oriented. The pathways were covered with slippery snow as were the rooftops and the ledges and the windowsills and since it was past the midnight curfew not a soul was on the streets except us. Even the white mice seemed to have hunkered down in their barracks for the night. Occasionally, we stopped and listened. Muffled shouts. Footsteps tromping on ice. Snake and his gaggle of fledgling Dragons were still following.

Finally, an alley we were traversing emerged onto the main drag just north of the King Club. Ernie peered around the corner. Then he leaned back toward me and whispered, "Looks like it's all clear."

"Let's hope," I said.

"Where to now?" Ernie asked.

The only place of safety I could think of was the Itaewon Police Station.

Ernie nodded. "It's a long straight run. They might've stationed some of their boys in the alleys off to the side, figuring we'd come this way."

"We'll have to chance it," I said.

Doc Yong tugged at my sleeve. I turned to look at her and in the darkness I could barely make out the smooth features of her face. I leaned closer until our noses touched.

"Across the street," she said. "Someone's waving."

I turned and studied the area she'd indicated. Rotating my head, using my peripheral vision, I finally saw it. Movement. And then I realized it was someone's hand, waving back and forth, trying to catch our attention while being careful to stay out of sight from the main street.

Ernie followed my gaze. "Who is it?"

I shook my head. I didn't know.

Doc Yong stepped between us and said, "Miss Kwon. She's trying to lead us to safety."

"Her?" I asked. "What's she doing out so late?"

"People must've seen your jeep entering Itaewon," Doc Yong said. "Word spread. Someone told her you were back. She knew you were probably looking for me so she's been standing here, waiting to help."

True dedication to Doc Yong. No time to discuss that now.

"I'll go first," Ernie said. "You two follow, if I don't get shot."

"No," I said. "I'll go first."

"Not a chance." Ernie dropped to the ground and low-crawled into the street. He moved amazingly fast, like a serpent slithering across tile. Seconds later, he was standing next to Miss Kwon, beckoning for us to follow.

I told Doc Yong that speed was more important than keeping a low profile so, instead of trying to crawl like Ernie, she darted across the ice-covered main drag of Itaewon in a crouch. I held my .45, ready to return fire if anyone took a potshot at her. No one did.

I was next and I sprinted at top speed across the road figuring that quickness and the element of surprise would keep me safe.

With her single crutch propped beneath her arm, Miss Kwon bowed to Doc Yong. Then, without a word, she turned and hobbled off into the dark maze, leading the way.

* * *

Ernie sensed it before I did. Footsteps behind us. Miss Kwon was moving faster now—one step and a thump, one step and a thump. We were still following a long, seemingly endless footpath.

Behind us, urgent speaking. Men's voices. Then footsteps, picking up speed.

"Bali," Miss Kwon said. She broke into a more rapid step, thump, step, thump.

We trotted forward, moving as fast as we could but our progress was impeded by Miss Kwon. Doc Yong stayed beside her, holding her arm, letting me know that there was no way we were going to leave Miss Kwon behind.

The footsteps were gaining.

Ernie turned, pulled his .45 and said, "You go on ahead. I'll hold them off."

"No. Come on. We'll make a turn up here and lose them," I said.

"There," Ernie said, pointing to an overturned handcart. It blocked most of the open space at an intersection of two narrow pedestrian pathways. Ernie crouched behind it. Looking back, he had an unimpeded line of sight of about ten yards. In the middle of the ten yards another extremely narrow alley—just a fissure between buildings—ran off on one side of the pathway. It was unlikely that Snake's boys would find cover there.

"When they round the corner," Ernie said, "I'll fire over their heads. That'll give you guys time to get away. Then while they're hiding and trying to figure out what to do, I'll sneak off after you."

"OK," I said, "but remember, only fire over their heads."

"Don't sweat the small stuff, Sueño. Where will I meet you?"

It would be impossible to reach the Itaewon Police Station. They expected us to head there and they'd have plenty of men, and firepower, waiting for us. I was still thinking this over when Miss Kwon piped up.

"Itaewon Market," she said. "I know good place."

"Where?" Ernie asked.

"No sweat. We hide. Warm place. Wait till sun come out."

Footsteps crunched on ice. We turned. Doc Yong dragged Miss Kwon off into the shadows. Two shadows emerged from around the corner ten yards away as Ernie and I crouched behind the handcart. More shadows joined the lead two and, like a phalanx of ancient warriors, the men marched down the narrow pathway.

Ernie leveled his .45 at them.

"Higher," I said.

The barrel didn't move. The men continued down the pathway. Ernie's fist tightened. Just as the gang of thugs reached the halfway mark, another shadow emerged from the fissure between the buildings on the other side of the road. It was huge, like a tall stick figure, and something long and dark swung in a wicked arc. The *thump* was so loud I felt it rather than heard it. The first two shadows at the head of the formation crumpled to the ground. Then the stick swung again and another *thump* ensued, and then another.

The formation backed up around the corner, away from us. The stick figure ran toward us, rod upraised, like a gangly avenging angel. Ernie pointed the barrel of his .45 right at him. When he was a few feet away I recognized him from the thin, angular shape of his body.

"Cort," I said and Ernie lowered the barrel of his .45.

"How'd you find Miss Kwon?" I asked.

"I've known her a long time," Cort answered.

We sat in a wooden enclosure about ten feet by ten feet and only four feet high. The floor was stained with purple dye and the entire enclosure reeked of lard.

"Pigs' house," is what Miss Kwon called it as she'd led us into the Itaewon Market. We moved through abandoned stalls laden with freshly fallen snow and then beneath canvas overhangs to a tightly packed grouping of wooden counters. We crawled beneath the counters and then through a low wooden door and entered a man-made tunnel that twisted twice before ending in this vile enclosure. The place reeked of flesh and a sheen of ice covered the cement, as if it had been thoroughly washed as the freeze set in.

It didn't take a genius to figure out that this is where the butchers kept their hogs. Outside was a contraption hanging on a crossed wooden peg that looked like a medieval torture device but I knew what it was used for. To hang the hogs by their hind legs while the butcher slit their throats and allowed the blood to drain into a cement sump. I'd walked past here early in the morning on more than one occasion and heard the screams. At first I'd thought the sound was human. And then I realized that it was the last anguished cries of a pig being slaughtered.

Five minutes after our arrival, footsteps approached in our wake. Snow had been falling steadily so it was unlikely that whoever was outside had seen any traces of our arrival. We sat motionless, breathing as little as possible.

The footsteps searched through the market area, paused for a moment, and then two men started chatting in low tones. I couldn't make out what they were saying. Someone lit a cigarette. Then more footsteps as they moved on. We sat for another half hour in the cold, dank slaughterhouse.

No one approached.

Miss Kwon had somehow come up with a single short candle which she lit and stuck in the middle of the floor of this porcine abattoir. Even that tiny amount of heat brought to life the stale odor of pork flesh. It hovered around us, poking fat fingers into twitching nostrils, causing us to cough and wave our hands, as if chasing away the last vestiges of an evil cloud. Then she and Doc Yong left the enclosure.

"Miss Kwon," Cort said, "was one of the orphans. She was brought from Itaewon by the nuns while she was still an infant. On the trip she developed a fever and they thought she would die. Somehow, she pulled through. We've always been proud of her for that. We always knew she was a survivor."

"'We?'" I asked.

"I joined the temple a few months after the Itaewon Massacre. I sometimes helped take care of the kids and grew to love them."

"I thought Buddhist's weren't supposed to love people," I said.

"It's difficult," Cort replied. "Love ties us to this world, making it harder for us to eliminate desire. But it's a powerful force. We try to understand it and thereby, ultimately, conquer it."

The two women reentered the pen. They'd been to find a place to pee.

"How'd you find this hiding place?" I asked Miss Kwon.

She lay down her crutch and squatted awkwardly, keeping her injured leg straight out in front of her.

"Find up," she replied. "Before I work this kind work."

I glanced at Cort.

"During the years after the war," he said, "the nuns were short of money, like everybody. They sent some of the kids to live with foster families. Temporarily for most of them but some of them stayed, especially if the family needed them to work. From the time she was a little girl Miss Kwon was a hard worker. She stayed with a family of butchers. Over time, they became her real family at least emotionally."

These were the people who'd recently told Miss Kwon that they couldn't take her back because they couldn't afford to support her, that she must return to Itaewon and continue to earn money as a hostess in the King Club.

"They aren't Buddhists, right?" I asked "Because they're butchers."

Cort shrugged. "Maybe they are. Probably they are. Not everybody can follow the teachings exactly. People have to live."

Ernie was restless. He crawled outside through the tunnel and returned when he heard noises.

"They already searched the market," he said, "but not thoroughly. They'll be back."

"Not for hours," Cort said. "By then the sun will be up."

We slept as best as we could, on the cold bloody slab.

Maybe an hour later, I awoke with the hot gritty odor of smoke shoving up my nostrils. I was dreaming of a barbecue in East L.A., after someone had slaughtered a goat. But then I realized that the smoke was real and it was all around me.

"Fire!" I shouted, reaching in the darkness for Doc Yong. At first my open palms slapped only flat cement. But then I hit a shoe and then a shoulder.

Doc Yong sat up.

"Fire. We have to get out of here."

She grabbed Miss Kwon. The three of us started crawling. I wasn't quite sure where Ernie and Cort were. A wall of smoke floated between us and the other side of the abattoir. The tunnel heading toward the back of the butcher shop, away from the counter facing the center of the Itaewon Market, was closer. On all fours, I led the way. Light was no longer a problem. Off to our left, the wooden stand next to the butcher shop was fully ablaze, casting rays of quivering brightness through cracks in the woodwork. I had almost reached the end of the tunnel when a wall of fire, like a flaming blanket, stopped us. I recoiled from the heat. Doc Yong bumped into me.

"What is it, Geogi?" she asked.

"Canvas," I said. "It fell from the roof and it's about to set these wooden walls on fire."

I crawled forward as fast as I could, doing my best to ignore the heat. When I was as close to the burning canvas as I could stand, I turned over, flopped on my butt, and crawled forward feet first, kicking at the burning material. The wooden walls of the tunnel were beginning to smoke now.

"Hurry!" Doc Yong said.

I kicked at the canvas, it bounced away from the soles of my shoes, but then flopped back into place, still blocking our way. I had to have something with which to push it out of our way.

I studied the smoking walls surrounding me. One of the support struts was made of dried wood with a few rusty nails holding it loosely in place. I grabbed it and yanked. It didn't budge. Doc Yong tried to pull at the top of the strip of wood while I worked at the center. Still it didn't move. Miss Kwon cowered, her eyes wide. I saw no other likely loose struts of wood.

Her face streaming with perspiration, Doc Yong reached past me and frantically pulled the strut toward her. I pushed her out of the way. This time I pulled steadily, applying pressure with my foot as I heaved and then ancient metal nails groaned, started to slip, and then released violently.

I wrenched the strut away from the last nail holding it and turning my face away from the heat, I poked the canvas up from the ground a couple of feet,

"Crawl through," I shouted.

The world around us was not only growing brighter with flame but hotter. Breathing was increasingly difficult as clouds of smoke enveloped us. They both crawled forward, Doc Yong first. Laying flat on her face, she wriggled beneath the burning canvas and beyond it and then Miss Kwon, still holding on to her crutch with her right hand, crawled about halfway through. She paused, exhausted, and just as I was about to reach for her, from the other side of the flames, someone pulled and Miss Kwon's good foot kicked forward and then she was out.

I slid back, away from the burning canvas. I gazed behind me back down the tunnel. Just smoke. It was not possible to go back for Ernie and Cort now. They'd either escaped to the other side or they'd already been overcome by the heat and smoke. I shoved at the flaming material with the stick, and holding it up as high as I could, I crawled under. About halfway through the flaming canvas fell onto my back. I wriggled forward as fast as I could and then I was out and Doc Yong was beating my back with her hands as sparks singed and sputtered against my flesh.

"Come on!" she shouted.

We stood in the center of a wooden warehouse, large enough to hold about four trucks abreast. The walls surrounding us were completely enveloped in flame. Miss Kwon waited near the big double door where, on a normal day, delivery trucks would back in.

I wondered why she didn't open the door and then I realized that it was held shut by a rusty hasp secured by a heavy duty padlock.

Doc Yong grabbed the padlock and pulled, accomplishing nothing, except making the heavy wooden door bounce up and down on its hinges, as if laughing at her. Within seconds, those doors too would be on fire and we'd be trapped. The roof above us was burning now and if it fell we'd never live long enough to see the exit door burn.

"Stand back!" I shouted.

I grabbed the women and roughly shoved them out of the way.

I stepped back a few feet and slammed my heel into the padlock. It shuddered but held. Doc Yong's eyes grew wider. More smoke enveloped us; the roof sizzled. I figured I had one more try.

I backed up a few more feet and tried to remember what I'd been taught in marital arts class. Think through the problem, envision only the solution. I stood with my side facing the padlock. A sidekick is the most powerful kick in the tae kwon do arsenal and I was good at it. Trying to make my mind blank, I hopped toward the door, bringing my foot up and using the momentum of my body and the strength of my muscles to slam into the padlock. The rusty hasp screeched in complaint and then the door burst outwards.

Doc Yong plowed into my back, and she and Miss Kwon and I stumbled into air that was cool and fresh and clean. Then we were on the ground, crawling forward, rolling on the cold frosty earth, laughing, hugging one another, wiping soot and perspiration from one another's faces.

Doc Yong kissed me. I kissed her back.

But my joy was short-lived. Behind us, about twenty yards away in the center of the Itaewon Market, a gun fired.

"Hide!" I told Doc Yong and Miss Kwon. "I'll be back."

Doc Yong tried to hold me but I wrenched myself loose and ran toward the sound of the gunfire.

Ernie fired. And then fired again. He was squatting behind the rim of the old brick well that marked the center of the Itaewon Market. One or two rounds whizzed past us but the light was moving crazily now.

We kept up a steady fusillade of bullets at Snake's men. The fire behind us raged, all the dried canvas and rotted wood that composed the Itaewon Market had gone up faster than even Snake could have imagined. That's what saved us. The abundance of fuel for the flames and therefore the intensity of the heat. Snake's thugs had been forced to retreat in order to save themselves.

I reloaded my .45 and kept firing. I knew Ernie was still on the other side of the well because I heard the steady bark of his pistol as he took aim and popped off rounds. I didn't know where Doc Yong, Miss Kwon, or Cort were. I could only hope they'd sought safety.

Ernie and I dragged ourselves farther from the flames. Sirens wailed in the distance. Strange voices were shouting—people who lived in the area. Then we heard the voices of Korean cops trying to take charge of the situation.

I crawled over to Ernie. His face was black with soot. I grabbed his right arm and held his pistol down.

"Enough," I said. "They're gone."

Ernie glanced around. "What about the others?"

"Not in the fire. Doc Yong and Miss Kwon escaped. They crawled out right behind me. How about Cort?"

"I'm not sure."

As the firemen started dousing the flames and the policemen held back the gathering crowd of neighbors, Ernie and I rose to our feet. I trotted out back behind the burning remains of the butcher shop. I searched for a few minutes but found no sign of Cort. I returned to the well. Ernie was waiting for me.

"They're gone," I said. "Miss Kwon, Doc Yong, Cort. I can't find them."

Ernie spit on the ground. "They have a reason to run."

"What do you mean?"

"Come on, Sueño. Come off it. You're not so blind with love for Doctor Yong In-ja that you can't see what's right in front of you."

"What do you *mean*?"

"I mean the reason she took you to see that fortune teller. The reason she convinced you to look for Mori Di's bones. The reason she sicced Miss Kwon on us through every minute of this investigation."

I was becoming angry and I stepped toward him, my .45 still hanging at my side.

"Spit it out, Bascom. What the hell are you talking about?"

"She *used* you. To get at Snake. Don't you see? Miss Kwon's one of the orphans of the Itaewon Massacre. So are the people who hacked Horsehead and Water Doggy to death. And so is Doc Yong!"

I hit him.

It was a straight left, right to the nose and Criminal Investigation Division Agent Ernie Bascom reeled backwards like a man being pulled by a rope. He collapsed against a pile of smoldering lumber. When I smelt burning, I leaned down and rolled him away. One of the firemen doused him with water. Sputtering, Ernie rose to his knees, shook his head for a moment, took a weak swing at me, and then collapsed back to the ground.

I used a thin screwdriver to pop the front lock to Doc Yong's medical clinic. My search was systematic, thorough, in accordance with my police training. It didn't take long to find what I was looking for.

On a previous visit, I'd seen Korean workmen in the clinic. They had broken through one of the walls to install the new wiring for Doc Yong's electrocardiogram equipment. At the time, I wondered why she'd needed such expensive equipment when most of her clients were young business girls whose hearts might be broken but were still beating. The older clients, like the friends of Two Bellies, could take a bus down to the Main Yongsan Clinic. Doc Yong had possessed an ulterior motive. She wanted the space opened so she could inter something valuable to her.

I kicked the flimsy wall in. Then, using the screwdriver, I scraped away plaster until the opening was large enough and I leaned in. I saw a square white box, wrapped in black ribbon, the type used in Korea to transport honored remains.

I lifted the box, placed it on Doc Yong's desk and opened the top. After a quick survey, I closed it again. Then I left the clinic, stepped carefully down the creaking metal stairs, and marched through the early morning dawn to the Itaewon Police Station. Because of the fire at the Itaewon Market and the reports of gunfire, Captain Kim was already there. He wore his khaki uniform, neatly pressed, and his big square chin had been recently shaved. The pungent tang of aftershave battled with the fragrant remains of morning kimchee.

He stood as I walked into his office. I must've looked a sight: dirty, muddy, covered with soot and pig's blood. I plopped the white box down on the center of his desk.

"Here," I said

Captain Kim stared at the box suspiciously. "What is it?"

I took a deep breath and let it out slowly. "The bones of Mori Di."

His face contorted and his lips twisted in disgust. He didn't want this box. It represented trouble. But now he had no choice. The remains of Technical Sergeant Flo Moretti had been presented to him by a representative of the United States Government.

Finally, after twenty years, Mori Di could no longer be ignored.

18

Bureaucratically, 8th Army had a spaz attack.

Back at CID headquarters, I made a complete report. Well, not exactly complete, I left out a few details. For example, I didn't mention the kidnapping of Doctor Yong In-ja. I didn't want to bring her into all this. I wasn't sure exactly how deeply she was involved in the murders of Horsehead and Water Doggy but I figured Ernie was right. She must have been implicated.

What I said in my report was that Ernie and I were reconnoitering last night in Itaewon, searching for the remains of our late 8th Army comrade, Tech Sergeant Moretti, when we were accosted by person or persons unknown. That led us to take refuge in the Itaewon Market where someone committed arson and as we tried to escape the blaze we'd been fired upon, once again, by person or persons unknown. Of course, we returned fire.

According to the KNPs, we were all lousy shots because no one was reported to have been wounded.

Afterward, my report continued, I decided to search the Itaewon branch of the Yongsan District Public Health Clinic, Doc Yong's office. After finding the front door open, I noticed a package hidden in a wall under repair. The package was presented to Captain Kim who ascertained that it contained the remains of Technical Sergeant Florencio Moretti, an American soldier who'd been carried on 8th Army's books as missing-presumed-dead for over twenty years.

The find was the talk of the 8th Army Officers' Club and the story was even reported in the *Pacific Stars and Stripes*. The fact that the item appeared in that official rag, albeit on page eight, was proof positive that the 8th Army honchos approved. So Ernie threw himself at the mercy of the provost marshal. Ernie had been in Itaewon, assisting me, despite being restricted to compound. Conveniently, Colonel Brace decided to set aside the previous restriction and, although we weren't commended in any official way, just the fact that we weren't punished told us both that we were no longer on the provost marshal's shit list.

Ernie forgave me for punching him but said he'd return the favor one day, at a place and time of his choosing. Some forgiveness.

But the biggest brouhaha was with the Koreans.

Captain Kim had no choice but to reopen the investigation into the death of Technical Sergeant Flo Moretti. At the KNP medical facility in Seoul, a complete forensic examination of the bones was conducted. The conclusions were much the same as I'd drawn when I'd first seen the bones in the basement of the Grand Ole Opry Club. Flo Moretti had been tortured and then he'd been bricked up behind those cold walls while still alive. He'd been bound and gagged and within days he died of hunger and dehydration.

A tough way to go.

The Korean newspapers made much of it, and recapped the good that had been done in the postwar era by 8th Army's reconstruction projects throughout the country.

Another thing that the Korean investigation pointed out was the Buddhist overtones of the way Moretti had been killed. In ancient times, people were executed by strangulation or by having heavy weights piled atop them or even by having foul things shoved down their throats so they couldn't breathe, but blood was not shed. Whoever murdered Moretti probably had that in mind. They'd left him there to die on his own, not having the nerve to end his suffering and do him the favor of cutting his throat as somebody had done for Two Bellies.

Snake was charged with the murder of Mori Di. So were Jimmy Pak and the two other surviving charter members of the Seven Dragons. They did what all good gangsters do: they said nothing and hired good lawyers. As a result, their interrogation by the Korean National Police was brief and they were released on their own recognizance. The investigation into Moretti's death promised to drag on for months.

Meanwhile, I started thinking of how different the follow-up murders were. The throat of Two Bellies had been expertly sliced, while Horsehead and Water Doggy had been hacked wildly by at least three blades. Auntie Mee, meanwhile, like Mori Di had been killed without bloodshed.

I wanted to talk to Doc Yong but she'd disappeared. According to the Yongsan Health Clinic, she'd resigned her job and moved with no forwarding address. Ernie and I checked her apartment. Empty. We talked to the landlady and she was just as surprised as we were. Without giving notice, Doc Yong had moved out all her stuff and left without so much as a goodbye.

I talked once again to the friends of Two Bellies. They'd told us previously that just prior to her death, someone had been following Two Bellies. I thought now I knew who that someone was. I confronted them with my suspicion.

The women looked away from me. "Maybe," one of them said.

"Two Bellies caught her following?"

"No." The *hwatu*-playing women all shook their heads. "Daytime, Miss Kwon come look for Two Bellies. Together they talk. Whisper, we no can hear. Argue about something. Later that night, Two Bellies go out alone, never come back."

I asked them why they hadn't told me this before.

One of them set down her still-burning cigarette and in her whiskey-shredded voice said, "You no ask."

I was walking through a dark Itaewon alley, pondering that information, when a short figure stepped out of the darkness.

"Geogi," she said.

The amber light of a streetlamp shone on her unblemished face. Doc Yong.

We embraced.

"She's using you again," Ernie said.

We were sitting at the 8th Army snack bar. It was lunch hour and the place was packed with G.I.s in uniform and a smattering of 8th Army civilians. I sipped hot coffee while a bacon, lettuce, and tomato sandwich grew cold in front of me.

"What do you mean?" I asked.

"I mean you're doing everything you can to keep her out of the Mori Di murder investigation."

"It's not my investigation," I said. "It belongs to the KNPs. Besides, she was just a kid when Mori Di was murdered." Ernie sighed with exasperation. "You know what I mean. The murders of Two Bellies and Horsehead and Water Doggy. It's obvious."

"It's not obvious."

"It is."

Ernie went on to explain what he meant.

When Doc Yong took me to see the fortune teller, Auntie Mee, she hoped to give me a reason to search for the bones of Mori Di. She did. And when I found them she hoped that turning them over to the Korean National Police would cause the Seven Dragons to be investigated for murder. Why had she involved me rather than looking for the bones herself? Because if a Korean found them, the KNPs could easily hush up the entire affair. But if an official of the 8th United States Army presented them with the remains of an American G.I., official action would be compulsory.

Ernie was convinced that the two men and three women who'd murdered Horsehead and Water Doggy were orphans of the Itaewon Massacre. Probably in league with Doc Yong. Reluctantly, I conceded that he was probably right.

"And about Auntie Mee," Ernie said. "She was killed in a Buddhist manner, probably ordered by Snake."

"Why?"

"Revenge for Two Bellies. And a warning to whoever had the bones not to let them see the light of day."

Still, that didn't explain why someone had murdered Two Bellies. Ernie set down his coffee cup and took a deep breath.

"No hitting," he said.

I promised I wouldn't.

"The slice across the throat was expertly done," Ernie said. "Like a doctor with a scalpel."

I surprised him; I remained calm. In fact, I picked up my BLT and took a huge bite. He waited patiently while I chewed and finally swallowed.

"I thought of that," I said.

"And?"

"It doesn't make sense. If she wanted the bones of Mori Di revealed, why would she kill Two Bellies and then hide the bones again?"

Ernie crinkled his brow. "I don't know." Then he looked up at me. I sat calmly, waiting. "You son of a bitch."

"What?"

"You know, don't you?"

"Know what?"

"You know who murdered Two Bellies and why they did it."

I shrugged.

"You're holding out on me."

I shrugged again. "I have theories."

"But you're not sharing them with Captain Kim."

"No reason to share them with him."

"But you're going to share them with Doc Yong."

I shook my head negatively. "Actually," I said, "I'm waiting for her to share them with me."

Hilliard was incensed.

"What the hell you mean, coming over here at oh-dark-thirty in the morning and rousting me out of my crib?"

Actually, it wasn't his crib. It was the room rented in a brothel behind the King Club by our favorite peg-legged business girl, Miss Kwon.

Ernie told Hilliard to go back into the hooch and keep quiet, which he did, grumbling to himself all the while. Wearing a cotton robe, Miss Kwon stepped into sandals and shuffled out onto the cement balcony where we could talk beneath the light of the moon. I pointed at her name on the nunnery's list of orphans.

"Who are the others?" I said. "The women and the men."

She started to cry. But after a few minutes, she started talking

It all made sense. Doc Yong was trying to keep Miss Kwon out of harm's way so the actual killing of Horsehead and Water Doggy had been done by people, now grown, who had once been orphans on the Buddhist nun's list. One man was a cab driver, the other a house painter. They were accompanied by a female chestnut vendor and two other women. Auntie Mee's real name was also on the list of orphans. She had been one of the oldest of the children brought to the nunnery after the Itaewon Massacre and she'd been one of the first to leave. When Auntie Mee saw Doc Yong and the others return to Itaewon and take up jobs around town, she knew that something was up.

I finished questioning Miss Kwon. Then I told her what I suspected. She became hysterical. Hilliard rushed out of the room. Ernie held him back. I put my arm around Miss Kwon and whispered Korean in her ear. "Don't worry," I said. "It's our secret." Then I told her to return to her room.

"Please," she said, grabbing my arm. "Think about them. When they were little children, they walk so far through snow. Mama and daddy dead. Think about that."

"I will."

Miss Kwon trudged slowly back into her hooch.

It was easy to see why the grown-up orphans of the Itaewon Massacre would want to take revenge on Horsehead and Water Doggy, and all of the Seven Dragons. Snake tried to send a warning to those unknown killers by murdering Auntie Mee. He ordered Aunite Mee's murder be without bloodshed so she was strangled with a silk rope.

Who had murdered Two Bellies? At first I'd thought it was the remaining Seven Dragons. But that idea troubled me. Snake and his brethren could have frightened Two Bellies into leaving town. That would have been much safer than inviting a murder investigation.

The Seven Dragons were hoping Ernie and I wouldn't find the bones, that they'd remain undisturbed for many decades to come. I concluded that Two Bellies had been made an offer she couldn't refuse, as insurance. She was to follow us, and if we actually found the bones, steal them and turn them over to Snake. Miss Kwon suspected Two Bellies so she'd stayed close to her; pretended to help Two Bellies in return for a 10 percent cut of the reward the Seven Dragons were offering for the bones.

When, against all odds, Ernie and I did find the bones, Two Bellies was right behind us. And so was the resourceful Miss Kwon. When Two Bellies climbed inside the makeshift ossuarium and piled all the bones into a cardboard box, Miss Kwon knew that Two Bellies would turn the bones over to the Seven Dragons. She knew that when Ernie and I returned we would find an empty crypt and she also knew that the truth about the murder of Mori Di, and therefore the truth about the murder of her parents in the Itaewon Massacre, would never be revealed. This was more than she could bear. While Two Bellies was preoccupied with gathering the bones, Miss Kwon reached in, grabbed a clump of Two Bellies' hair, and cleanly sliced her throat.

The move was one she'd learned when she was sent to work for the butcher family in the valley beneath the Temple of Constant Truth. She had used a hooked blade attached to a wooden handle, almost as sharp as a scalpel, the one she'd pilfered from her friends at the butcher shop counter in the Itaewon Market, the same type of blade that is used to slaughter hogs.

Conveniently, Two Bellies had already packed the bones into a square white box so Miss Kwon picked it up, tied it with the black ribbon Two Bellies had provided, and transported the remains to Doc Yong's clinic for safekeeping. Doc Yong couldn't turn the bones over to me because if she did, then I would have suspected her, or possibly her little friend Miss Kwon, of having murdered Two Bellies. Doc Yong was holding onto the bones, waiting for a more opportune time to allow them, somehow, to be brought to light.

Later that evening, filled with remorse for what she'd done, Miss Kwon leapt off the roof of the King Club. But, her survival instinct kept her alive and, for the most part, whole.

Then Horsehead and Water Doggy had been killed. Shortly thereafter, Doc Yong was kidnapped by Snake.

Doc Yong lay still.

Awake, but unwilling to talk to me. She was smart enough to know that I thought I'd figured it all out. We were holed up in a small room in a rundown tourist hotel on the eastern outskirts of Seoul in a district known as Kui-dong. In order to get her to talk, drastic measures were in order. I switched on the small lamp on the night-stand. Then I pulled out the photograph the nun at the Temple of Constant Truth had given to me and placed it beneath the glow of the green lamp.

"Is that her?"

"Yes."

"She was beautiful."

"Yes."

The photo showed Moretti, in full uniform, standing with his arm around the tall, handsome Korean woman.

"My mom," Doc Yong said. "She always told me, Mori Di, he good man. He come visit us, always bring nice things. Food, cooking oil, money for charcoal. He played with me, even helped me study English. When he was alive, everything good."

We lay like that for a long time, both of us staring at the photograph. She didn't cry, neither did I.

"It must've been rough for you when you went to the orphanage," I said.

She nodded slowly. and then started to speak. "When she was old enough, Miss Kwon was sent to a butcher family to learn a trade. When there wasn't enough work to do, the family would send her back. They didn't want to feed her unless she could earn money for them. The nuns always took her back and fed her. Often, I watched over her. She was so little, so helpless, so lost. She wanted so much for the butcher family to accept her but they were poor and I suppose, they were cold-hearted. They never accepted Miss Kwon."

I waited for Doc Yong to compose herself. Then I said, "When Auntie Mee left the nunnery, she relied on skills she'd learned from her mother and she became a fortune teller, famous and rich. But Miss Kwon didn't have any such skill so she did what she had to do." I paused for a moment, letting my words sink in. "But what about you? How did you become a doctor?"

Doc Yong smiled at the question but kept staring at the tattered wallpaper of the little room. From the faraway look on her face, the dingy furnishings might as well have been the stars of the Milky Way. Finally, she spoke.

"I did well in school," she replied. "The nuns saw that I had the ability to learn so they scraped together the money to send me to middle school. Still, high school would've been out of reach. But someone stepped in to help."

"Who? Certainly not the Seven Dragons?"

"No. Not them. Of course not. I doubt that they even knew we existed. It was someone else, someone who knew my mother."

"A friend of Moretti's?"

"No. From before that time. From when my father was alive. From when we lived in North Korea."

After that, she didn't want to talk anymore. I let her be.

As we lay there, I wondered what I was going to do. So far, nobody in law enforcement had put all this together except me and Ernie, and Ernie would go along with whatever I decided. Finally, I asked Doc Yong.

"Why did you start?"

"Start what?"

"Start killing the Seven Dragons. First Horsehead and then Water Doggy."

"I didn't want to," she replied. "They wanted to, the other orphans. But I told them no, there was a better way. We'd arrange for the bones of Mori Di to be shown to the world and then the Seven Dragons would be punished. Punished properly in a court of law. Not by, how you say? Vigilante justice?"

"That's correct."

"Right, vigilante justice. I didn't want that. That's how our parents were killed, trying to take the law into their own hands."

"But you changed your mind."

"Yes."

"Why?"

"Because of you."

"Me?"

"Yes. Because of you. Remember? You told me that you fought with Horsehead. Horsehead was mad at you for interfering with his plans with that American girl and everybody in Itaewon said that maybe he would kill you."

"That was just Horsehead blowing off steam. He didn't mean it."

"How do you know?" When I didn't answer, Doc Yong gazed back at the wallpaper. "Anyway, I didn't want to take a chance."

I paused at that statement, overwhelmed for a moment. I felt gratitude that someone—after all my years of being an orphan, all my years of being alone—had felt so strongly about me.

I waited until I regained my self-control. It took a couple of minutes. Then I said, "So that's what started it?"

She nodded her head slowly.

"And Two Bellies?"

"Miss Kwon. She try very much to help us. To protect us."

We sat in silence. I thought about all that had happened: tragedy, revenge, miscalculation. The usual.

Finally, I turned to Doc Yong and said, "What should we do?"

She shook her head. "You don't have to do nothing. I do everything."

The honchos of 8th Army were still pissed about Jessica Tidwell. And the fact that we had yet to find her and bring her in was still making Colonel Brace's life miserable at the 8th Army Officers' Club.

"Whatever happens to her," Colonel Brace said, pointing his forefinger at us, "is on you two."

"How do you figure that?" Ernie asked. He didn't say "sir."

The pressure we were living under had made him even more

reckless than he usually was. Fortunately, Colonel Brace chose to ignore the lack of military courtesy.

"That's what her father, Colonel Tidwell, is saying," Colonel Brace replied, "as well as the Eighth Army commanding general. You two left her out there. You didn't pick her up when you should have, when you shot that corporal at the White Crane Hotel, when you had the chance, and now whatever happens to her, whatever she does, whatever trouble she might stumble into, is on you two. And nobody else."

"Maybe the blame," Ernie said, "should be on her parents."

"Don't get smart with me, Bascom."

Before Ernie could say anything more, I jumped in. "We'll find her, sir."

"You'd better. Immediately if not sooner. Because whatever crimes she might commit or, worse yet, whatever crimes might be committed with respect to her, are going to be your responsibility."

He pointed his forefinger at us once again, the finger of blame.

This was nonsense. Ernie knew it and I knew it. Even Colonel Brace secretly knew it. But the military mind has a tremendous capacity for passing on blame. And the collective wisdom of the officer corps of 8th Army actually had a genius for diverting blame and sliding it on down the line toward the lower ranks. And the better an officer is at that particular skill, the higher his rank.

When I dragged him outside, Ernie was still sputtering with rage, looking to punch somebody. I stayed just over an arm's length away from him.

Mrs. Tidwell was waiting for us in the parking lot.

She wore a neatly pressed dress and she was fully made up but she still looked like hell. No amount of makeup could hide the bags beneath her eyes.

"What are they doing to my Jessica?" she asked.

"What is who doing?" I asked.

"Those Korean gangsters."

"I don't think any gangsters are around her now, ma'am," I replied.

Ernie sidled over to the jeep. He knew better than to try to face an irate mother in his current emotional state. I was glad he did.

Mrs. Tidwell looked confused. "If she's not being held by gangsters," she asked, "then why doesn't she come home?"

"She's young, Mrs. Tidwell. Young people like their freedom."

"Freedom? Freedom to live amongst animals?"

I didn't bother to answer. Mrs. Tidwell turned her head away. "No," she said. "I didn't mean that. I'm just so worried about her. Doesn't she understand that I can't sleep at night and that I sit by the phone all day waiting to hear from her?"

"She probably doesn't think about that. She's young and she's just enjoying her freedom, ma'am."

"What is she doing out there?"

"I'm not sure."

"Why haven't you found her?"

"We will."

"When?"

"We're going right now, to see what we can find out."

Mrs. Tidwell grabbed my arm. "Hurry, won't you?"

"We'll try."

"This is causing a great emotional strain on her father."

A great emotional strain trying to point the finger of blame over at the 8th Army Officers' Club, I thought. But I didn't say anything.

Instead, I patted Mrs. Tidwell on the shoulder and said, "We'll do our best."

Walking the streets of Itaewon, Ernie grinned at me. "Mrs. Tidwell really gave you the business, huh?"

"She's worried."

"Can you believe that asshole, Brace? Saying we're responsible for anything that happens to Jessica Tidwell."

"That's the way the military mind works. If something goes wrong, it's the fault of the lowest-ranking man."

"Which in this case is us."

Two kids holding wooden boxes accosted Ernie, asking if he wanted to buy chewing gum. Ernie rummaged through their wares, found some stale ginseng gum, and tossed the kids a quarter. They took one look at me, spotted a cheapskate when they saw one, and ran off for greener pastures.

"So after you rousted Jessica out of that hotel," I asked, "where would she have gone?"

"You mean the time she kneed me in the balls?"

"There was another time?"

"No, that was it. She had money, left over from that pile of yen she had in her purse at the White Crane Hotel, so she could've gone anywhere."

An MP had been assigned to guard Paco Bernal's ward at the 121 Evac and, so far, Jessica hadn't turned up there again. She had, however, made a couple of phone calls. Paco wasn't well enough to talk to her yet, although his condition was improving, but one of the medics had taken pity on Jessica and told her that Paco would be flown out next week to Tripler Army Medical Center in Honolulu. They had a large rehab center and the doctors thought he'd make faster progress there. Of course, if I were him I wouldn't be in any hurry. Once he was well enough, the judge advocate general already had plans to press charges against him for the theft of the $1,000 from Colonel Tidwell and for the statutory rape of Jessica Tidwell. On those charges, he could easily do five years at the federal penitentiary at Fort Leavenworth, Kansas.

"So Jessica has money," I said, "but she also knows that Paco will be transferred soon to Hawaii. And her money must be running low."

"So maybe she wants more money," Ernie said.

"Maybe. And if she wanted more money, how would she get it?"

"Contact one of the Seven Dragons. Have them get her a job."

"Doing what?"

Ernie shrugged. "Who knows? There's plenty of Japanese gangsters available."

"But Paco didn't like that," I said. "He called her a very bad name in Spanish."

"Oh, yeah. What was it?"

"Never mind. But maybe Jessica will want to try another line of work."

"A pretty girl, redhead, nice figure. Shouldn't be difficult."

Somehow, we'd wandered toward the UN Club. Ernie and I checked our .45s, making sure they were loaded, and pushed through the big double doors.

Two goons stood in front of the entrance to Jimmy Pak's office. I told them in Korean, gruffly, that I wanted to see Jimmy. Words were whispered and relayed through the door and, within a few seconds, we were told to enter.

The dapper entrepreneur sat behind his desk, a low green lamp illuminating paperwork spread out before him. Jimmy Pak smiled and bade us sit and generally acted as if it wasn't our fault that he had been formally charged with the murder of Technical Sergeant Flo Moretti. Civil of him. But maybe that's how Jimmy Pak had survived all these years, by never burning bridges. Instead of becoming angry, he offered us a drink. This time, both Ernie and I refused.

"Where is she, Jimmy?" Ernie asked.

"Who?"

"The redhead Horsehead was trying to pimp. Jessica Tidwell."

Jimmy Pak frowned as if acid were pumping out of his stomach.

"That's all you want?" he said.

"That's it."

"After all the trouble you cause, you only worry about her?"

"We don't give a shit about you," Ernie told him.

"Why I help you?" Jimmy asked. "You do nothing but cause me trouble."

I leaned forward on the leather seat.

"You're going to help us," I told him, "because if you don't, we're going to return to Eighth Army and tell the honchos there that Jimmy Pak has Jessica Tidwell. We're going to tell the honchos that Jimmy Pak is pimping one of their daughters and we're going to tell them that if they're smart, Eighth Army will never do business again with Jimmy Pak or with his asshole buddy, Snake."

Jimmy's round paunch seemed to convulse and even more acid rumbled up his throat, causing him to swallow with a sour frown on his usually jolly face. He sat still for a moment, considering what I'd said. Then, without saying another word, he reached across his desk and grabbed a pen and scribbled an address on a piece of paper. He handed it to me.

"You go find," he said. "She small potatoes. Horsehead dead. Water Doggy dead. Nobody care about her now. You go find up."

I stuffed the address in my pocket.

With manicured fingers, Jimmy Pak waved us away.

When I stood up, I said, "You gonna beat the charges, Jimmy?"

I was referring to the murder charge for the death of Mori Di.

"Of course I beat," he said.

"Too bad," I replied. "If Korea was still under Eighth Army martial law, I'd pull out my .45 and shoot you right now."

Jimmy Pak stared at us, calculating how serious I was, calculating how far away his bodyguards were and how close we were.

Before his calculations were finished, Ernie and I walked out.

The joint was called Myong Lim Won, the Garden of the Shining Forest, a *kisaeng* house in the downtown Mugyo-dong district of Seoul. *Kisaeng* are fancy hostesses, similar to Japanese geisha but in modern Korea they seldom wear the traditional gowns or pluck the strings of the *kayagum* or perform the traditional drum dances that they once performed during the Yi Dynasty. Pouring scotch, lighting cigarettes and laughing at businessmen's jokes, in these modern days, are enough skills to entitle a woman to be called a *kisaeng*.

We flashed our badges and pushed past a doorman into a room lit by low red lights and filled with about ten large booths encased in leather upholstery. In the largest booth, a half-dozen Korean businessmen, all wearing suits, and three *kisaeng*, celebrating whatever in the hell it was they were celebrating. Just being rich, I suppose. One of the *kisaeng* had a long nose, red hair and fair skin: Jessica Tidwell. As we approached, she stood, reaching as she did so into a leather purse at her side. The red blouse she wore was low cut and the skirt barely reached halfway down her thigh. She bowed to the Korean gentlemen and excused herself and stepped out on the carpeted flooring.

An old woman wearing a floor-length dress and heavily made

up, scurried out from the back room. She waved her open palm from side to side and said, "G.I. no! No can do! *Bali kara!*" Go away.

Ernie stepped in front of her and turned his side to the old woman to block her way. She plowed into him, grabbed his coat, and kept shouting, "G.I. no! G.I. no!"

Businessmen from various booths around the room were standing up now, murmuring curse words that had something to do with "base foreign louts."

The old woman jerked on Ernie's coat and he jerked back and then shoved her. He miscalculated a tad. The heavily painted old crone reeled back and crashed into a cart that held a bucket full of ice and a half-full bottle of Johnny Walker Black. The woman and the cart and the ice and the booze all crashed to the carpeted floor.

Kisaeng screamed. The Korean men were up now, surrounding Ernie and me, some of them pointing and shouting, others being held back by their brethren.

Ernie held his palm out and said, "Back off!"

Jessica Tidwell pushed through the crowd. Some of the Korean men made way for her. She stepped in front of me, reached into her purse, and whipped out a bayonet. As one, the crowd gasped at the gleaming metal blade and everyone took a half step back.

Koreans argue in public often—they aren't called the Irish of the Orient for nothing—but they seldom get violent. Everyone shoves and pushes and grabs coats but only occasionally does the altercation devolve into fisticuffs, and virtually never into assaults involving a weapon as deadly as a sharpened bayonet.

Still a half-an-arm's length away, Jessica Tidwell pointed the tip of the blade at my throat.

"I ought to cut you," she said.

She might try but she wouldn't make it. Not only was I ready to deflect her lunge but Ernie had turned his back on the stunned Koreans and stood less than a step away. The Korean customers and female hostesses sat immobile, barely breathing, watching a tableau involving the exotic rituals of three long-nosed foreign barbarians.

"You shot Paco!" Jessica shouted.

I stared at her, not bothering to offer a defense. She'd been there. She'd seen what happened. She knew that Paco Bernal had attacked Ernie with the very bayonet she now held in her hand. She knew that I had no choice but to shoot. We stood like that for what seemed like a long while but was, in reality, probably only a few seconds; she staring directly into my eyes, me staring back.

Finally, she twisted the bayonet with her narrow fingers until the handle was pointing toward me. "Here," she said. Ernie snatched it out of her hand.

The Koreans surrounding us let out a sigh of relief. The stepped back even further—not so far that they couldn't observe, but far enough so they wouldn't be hurt by the crazy foreigners.

Jessica swept red bangs from her forehead. "So now you have the bayonet," she said. "The 'assault weapon' I guess you'd call it. So why don't you get out of here and leave me alone?"

"No way," Ernie said.

Jessica screamed. "What do you *want* from me?"

"You're coming with us," Ernie said.

"The hell I am." Jessica's green eyes flashed in the dim light and she rummaged back in her leather purse. I almost expected her to pull out a pistol this time but instead a laminated card emerged. She flipped it at Ernie. He grabbed it in midair.

He twisted the card toward the light, read it, and then handed it to me.

"What of it," Ernie said. "We've seen it before. Your dependent ID card."

I studied the card. The same military dependent identification we'd seen when we first found the sleeping Jessica Tidwell in Corporal Paco Bernal's room in the barracks at 21 T Car.

"Check the date of birth," she told me.

I did. Then I did the math.

"That's right, Einstein," she said. "I'm eighteen years old now. No longer a minor." She grinned a lascivious grin. "You can't touch me."

She was right. Under the Uniform Code of Military Justice, once a military dependent turned eighteen years old we could no longer take her into custody and turn her over to her parents. Not legally.

"Eighth Army doesn't give a shit about that legal crap," Ernie said.

"My ass," Jessica replied. "I'll hire a civilian lawyer and burn both of you and sue the freaking fatigues off the provost marshal and the commanding general of Eighth Army if I have to."

Jessica Tidwell grew up as an army brat. She knew all the ins and outs of how to strike terror into the heart of a military bureaucrat. And she was right. She was no longer a minor. Ernie and I couldn't take her into custody.

I handed the ID card back to her.

"So what do you plan to do, Jessica?" I asked. "Work here, lighting cigarettes and pouring scotch, for the rest of your life?"

I glanced around at the half-drunk businessmen and the startled *kisaeng*. Mouths hung open, some of them twisted in sneers of disgust. But one thing they all had in common is that they were all tremendously interested in what we had to say and they were all straining to understand our English.

"No way I'm going to stay here," Jessica replied. "Not hardly. Paco's being transferred to Tripler Army Medical in Honolulu. I'm just working until then so we'll have some cash to start out on."

"You're following him to Hawaii?"

"What did you expect?"

I'm not sure what I expected. But it was clear that from here on out that Jessica Tidwell, adult, would make her own decisions.

"You'll say goodbye to your mother," I said.

"Her, yes. But not to my dad."

I wanted to ask her why not but thought better of it. That was her decision. Not my business.

"Your mom's worried sick about you," I said. "We're going to tell her where you are."

"Just don't bring her down here."

"That's up to her. Not us."

"I'm not worried about that. She won't come down here without an escort. Even in the States, she's afraid to leave the compound by herself."

"All right then," I said, "It's settled. You're going to watch out for yourself from now on. Be careful."

"I will." She turned to Ernie. "Sorry for kneeing you in the balls."

"Don't mention it," Ernie replied.

19

Sergeant First Class Quinton "Q" Hilliard looked great in his papa-san outfit. His silk vest was fire engine red and his pantaloons were sky blue. He also wore a jade pendant around his neck and his pipe was made of hand-carved bamboo.

Ernie shook Hilliard's hand in congratulations and so did I and then we bowed to the bride. Miss Kwon wore a bright red traditional *chima-chogori* dress with yellow and green stripes on the arms. A silver tiara sat atop her intricately braided black hair. She bowed back to us and we wished her every happiness. A lot of soul brothers were enjoying themselves with the free-flowing *soju*, Korean rice liquor, and Ernie mixed with them easily, shaking hands and laughing, patting them on the back.

That was Ernie. He'd fight you or love you with equal alacrity. I'm not sure he saw a difference between the two.

Miss Kwon confided to me that at first she'd seen Hilliard's pursuit of her as being pressure that was more than she could bear. But later, she realized that he was going as far as he did, and using every power at his disposal—ethical or not—because he truly cared for her. Yes, he was over ten years older than her and yes, he was a foreigner but Miss Kwon's ancestors were far away in North Korea behind a bamboo curtain that couldn't be breached and her parents were dead and her foster family of butchers saw her only as a source of income. She was alone in this world. And besides, she told me in Korean, she thought Hilliard was *kiowo-yo,* cute. I wasn't sure I agreed with that part but the more I got to know him, the more I realized that he was fundamentally a decent guy.

I wandered over to the table with the *soju* and poured myself a shot. So far, Miss Kwon's name hadn't come up in Captain Kim's murder investigation. I don't think he was worried about who had murdered Two Bellies; he was concentrating on the political hot potato of the twenty-year-old murder of Moretti. In the States, some hotshot reporter would be interviewing the relatives of the people who had been murdered in the Itaewon Massacre, printing stories about them crying for the blood of Jimmy Pak and Snake and the other surviving Seven Dragons. But in Korea, there was no such publicity. Under the Pak Chung-hee regime, the press was controlled. And with millions of dollars in United States military and economic aide flowing into the coffers of the government, President Pak stepped on stories concerning a murdered American G.I. He wanted nothing to hurt relations between South Korea and its most important international ally.

Captain Kim was probably feeling the pressure too. My guess was that he wouldn't come looking for the weapon that had been used to murder Two Bellies and, even if he caught wind of Miss Kwon's involvement, once he realized she was marrying a G.I. and moving forever to the States, he'd be relieved.

I'd been pondering whether to turn her in. Two Bellies might've been a washed-up prostitute but she was a human being, a child of god just like the rest of us. Murdering her wasn't right. Still, I'd promised Miss Kwon that her secret would be safe with me. I managed to ease my conscience somewhat by telling myself that the case didn't fall under my jurisdiction—and it didn't. But mainly I calmed myself during restless nights by remembering Miss Kwon standing on the ledge near the roof of the King Club, staring at the fall below her—at her own death. Miss Kwon would have to live with what she'd done to Two Bellies. And Hilliard, now that he was her husband, would have to help her get through it.

I poured myself another shot of *soju*.

Some soul sister—Private Wallings, the one who'd blasted us at the EEO office—had dragged Ernie out on the dance floor and he was dancing as if he hadn't a care in the world. I searched the faces of the other guests, those on the dance floor and those off of it, hoping that Doc Yong would be among them. But, of course, she wasn't.

After a couple of more shots, Hilliard stepped over to the table and took me aside, leading me out into the open foyer. He placed his hand on my shoulder.

"What about Doc Yong?" he asked me. "How is she doing up there?"

"I can't be sure," I said. "Not good according to MI."

"MI," Hilliard said. "What the hell does Military Intelligence know?"

Doc Yong had asked me to hold off telling the Korean National Police until she and her friends—the two men and the three women—could make arrangements to flee the country. They couldn't obtain a passport—those were husbanded carefully by Pak Chung-hee's military regime—but she could obtain a fishing boat.

I tried to talk her out of it.

She took me by the hand and stared into my eyes.

"My mother was an activist for labor unions," she said. "So was my father. In the eyes of the people running South Korea at that time, joining a union was the same as being a Communist. The more well known my father became, the more danger he was in. He was assassinated by the Syngman Rhee regime. The leaders of all unions and the leaders of the Workers' Party, the ones who survived, fled north. But they never forgot me. A North Korean agent operating here in the south contacted the Buddhist nuns and gave them enough money to send me to school. It was because of him that I was able to become a doctor. It was because of him that I am now able to help my people. And it is to him, and the Communist Workers' Party of the north, that I owe my allegiance"

"But you can't go up there," I said, tightening my grip on her hands.

"My ancestors are in North Korea," she told me. "I'm going to take the photograph of my mother and return to our home village of Simsok-ni. There I can pray at our ancestral burial mounds."

"But the North Koreans will arrest you," I said. "In their minds, you've been tainted by living down here. The commissars will throw you in a prison camp."

"Maybe. Maybe not. They need doctors. Anyway if I stay here, I spend the rest of my life in the monkey house."

"I won't tell anyone. Neither will Ernie."

"Someday Captain Kim will find out."

She was right. Captain Kim was a smart man and a good cop. And now that the case had become public, and both the Korean and the U.S. government were demanding justice, Captain Kim was bound to provide it. Eventually. Still, I tried to give Doc Yong some reason to stay.

"South Korean prisons," I said, "beat the hell out of North Korean prisons."

She looked at me with that look again, as if to say I wasn't too smart.

We spent our last night together. I couldn't sleep. Before dawn I woke her and promised her again that I would tell no one what I knew and that I would do everything to make sure that she was never punished for her crimes.

She patted me on the cheek and told me to go back to sleep.

The next morning, I saw Doctor Yong In-ja and her five compatriots off from a rickety wooden pier on a wharf at Kangnam Island. They were bundled warmly against the cold air and wore rain slickers to keep dry. She squeezed my hand as she climbed down into the skiff. The women unfurled a sail and the two men started heaving at the oars. They pulled away from the pier, confident that in the heavy fog they'd be able to slip past the South Korean coastal patrols and make their way into North Korean waters.

She waved to me one last time. As I waved back, she pointed at her belly, cupping it tenderly with splayed fingers as if embracing something precious. Then she smiled.

I watched helplessly as the smooth complexion of her face was enveloped by the cold morning mist.